DRAGON'S TEAR

BOOK 3 OF THE BLOOD OF THE COVENANTS SERIES

LEAH E. WELKER

LIGHTBOUND MEDIA

CONTENTS

To my oldest friend/adopted sister, Katelan, for all those late-night readings, with all their laughs and tears. I hope you knew your turn was coming. So yes, this one is for you.

And you, my father, there on the sad height,

Curse, bless, me now with your fierce tears, I pray.

Do not go gentle into that good night.

Rage, rage against the dying of the light.

Dylan Thomas

KEY TERMS & TRANSLATIONS

Races

draká ("druh-KAH"): the original "dragons."

amá ("ah-MAH"): human(s); the sentient inhabitants of Earth.

dramá ("druh-MAH"): the race that emerged from the combination of draká and humans.

Blood Manifestations

drakón ("drah-KOHN"): dramá chosen to have far greater magic and gain a drakáform.

amón ("ah-MOHN"): dramá who are not chosen, yet still have the Blood of the Covenants and cannot accurately be called "human."

Distances

Rough equivalents

ild: inch.

foot: literal translation.

erd: yard (only a couple dramá feet).

ald: 100 dramá feet.

eld: half an English Imperial mile.

elden: an English Imperial mile.

Time

dek: Roughly 1 minute, made of 56 moments.

deken: Roughly 1 hour, made of 56 dek.

day: 28 deken.

THE SIX REALMS

Sun	Planet	Capital	Clan	Color	Specialty
Kaldrir	Ythra	Crownhold	Sunfilled	Gold	Central governance, priesthood, guarding Tree, maintaining sungates
Kyalid	Ekrel	Krevenyir	Battleblood	Violet	Battle, smithing, exploring, peacekeeping
Ashga	Oshal	Rosin	Starkissed	Sapphire	Magic, scholarship, diplomacy, artistry
Olmen	Romskal	Palla	Strongshield	Scarlet	Civil service, law, administration
Winalken	Yonvey	Remik	Brightflare	Orange	Tinkering, financing, mining, farming
Yedrik	Ykran	Danyeth	Peacegrowth	Emerald	Healing, farming, conserving

PROLOGUE

JACOB

EARTH, THE THIRD PLANET in the solar system, the birthplace of humanity, was dying.

Jacob Lind had already known this, but the evidence was now everywhere around him as he walked across barren fields of black rock, under an even darker, starless sky. How he could still see, he didn't know. The one thing he knew for certain was that he was dreaming, so it seemed pointless to question that aspect of his vision.

Jake never indulged pointless questions.

But here...here, all around him, was the most important of questions, and perhaps if he looked and searched hard enough, he would find the answer: how Earth would finally die. So he walked for what felt like hours over black rock—devoid even of soil.

Or any other organic material, Jake noted with a clinical eye. That was the first clue he had gleaned from his search, and he was frustrated with himself that it had taken him this long to realize it.

Then again, nothing about this utter destruction made any sense. None of the hundreds of ways Earth could have met its end fit with what he was seeing now.

Jake was not ignorant of humanity's foolish, headlong rush toward self-annihilation. He had become an engineer out of faith in the ingenuity of his species to solve their problems. He was often surprised to find that faith was still burning, even though he had long since grown weary of trying to create solutions in the face of humanity's equal unwillingness to use them.

Jake had always taken the long view, calculating with excruciating exactness how his actions now shaped his future and that of his family. It always aggravated him how few others did the same.

So he was saddened but unsurprised to be walking the land of humanity's ultimate demise. Yet he was also increasingly puzzled as to what could have brought that end—and increasingly intent on knowing the answer. If he knew how, then perhaps, just perhaps...he could prevent it.

However unlikely that was. He was realistic about his odds of saving the world—one lone engineer working for a small firm and teaching night classes at an insignificant college in suburban Pennsylvania, with a wife and eight children to think of. True, his oldest had begun his own career and family, and his second could support herself if she had a mind to. His third....

He pivoted his mind away from his third, with recent events making thoughts about her too laden with emotion for his current task. Though he had an inkling that her disappearance and this dream weren't unrelated.

Ever self-aware, he admitted to himself that was one reason he was becoming so determined to find the answer.

Yet it eluded him. Disease would have left the buildings intact, even if they might have crumbled a bit from neglect, yet only shells or fragments remained. Besides, a disease that would have wiped out humanity should have left most other life flourishing, perhaps even more so for their absence. Yet *no* life lay in sight.

None.

Global warming would have disastrously upset world order, and yet there still should have been life *somewhere*, even if in a vast sea. Yet there was no water, either. Not a single drop in this dark, desiccated waste, not even after hours of walking.

Conventional or nuclear bombardment would have created the broken structures he occasionally passed, but why would it leave steel frames or stone pillars intact and little else? Those shells of buildings were charred black, true, but they still stood as recognizable ghosts of what they once were, like the bones of enormous beasts left on a cracked earthen waste, every scrap of flesh picked clean.

Jake wasn't one for dramatic imagery, but that last uncharacteristic simile his mind had produced gave him pause. Perhaps his answer lay therein.

Organic matter, he repeated to himself. *Or anything remotely able to support life—it's all gone. All of it.*

As if there were some unimaginable beast that had consumed everything with the potential for life and had left Earth as no more than a spit-out husk.

But what sort of monstrosity could that be?

For the first time, he felt a chilling realization that humanity might not have been the cause of its demise. At least...not directly.

He was surprised by how much that conclusion troubled him. Humanity was both bright and dark, but at least he had some idea of what that darkness was, and how to combat it. As increasingly hopeless as the efforts of the bright ones such as him were, still, he thought he knew his enemy. Yet this was something so entirely outside his knowledge, let alone his toolset to fight, that for the first time in this dream, Jake felt his blood go cold.

He had perhaps found the answer, but it gave him no comfort—only fear. Instinctual fear that he had felt the moment he "woke" in this dark waste and yet suppressed through the ferocity of his focus on the problem before him. Now, having concluded that this was something beyond his power to even understand, let alone fight....

He felt true fear.

Not for himself, but for his family. His children. His beloved children. Stubborn Michael, dazzling Rachel. Steady David, charming Lizzy. Mischievous Jonah, eager Noah. Sunny little Abby.

Quiet, bright Sarah...the child most like him, yet hopefully spared his worst flaws.

He had fought the good fight, as best as he had known how, even despite ever-increasing weariness and disillusionment, to create a better world for his children. He would have given his life to see that theirs went on.

Now, to see that all that remained for them was to meet this inescapable doom....

All the emotions he had blocked off behind the dam of his formidable mind and will broke free. Rage and grief and bone-deep fear for them finally overcame him, slowing his formerly firm steps one by one...until he came to a halt.

There, in that land of death, unable to go another step...he fell to his knees.

For the first time in his life, he truly prayed.

It wasn't a reverent prayer. It was a cry of rage and despair.

Why show me this? Why take her, why take my Sarah, why send us her image in ice, then why show me this? *What is the point, if all hope is lost for my children? WHY?*

Then, for the first time in this nightmare of darkness, Jake saw a light.

It blossomed amid the shadowy mists ahead of him, like a lighthouse shining in a storm.

Jake hesitated. He was so furious at this point that he wasn't certain he wanted an answer. Wasn't sure, even despite the light, that there was any meaning left to be found in this purposeless waste. Even when he reached it, it would probably only lead to more disappointment and despair.

He had never believed in a higher power before. He wasn't particularly opposed to the idea, but neither had he been convinced of one's existence. He had been, and thought he would always be, a firm agnostic.

Then...Sarah had disappeared, without a trace. That same day at sunset, ice had come for the first time, and had every sunset since. Now here he was, over seven days later, in this most terrible and yet tangible and visceral of nightmares.

His life had taken a dramatic turn, and he was too intelligent and aware to deny that there was something else out there, something more than he had previously imagined.

That didn't mean he thought it was good.

And yet....

There was something about that light. Something that felt so different from the wastes.

Something that felt like life.

It was that difference that persuaded him to move, getting to his feet before his mind made a conscious decision. Then he was moving forward again, pressing through the mists toward the light.

Even after minutes of walking, the light still seemed distant, flickering vaguely and shapelessly through the walls of dark mist. Had they been so thick before? He hadn't thought so. There had been *nothing* before, nothing but rock and twisted metal, and now a light that seemed alive and a darkness that...wasn't. For all its hunger.

The darkness pulled at him now—like a thing alive, but in a solemn mockery of life. Its fingers on his skin imparted the cold of nothingness, of the utter rejection of any order of creation Jake knew. His steps quickened. Someone less level-headed and clear-sighted might have tried to delude themselves by saying it was only mist, only darkness. But even in his despair, Jake was always taking in information and analyzing it with cool impartiality.

He had already determined that some force previously unknown to him had consumed Earth. Now he was encountering a force whose malevolence was so great, he couldn't help but feel it in its very presence. To Jake, the logical connection was obvious. So was the next: this thing, this destroyer, must have returned for a reason, and the only reasons he could think of were to consume him...or to prevent him from reaching the light.

He saw no reason why it couldn't be trying to do both.

He broke into a run.

The darkness surged thicker, becoming almost solid, its touch as it grabbed for him imparting agony the likes of which he had never felt before. The pain staggered Jake, making him stumble. He thought he had known fear before, but that was nothing compared with his primal terror now. Just in the moment he was about to give up all hope....

Please, Jake gasped, making his choice.

The very next moment, the light flared brighter.

The darkness hissed like water vaporized by flame. Which was strange, because there was nothing hot about the light. In fact, it was accompanied by a wave of cool air—coolness quite unlike the darkness's void-filled touch. It was the cold of stillness, of rest, of life in its slowest, most ponderous, most eternal state. It soothed away his pain to nothing.

That flare of light and blast of cold air drove the darkness away from him, and Jake wasn't about to take that life-saving gift for granted. He rushed forward, now with the source of the light clear.

It was...a Tree. A Tree so vast, Its trunk must have been a hundred feet wide and perhaps hundreds tall. It towered over him like a skyscraper, Its branches forming a canopy that seemed to eclipse the sky. Its roots—most of the ones he saw were bigger than him—broke through even this barren rock and stretched in some places nearly as far as the canopy. Every surface, every line of Its bark, every crevice in Its roots shone with cold light. Especially the leaves high, high above, so bright against the starless sky he couldn't even discern the shape of them.

Jake realized with a start that his run had petered out into a slow walk as he took it all in, but when he glanced back, he saw the mists held back, staying feet away from the roots at all points around the Tree. Now that Jake was under Its canopy, walking among Its roots, he appeared to be safe.

But...why?

Again, his curiosity burned, this time with renewed hope. Here was something that could drive back the hungering darkness. That could deny it its prey, so long as that prey remained within the Tree's protection. If he could get his family here, before the end came in truth....

But where was here? *What* was here? What was this Tree? Was it a metaphor produced by his mind, or by whomever or whatever had given him this dream?

"No, Jacob Lind, My son."

Jake spun back toward the Tree and the sound of the voice—a voice unlike he had ever heard before. He felt it in his chest almost as much as he heard it with his ears. It was mild, like the whispers of cool winds rattling through bare branches on an early spring day, but it struck to his core and set it on icy fire.

There, where nothing had been just a moment before, stood a Woman made of ice.

She was taller than him, with long hair that reached nearly to the ground, and She was either wearing a crystalline gown or was simply shaped like one from the shoulders down to the floor. With all Her being made from the same living shards of ice shining with an inner light, Jake couldn't tell, and he didn't much think it mattered, so he immediately dismissed the question as frivolous.

Especially when She spoke again, Her lips pulled into the smallest of smiles. *"I am very much real, and I am precisely as you see Me now."*

Jake tried to harden himself, but he found that difficult. The contrast between the destroying mists and this Tree and Woman of life was too stark. He knew who his true enemy—the enemy of all life—was now. He likewise knew who was its protector. But that made no sense.

A Woman of ice, connected in some way to a Tree. Just as Abby, his five-year-old, had said.

"You're the one who took my daughter," he said flatly.

"Yes," the Woman replied with perfect peace.

His fists clenched and unclenched, resisting that peace as it tried to settle into his soul. He told himself that he was being unreasonable; he reminded himself of the contrast, that this couldn't be his enemy. Yet he was a father, and when it came to his children, his emotions weren't as easily controlled as they were in all other cases. In no other realm did his feelings cloud his judgement and influence his behavior so readily.

"Why?" he demanded.

If the Woman was offended, She made no sign of it. Her voice retained its mild—yet piercing—nature. *"For the same reason I do all that I do. To ensure that this..."*

She gestured out into the darkness. *"...does not come to pass. Inasmuch as it is in My power to do so."*

"What does taking my daughter from us have to do with preventing this?"

"Sarah, as you know, is as precious and bright as a diamond. As such, I have chosen her as the vessel of My power, so that she may fight at the side of another to drive off the darkness you witnessed before it can consume your world."

Jake's heart sunk. "Fight?"

The Woman's eyes became sad. *"The hunger cannot be bargained with nor sated. It must be driven, and that is a danger she must face, or she will perish with the rest when the end comes."*

Jake took a shuddering breath. He picked through all the things he could do or say, all fits of temper, useless denials, or ultimately meaningless questions. With his usual stoicism, he forced himself to view reality as it was and accept it, then move on to what he could control.

Still, he couldn't help one, probably unanswerable question.

"Why her?" he rasped. "Why my daughter?"

Yet She answered. *"Because she has the greatest chance to succeed."*

Jake slowly nodded.

He had always known Sarah was special, from the first time he had held her in his arms, walking the floor of that hospital room to soothe her cries. Jake had two children already by then, so he knew it wasn't just the warmth of new fatherhood clouding his reasoning. He had examined the feeling long enough over the years to determine that it wasn't fatherly bias, either. It had never been a happy knowledge; it had always been a heavy foreboding. For her sake, he had sometimes wished she were more like the others.

Because he had always sensed in her the light that would be called on to struggle against the dark.

The same light he had felt within himself, except even brighter.

In a way, he had been waiting for this moment her entire life. Not in such a drastic, world-shattering way, true, but when the Woman said Sarah was the one She needed, Jake felt the culmination of over eighteen years of impressions, each individually too subliminal to be understood, finally coalesce into the heaviest of truths.

His daughter would bear the fate of their world on her shoulders.

"Not alone," the Woman whispered, once again answering his thoughts.

The mind-reading didn't surprise him. This was Her dream, after all, and even if that wasn't the reason, She was unlike any being he had previously encountered, and would no doubt have abilities beyond his current understanding. He spared no thought for this aptitude other than to catalog the information away, and he refocused on what She had said.

Her words gave him the first lift of hope he had felt since he had entered the Tree's protection.

"Can I help her? Bear some of that burden for her?"

Why else had he felt this light within him his whole life, the heavy calling that made him constantly struggle to solve the world's ills?

"You may, in part. But the one who will primarily share her burden is My Sister's chosen vessel, as Sarah is Mine."

"Who?" Jake asked in surprise.

"I have shown his visage to you before."

The Woman spread Her hand. A sheet of the smoothest ice appeared between them, and in it, Jake saw colors appear and form an image of a pristine quality no screen he knew of could match. This was almost exactly like the ice and images that had appeared at sunset every day since Sarah had disappeared.

This time, however, there were two distinct differences. First, the image moved, like a video rather than a photo. Second, Sarah was nowhere to be seen.

Instead, the principal subject was a young man, walking down a large stone hall. The Woman was right. Jake immediately recognized him from many of the images he had seen before.

His exact age was a little hard to determine because of his short, blond beard, shoulder-length blond hair, towering height, heavily built musculature, and occasionally commanding presence. There was also sometimes a hard or weary look in his golden eyes that no one so young should have. But Jake had seen enough of him by this point to determine that he was probably not much older than Sarah. Certainly he and Sarah acted like peers and friends.

Or more than that.

The Linds had seen nothing yet in the ice to explicitly indicate something more than friendship, but Rachel swore there was something going on between the two of them, and Jake had to admit there was probably something to that, if only from the fact that Sarah was with the young man more often than with anyone else. A less objective yet still undeniable data point was the tender adoration on Sarah's face that was clear to every member of her family every time an image showed her looking at him.

Jake had never seen Sarah so infatuated with anyone, and that had troubled him a great deal. Mixing with a father's protective instincts was all the uncertainty around Sarah's situation. If the images could be believed to be real—and they had had no reason to assume otherwise; why would any mystic force that could take her with impunity bother deceiving them?—Sarah wasn't currently in any danger. She seemed to be comfortable and friendly with the people around her. The images often showed her smiling, laughing, or with her neutral, thoughtful expression. They showed her doing normal things. Sleeping, eating, walking, talking. She seemed to have freedom of movement and control over her situation.

Then why was she *there* and not home? It was impossible to tell from just the images whether she was trying to find her way back or if that was even possible. She clearly wasn't on Earth anymore, judging from the otherworldly places they had seen her in; the unusually tall, colorful, strangely clad people they had seen her with; and the glimpses of technology so beyond his understanding that the only adequate term he had for it was magic.

After all, weren't the ice messages magic?

Assuming the messages could be trusted, the most logical conclusion was that Sarah was currently happy and safe in another world, and the only reason she hadn't come back to or otherwise contacted them was because she couldn't. But Jake *didn't know*. Not for certain. So his daughter's clear infatuation with this young man troubled him. Was it developing naturally from mutually chosen companionship after circumstances had thrown them together? Or was it Stockholm syndrome? Was he a true friend...or something more sinister?

So Jake had studied the young man in those images with almost more scrutiny than his daughter. For reasons he couldn't name, this young man had seemed to be the key in all of this—possibly the one who had taken her in the first place. Yet Jake's sharp eyes had caught nothing remotely sinister in him. In fact, as Jake learned his expressions, he thought the young man seemed quite fond of Sarah, perhaps even just as infatuated. His posture toward her was always friendly, warm, even protective. By this point, Jake had found it hard to keep examining him with suspicion.

Still, Jake's instincts had been right, in a way. He was the key.

"Him?" Jake asked, but there wasn't any surprise in his voice. "He is this other...vessel?"

That was the word the Woman had used, wasn't it?

"He will be. He is only partially invested with My Sister's power now, as Sarah is only partially with Mine. But soon that will change for both. Sarah will become My chosen Queen...and he will become My Sister's chosen King."

Jake looked up at Her sharply. The parallelism of their titles hadn't escaped him. "When you said he is meant to help share her burden...."

The Woman gazed back at him solemnly. *"If they are to have the power necessary to drive back the Devourer, the Queen of Ice and the King of Flame must become one."*

"I...see," Jake said heavily, looking back down at the ice.

Perhaps it was just as well that Sarah was infatuated with the young man. Perhaps then she could find *some* happiness in her fate. Jake desperately hoped so. What other hope did he have left to cling to, now that he knew he could not save her from it?

"Is he good?" he whispered, looking at the young man as he continued to walk down those empty stone halls.

He looked even wearier than usual, his golden hair was even untidier, and he was still dressed in the black clothing they had seen him wearing in the images that evening. Normally, he seemed to wear gold clothing and undyed leather belts and boots, without deviation, yet last night and now, everything he wore was black. Embroidered and ornamented with gold, but still the sudden change was troubling. Was he in mourning? Assuming black was a mourning color in his culture. At the least, his expressions had been unusually sober in the stills they had seen of him that evening, especially the one with Sarah and him facing each other in the middle of a dark, crowded room. Sarah, too, had been serious as she gazed up at him, even though she was resplendent in a glowing white, effervescent dress. Even her skin and eyes had seemed to glow, making her shine like a star in that darkness.

Now that scene made more sense in Jake's mind, having heard what this Woman intended them to become. The future Queen of Ice, facing the future King of Flame. Perhaps as they realized themselves what fate lay in store for them.

"He is, or My Sister would not have chosen him."

Jake took a deep breath. "Will he make her happy?"

"He could, if he chose. There is great sorrow ahead, no matter their choices. Yet they can have bright moments that will make the dark bearable, if they reach for them together. That is up to them to decide."

When Jake looked back at Her, She smiled as softly as Her icy lips could. *"We never force or coerce Our children, Jacob Lind. We can only guide and protect them...when they will let us."*

Jake waved at the ice. "So this destiny you have in store for them. They could reject it? You would allow that?"

"Yes, We would. But even greater tragedy will result. As I said before, she and he, together, stand the greatest chance to save our worlds...and all life therein. Yet the choice is always theirs. We only have the power to save Our children that Our children in turn give us."

Jake looked back at Her. He could sense that this dream was coming to an end. Only one more question mattered deeply enough to ask now.

"Why are you telling me this?"

"Because I do not need just Sarah. I need her family as well. All twelve of you."

"Twelve...." Jake paused for a moment in puzzlement, then understood. "You mean Laura and Tommie, too?"

His daughter-in-law and grandson.

"Indeed. I cannot stop the devastation you have seen, not alone. I require Sarah most of all, but she will require all of you. She is striving now to find the way We have prepared for her to return to you."

Jake's heart leaped. "Sarah is coming back?"

If, for all their sakes, her destiny indeed lay with that young man, then Jake had begun to despair that he would not see his daughter in the flesh again. He had assumed that was the reason for this dream when he had first asked his question—to show him why Sarah would never return home.

The Woman nodded. "*When she does, I will have a work for you to do together. I have shown you and told you all of this to prepare you to be ready to help her. Yet that is not all.*"

She raised her hand. A light from the Tree above floated down to them slowly. As it did, She said, "*I offer you a gift, My son. A gift I have not bestowed for nearly a thousand years. It is the greatest gift that is in My power to grant save My power itself.*"

The light finally rested in Her palm. It was a leaf, made from ice that glowed with a cold inner fire. She held it out so that he could see it, but not so far as to invite him to come forward immediately to take it.

"What is it?" Jake asked quietly.

He was wary now. He saw no reason to distrust the Woman; in fact, he felt in a way that even he couldn't logic away that She was the epitome of trustworthiness. Yet She herself had made it clear this gift wasn't to be taken lightly. Before he took it, he would have to be willing to bear the burden that would come with it.

"*It is the gift of Sight,*" She said, with the softness of a whispering winter wind. "*Should you accept what I offer, you will be able to see what I give you of the past, the present...and of the potential future.*"

That was, indeed, no small gift, and the implications already staggered him, both good and bad. But one word needed clarification before he could decide.

"Potential?" Jake said intently.

"*The future stretches before you in a thousand upon thousand branches, with each decision one of Our children makes creating another. We Eternal Ones of the First Creation can hold all the possibilities in Our minds at once. In fact, We exist outside of them, as if time were a tapestry before Us already complete, and We have only to touch one strand to see all futures that could have been and yet were not. Yet that is too much for any mortal mind to bear. To be merciful, and to respect the sanctity of choice, I will only show you possibilities, just as I have shown you the possibility of one this night. Nothing I show you beyond your present will be set in stone; they will be messages of comfort or warning only. You and your family will still be free to choose your paths."*

"So you *know* what will happen in the end," he said dryly. "Yet you would show them as possibilities, so I still have an illusion of choice."

"Knowing what you will choose does not take that choice away, My son."

Jake pondered that for a moment. "I suppose…it does not. Unless I thought it did. Unless I thought what you were showing me was inevitable and acted accordingly. There is an element of illusion here still, but…it is actually in my favor."

The Woman simply smiled.

"Why give this to me?" Jake asked slowly. "If Sarah is your chosen Queen, what am I to you?"

"You have always been My servant, Jacob," the Woman said gently. *"Though you did not know it, because you were prevented from knowing Me. I offer this to you to change that. To prepare you. To give you the chance, as you asked, to share something of your daughter's burden. For she will have great need of you."*

"In that case…" Jake's eyes fell on the leaf, and he held out his hand. "…I will take it. For Sarah."

His daughter.

He would have given his life to save her. What good father wouldn't? And he would have given his life to spare her this kind of burden. But he couldn't. So he would live, and he would share it with her, no matter the heavy cost of that gift.

That seemed a small enough price to pay.

Chapter One

CHOICE

Koriben

It was nearly dawn before Kor could finally lead me to Sarah's gate.

Kor's elaborate plan to debut Sarah during the Moonfair pageant was, in everyone else's mind, a resounding success. Her guileless yet breathtaking performance and symbolic participation as the Moondaughter won over every Starkissed who had been in attendance and captured the hearts and imaginations of everyone else, and word spread almost instantaneously through Olsdak and then through the Six Realms.

The aftermath required hours of Kor and I explaining to the people across the Realms who had a right to know as much as they had a right to know about Sarah and what her presence meant for them, and deflecting questions and giving vague answers to the people who didn't.

Unsurprisingly, Kor had already laid some of the groundwork by informing the Lady Starkissed and Olsdak elder in advance both of Sarah's presence in Olsdak and the Crown's intentions for the pageant revelation. The Crown, meaning Avva, his wings and their people, and both of my wings and theirs. All of them had been in readiness that night: the rightwings and their elites for handling anything from a full-scale Devourer assault to attempted assassination to simple crowd control; the leftwings and their people had been in readiness for the flood of questions and careful handling of the narrative, which they sprang into action to manage as soon as the lights came on.

In fact, every member of the entity we called the Crown was to some extent informed and prepared for every scenario of that night...except me. Because, of course, I was the only key stakeholder *not* informed. Even Sarah had been given the choice to reveal herself or not—even if she'd been tricked into attending the pageant as a participant.

No one told me that last part. Kor glazed over it as if Sarah had been aware of the entire plan. But I knew her too well for that, and I had seen the look of terror on her face when the Moonstar had stopped in front of her, choosing her to be my counterpart in that blasted pageant's finale. She may have been given the choice to reveal her Moontouched identity...but other than that, she had been left in the dark just as much or even more than I had been.

The moment I first saw her in the back of that dark crowd, the pieces fell into place—but not in time to save her. She hadn't deserved to be dragged into this charade with me. She didn't deserve to feel all those expectations descend on her and all those stares follow her every movement as she stumbled to obey them. She shouldn't have had to kiss me, and in front of all of them, just to avoid ruining the production. She *shouldn't have had to do any of it.*

Yet they had given her no choice.

At first, in the moment, all I had felt was numb horror, only overcome with wonder and longing. Sarah could not have known how she looked to all of us, glowing brighter and more beautiful than a star in that darkness, even so stiff with fear. Perhaps even more so, with her noble chin lifted in such self-sacrificing courage. Never had she embodied her name more, in both its senses of *Heir* in her own tongue and *valiant* in mine. But in every moment since she'd surged from me to the safety and privacy of her hold, my horror for her heated to an ever-increasing rage.

That was why no one had told me.

I was the only one left completely in the dark because everyone just assumed that I either would throw a fit and refuse to put Sarah through that torture or that risk, or I would be incapable of acting out my role if ordered to do so. And...torch it, they were right. That didn't mean I wasn't tempted to strangle Kor as he was hurriedly explaining things to me, but fortunately for him, there wasn't time to murder him, and I needed him now more than ever to handle the aftermath of what he had done.

What made me want to scream was that *no one* thought we had done the wrong thing except me. Everyone was full of triumph and relief at how incredibly *well* everything had gone, how clever Kor and Eskala had been for being the masterminds of all of this and remarking at the fruit it had already borne. Even Yvera's brusque assessment was "Seems like Kor didn't mess up this time." Aside from Kor's barest of hurried apologies to me, no one stopped to think how even I felt about being used in such a way, let alone what Sarah felt.

Even though *Sarah* was the beloved name on everyone's lips, once they had it. All anyone outside the Crown wanted to know was where Sarah was, why I was answering their questions about her for her, and why the Crown was still holding her back from them. They always seemed flabbergasted when I would explain to them time after time (losing patience with each repetition) that she hadn't yet been invested, that it wasn't yet time for her to take her place as Queen of Ice, that she might yet decide to pass the role to another, and for the last time, *no* we were not betrothed, and might never be.

Flame help Sarah if she *didn't* want to marry me, because after tonight, she would have to fight a crushing mountain of expectation to avoid it.

A mountain made larger than should have been possible by the nonsensically reverent notion that began gaining traction the moment of Sarah's breathtaking reveal: a disturbing number of people—increasing the longer that interminable night wore on—began elevating the Moonfair play to the level of sacred, Tree-inspired prophecy, and Sarah and me as its fulfillers, *and that sect wasn't just Starkissed.*

I could have expected such absurdity from their clan, but I had underestimated how deeply their yearly Moonfair reenactment and frequent productions of the full-length version had penetrated the hearts and imaginations of the Six Realms over the centuries. Intentionally or not, they had planted in every mind the subliminal expectation of a Moondaughter and a Golden Heir as their beloved saviors.

Perhaps if this had happened at another time, they would not have made that leap with quite such fervor, but all the previous signs this hard year had pointed to darkness. The increased numbers and aggressiveness of consumed attacks, the droughts, the fires, the malfunctions, my unexplained travels, my recent raging feat of impossibility, preparations for war, and rumors about the King's health, all culminating days before the Dark Solstice....

Then, give them a sign, a bright moon in the darkness, that things would be alright....

Well, perhaps their belief was inevitable.

If as crushing as an avalanche.

"YOU *KNEW* THIS WOULD happen," I accused Kor as we waited, alone, at long last, in front of the moondoor that led to Sarah's gate. At least, where he swore the door was, since it wasn't currently visible.

Kor just raised a weary eyebrow at me, too tired to even smirk. Yet somehow, even after the night we'd had, he was still as presentable as ever, which only made me even more irritated with him. I was certain my hair was a frazzled mess by now, and my black pageant finery was all rumpled and stiff, but Kor? His midnight-blue curls were still perfectly styled, his blue silks crisp and straight and laying just so, his brown-skinned, angular cheeks appearing as clean-shaven as ever. The fact that those cheeks could not even *grow* stubble only made me more irritated with him, not less.

"Of course I did," Kor said. "I *made* it happen."

"You...." That was all I could manage, rage and frustration choking my throat.

Kor met my eyes. "You've seen the hope you've given them. Would you rather they didn't have it?"

For Flame's sake, why? Why did he always have to be so *right*?

"No. I would rather have been given a choice."

Kor's midnight-blue eyes flashed with soulflare. "You made your choice when you became Heir. 'My life for the Realms, my life for my Tree.' *That's* what you swore. Ever since that moment, your life wasn't yours anymore. It was your people's and your Tree's. If I sometimes have to trick you into keeping your oaths until you grow up, well...I am sorry. But maybe think a bit more about how you took away *my* choice when *you* choose *me* to be your leftwing."

I closed my eyes and took deep breaths. "You had a choice."

Kor laughed coldly. "Did I?"

I opened my eyes. "More than I did."

Eyes burning, Kor smiled humorlessly and shook his head at me. "You know what I gave up for you. For all the Realms."

I flinched. I knew. Even though he so seldom brought it up, I never forgot.

"Everything," Kor finished. "Everything, Ben. Because there's no point in having that if the Realms fall."

I sighed, running a hand through my hair. "Alright, you know what infuriates me about what you did? Sarah hasn't chosen yet, Kor, yet you still took that from her."

He stiffened. "She had a choice—"

"That she had to make after you *trapped* her down there with me! And after being trapped, you knew what she would choose. Because she's Sarah. You used her even more than you used me, and that's the part that I can't forgive you for."

Kor clenched his jaw. "She can still give it all up. Unlike us, she can walk away."

"Walking away won't erase what you made me put her through. Flame, Kor, you made me *kiss* her."

"Oh, don't pretend that you two *suffered* through it."

I gritted my teeth. "Whether or not Sarah enjoyed it is beside the point. Our first should have been her choice."

"Oh, that was your first?" Kor said flatly. "I'm sorry, but given your behavior toward her, that would have come as a surprise to anyone."

I lowered my voice to a soft, dangerous volume. "Do you really want to get me started on *your* behavior toward her?"

Kor slowly smiled, eyes as cold as ice. "Oh, please do."

Just then, the moondoor flared into being and began grinding open. We both stepped apart as Sarah came through, yawning and rubbing her eyes.

"Sorry about the wait. Still waking up, and I had to run to the...."

She looked between the two of us, registering the tension there.

Her brown eyes sharpened. "What's wrong?"

"Nothing!" Kor and I blurted at the same time, like naughty hatchlings caught stealing hotsweets.

I glared at Kor, but of course he had already smoothed himself over and was turning to her with real exhaustion.

"It's been a long night for both of us, that's all."

Sarah gaped. "You two stayed up the entire *night*?"

"A long, long night," I repeated, going to her. I took her smile and brightening eyes as invitation enough and bent down to kiss her.

Oh, but to taste her again, to breathe her deliciously cool scent in straight from her skin and feel her pulse thrum under my fingers at her neck...

...made the tension from the night fade like a dream and the brightest part of it come back in force.

"Getting longer while we stand here," Kor said pointedly.

I only broke from Sarah's lips long enough to say, "You're welcome to go."

In fact, please do, I thought.

I was more than ready to be *alone* with her.

"Ben," Kor said flatly. "We came to get Sarah because the Lady Starkissed has requested an audience and is *waiting* for her."

Sarah broke from me with a start. "Wait, what?"

I sighed and straightened. "Unfortunately, yes. *I* wanted to let you stay in your hold until we were ready to leave, but...let's just say that you...made quite the impression last night."

"What *kind* of impression?" she asked suspiciously.

Kor gave his signature smile. "Only the *best* kind. Everyone loved you. The downside is...everyone is now dying to meet you."

When Sarah's eyes widened with horror, I put a comforting hand on her shoulder. "Don't worry. We handled the worst of all of that. That's what we've been up doing. But the only one we couldn't put off was the Lady—because you made your debut here, in her Realm, at her festival."

Not to mention she gave Kor her full cooperation in pulling the night off, but I wasn't about to mention that. Not only was that going into more detail than Sarah needed to handle now, I was still too mad at Kor about it all.

Sarah looked down at herself. "You could have told me that before I picked something to *wear*."

"Why?" I asked in surprise.

I looked at her form-fitting sweater, trousers, and boots, all of which tantalizingly displayed her slender frame and subtle curves. Her dark brown hair was done up in a simple, yet pretty braid, and though her heart-shaped face and light brown skin had none of the elaborate makeup and body paint from last night, she somehow looked lovelier to me than ever.

"You look perfect, as always."

Not that I would have minded if she'd worn that delicate white dress again....

Her lips twitched. "Thanks, Ben, but—"

"The Lady will understand the circumstances, Sarah," Kor said smoothly. "She knows something of the urgency of our mission and what a wild night it has been. All she wants is to meet you for a few dek before you're whisked away again."

As she processed, I watched the anxiousness in her eyes, the desire to flee in her hunched shoulders...fade. It didn't entirely leave, but she set her shoulders and raised her chin.

"You know what? Why not? I've been through worse and somehow survived. Let's go meet a Lady."

She strode forward imperiously, and my flameheart flared for her.

"Well, technically," Kor said cheekily as she passed him, and he followed. "Ben and I have already—"

"Shut it, Kor."

I followed the two of them with a grin. Oh, yes. The day was looking up. Or so I thought.

Little did I realize then that I would look back on that brightly dawning day as one of the darkest of my life.

Chapter Two

PIECES

Sarah

I SHOULD STOP HAVING expectations of people, because the Lady Starkissed wasn't anything like I expected.

Ben, Kor, and I had avoided any of my new "fans" through a combination of scarcely used passages and careful crowd management by the guards who joined us a safe distance from the moongate. (Only Ben and Kor had come all the way to get me to reduce the number of people who knew its location, and the guards who had been with me last night when we'd discovered it had taken blood oaths not to reveal it even before they began their assignment.)

But the moment I walked into the audience chamber in the King's Wing, two giggling girls of about three and six assaulted me, screaming, "Moondaughter! Moondaughter!" A statelier tween boy followed them and clasped arms with me far more seriously than his age seemed to warrant; but then again, from his cornflower blue hair and eyes that matched the woman behind him, I guessed he was the Starkissed Heir.

The Starkissed Lady, Winthra, seemed much more like a tired, doting mom than the sultry, conniving leader I would have expected to be at the helm of the Starkissed clan. Oh, she had cheek, but I got the impression that half the reason she had asked to meet me was so that her kids could—and, from her most serious moments and questions for me, the other half was to find out if I was the sort of person she could count on to help save them.

The older two children, Okyo and Asha, were alright, but little Yira won my heart. She snuggled up in my lap the entire time and seemed to content to stay there and listen to the grownups talk, playing with a string of blue beads that glowed when she would touch them and beaming up at me as if I were a Disney princess and she the luckiest girl in the Realms to have met one.

When Lady Winthra stood and picked up her daughter from me, Yira shyly handed the beads to me. "That's for you."

"Oh, take it, please," Winthra said before I could protest. "You'll make her sevenday, and I can easily get her another one."

"Alright." I smiled at Yira. "Thank you very much."

The Lady grabbed her other daughter's hand and started leading them out, but Asha turned and said boldly, "When are you going to heartbond with the Heir? And why aren't you wearing his earring?"

As I had learned only a couple days ago, a heartbinding was the dramá term for *wedding*, and an earring was their equivalent of an engagement ring.

My cheeks heated. "Er, well, you see. We haven't...decided if we're...doing that."

"What?" the girl said in consternation. "Why?"

"Because...it's a big decision that needs a lot of thought and discussion."

Like, any discussion would be nice. Any at all.

Ben hadn't even told me how he *felt* about me yet. I knew he cared for me because, well...that much was obvious to even me by now. But at Kor's advice, I hadn't yet talked to Ben about it, and especially not about how I felt. After losing his mother years ago and bearing the burdens of being Heir during these dangerous times, Ben had an unhealthy tendency to push away the people he cared about for fear of hurting them. Kor claimed that if we didn't first convince Ben that he *couldn't* live without me...he would find a way to do just that.

I fervently hoped last night and especially Ben's greeting this morning meant we were in the clear. After the adrenaline from the pageant had worn off, and I paced alone in my hold, worry had settled in, with all Kor's dire warnings replaying over and over in my head. That worry had reached a fever pitch by the time I'd stumbled through the moondoor this morning, wondering what I would see in Ben's eyes after a night apart. Then his golden eyes glowed like twin suns when they rested on me, melting every single doubt.

Then, after that kiss, almost as good as our first...we had to be good, right? But that meant we finally needed to talk about...us, and that thought gave *me* butterflies of uncertainty. I cared about Ben—loved him, to be honest. So much it frightened me.

That was part of the problem. This was all happening so fast, yet it all felt so *right*. And it still wasn't a simple decision. Because choosing Ben also meant choosing a destiny I wasn't one-hundred-percent certain I could bear.

According to the Tree of Flame, Ben *had* to marry the Queen of Ice. Whether that was me or...someone else.

My gut twisted painfully—even more so for the butterflies that had been bouncing around in there.

"Ashes," the girl pouted, thankfully oblivious to my inner turmoil. "*You're* the Moondaughter, and he's the Golden Heir. He's waited eighteen years for you, and now he's found you, you're supposed to be together."

I blinked at her. Did Ben have to deal with these kinds of expectations *every* year? No wonder he dreaded the Moonfair so much.

"Honey," I said gently. "I think you're getting me confused with the *real* Moondaughter."

The real...fictional Moondaughter, that is.

Ben had said the play was fiction, right?

"No," she said, growing even more upset and pointing at me. "*You're* the real Moondaughter. The one we've been waiting for. The Moontouched returned."

Did I see...a flicker of alarm in Lady Winthra's eyes? Did she and her son share a quick look?

"*Suki*," she said soothingly to Asha.

The translation magic Ben had placed on me literally interpreted *suki* as "candle flame" in my head, but the English didn't sound nearly so much like the short-and-sweet term of endearment it was meant to be.

"*Suki*," the Lady repeated, "remember that she doesn't remember him from before. She's been reborn. Now the Golden Heir needs to be patient while she gets to know him again."

Winthra met my eyes with a pleading look that said, *Please, just go with it.*

"Right," I said slowly, nodding. "I...um...don't remember any of that. I still have some getting to know him to do."

"Oh." Asha calmed down immediately. "That makes sense. But you *are* going to like him. After all, you died for him."

This was getting weird, but for the sake of her mother, I just smiled. "I'm sure you're right. I can already tell he's a good guy."

"He is," Asha declared, as if she were the expert on such things. Then she finally let her mother lead her out of the room.

Just before they were out of hearing, I heard her ask, "Does this mean we can't have the Moonfair anymore?"

"Of course not, *suki*. We can still...."

The rest of the Lady's answer was lost in the bustle of the central court.

Huh. I would have written all of that out as girlish whimsy...except for the Lady's alarm and the look she traded with the Heir.

Was there...something the Starkissed weren't telling the rest of the clans?

Oh, who was I kidding? Of course there was. The only question in this case was *what*?

Well, I thought I knew what thread to pull next: I made a mental note to ask Kor if this playwright had Moontouched ancestry—and watch his reaction carefully.

Because, even if Kor *could* be trusted...he wouldn't go spilling cherished Starkissed secrets just for the asking.

Kor.... There was yet another matter to figure out, one that twisted my guts yet again, this time in a different way. *Could* he be trusted? Was he simply a brilliant and sometimes arrogant leftwing, or was he something more sinister, as Svyer claimed?

Though Svyer—Ben's Peacegrowth cousin—was one of the most compassionate people I knew and was fast becoming one of my best friends, I doubted her objectivity about Kor, and that of her unclear source. Svyer had been right about Kor's betraying his own brother for power; Kor hadn't even tried to deny it when I confronted him with the information last night during our hunt for the moongate. Except...he said that everyone knew that. If everyone, especially Ben, knew...what made them still trust him?

Could he really be fooling them all? Could he *really* be plotting to kill Ben's *father* to make Ben King, giving Kor as much power as he could hope to get in the Six Realms?

I didn't want to believe him capable of that. Though most of the time he put on a veneer of clever, charming callousness, several times by now, he had been vulnerable, human, even caring toward me. I'd begun to think of him as a friend, as he claimed he was.

Although his deceitful machinations over these past couple days hadn't helped dispel the seed of doubt Svyer had planted, and something was *still* going on here that he wasn't telling us; I'd had a vision in ice of a conversation he had with Eskala that hinted at some danger that Kor thought he had under control, enough so that he refused to tell Ben about it.

That last thought—the reminder of a lingering danger that I'd blissfully forgotten about until now in the glow of last night—wrenched my gut once again, making me glad I'd only grabbed a roll for breakfast. (Even though Ben would scold me for it when he found out.)

As I muddled over the thorny enigma that Kor was, I found myself frowning in one of the audience room mirrors.

Then it rose inside me, unbidden: power unfurling, *asking* to be released.

Heart pounding, I cast a glance around the room, but for the moment, I was still alone.

Make it quick, I told the magic.

Then I reached out and put my hand on the mirror. As if heeding my request or simply because the need was urgent, the ice creeped across its surface much more quickly than last time, forming the image even before the mirror was covered.

It took me a moment to realize what I was seeing, since the scene was dark and only somewhat moonlit, and outside, somewhere I had never seen before. Once I understood, I immediately felt queasy.

Even with his back to me, Kor's dark blue curls, broad shoulders, and trim waist were unmistakable. Even as he was tangled with a woman. This wasn't the fake make-out session he'd put me through last night as part of my "disguise." In far more detail than I ever had wanted to, I saw what it truly meant for Kor to seduce someone.

But when he pulled enough away to trail kisses down the woman's neck, and I saw her face, my stomach dropped, and I nearly broke off the magic.

Svyer.

Now I also had a hint at *when* this was, because that was Svyer's updo and dress...from last night.

"Please, flameheart," Kor said huskily, brushing his lips along her jaw. "For me."

Numbly, I remembered Svyer's angry words to me, when I'd told her Kor had begun flirting with me but that it was nothing. *With Kor, it's never "nothing." It means he wants something from you, Sarah.*

Svyer hesitated, panting. "I...don't know. Why can't you just give me a mess—"

Kor cupped her face. His voice was still husky, deeper than usual. "No, no, not for this. I need time with him, alone with him. It's the only way to make him see. Don't you understand?"

That man would do anything for power.... What's keeping him from betraying his own King?

Svyer, I thought in horror. *What is he asking you to do? And why are you considering it?*

Because she was. Kor covered her mouth, and her eyes closed again in pleasure. Caving.

"Sarah?"

I jumped, breaking the connection. The image vanished, and the ice retreated, leaving not so much as droplets behind.

I turned, heart pounding. Yvera—Ben's rightwing, primary bodyguard, and lifelong friend—stood in the doorway, arms folded, scowling.

Even more than usual. Yvera normally had a hard look on her face, made even more intimidating by her over-six-and-a-half-foot height, muscular warrior's body, customary violet scale-plate armor covering almost every inch of her olive skin up to her neck, high cheekbones, severe braid restraining her kinky violet hair, and scar through one eyebrow.

Right now, she was taking the hardness up another notch. She was *not* in a good mood.

"What in Flame's name were you doing?"

"Er...." I said, heart still pounding rapidly, mind reeling. I felt like I needed to throw up. "Moontouched stuff."

I don't know what I'm supposed to do with this! I told the magic. *I didn't ask for this!*

I most definitely did *not* ask to have forever seared in my mind the image of Kor sucking the face off my friend.

You gave me this. Now help me figure it out!

Yvera snorted and slumped on the wall next to me. "I figured it must have been something like that. You're not one of those egocentric girls who are always checking themselves out in a mirror. Ashes, I *hate* them."

I stared at her. "Why are you here?"

What I wanted to ask was, *Why are you being kind of...nice?*

Especially given her mood. These days, I was normally the *cause* of her bad temper—or at least a convenient target.

Yvera scowled and waved her hand. "Why else? Ben told me to keep an eye on you while he's off somewhere."

"And you're...listening to him?"

She shrugged. "Why not? Gives me something to do."

"I thought you didn't like...hatchsitting me," I said slowly.

"I don't," she said bluntly. "But it's the job."

Then cocked her head. "Oh, but you're talking about last night, aren't you? Well...that was even worse than usual, obviously. What with...the pageant and everything."

I stared at her, then finally understood. "You knew I would probably be chosen...and you went along with it anyway. Why?"

I could hardly believe my daring, as if I were asking an angry bear how it had gotten the trap marks on its paw. But she'd never been in a communicative mood around me before; would I ever get another chance like this again?

Maybe solving this much smaller mystery would help me unravel another.

Yvera gave me a hard look, and for a few moments, I thought I'd pushed my luck too far.

Then she looked away and spoke quietly. "If I hadn't...then I would always wonder."

I waited three beats of silence before asking, "Meaning?"

Still without looking at me, Yvera said dispassionately, "The Tree told me years ago that I would never marry Ben. But She told me I would know the one who would, because I would stand beside her when the Moonstar chose her."

I became still, heart pounding again. I swallowed, then rasped, "She...said that, did She?"

Where was there the *choice* in all of this? That choice everyone kept talking about?

Do you really want to make any other? the quietest voice in my mind whispered.

Shut up! Just...just shut up!

"Yup," Yvera answered tonelessly. "So. Like I said. I don't like living with regrets. Or questions of 'what might have been.'"

"Does that mean you've...told Ben?" I asked tentatively. "How you feel?"

Yvera slowly smiled. "In a manner of speaking. He said no, of course. In no uncertain terms."

That...made me a lot happier than it had any right to. It also made my heart hurt for her at the same time.

Especially when her smile faded. "In his mind, I'll always be his sister."

After a pause, she looked at me sidelong. "What? No pitying, 'I'm so sorry, Yvera'? 'That's such a shame, Yvera'?"

I smiled thinly. "I figured you didn't want to hear it. Especially coming from me."

She slowly smirked. "You know, if I wasn't destined to forever hate your guts...I might have come to like you."

"And if you didn't scare the heck out of me...I might have come to like you, too."

Her grin turned feral, showing teeth. "Aw, you flatterer."

My smile faded.

"What?" she said, raising an eyebrow. "Come on, you're nearly as transparent as Ben. Something's clearly eating you, and has been ever since I came in."

Yvera...might just have something that might help me. No one was more paranoid about Ben's safety than she was.

"Speaking of flatterers...." I looked around and listened, but I didn't see or hear him nearby. That didn't always mean much, but didn't he say he would be taking a nap to rest up before we had to go? He'd looked tired enough that might be true.

I looked back at her. "Do you trust Kor? I mean *really* trust Kor?"

Yvera's eyes narrowed. "What kind of trust? As in, would I trust him with my last cask of wine, or...?"

"I mean with Ben's life."

Her face became grave, her eyes hard. "If I didn't, I would have killed him a long time ago."

"What about...Ben's happiness? Wellbeing?" I said carefully.

"What are you getting at?" Yvera demanded.

"I guess what I'm asking is, *why* do you trust him with Ben? I...need to know."

She pressed her lips thin. "I trust him with Ben's life...because if it weren't for Kor, Ben wouldn't *be* alive right now. He protected Ben...when even I couldn't."

"What, he just...threw a shield around him once or twice?"

"No." Yvera scowled. "I mean, he turned in his own brother to save Ben. If that doesn't prove it, I don't know what would."

"What?" I whispered. I could feel a numb horror seeping up from my gut to my brain.

Yvera must have thought that was a question for more details. She sighed and settled in, propping her leg on the wall behind me.

"If you think *Kor* is unbearable, you should have met his older brother. Solim was a two-faced *snake*. I told Ben so. But Ben...it was after his mom died. He...he was going through a rough time. And Solim...."

Yvera ground her teeth. "He was trying to get Ben to choose him as leftwing, see? Ben was getting to the age when he was supposed to pick, but he wasn't in his right head, couldn't see that Solim's *niceness* was just an act. He wouldn't listen to me. He thought Solim was his hero."

My heart thumped wildly. I could see it all now. Ben, lost and grieving. A cool, clever older boy showing him attention, seeming kindness....

Hadn't Kor himself described that very scenario to me?

Yvera snorted. "But if Ben thought Solim was a hero, then Kor worshiped the ground Solim walked on. Followed him around like a little, pathetic shadow. When his dweeby nose wasn't stuck in a book, of course."

"What?" I breathed.

Yvera grinned at me. "You'd never know it now, but Kor is nothing like he was back then. He was small, tiny for a drakón, skinny as a twig, and he wore these *spectacles.*"

She chuckled with relish. "Said they helped him read for longer or in different lightings or something. I didn't care. They made him look ridiculous. He was always reading something or other, said he wanted to teach *history.*"

Yvera gagged.

"Even when Solim could drag him out of the Library, Kor would never talk to anyone but Solim, and occasionally Ben—but not in the same way Solim did."

She hesitated, then grudgingly admitted, "Kor was different back then. He was...*nice.* What you saw was what you got with him, and when you could get him to talk...he was nice. In a weird, awkward sort of way. He tried to be kind to Ben, I'll give him that."

Yvera's face grew serious. "When the time came, I thought for sure Ben was going to choose Solim. He told me he was, and I couldn't talk him out of it. Then...Kor found out about something. I don't remember what. Just something that made him think his brother wasn't so great after all, and he warned Ben, just before the ceremony.

"Whatever it was, it finally made Ben realize that Solim just didn't feel right. So, after picking me, he picked Kor. Everyone was shocked. And *no* one was more shocked than Kor. People who say that Kor aimed to be leftwing just like Solim did weren't there, didn't know them. Not like I did—and I'll be the first to tell Kor he's a torched ass to his face. But back then? He was shocked. He went as pale as I'd ever seen him, tripped on his way up the steps, whispered to Ben that there must be some kind of mistake. But by then, Ben was sure. He said his leftwing was supposed to be Kor, and the King and Tree approved. So, Kor finally accepted."

That man would do anything for power....

I had gone numb. "Is that what you meant? About Kor turning in his brother? To protect Ben?"

"No." Her violet eyes darkened. "That came right after. See, Solim was *mad.* Oh, he pretended to be happy for Kor, that he had never wanted the job for himself. He was still as 'nice' as ever to Ben. But in secret? He started planning how to kill Ben."

My heart iced over. The premonition I'd felt in my gut was spreading. "*What?*"

Yvera nodded shortly. "No one knew, the asher was so good at hiding what he was. Not even I saw he was that mad. His only mistake was in trying to get Kor to help him. Telling Kor some torched ashdust about how, if Ben was gone, everything could go back to the way it was, the way it *should* be. Kor could go back to his books and *history,* and Solim could try to be the next Heir's leftwing."

Yvera snorted. "Well, you can guess what Kor did. I just told you. He turned Solim in, gave the court the proof they needed to convict him and everything.

Even though that puny kid looked about ready to puke the entire time, and he *cried,* like a baby, when Solim cursed him and said they were no longer blood."

My heart was pounding a raging staccato now, my mind putting together the dots. "What happened to him? Solim?"

Please say he's dead or locked in some high-security prison. Please. Please.

Yvera ground her teeth. "He...got away. Torched clever and powerful as he was. We've been searching for him ever since."

Kor's words to Eskala came back to me. *I knew him better than anyone. Still do, I think. He is here, somewhere. He wouldn't be able to resist a chance as good as this.*

"He's actually our top suspect for that lish that attacked us," Yvera continued, oblivious to my inner crisis. "It would be just like him to turn to the Devourer. It's probably why we haven't caught him yet."

Eskala. *Even if what you suspect about him is true?*

Kor. *Especially then. After Ben's challenge, it would be too perfect. Don't you see?*

A few days ago, Ben, driven to a berserk rage by my assumed death, had challenged the Devourer to send its legions...its lish.

I hunched over in horror, feeling about ready to retch.

"Sarah?" Yvera said in surprise, finally noticing what state I was in.

I grabbed her arm. "Yv," I rasped. "Do Kor and Solim...look anything alike?"

Yvera's brow furrowed. "Well...they didn't at the time...but now that you mention it, they would. Kor looks now pretty much like Solim did."

When I asked Svyer how she had gotten her information, she said, *From the person who knows him best. Sol—*

Solim.

I bolted.

"Sarah? Sarah!" Yvera shouted, running after me.

"I need to talk to Kor," I gasped. "Now!"

I had made a terrible mistake. I'd had so many pieces of the puzzle. Not all, but more than most. Although, thinking I was so clever, so objective...I had put them together *wrong.*

Because I hadn't bothered to get the entire picture fast enough. Because part of me had *wanted* Kor to be the bad guy.

And now Svyer could be paying the price.

People stared as we shot through the central court, but we ignored them. Yvera, bless her, didn't question me. She just kept pace.

"Where does he sleep?" I asked frantically, realizing I didn't know.

"This way."

Yvera led me down a corridor I hadn't in been before. It was nice, but the doors were much closer together, indicating normal-sized rooms instead of the expansive suites in my hallway. Just like the guest wings in other holds I'd been to, they had gems of various colors in the centers.

Yvera brought us to one gem that was glowing with a familiar dark sapphire light and pounded on the door.

"You realize he's probably not going to be coherent?" she told me, referring to Kor's quirk of spouting only nonsense for the first fifteen minutes or so after waking. But she didn't stop pounding.

I swallowed, even though it felt like I didn't have any saliva to go down. "Let's hope he didn't get much sleep then."

"What in Flame's name—" Kor cried as he opened his door, blinking in the hall's light. He was bare-chested and bare-footed, and his room was dark, but he was the sort of grouchy you got when you'd been trying to sleep rather than succeeding.

And thank the Flame for that.

When he saw us, he cut off and took a step back, eyes widening. "Sarah?"

"I am so sorry, but this is a matter of life and death," I babbled. "As such, I need you to answer this question with absolute, one-hundred-percent honesty, no matter how bizarre or invasive it may be."

"What?" Kor said flatly, eyes narrowing.

"Did you or did you not make out with Svyer last night?"

Yvera snorted. "*That's* your life-or-death question?"

Kor blinked again, shaking his head. "*What*? Svyer? What would make you think that I...."

I swallowed. "Or was it someone who looks exactly like you from be-hind? Like...a brother."

Kor froze for one eternal second.

Then he abruptly grabbed me by the arms, his eyes burning. "Sarah, when and where did you see this? *Where? And when?*"

"In the ice!" I babbled. "It's started showing me things! Anywhere, not just in the hold!"

I thought he would be angry that I hadn't revealed my talent for spying, if that's what it was, until now. Instead, relief flickered across Kor's face.

He was glad that I hadn't seen it in person. That I hadn't been *that* close to...his brother. Whatever monster he was now.

"When did you see this?" he demanded again, hardening once more. "Where were they?"

"I saw it just now! But I wasn't there! I don't know! It wasn't *now* because it was night. The ice must have shown me last night. Svyer was in her dress...."

Kor shook me. "*Where were they?*"

"Outside somewhere. I don't know! It was dark. There was some moon-light, but they were in shade. All I saw was them, and all I heard was him asking Svyer to do something for him, to get him alone with...."

Even when I thought I had figured it out, I hadn't entirely. Now the last piece fell into place.

I...had thought Kor...Solim...had meant the King.

My frozen heart cracked and shattered.

Kor saw it at the same time as I did. His eyes went wide with horror, and his hands fell limply from me.

"Yv," Kor said numbly. "Where's Ben?"

"He...." Yvera's eyes widened. "He flew off with Svyer. Wouldn't let me come."

In the very next heartbeat, she was a violet bolt shooting back down the hall. She didn't stop to think, to ask what overly complicated things were going through our overly complicated brains.

If there was one thing Yvera understood instinctively, better and faster than anyone, it was a danger to Ben.

"All MY ELITES," she roared in the central court, the sound echoing back to us. "TO ME, NOW!"

Kor let out a livid curse, then grabbed me by the arms again. "Go tell Eskala exactly what you told me. Do you understand? Exactly. Everything. And for Flame's sake, whatever you do, stay with *her*, where it's *safe*."

"But I can help him—"

I could give him energy like no other could. Surely that was more necessary now than ever?

Kor shook me again. "*Think*, Sarah. Think what Ben will do if you get hurt. Think what the Devourer could do with your Blood. It's probably *waiting* for you to go after him."

"If Ben *dies*, that hardly matters!" I cried.

Kor clenched his jaw. "If Ben dies...then you are our only hope."

Without another word, he ran down the hall after Yvera—not quite a blur, but still faster than I had ever seen him run.

I stood there, frozen for far too long. Even as the King's Wing stirred like a kicked and maddened beehive, as shouts and commands rang out, as people rushed to and fro. I stood in that momentarily empty hall, feeling utterly helpless to do anything meaningful to save the man I loved from the danger I had seen too late.

Then...a quiet voice whispered, *You're not helpless.*

I couldn't fly out with the dragons to save Ben. I couldn't fight by his side. Not against a lish. Not without risking doing more harm than good.

But there was more than one way to help.

Even as the morning waxed toward noon and my power waned...it curled up with a precious offering.

CHAPTER THREE

BETRAYED

KORIBEN

SVYER FOUND ME WHILE I was packing, fit to bursting.

At first, like Kor, I thought I would take a nap to tide me over so that we could leave not long after Sarah's meeting with the Lady Starkissed was done, but I couldn't even get so far as taking off my boots. With the sun climbing and my brain whirling, I had gone past the point of exhaustion to jittery nerves.

Everything had felt so right when Sarah had come out this morning, so natural and effortless. Before, my mind had been too full of dealing with the aftermath of the pageant to think about the future. With her back, it had been easy to forget past *and* future altogether. But as soon as I set her off to meet the Lady in the audience chamber....

It all came crashing in like a tidal wave, nearly knocking me off my feet even as it knocked out my breath.

What am I doing?

Everything I had wanted was now so close, almost close enough to touch it. One more gate down, only two to go, and Kor's people had made good headway in identifying likely locations for us. We could do this. We could get Sarah to Earth and to her Tree. Avva would be healed, everything back to the way it should be. And Sarah....

Well, she might not be ready to take an earring from me right now, but even I could see now that she...wanted me. *Me*. Not Kor, not anyone else.

Cared for me, even.

That was...what I had wanted. More desperately than anything. Wasn't it?

Then why was I so *terrified*?

I had only barely gotten back to my rooms in a somewhat normal-looking outer state before I started falling to pieces.

Fortunately, I had long ago dismissed the couple of attendants that Eskala had half-heartedly tried to assign me. She knew I preferred to take care of myself, and attendants were essentially bodyguards, anyway—and, unlike Sarah, I had more than enough of those with my elites and Yvera around. Upon arrival, I had immediately exercised my right to politely tell them that their services wouldn't be required, and they'd left with no more than a shrug.

After all, even though the Starkissed pretended to "pamper" us Royals when we came to their "optional" events (as part of their whole insidious torture package), dramá didn't believe in spoiling our Royals. Doing the occasional chore like laundry or cooking, yes, since we simply did *not* have the time, but not waiting on us hand and foot. After all, if we couldn't so much as dress ourselves, how were we supposed to defend them?

At first after getting to my bedroom, I had paced while trying to control my breathing and too-fast flameheart pulses, telling myself I was being ridiculous. When that didn't work, I put my frantic energy to use by grabbing all the little things I had somehow scattered everywhere over one day and sleepless night. (There was a good reason I hadn't let Sarah see my bedroom at Crownhold.)

Just about when I was finishing up that task and starting to desperately think of another, I heard a knock on my outer door. Not sure whether to be relieved or worried at the interruption, I hurried to answer it.

Svyer stood there, in her normal healer's uniform, but her emerald-green hair was oddly loose and unbrushed, and she looked as tired as I felt. That off smell from before hit me, stronger than ever, and there was something in it that almost seemed...familiar.

She wasn't just experimenting with something. Was she...sick? In a way that neither she nor her colleagues could heal?

I felt a new spike of fear join the others inside me.

"Hey," I said, blinking. "You alright?"

"Thanks, Ben. You look great this fine morning too," she said with a weary smirk.

"No, I mean, are you really...alright?" I asked hesitantly.

Her smile faded. "I've...been better. You?"

I didn't want to make this about me, but neither did my sleep-deprived brain have the capacity to lie, even as poorly as normal. "Me...too."

She took a deep breath. "That's what I figured, after last night...."

I groaned, leaning against my doorway. "Don't tell me you were there, too."

For my sake, she normally skipped the pageant, if she went to the Moonfair at all.

Her expression remained unusually sober. "I wasn't. But I heard about it later, of course. Sounds like you and Sarah made quite the..."

At my pained grimace, she chose her last word carefully. "...impact."

"I hold you at least partially accountable for that," I said, waving a finger at her. "You, of all people, I would have expected to explain to Sarah just what she was getting into."

Her face darkened. "Kor didn't give me the chance. He showed up right after I did. Conveniently."

"Sounds about right," I grumbled. "Sorry for the accusation, then. That wasn't your fault."

She took another deep breath. "Anyway, I figured that you might want to talk to someone about it—someone a bit more sympathetic than Kor or Yvera—s o...."

"Oh," I said in surprise, then stood back. "Sure. Come on in."

I wasn't sure how much I *wanted* to talk about it, especially since I had done nothing but that all night, but it was kind of Svyer to offer, and if I gave her some privacy and let her think she was helping me, maybe she would finally let me help her.

"Actually...." she said hesitantly. "Would you like...to go flying with me? I figured you could use some wing-stretching first...."

It was as if she had thrown me a lifeline.

"*Hellwinds*, yes. Come on, let's go."

I stepped out and closed my door behind me, then began walking with her out the hall and into the central court.

"Ben!" Yvera called.

Svyer and I paused near the arch to the landing circle. Svyer ducked her head as if she had been caught doing something naughty. I put a hand on her shoulder.

It's fine, just ignore her, I told her with my inner voice.

"Where are you going?" Yvera demanded in exasperation. "I thought we were supposed to be getting ready to leave."

"Sarah's still with the Lady, I'm assuming?"

"Yes," Yvera muttered as she reached us.

"Then we can spare another half deken for me to spend some time with my cousin before we leave."

Silently, I told her, *You're the one who's always saying I should make more time for friends.*

Yvera rolled her eyes. "Fine," she huffed, and made as if to follow us.

Svyer raised her eyes in slight alarm.

Maybe Svyer had already been intending to tell me what was wrong all along, and she just needed some real privacy—not just a closed door—to do it.

"Alone," I told Yvera pointedly, blocking her way.

"What?" she said flatly.

"Yv," I said in a low, patient voice. "It's broad daylight, increasing to noon. I'm going with *Svyer*, my *cousin*, for a short flight around *Olsdak*."

Which was one of the safest places on Oshal, made even safer by all the extra patrols our elites had been flying. Any consumed that would have slipped through the combined net of our vigilance, the remoteness of the hold, and the power of Starkissed wards would have been one or two at best—hardly a threat to me under the circumstances.

All of which Yvera well knew.

Still, she ground her teeth, and it took a hard look from me for her to see a direct order was coming if she didn't bow out now.

"Fine," she muttered. "Go get torched, for all I care."

I smiled. "Thanks, Yv. Love you too."

I hesitated, then following a gut feeling, I said, "If you're done packing and need something to do, would you mind keeping an eye on Sarah for me?"

Yvera gave me a look that said, *Are you serious?*

I was, though, surprisingly. Even through my sleep-deprived brain, something was nagging at me. Something being not quite right. Drama and personal mortification aside, the Oshal portion of our mission had all been a bit too…easy, hadn't it? The Devourer hadn't tried to get one of its agents to Sarah, and surely it knew its window was closing.

That made me anxious in a different way. I was abruptly as reluctant to leave as I had been eager to go, and the only compromise I could make with myself to justify leaving Sarah was if the deadliest person next to me was guarding her.

"Please, Yv?" I said sincerely, eyes pleading. That was my secret weapon with her, which I used as little as possible to keep it sharp. She almost had the daring to defy a direct order…but she seldom seemed able to resist if I begged.

I felt guilty about that when I finally realized why that might be, but it was too late—the damage was already done.

"Alright, alright," she said, throwing up her hands. "I'll hatchsit your girl for you while you go off and have fun. But you *owe* me."

I winced at Yvera's calling Sarah "my girl." Beyond the crudeness, it sounded like too much at this point…and not enough…and too much again.

But I wasn't going to correct Yvera when, first, I didn't know what she should say instead, second, I shouldn't be having this inner crisis in the first place, and third, I did owe her. Especially for accidentally using her feelings for me to get her to guard the one I felt for.

"That I do," I agreed fervently.

THE FLIGHT WAS GLORIOUS, just what I had needed to blow off the worst of my terror. It still lay beneath, but it would wait for the time being. I could go back and face Sarah without falling apart again…probably.

Come this way, Svyer said, diving toward a small island, barely big enough to have a mound of trees and some sand. *I want to show you something.*

What? I asked curiously.

Something...interesting I found last night.

Svyer, you were out flying last night? I said uneasily. Clearly, she was fine now, but still. She had to be more careful than that, especially in times like these.

Just for a little, right after sunset, she said guiltily. *I...just had to get away.*

I supposed I wasn't one to talk about that. Especially since I had just dismissed my rightwing in front of her.

Since the beach wasn't an ideal size for us—or at least for me—to land, we glided into the water and then swam to shore.

Swimming as a draká was fun and surprisingly easy; many of our adaptations that suited us to the air transferred better than they probably should have to the water. Our eyes worked well under the water since the same clear lid that protected our eyes during flight also protected us from the water and acted as a second, more adaptive lens. Our nostrils could close like a sealen's, and if we took a deep breath first, we could hold it for dek at a time. The most practiced and adapted Starkissed divers could for nearly a deken. Much of the reason we could fly was pure magic, but there were a few natural innovations, such as sacks of air inside our torsos full of a highly buoyant gas, and those could keep us comfortably afloat on the surface of water as long as we liked, and we could let some of the gas out to dive.

Though I didn't find swimming as pleasurable as flying, I always enjoyed it when I got the chance. During the daytime, at least. As with all things in the Realms, we were the most formidable creatures of the water by day...but by night....

Yet another reason I was nervous Svyer had taken that kind of risk to come here. She might have been able to land on the beach, though, which would have been safer than the water.

We shook off, and with the sun, breeze, and our inner heat, we dried off within moments. Then on unspoken agreement, we both changed back into amáform. I presumed that whatever she had to show me, it wasn't on this empty beach, and when she started for the trees, I knew I was right.

"Come on. It's just a bit of a walk, but we can talk along the way."

Ah, yes, talk.

Before I found the best way to ask about her, she beat me to the punch, casting me a compassionate look. "How are you feeling, Ben? Really? I know this all must be a lot...."

As if the flight and refreshing swim had done little after all, it came rising up again. I found myself glad we still hadn't reached our destination, so that at least my legs could keep pumping. Although Svyer was walking slowly, so I had to force myself to match her pace.

Besides, this tropical jungle wasn't suited to marching along. We had to pick our way through the undergrowth, and if I hadn't been so distracted, I would have wondered why Svyer had done the same last night. In the dark.

"You...could say that again."

She looked at me in surprise. "You look...tense. I thought you would be...I don't know...a *bit* happier by now."

"I am," I said tightly.

I was. The realization that Sarah finally wanted something more from me and the literal glow of that first kiss were still searing in my flameheart. I knew that happiness was there. But it was trapped beneath a layer of ice now, and though I could see it, I couldn't reach it.

"Don't you...love her?" Svyer said hesitantly. "And...want her to love you?"

I did. Both, and with a ferocity that I had never felt before, and yet...that frightened me, more than ever before.

I swallowed as I put a name to the fear.

"Yes," I rasped. "That's the problem."

"I don't get it," Svyer said blankly.

"Svyer...I love her."

That was the first time I had ever admitted the truth out loud, and for good reason. The shockwave of it cracked the ice inside me, and that wasn't a good thing. Because what lay beneath was even deadlier than this numb terror that was holding me back.

Flame, how I loved her.

"But I don't know if I *should*."

Even with everyone's (rather too enthusiastic) expectations and support. Even if the Covenants could be restored, making my oath to never marry void. Even with the Trees' permission. Even with Sarah's.

"What do you mean?" she demanded. "Sarah.... Well, you're going to have to ask her how she feels about you, but even you know by now that it's not *nothing*."

I groaned. "I know, I know, but...*should* she? Is that...good for her? *Safe* for her?"

There it was. The deadly catch. The more I loved her, the more I wanted her to love me, stay with me. The more selfish and reckless I became to convince her to do so. But the more and longer she did that....

"Safe?" Svyer asked, troubled.

I swallowed. "People...who care about me...get hurt."

There. I'd said it.

And Sarah had more potential for both getting hurt and hurting me than ever before. After all, the higher the two of us flew together...the further she had to fall.

I had expected Svyer to jump in with meaningless assurances, but I had underestimated her. She was quiet for a dek as we walked, thinking, face pained.

When she broke the silence, her voice was soft. "Is this...about your mother again?"

I froze, nearly tripping, but I grabbed a vine to steady myself. "What?"

What did Svyer know?

Her face was only gentle when she stopped and looked back at me. "Ben. You *have* to let this *go. It wasn't your fault.* That was just...life. She had so much of life before you, even if you were one of the brightest parts of it. She was ready, though. It was her time."

I closed my eyes and bowed my head, sinking under the weight of how *wrong* she was.

Everyone thought that what took Avvi was the normal wasting sickness that otherwise strong, healthy, nearly immortal drakón got when the Tree had decided it was their time to pass on.

It had not been her time. Or it would not have been...if not for me.

To my surprise, I felt Svyer's arms going around me. I nearly pushed her away, especially as the new wrongness of her scent enveloped me, but in that moment, I needed my cousin, who had loved Avvi, her dearest aunt, nearly as much as I had. Even though Svyer was utterly unaware that I was the monster who had killed her.

"That's not going to happen to Sarah," Svyer said gently. "At least, not for over a century. After you have a long, full, *happy* life with her, and both of you are ready to return to the Flame."

"You don't know that's what will happen," I rasped, clinging to her.

You don't know that I won't kill her too.

"You don't know it won't," Svyer chided gently.

"Svyer," I said, voice breathless with panic. I pulled away from her, shaking my head. "I just...I don't know if I can do this. To her...or to myself."

She took a deep breath. "Well, what's the alternative?"

She flinched, as if an insect had stung her, but she ignored it.

"What do you mean?" I said, mouth and throat dry.

"If you can't let you and Sarah just be happy, for as long as the Flame wills...then you're going to...what? When you go back, what are you going to do? What are you going to tell her?"

I felt like my insides were curling up in the frost and dying off, one by one. "I...I don't know. I can't think. About either option. I just...can't...think."

"Alright, alright," Svyer soothed. "Maybe we take a break from this for a bit."

She flinched again, muttering under her breath.

My concern for her finally pierced through my blind, sleep-deprived panic. "Svyer, what's wrong?"

"I...have something to show you," she said slowly, and turned to continue walking.

We were almost to a clearing. I could see the opening in the trees and undergrowth ahead, but something...was strange. If it were an open space, should it have been so...dark?

"What...." I began, but I trailed off as we stepped into the clear.

Under a dark, spell-enforced canopy that severely dampened the strength I received from the sun.

In the center of that small clearing...was a rough stone altar. Newly made and charged with dark power, it throbbed with menace in my mind's eye.

"Svyer," I said, flameheart stopping. I reached blindly to push her back. "Run. *Now!*"

I was too late. I felt as much as saw a dark shield, like a tar bubble, spring up all around us, far more thick and powerful than it had any right to be.

Then that smell, accompanying the magic, was everywhere. It was different now. Decayed, festered. *Wrong.* But now I finally recognized who it belonged to.

Again, too late.

I wasn't even surprised when he stepped into view. Though the sight still felt like a punch to my gut.

"Solim," I said faintly.

I had almost forgotten. Not what he looked like, because he, and particularly what I remembered of him from the trial six years ago, was forever seared into my memory. Although, thinking of that time as little as I possibly could, I had forgotten how similar he and Kor had looked, and since Kor had grown into a man, now more than ever.

Right down to his clean-shaven face. Of course Solim would continue to hold on to that mockery of his birthright, of what he should have been—and forced Kor to be instead.

But never, ever had I or would I ever see the darkness in Kor's eyes that I saw in Solim's now.

His lips pulled into a polite smile.

"Ben," he said, greeting me as if we were friendly acquaintances meeting by pure chance. "How good to see you. And my, just look at you. All grown up."

"Ben," Svyer said quietly, urgently. "I know how this looks, but it's alright." Had she gone *blind* and *deaf*?

"Svyer," I said in a low voice, holding out my arm. "Stay behind me."

Solim tsked. "There's no need for that, Ben. I won't hurt her. Will I, flame-heart?"

He addressed the last to Svyer, voice dripping with cloying sweetness.

"Of course not," Svyer said with perfect, loving confidence.

I felt a stab of fear and rage that made the edges of my vision go red.

In a dangerous, low voice, deeper than my human voice should have been, I said, "What...did you do to my *cousin*?"

Solim ignored me for a moment and crooked his finger to Svyer. "Time to come over here, dear. Your Heir is getting a bit...unstable."

"Ben, it's alright," Svyer said urgently. "It's Kor that can't be—"

"Svyer," Solim repeated, almost bored now. "*Come.*"

There was a lace of power in his voice that slapped across the clearing. Still not thinking straight, I wasn't prepared for the effect it would have on Svyer.

She went. Ran, actually. Immediately, without thinking. Before I knew that's what she would do. Before I could stop her. She ran so fast that my fingers only trailed helplessly through the tips of her hair as I reached in vain for her.

"No!" I choked out, stumbling forward a few steps, but she was already at his side.

The Svyer I knew was gone, leaving her expression vacant, eyes empty, body stiff and still.

"Svyer," I gasped.

"This is what I did to her, Ben," Solim said, trailing a finger down her cheek. "Starting with love spells, of course, to get close enough to her. To get her to listen to my 'reasoning.'"

He chuckled. "Truth mixed with lies, of course, but Korinth *does* make himself such a good villain. Don't you agree? I can't imagine that you yourself haven't thought of killing him a dozen times by now."

I could hardly breathe now, but I forced my lungs to keep pulling in and out. I forced the red in my vision to retreat. Solim *wanted* me to lose my temper. Even if I shouldn't be able to go entirely berserk for Svyer, he knew how much this was torturing me. That was why he was doing this.

That was why he had targeted her at all.

"Then," he said with relish. "I could begin consuming her. Just a bit. Just the slightest skiff. But enough. You see, Svyer is my latest and obviously most successful experiment in creating consumed that are undetectable by any of the usual tests. Even...by you."

That wasn't entirely true. The smell. I had smelled the wrongness of him on her.

I just hadn't let myself process what that meant.

Because it couldn't have been.

Not Svyer.

"Perhaps the best part was that Korinth suspected what I was doing to her all along," Solim said, lips pulling into a smirk.

I felt like I'd received another punch to my gut. "*What?*"

"Yes," Solim said with a slight frown. "I'm not sure what tipped him off. Perhaps he is developing his own tests. That would be just like him—always trying to best me."

Solim shrugged, then smirked again. "No matter. It was a delight to watch Svyer's memories of his frustrated attempts to get *proof* from her."

He laughed. "Oh, the look on his face when Svyer passed the blood test in front of the King's Wing.... Priceless."

He shook his head, smile thinning. "In the end, the only person who truly frustrated my plans for Svyer was Eskala, by requiring those torched *blood oaths*. She even chose just the right words."

The blood oath...to not intend or bring harm to Sarah. Not intend...*or* bring harm. Because even if most of Svyer's consciousness thought she meant no harm, just enough of her knew to prevent her from....

My horrified eyes fell on the altar.

I saw red again. I trembled with it. The only thing that was keeping me from bursting right now was the fact that I could kill Svyer just in the transformation, let alone the rage—and Solim knew it.

"Yes, that's right," Solim said with a thin smile. "That was intended for your beloved Moontouched queenling. The Devourer was...displeased when it found out Svyer could no longer bring her to me, but I think it's better this way, don't you agree? More appropriate. Coming full circle. All of this between us began with you, after all. Even though you did me a favor by not choosing me as your leftwing, I see that now. Now I have far more freedom and power than Korinth could ever dream of. I probably would have killed you anyway, out of sheer boredom. But now, Ben, your death gets to *mean* something. Isn't that comforting?"

"Hardly," I said flatly.

Except that wasn't entirely true. If my death satisfied the Devourer today.... If it bought Sarah one more day....

Not that I was going to just lie down and take the knife without a fight. If only my exhausted, battered, raging mind could just *think* of how to do that without getting my only cousin killed in the process.

But Flame help me, I was trying.

"Oh, come now, Ben," Solim said, smiling icily. "You *asked* for this, after all. 'Send your legions. Send your lish.' The Devourer couldn't leave such audacity unpunished, but why bother sending legions...when it could send one lish?"

"You've sunk that low, have you?" I said coldly.

I wasn't surprised—all this reeking dark magic around me and his own stated allegiance pointed to that conclusion—but I needed to keep him talking.

Think. Think, torch you.

Solim smirked coldly, and with horror, I saw he knew what I was doing. "Hardly. I've risen that high. After all, I had you and your wings scurrying like insects on that mesa in Ykran, did I not? The only reason you survived is because you fled, like cowards. Well, the time for fleeing is over for you, Ben. It's time...to take your rest."

He pointed to the altar.

I clenched my jaw. "Do you really expect me to make it that easy for you?"

"I do, actually." Dark talons formed on one of his hands, and he used it to grip Svyer's throat. "You see, however stupid it might be for you to do so, I think your flameheart is still too tender, even after all these years, to watch me murder your cousin in front of your eyes."

He was right, on all counts. It *was* stupid of me. Inconceivably stupid. I could hear Kor screaming at me in my head.

I should just change now and begin the fight that would end both Svyer's and my life anyway...but at least I would die *trying* to save us, or at least make our deaths mean something. That's what a hero would have done. But I couldn't. I couldn't be *the one* to kill Svyer. That would destroy me just as much as the sacrificial knife could.

What a true coward would have done was surge to the Olsdak sungate; none of the barriers and protections Solim had put in place could have stopped me from doing that much. He knew that. That was why he needed Svyer—to tie me down more securely than chains ever could. Because in an instant, I could be safe. I could be back with Sarah. Even now, I could see her star in my mind's eye, beckoning me to return to her.

But Solim would no doubt kill Svyer instantly as punishment and then escape unscathed, and I would be a monster unworthy of anyone, let alone my star. Even if so many arguments could be made otherwise—that my life was more valuable than Svyer's, that Realms could not afford to lose an Heir *now*, that Sarah needed me to finish her task. I couldn't do it.

I wasn't a hero...but I wasn't that kind of monster.

I was something in between.

That was, perhaps, something far worse.

Solim watched me fight my inner battle against my flameheart...and lose.

He smiled, eyes flashing in icy triumph.

"If you would be so kind, Ben," he said, pointing again to the altar.

With a flameheart being further quenched with each step...I slowly walked to my death.

Just when I was right in front of Solim, close enough that his fetid stench made me want to retch...

...I heard a sound that extinguished my flameheart.

"Ben, it's a trap—" Sarah shouted.

Then, in an abrupt change of tone that would have been hysterically funny if I weren't dying from horror for her, she said in a much smaller voice, "Oh. Oops. I guess you've already figured that out."

Solim turned, eyes glowing darkly with greed, as if he could hardly believe his luck.

I didn't turn.

I didn't think, didn't question, didn't wonder.

Sarah was in danger.

So I acted.

My fist flew, clocking Solim squarely under the jaw with what should have been bone-shattering force.

Flame, that felt *good*. I'd wanted to do that for six years.

For me, of course. One of these days, I'd plunge my sword through his torched chest and slowly burn him from the inside out for Svyer.

But I couldn't stop to think about that, because Solim, torching lish he was, only stumbled backward. All that unexpected punch had given me was a moment.

I took it to grab Svyer, throw her over my shoulder, and dash toward Sarah.

But I didn't see her. Anywhere. Or smell her, either. In fact, now that I had a split second to *think*, I saw her star in my mind's eye was still *far away*. Right beneath the Olsdak sungate, in fact.

Bless the Flame, she was *still safe*.

Then how had I heard her voice?!

Solim roared, sending a crashing wave of dark power toward me that I only just blocked in time with a golden shield of energy, and even then, the force of Solim's wave breaking against my shield made me stumble.

"Ben!" Sarah screamed. "Come to me! Surge to *me!*"

I didn't know how this was happening, but I didn't waste the time to question it.

"I can't bring Svyer with me, Sarah!" I shouted, turning back to face Solim. If Sarah was safe and Svyer was now out of my line of fire....

Well, this was where I made my stand.

As Solim sent another raging wall of black power that sent trees crashing, and plants, stones, sticks, leaves, and dirt flying, as I braced myself, raised my hand, and summoned another golden shield and *held* with all my might....

Sarah shouted, "Yes, you can! I'll give you the power! Just take it and bring her to me!"

Sarah, I thought but didn't say. *It's not a matter of power. It's that I can't.*

Then she poured power into me. Just a small stream, perhaps all she had, but it felt like liquid sunlight inside of me, setting my entire being on fire with the force of her valiance. She used it to lasso me and even Svyer to her, and then *pulled.*

Suddenly, I saw it, felt it. What was impossible, she had made possible. Like she always did.

When was I going to stop doubting her?

I grabbed onto that pull and surged for Sarah.

Taking Svyer with me.

CHAPTER FOUR

FAULT

SARAH

IN ESKALA'S STUDY, I watched the icy panel in front of me in horror. Whatever ice shard had formed on the other side to give me this perspective, it was high in some tree, so I had a terrifying view as the second dark wave crashed over Ben. Only a split second later, my optic went wild as the tree thrashed from the force of the blow, making me lose sight of him.

Was I too late? Was Ben overcome? Both he and Svyer lost?

"NO!" I sobbed, pounding the wall on either side of the ice. Eskala put a comforting hand on my shoulder, but I hardly felt it.

Damn it, Ben. Take what I gave you and—

He crashed into me—really, both poor Eskala and I—with a force that bowled all four of us over, counting Svyer. It was a good thing that Eskala had a nice, plush rug in the center of her study that prevented any concussions, but I still had the air knocked from my lungs.

Then Ben was pushing up and off us, panting, pulling Svyer's limp body to the side as well.

"Sorry," he gasped. "So sorry! Are you alright?"

I could only wheeze, lying dazed and still as my narrowed vision slowly expanded again. I had gotten the worst of it, since he'd come directly for me. Eskala was already sitting up, but I thought her daze was more from shock at what Ben and I had just done than anything.

"I am so sorry, Sarah," he said again, kneeling over me on all fours as he put one hand on my throat. He *dumped* healing power into me. If I'd had so much as a scratch before, he scorched it away. In fact, the force of his healing was almost as dizzying as his crushing weight had been.

"You're alright," he gasped, dry sobbing in relief. "You're alright. You're safe, and you're alright."

All I could do was nod weakly in reply.

"So are you, Koriben," Eskala said gently, putting a hand on his shoulder. "You're back in Olsdak. Both you and Svyer."

"Right," he said, his voice gaining strength as he shifted off me and sat up. "Right."

He looked to the side, where people were already bending over Svyer. His face hardened. "How...is she?"

"I don't know," the gold-uniformed attendant told him frankly but kindly. "We need to get her to the healing wing, now."

A Battleblood guard picked her up in his arms as she spoke.

"Don't leave her," Eskala said sharply to the guard. "Watch her, even after the healers are done."

"Yes, Leftwing," he said with a nod, and he and the attendant hurried out of the room.

"Was that necessary?" Ben asked Eskala in a hard voice as he put an arm around me and lifted me up into a sitting position.

"Perhaps not," Eskala said, "but the time for taking chances with her is passed. Her consumption is now proven."

"She wouldn't—" Ben began hotly.

"She may have sworn a blood oath not to harm Sarah, but do you really want to risk another of your people's lives, Koriben?" Eskala said coldly. "Or is Sarah the only one who matters?"

Because I was leaning against him, I felt Ben stiffen. "That wasn't what I meant," he said icily.

"I know, but *think*. We *keep* Svyer innocent by protecting her from others. We protect them, we protect her."

"Fine," Ben said, shifting back. He stood and pulled me to my feet as well. "Do what you think is best. I have my own job to finish."

He turned to leave.

"Ben," I said in outrage, pulling him back. "What are you doing?"

I didn't save his damn life to have him go straight back out there to throw it away again!

His face didn't soften, even when his eyes met mine. "Solim might still be out there, Sarah. I'm guessing that if you knew I was in danger, and from the fact that Yvera isn't here right now pounding out my guts, that people have gone after me. Am I right?"

"Correct," Eskala said, coming to stand beside me and put a hand on my shoulder. "Go, Ben. Finish it, if you can, but at the very least, bring them back safe."

"Don't send anyone with me," Ben told her. "I don't want to weaken Sarah's defenses any more than I already have. With innocents out of the way, I can always surge back to Olsdak if need be."

She nodded sharply. "Go, and Flame go with you."

Ben looked back at me, and his eyes softened. "I have to do this, Sarah."

I slowly nodded, but dang it, I hadn't recovered yet from all my emotional pendulum swings of the morning, and tears stung my eyes.

I blamed hormones. This was the most *horribly* timed period of my life.

Ben ducked in and gave me the fiercest kiss yet, lips seeming to literally burn against mine in the force of his barely suppressed energy.

Then he tore himself away and was gone, a gold blur running through the door.

Eskala put her arm around my waist and pulled me in. "You saved him, Sarah. Remember that. You saved him by saving Svyer. He'll be fine now. You'll see."

He had better.

I didn't think my heart could take another scare like that again and keep beating.

SOLIM WAS GONE. HE vanished before the rescue party had even reached the scene of destruction, though they, with Ben once he caught up to them, searched long and hard for him.

Svyer never woke up. Though her body was healed, and even purged of the love spells that had so clouded her judgment, the consumed taint remained, and Solim had taken her spirit with him.

Just as he had briefly done with Kor's, back on the mesa.

"That's how I knew it was him," Kor said grimly.

They were all back now—Kor, Yvera, and Ben—and they had all come to where I was sitting with Svyer in the healing wing, in her own private room. Her cell, essentially, the distinction made clear by the guards posted outside her door. There had been guards on the inside, too, until Ben came in and told them their services weren't necessary during his visit. It was a carefully worded way to tell them to get lost, the subtext made clear by his glare.

"What?" Ben said to Kor.

I looked at him in concern. From the moment he had walked in, there had been something different about him. Something hard. Something...dead. Not even a brief hug from me and his hand on my shoulder now had softened him.

"You *told me* you didn't know who the lish was," Ben said flatly. "That you didn't recognize him."

"I lied," Kor said bluntly, arms folded. "I reported the truth to the King and Eskala as soon as I could, and I asked for permission to conceal it from you, so by the time you asked me, I lied."

"Why?"

But Ben looked like he already knew the answer.

Kor took a deep breath. "Because, as your leftwing, I judged that if you knew Solim was a lish and was after you *and* Sarah...that it would detrimentally affect the performance of your duty."

"You—" Yvera called him a name so foul, I won't repeat it.

Ben held up a hand. "Yv," he said in simple warning. "Let him finish."

"What good would it have done, Ben?" Kor said, a pleading note entering his voice. "All that could be done was already *being* done to find him. You knew that much. You also knew that the lish remained a risk to us, regardless of his identity. The only thing that would have been accomplished by telling you who he was would have been increasing your mental strain, and you were already pushing yourself to the breaking point. You had to focus on Sarah. Your duty, and thus mine and Yvera's, was to her, not to track down Solim. What good would it have done if I had told you?"

"And Svyer?" Ben said. "Solim said you always knew."

Kor flinched. "I didn't tell you about her for the same reason, with the additional motivation that I didn't have *proof*. I first suspected when I encountered her at Elspeth Hold, when a...charm I had been working on to detect faint traces of consumption—the new kind the Devourer has begun to employ—went off."

He held up the blue stone that he frequently wore on a black cord around his neck. Especially, I realized...since we had arrived here. From the way Ben's eyes narrowed as they fell on it, I knew he was realizing the same thing.

"But the charm was—is—still in a very experimental phase. Obviously, test subjects are a bit hard and unethical to come by. That wasn't *proof*, Ben, and you know for accusations of consumption, you must have proof. My hands were tied. *Eskala's* hands were tied, even though we immediately asked for and received an observation order from the King. We couldn't tell our people to do anything except observe, and somehow we tipped Solim off, and he was more careful than ever in handling her after that. We never caught him, and we never got proof. And without proof...."

"There was nothing you could do," Ben finished. "But you still didn't *tell* me. Even after Svyer showed up so conveniently and ingratiated herself with Sarah again."

"Ben," I said quietly.

I'd had a lot of time to think, sitting at her bedside while the others searched for Solim, and I had concluded that she was not just innocent but still, at heart, my true friend. I refused to think Svyer's motivations were impure, even if her actions were somewhat controlled.

She cared about me. I knew that. She'd had a piece of cloth with my *blood* on it, and she had thrown it away to be neutralized—perhaps too quickly to have been unconsciously done. Might she not have been at the Moonfair if she hadn't been ordered to be? Maybe, but she always cared about me. That's perhaps why she revealed more to me than Solim would have wanted her to.

"We couldn't stop her," Kor said. "Don't you think it killed me to let her in, to let her be near Sarah? But she passed the consumption test, Ben. Right in front of my eyes, *and* she took the blood oath. We had no right to infringe on her rights. All I could do was watch out for Sarah."

Kor's caution to me to not tell Svyer anything. His convenient interruptions of our call in my hold and our conversation in my room. His demand after the feast that I tell him everything Svyer had told me...for her own good.

"But you still didn't *tell* me, Kor," Ben repeated. "You let me vouch for Svyer, otherwise she wouldn't have had free access to the King's Wing. Because I trusted her implicitly, Sarah could have...and now Svyer is...."

He put a hand to his forehead and took deep, shuddering breaths. I stood back up again and put my arms around him. He rested one arm around me, but only lightly.

"That...I regret," Kor said quietly, voice laced with pain. "That was my crowning mistake, which you both paid the price for today."

"You—" Yvera swore at him again. This time she threw herself at him, shoving him against the wall. Kor let her, his head *thunking* limply against the stone, his arms unresisting by his sides.

I knew better by now than to think that meant Kor couldn't stop her if he wanted to.

"Yvera," I said in alarm, pulling away from Ben.

"*I'm* a failure?" she spat in Kor's face. "*You* failed him, Kor. Because of *you*, Ben was nearly not just killed but *sacrificed* today, and his cousin is—"

"Yv," Ben said wearily. "Stop. Please. Kor was right. Probably about everything."

Kor's dull pain broke as he looked at Ben with increasing alarm. Even as Yvera pushed away from him in disgust.

"No, Ben, this is all, entirely my fault. I let my arrogance and my vendetta with Solim blind me, and he used that, the torched asher. I...I'm not worthy to be called your leftwing anymore. I probably never was."

I stared at him.

"Resignation not accepted," Ben said. "We all make mistakes, Kor. Just because you make them so seldom doesn't make you any less mortal than the rest of us. In fact, you have carried the heaviest burden of all of us since Sarah got here. I'm the one to blame that I couldn't handle my share."

His dull eyes rested on his cousin's lifeless body. "You were right about me, as always. If there's anyone to blame for the fact that Svyer's lying there...it's me."

My heart wrenched. "Ben...."

Kor blanched. "Ben...no, it isn't."

"Of course it is. Isn't it always?" Ben said in a dead voice.

Before we had time to recover from that, he turned to leave. "Get a bit of rest, if you can, then meet me on the landing circle in a deken. It's time we left, while there's still daylight."

"Ben," I said, grabbing him by the arm.

For the first time, he flinched away from my touch.

No, I thought in horror. *This can't be happening. Not now.*

He closed his eyes from the sight of me, even before he turned away. "Sarah, just...just don't. Please don't."

He turned and left.

I stood there, heart breaking, as I felt the pull—that magnetic force I had felt from him for days now that represented the magical, symbiotic bond growing between us—weaken far more quickly than it should have with the distance between us.

Kor was right.

He was pulling away.

CHAPTER FIVE

SNOW

SARAH

ONE OF THE CRUELEST ironies of my life yet was that the first time I rode on Ben's dragon back since discovering my inner voice, the first chance we had to use that time in the air to *talk*, just the two of us, with no one the wiser...was after he stopped speaking to me.

Oh, he greeted me when I came out to the landing circle, but he was merely being polite, as if I were an acquaintance he were giving a lift to. His eyes never met mine. He didn't touch me.

Just like that, it was as if the last six days, and most especially last night, had never happened.

I would have been mad at him if I could. I tried, as we flew. I tried hard.

But all I did was ache. For myself. For him. For Svyer.

Knowing he was doing this *because* he loved me only made it more painful.

It meant I couldn't hate him. It meant that half the tears that the wind whipped away from my cheeks were because of him...and half were for him.

It was a good thing I was on Ben's back, so he didn't see them.

But Kor, flying at his side, could.

A half hour after we had passed through the Olsdak sungate and entered the Battleblood Realm of Ekrel, as we were soaring over breathtaking highlands and heading to snowy peaks that would have rivaled the Alps, Kor spoke to me for the first time since Svyer's room. He must have seen the streams running down my cheeks—or, perhaps more likely but less heroically, the many times I had to blow my nose.

Sarah.... Kor said, voice in agony.

I don't want to hear it, Kor, I said wearily. *You've already told me why.*

I am so sorry.

It's not your fault.

It was no one's fault. No one's...but Solim's and the Devourer's. Why couldn't Ben see that? The common factor in all his tragedies wasn't *him*. It was the evil we were fighting against, the true monsters we were resisting—to save everyone. The people that got hurt around him wouldn't be any better off if the Devourer consumed them.

I feel like it is, Kor said in audible distress. *Tell me what to do to make it right.*

My lips pulled into a humorless smile. *I thought you were the one with all the answers.*

A long pause. Then, sounding smaller and more lost than I had ever heard him, Kor said, *I don't have them now. I don't know what to do anymore.*

I doubted that bewilderment would last for very long. Kor's mad genius was too irrepressible for that, but I wasn't about to minimize his pain now by saying so.

Instead, I said gently, *Welcome to being mortal, Kor.*

Another pause, but a shorter one this time, and some of the Kor I knew had returned to his voice. *Really? Is this what you all feel like, all the time? Well...it's a torched bother.*

I found a weary laugh escaping my lips.

That's it, Kor encouraged. *Be our* sera *for just a bit longer. I hate to say it, but any more tears will have to wait. It's time to dry them and put your cold-weather gear on.*

Since we would be flying into the winter-bound Moldeth Mountains of Ekrel, heading for a remote hold within its peaks that Kor's analysts had identified as the likeliest location for the next gate, my attendants had dressed me in insulating layers, heavy outer pants, and snow-worthy knee-high boots. Then, so I wouldn't be completely suffering in Olsdak's tropical warmth, they stowed the heavy-duty coat, gloves, balaclava, and goggles in a bag hooked to Ben's saddle for me to put on later.

I thought we were going to land first, I said, slightly nervous. For the first time, I noticed that Ben, far from slowing before the mountains, had picked up the pace significantly, so that Kor, Yvera, and the elites accompanying us appeared to be struggling to varying degrees to keep up.

I could only think of one reason for the sudden change of plans and increased speed: danger.

A blizzard is brewing ahead, Kor said grimly.

I looked at the giant clouds forming, creating dark puffy mountains of their own over the snowy range, with the air between land and sky hazy.

I didn't know whether to be relieved that the danger wasn't a Devourer attack or not. From Kor's tone, a blizzard still wasn't a good thing.

So we're going to head right for it? I began getting out the gear, using my best guesses on which order to put things on and how.

Ben's call. He thinks we can beat the worst of it to Roddan Hold. If we don't try now, it could be inaccessible for days.

Days we didn't have to waste.

I understood now. Something seemed off, though. It took me a moment to realize what it was, and then another shot of pain went through my chest.

Ben would have normally told me all of that himself. Discussed it with me, even.

Ben...told you to tell me, didn't he? I asked quietly.

Kor waited a moment too long to answer. *Yes.*

I wasn't offended by Ben taking command, since I deferred to his judgement on this and was relieved he'd made the quick decision when he had to, but I was disturbed and pained by how he'd used an intermediary to tell me about it.

He's in pain, I thought. *So much pain.*

In one morning, he had drudged up memories of the darkest days of his life, had his former hero-turned-would-be-murderer reemerge as a lish for round two, and lost his beloved cousin, perhaps forever. Solim may not have succeeded in plunging a dagger through Ben's flameheart, but he had blown a cannonball through Ben's soul. Here Ben was, taking on water, yet trying to press on, in the only way he thought he could. Could I blame him that this was the only way he knew how to even keep *functioning*?

No.

But I could break my heart from longing to wrap my arms around him, for just wanting to cradle his heart in my chest and keep it from any further harm, forever.

Tears stung my eyes again, and that wouldn't do, so I tried to think of other things. Things like those brewing clouds ahead.

That wasn't hard, since the storm hit us moments after that.

One second, the air was calm.

Then the next, Ben was thrown to the side with a squall, and I couldn't help but let out a yelp of fear and surprise. Snow was suddenly everywhere, all around, a whirling wall of white. Ben labored through it as best he could, wings beating, lungs heaving, steam billowing from his mouth that blew back in my face and fogged up then quickly iced over my goggles, making my visibility next to nothing.

Lean into him! Kor urged. *Lean down in the saddle, grip the straps there!*

That's when I realized the saddle had been made for sitting or lying down. With a bit of difficult adjustments to my straps, I was able to shift my weight forward and lie down, gripping hand straps there for added stability. The new position reduced the force of the wind on me and brought me closer to Ben's radiating warmth. My goggles defrosted a bit, but I still couldn't see much, especially from my new position.

How are you going to find the hold in this? I asked Kor, trying to keep the nervousness from my voice.

We still know our heading, Kor said. *As long as we don't get too blown to one side or the other, we should be alright.*

How?

We can sense the pole's pull to the north, and conveniently, we need to head north, Kor said. Even the tense, distracted tone in his voice couldn't dispel his snark.

Of *course* drakón had internal compasses. Silly me.

I didn't dare distract Kor after that, because from the way even Ben began to be tossed back and forth, I realized the risk of being blown off course might have been greater than Kor had let on.

It felt like I was riding a bucking bronco in a shaken snow globe—a very, very cold snow globe, no fake snowflakes here. The air was so frigid, it burned my throat to breathe it in. The portion of the balaclava over my mouth was at once soaking and freezing my skin, and despite the goggles, my eyelashes stiffened and eyeballs hurt.

Then a giant of a squall threw Ben, as enormous as he was in this form, against a mountain, as a child throws a ball.

As we crashed and snow and pebbles exploded around us, I screamed, but more for fear for Ben than for myself. I was so tightly bound to him, I was mostly unscathed by the sideways impact, the straps and my position holding me in place, but even through the grinding, shuddering crash, I heard the terrible cracks of bone, and though I could hardly see when I glanced back, I knew from how the golden dragon underneath me was pressed against the mountainside that Ben's left wing must have been crushed.

"*BEN!*" I screamed with both mind and voice.

But he lay still, far too still with how much agony he must be enduring. His great neck just lay limply on the snow in front of me, and faintly through the whirlwind of white, near the vague outline of his head, I saw streaks of gold.

Gold where it shouldn't have been, blurring the white snow. Like a child had colored outside the lines.

Blood.

His blood.

"*NO!*" I sobbed. "*BEN!*"

This couldn't be happening. Not to Ben. Not to my enormous, powerful, indestructible dragon, who had survived uncountable dangers just since I had known him with barely a scratch. I could *not* have saved him just this morning from being killed by the most formidable kind of monster save the Devourer itself, only to lose him now to a bit of *wind* and *stone*.

Then...we began to slide.

Judging from the tilt of his body, I realized the bit of mountain we were on wasn't level. Perhaps if it had been clear of snow, it might have held him, but as it was, his giant, heavy, still body began to drag across the soft, slick white, leaving streaks of gold behind him.

SARAH, GET OFF HIM! Kor shouted, voice wild with panic.

I suddenly understood with fatalistic calm: We were going to fall, plummeting off the mountain to the depths below, and, from this angle, odds were good that Ben would fall on his back...on top of me.

That would be a different matter than when he had bowled me over as a human this morning. No plush rug, and no thickness of snowbanks below, would save me. Even *if* the combination of the fall and his crushing weight didn't *instantly* kill me, then he could swiftly suffocate me before the others could unbury me.

One didn't have a multi-ton, scaly boulder fall on them and live.

I understood all of that in an instant, and yet, I could not move. Not from terror, but from...something else entirely. The same sort of lost bewilderment that had been in Kor's voice before.

How...could I just...leave him?

Lashes of sapphire power whipped out, cutting with surgical precision across the straps holding me in place. At this tilted angle, I began to fall before I even realized what was happening.

Then something—some*one*—crashed into me. Human arms wrapped around my chest, and my captor-savior pushed off Ben's back in a mighty leap just as the dragon slid fully off the mountain and tumbled down below.

We didn't fall with him.

At least...not in the same way.

If *Ben* in dragonform had had difficulty flying straight in this...well, Kor, as he was, stood as much chance as a pebble in a tornado.

All he could do with his half-form wings and the momentum from his push-off was only slightly control the trajectory of our fall, creating an arc only *less* deadly than Ben's sheer plummet.

His arms wrapped around me like soft, hot iron bands, his legs wrapped around mine, his blue shield emerged around us, and just before we hit, Kor pulled his wings around me as a sacrificial shield and turned so that it was *his* back that hit the ground with a tremendous, ominous *snap*.

The ground, not so solid after all, gave way immediately, only slowing our fall by a fraction of a second.

Then we plunged straight through it into the darkness below.

Chapter Six

AGONY

Koriben

Ben, Ben!

Yvera's cry was the first thing I remember.

Then pain.

So. Much. Pain.

I roared with it, even though that motion doubled the lancing spears at my side and pounding hammers in my skull.

Agony, everywhere.

And cold, such cold it was its own kind of pain, leeching my strength.

Ben, change back! Ordran, Yvera's rightwing and captain of my elites, ordered sharply. *Heal! Change back! We're doing what we can for you, but we can't get you inside like this!*

What was happening? Why such pain? Why such cold? Why such white everywhere, burying me with it, and none of it....

Sarah.

SARAH.

I roared again, this time from memory, from mental agony far more potent than any my body could produce.

I was on my back—and on my back had been....

No.

No, no, no, no, *no.*

NO!

Heedless of the price I immediately paid in white-hot agony, I rolled over, pummeling into giant scaled bodies that had gathered around me as I did so, but I felt no guilt. They were large enough to take no great injury from me, and what bruises and scrapes I might have given them would heal swiftly, even in this cold.

But the one beneath me would not.

SARAH, I sobbed, shouting the word indiscriminately with my mind as I roared with my throat, letting it ring in the minds of all around as I raked my talons across the earth and snow. *SARAH, NO!*

We're looking for her, Ben! Ordran said swiftly.

But I knew what they would find—something far worse than nothing. There was only darkness in my mind.

My star, my beautiful, brilliant, valiant star...was gone.

Because I, the monster that I was, had killed her.

I roared, letting the whole world know my agony, my unworthiness to live.

Then blessed darkness took me again.

Chapter Seven

BIRTHRIGHT

Sarah

Kor hit the last layer of ice with a sickening crack, and his formerly iron grip around me went slack. I tumbled off him, too winded to move for the second time that day.

This time, there was no Ben to heal me.

To heal either of us.

"Kor," was my first choked gasp.

The second mobility returned to my limbs, I pulled off my frozen goggles, rolled over, and dragged myself on my belly to him.

For a moment, his wings spread around him, partially hiding him from view with my perspective on the floor—though the wings were awful enough a sight as they were, cracked and bent and torn in horrifying angles, like blue kites that had hit too many trees. Then the wings shrunk into him, the scales disappeared from his arms and chest, his talons withdrew from his fingers, and horns retreated into his curls. In just a few heartbeats, he was only Kor. Human Kor.

Or...as human as he ever was.

His head was turned toward me, so I saw his eyes were closed. Hot, sapphire blood pooled around his head, hissing and sinking into the icy floor.

No.

NO.

Not him *too*!

Not because of me.

"Kor!" I rasped, pulling my balaclava down off my mouth. "Kor, you have to heal."

He didn't move, didn't respond. I had never seen that animated, brilliant face so dull, so dead.

I reached him then, sitting up next to him. I leaned over him cautiously, not daring to press any part of him lest I do more damage. I put a hand against his face, stroking his sharp cheekbone with my thumb.

"Kor," I sobbed. "You have to wake up. You have to heal yourself. You have to tell me what to do. I can't heal you. I don't know if there's anything I *can* do. Kor, *please*. Please, Kor."

Shouldn't his body continue to heal him even in unconsciousness? Then why did the blood continue to pool? It didn't seem to be slowing!

Cursing myself for my lack of first aid knowledge and praying with all my might that I wasn't doing more harm than good, I turned his head to expose the wound and pressed my hand against it, begging it to heal, or at least for my pressure to slow the bleeding.

Something about the relative paleness of his dark skin finally hit me. Not leaving off the pressure with my left hand, I yanked my right glove off with my teeth and put that hand over his bare chest where his heart...his flame-heart...should be.

I couldn't feel anything. I could feel a pulse at his neck when I checked, but no heat over his heart, and I knew by now that was wrong.

I ran my hand all over his chest frantically, but only met ice-cold skin.

He was too cold. A drakón shouldn't be this cold. Though now that we were *relatively* warmer, in this strange, icy tunnel, being out of the wind and even the worst of the drifting snow that I could glimpse high above, we were still surrounded by ice, so the temperature was at least freezing. That could not have been good for him, perhaps leeching what little power he had left....

I abruptly came to a horrifying conclusion: Kor wasn't healing...because he didn't have the power left to do so.

I had no way to give him energy through the normal drakón ways—sunlight, heat, or food. Not in time. If ever.

Though he had given everything he had to save me from sharing Ben's fate, I couldn't save him from the same....

Through any normal way.

I wasn't sure if what I was about to attempt was possible. I hadn't previously wanted it to be. I had given Kor a spark of power before, but I had a feeling that this would require a lightning bolt, and I was afraid of what that bolt might create between us; after all, the first time I'd attempted sharing power at that scale, it had formed my connection with Ben. If I were to have ever willingly picked someone to risk forming a second connection to, it would not have been his leftwing.

But damn it, I would not let *Kor* die for me.

Especially not after Ben....

Carefully not letting myself think about what was in the past, what I was doing now, or what it might mean for after, I took a shaking breath and put my hand over Kor's cold flameheart again.

And I *pushed* all the power I had into him.

Forcefully.

Once the channel had been established between Ben and me, the power flowed naturally, almost too easily, like water running downhill. I had no such channel with Kor, which was perhaps why I could give him only a trickle before. I had to make one now with him, shoving the water through the unbroken soil with the force of a firehose.

As if I had hit him with a defibrillator, Kor's body trembled. His eyes shot open, sapphires blazing, and he let out an inhuman roar, arching his back. For a few terrible heartbeats, I worried I had merely made his end agony.

Then he collapsed back, panting, but his eyes didn't close again. He blinked rapidly, eyes slowly regaining focus as they continued to blaze, and his hand reached dazedly for his head. My hand, still resting over his flameheart, began to feel heat spread under his skin—the contrast all the sharper to my now-freezing hand.

"Kor," I babbled. "You've hit your head. You're bleeding. You have to heal yourself. Please, *please* heal yourself."

"It's healing, Sarah," Kor croaked, wincing. "Torch me, it hurts too much to not be."

I pulled my now blood-soaked gloved hand away from the wound. It was hard to see whatever might be going on underneath that mat of hair and blood, but I *thought* it was no longer gushing.

Kor moaned and gingerly touched his own fingertips to the area. He squinted his eyes shut and took a quick, deep breath. I felt him send a surge of power to the area and saw him instantaneously stiffen, but after only a few moments, he slowly relaxed and let his hand fall back to his side.

"That's the worst of it gone, I think," he rasped. "The rest should heal on its own quickly enough from the way I'm—"

Kor froze, eyes widening with horror. "Sarah...."

He slowly sat up, propping himself on one hand while he curled the other over his flameheart. "What...did you do?"

"The only thing I could," I whispered. "I'm...sorry. You were dying."

Kor looked up at the shattered layers of ice he and I had crashed through. Then back down, at either the sapphire blood in varying states from hot liquid to icy slush, or its remnants in the pitted ice and stained dirt beneath, and finally, on my soaked glove.

He scowled. "Hmm. You might be right. You may have just saved my life. That is...inconvenient."

I was abruptly so furious, I could have killed him. "Well, thanks so much for informing me of your do-not-resuscitate form *after* the fact, but I'll keep it in mind for next time."

"That's not what I meant, Sarah," Kor said impatiently as he pushed and stumbled to his feet. "It's not that I'm...ungrateful. It's that it should not have been necessary. This could add complications that we really didn't need right now."

"What was I *supposed* to do?" I said, standing up.

"That's precisely the point," Kor snapped.

As he spoke, he flexed and shifted his hand to bring items of clothing out of his ether storage, putting on each one before bringing out another: socks, boots, a shirt, a coat, and finally gloves.

"Given the circumstances, you couldn't have done anything else. You were trapped, you were cold, you had no more supplies than what's on your back right now, and if no one has come for you by now, then they must not know where you are, and probably wouldn't have been able to find you before you either froze to death, became some creature's dinner, or ran headlong into the Devourer's welcoming arms. I got you into this mess, therefore, I was your only hope to get you out of it, so with me so inconveniently dying, *there was nothing else you could have done.*"

I just stared at him as he tugged on the final glove. I honestly couldn't tell whether he was apologizing for failing me, was putting me down, or was raging at the unfairness of the circumstances, or all of the above.

"I hate you," I said flatly. "I *really* hate you."

He didn't even smirk. "Not as much as you're going to when what you had to do to save your own life finally sinks in."

My heart sank. "What do you mean?"

Then I felt it.

The pull. Far, far closer than it should have been, and far stronger, after Ben had weakened it this morning.

My stomach dropped, and my heart froze.

There was just the one, leading straight to Kor.

Just the one. Nothing, nothing at all led to Ben anymore.

"No," I breathed.

Kor turned away, face hardening. "Come on. We can sort through this later—"

"Tell me it isn't true," I said, voice trembling.

Kor flinched. "Sarah, I'm sorry that a connection to me disgusts you so much, but I promise we'll figure out a way to—"

"*Tell me it isn't true!*" I cried, bending over from the pain. "Tell me he...he isn't...."

I collapsed to my knees, all my fears and pain coming crashing down now that they could be allowed to break free. I had only suppressed them thus far by sheer terror and guilt for Kor, but now that he was alright, now that I had the full evidence of Ben's absence in my soul slapping me in the face, I shattered with it.

"Sarah?" Kor said in alarm, putting his hand on my back as I curled into myself.

"Tell me..." I sobbed, tears freezing almost as soon as they could streak down my cheeks. "...he isn't...*gone.*"

"Sarah," Kor said tentatively, moving his hand to my shoulder. "If you're talking about Ben, I can't say for certain, but probably not."

I looked up at him, blinking through my sticking eyelashes. "What?"

"He was still alive when I pulled you from him," Kor said grimly. "My guess is that the fall wouldn't have been enough to finish him, either. Not Ben, not in his drakáform, and especially not with Yvera and all his elites there to immediately swoop in to help, and perhaps more besides with him falling practically at Roddan Hold's doorstep. Again, I can't tell you for certain...but I would say his odds are better than ours right now."

"But...I can't feel him anymore," I rasped. "The pull, the connection with him. It's...."

Still, my heart was fluttering dangerously with hope.

"There is...a likelier explanation for that than Ben's death, Sarah," Kor said, grimacing.

When I just continued to stare at him, he said through gritted teeth. "It is more likely...that only one...connection...is possible for you at a time."

I hiccupped.

Then said, "Oh."

My fears weren't entirely allayed, but I knew by now that Kor genuinely cared about Ben. He'd been frantic to save him just that morning when convinced that Ben's life was in danger. Right now, with Kor grim but calm....

My fears weren't gone, and I still felt Ben's absence as if a vital, life-sustaining piece of me was missing, but I could function again, at least for now. I could slow my heart and my breathing. I could start thinking again.

Kor kneeled in front of me, gripping my shoulders. His eyes glowed faintly as he spoke. "Sarah, I tell you now in good faith that I think Ben is alive and will be well, and I promise you, I'll get you back to safety at the least, and to him at the best. Once you've returned to him, we'll figure out how to restore what should be between you...and knock some sense into him while we're at it."

I took a deep breath, then nodded. "OK. Thanks. I'm...I'm alright now. Sorry...about that. It...kind of hit all at once."

Kor smiled thinly and gave my shoulders a squeeze. "It's been quite the day for us, hasn't it?"

I laughed shakily. "You could say that."

"Here," he said, taking off his gloves and putting his hands through the hood of my coat to place them on my neck. I shuddered under the warmth of that touch—probably a bad sign.

From Kor's grimace, he seemed to agree. "The least I can do is use some of this molten moonlight you dumped into me to warm you up and give you a good once-over."

His power poured through me, as warming and soothing as a soak in a hot tub. In fact, I had never had a healing quite this...soporific....

I only realized what he was doing when it was too late. I collapsed into him with a sigh, not even able to work up proper alarm or anger.

"Kor...." I mumbled.

He chuckled as he pulled me into his arms, his nose brushing mine. "Sleep, Sarah. You have done enough for now. Allow me to handle things for a bit."

You've handled enough, I thought, but didn't have the energy to say.

I meant that in both the good and the bad way, but, surprisingly, the good more than the bad. The scales of my judgment had shifted that day, in so many ways, and the implications were only just beginning to hit me.

My last thought was a memory: the image of Kor's mangled wings, broken like a fallen angel's.

THAT LAST MEMORY WAS also my first when I began to stir, and its sudden significance woke me with a start.

Then, when my eyes opened, and I realized where I was—and particularly why I was so comfortably warm—I shot up so fast that my head spun.

Kor grunted as his arms fell off me and the top cover of the bedroll we were sharing shifted off his shoulders, exposing him to the cold air.

"Kor!" I said, throat choking with outrage.

His eyes blinked open blearily. "M'wha? Ishcold."

Well, at least I had my evidence that he had truly been sleeping. For at least a little while. Of course, that also meant there wasn't a point in strangling an answer out of him for another ten minutes or so.

"Cmer," he said, closing his eyes. He pulled me back down and snuggled us back under the cover again, and I was too stunned to stop him. His eyes half-opened, and he smiled at me in a way I never would have ever thought to see. Ever.

Fond. *Dopily* fond.

"Y'warm. N'smell nice."

I stared at him.

He sighed happily, content as a puppy as he resettled against me—seemingly so innocent that I didn't know whether to push him away or laugh.

Did...Kor have a curse? Was that a thing? If there were such things as love spells, which I'd sadly found out today that there were—a sharp pang went through me at the memory of Svyer—were there such things as fairytale-style curses? With Kor's being that he became an absolute idiot for ten to fifteen minutes after waking. Because this seemed a bit too much to be anything other than magic induced.

Either that, or some experiment of his had gone horribly wrong, and he now had a split Jekyll-Hyde personality. This version of him *did* seem to be the opposite of his normal self in every way.

"Er, Kor?" I said, my voice tight not with tension...but suppressed laughter. "Mind letting me go?"

His eyes cracked open again, and his lips pursed. "Cold," he repeated. "S'night."

"Yes," I said with surprising patience. "But that's exactly why I'm *awake*."

My blood was buzzing again, magic curling up in tantalizing tendrils from the shadows inside me, and now that I was focusing on it....

Kor's pull hummed dangerously.

I lost any trace of humor.

Kor glared sleepily at me, but he finally pulled his arms away and mumbled, "Wear coat, light firecrystal."

I had no idea what he meant by that last part, but I wasn't going to linger to find out. I rolled out of the bedroll, ignoring the discomfort of the cold that had immediately hit me.

In the light of the glowing stone that Kor had left "on," I quickly found my gun, holster, coat, and boots, and on top of the coat was a new pair of gloves (a bit large, but they would do), and a scarf. My old gloves, balaclava, and goggles weren't anywhere to be seen, so I assumed that Kor had either dumped them—or, more likely, since they contained dangerous bits of both of us—stowed them away in the ether. I wondered idly what he had done about all his blood on the ground.

I tried not to let the fact that he'd taken care to replace my things and lay them out so that I would find them soften me.

Just a few feet away from us, I found...a crystal: a chunky orangish block about the size and height of a football sitting upright but with a wide, flat base. The firecrystal?

Curiously, I touched it, giving it a spark of power.

It began to glow like a flickering coal, and it let off more warmth than its size and the amount of power I had given it should have warranted.

Ah. Firecrystal indeed. Probably superior to an actual fire in this case because, when I looked up, I saw we were in a dome-like cave, so there was no way for smoke to escape.

Although the firecrystal wasn't as comforting as a crackling fire would have been, even to my Earthren sensibilities. That, combined with the fact that dramá just plain liked fire so much, was probably why they didn't use them everywhere.

With the lit firecrystal, my coat, my insulating layers, and my already warmed body, and the fact that we were now deep within the bowels of the earth, far beyond the ice cave we had fallen into, I was comfortable, but without feeling like I was in danger of sweating and then freezing as the moisture on my skin did. Dramá simply knew how to make warm clothing; only the extremity of the blizzard and my exhaustion had tried the effectiveness of what I had been given today. I would have expected no less by now.

For lack of anything better to do, I picked up the small glowing stone and walked around a bit.

"Don't go far," Kor muttered, sounding almost normal now, though his eyes were closed again. "Protections."

Of course. Now that he pointed it out, I could feel the layers upon layers of magic that he had put around the borders of that small cave, and especially across the threshold of the one slight passage that led out of it. That was why he felt comfortable sleeping with me.

Er, at the same time as me, that is.

Kor had really set up camp, too. I found the same sort of bucket-and-curtain toilet setup we had used on the mesa, and I hastily took advantage of it before he could become fully conscious. When I came back out from behind the curtain, I saw he had rolled over with his back to me, perhaps drifting off again. Which made me relieved and irritated at the same time.

On the one hand, I didn't want to face him, talk to him, process with him. On the other hand, there seemed to be pretty much nothing else to do, and the thoughts were just going to keep driving me mad until we did.

"Kor," I said, testing the waters.

"I'm awake," he said irritably.

Now he actually sounded like it.

He sat up haltingly and blinked at the firecrystal. "Oh. Good. You lit it."

"You told me to," I said in surprise.

He frowned. "I did?"

I stared at him. Was he really cursed? To not just be stupid but also forget the entire experience?

Well...that was a bit of a relief. I didn't know why, but I didn't want to go into his odd behavior after I woke up. Probably just because it was nice to avoid yet another thing. We had enough to talk about as it was.

He finally just shrugged. "Of course I did. Because I'm intelligent like that."

I had to fight very hard to keep a straight face.

He groaned and stretched.

"Well," he said with a wink, some of the cheek that had been gone all day finally returning. "Though I didn't sleep long, I slept surprisingly *well*. I can see why Ben recovered so quickly that one night."

I glared at him. "About that."

"What?" Kor said innocently. "I kept you warm, didn't I?"

I pointed at the crystal. "Why couldn't that have done the same thing?"

Kor snorted. "*That* thing needs a spark about every fifteen dek or so. Not an ideal refueling schedule for sleeping, don't you think?"

"Oh," I muttered.

"Besides," Kor said, turning grim as he kneeled and began stowing his bedroll. "If we had to be stuck with this...connection, then we might as well reap some of the benefits. We're not out of danger, after all. We both had to rest and heal, but we had to do it quickly and efficiently, and so together, we did."

I hated that I didn't have an argument against that logic, so I said changed the subject.

"Speaking of danger, have you tried contacting Ben?"

"I made some calls, yes," Kor said with suspicious vagueness. He had sat down on the ground next to the firecrystal and began pulling out some food, which he handed to me. Reluctantly, I sat down and picked at it.

"I am happy to inform you that I was correct: Ben survived, and he is now healed and as safe as he's going to be inside Roddan Hold. Like I said, his odds were much better than ours."

"Really?" I gasped, feeling weak with relief for a moment.

Kor gentled. "Really."

I knew I shouldn't ask, that it only showed how pathetic I was to do so, but after squirming for a moment, I blurted, "Did he...say to pass along anything to me? A message?"

The smile left Kor's lips, and my heart wrenched.

"Oh," I said, taking a swig from my canteen to hide my rapidly blinking eyes. "Never mind. Forget I asked."

"Sarah," Kor said hesitantly. "It's not that he wouldn't have, if he wasn't...."

"I get it, Kor," I said, more sharply than I had intended. "He's in pain."

"You don't know how right you are," Kor muttered.

"What do you mean?"

He looked at me, then swore. "Torch it, I wasn't going to tell you this yet, but I probably shouldn't make the same mistake of assuming I know when it is best to withhold information. At least not twice in two days."

I blinked. "Tell me what?"

"Ben didn't say anything...because he hasn't woken up. Not after he realized you were gone."

I froze. "*What*?" I choked. "You just *told* me—"

Kor threw up his hands. "I said he was healed. Physically. His mind right now...is another matter. That's something we can't do a lot about, not when he is refusing to let us help him. He's buried himself deep, deeper than we can reach him."

"Why?" I breathed.

Kor took a deep breath. "Because right now, he thinks you're dead. Again. Except this time...he thinks he killed you himself."

I stilled. "Oh."

He wouldn't have known that Kor had gotten me off his back, and if he were even somewhat conscious of the loss of the connection between us, what other conclusion would he have come to? I'd immediately done the same about him.

Except I hadn't had to deal with his guilt. This...was his worst nightmare come true. Final proof he was what he feared himself to be: a monster.

Still....

I swallowed. "He's really made himself *catatonic*? Because of me?"

Kor sighed. "I know it seems a bit much, but it's more likely a culmination of...everything. And I don't mean the past eight days, or even the past year. What with...Solim, this might be stretching back six years. Hellwinds, this might be going back to when he was confirmed as Heir. I think that all those twisted knots that he just kept trying to push through instead of untangling...all those burdens that became too heavy because he wouldn't share them...finally became too much, and he just...broke. In a way that he knew wouldn't get anyone else hurt."

I put a hand to my forehead, sighed, and nodded. That made too much sense to me.

"Sarah, I know you judged me for not telling him about Solim and Svyer," Kor said, pained. "And I know I failed to protect Svyer and thus Ben as I should have, but...."

I sighed again. "I understand, Kor. You could see he was getting close to the breaking point. It's not your fault Solim pushed him over."

Kor grimaced. "Well, it's not Ben's either. I hope you're not judging *him* for his current state. As torched impatient as I get with him...I know I don't bear the burdens he does. None of us, except you, might ever understand just what it means to be a Tree's chosen vessel, to have to bear that kind of power and responsibility...and not go mad or cruel with it."

"I don't judge him," I said quietly. "I hurt for him. I love him."

There. I'd said it. Out loud.

When it was too late.

My eyes burned with tears I was trying very hard not to shed. "I just wish he would *let me help him*."

Kor sighed. "You and me both, Sarah. You and me both."

After a moment to recover, I asked, "Has anyone tried telling him I'm alright?"

Kor sighed again. "Yes, but if he can hear us, he doesn't believe us, and this..."

He waved between us with a grimace. "...might not be helping."

"He said he could always see me," I whispered. "Like a star in his mind's eye. Like a gate."

Kor stilled. "Really? Interesting."

I rolled my eyes. "We felt like gates to each other. How else do you think he surged to me?"

Then Kor's too-neutral expression finally hit, and I groaned. "How do *I* feel to *you* right now?"

"Well," he said clinically. "Unlike you and Ben, I've never felt gates before, but now that you point it out...."

He closed his eyes, focused for a few moments, then slowly nodded.

"Interesting," he repeated mildly.

"Congratulations," I said dryly, mock toasting him with my canteen. "You now have a gate."

"Lot of good that does me when I'm sitting right next to you," Kor said, opening his eyes and smiling thinly. "Actually, one of the many torched inconveniences of this right now is that *you* can't get to safety by simply surging to Ben."

I snorted. I didn't bother to mention that I wasn't sure I could surge from that distance anyway. "Then what would you have done?"

"Oh, I could have found my way back well enough," Kor said vaguely.

I sighed. Without me to protect...he probably could have.

Which reminded me.

My eyes narrowed on him. "Kor. Is there something you're not telling me?"

He grinned slowly. "My dear Sarah. What kind of question is that?"

I rolled my eyes. It *had* been a stupid question, or at least, a very unspecific one. "I'm referring to the fact that you maintained a half-form for at least a minute, only losing it after you went unconscious and your power drained out of you."

His smile disappeared. "Ah. That."

I raised an eyebrow. "Yes, that. Don't get me wrong. I'm...."

I gritted my teeth and forced myself to say it, because he *had* earned it. "I'm grateful. You saved my life, and probably Ben's sanity, too, but I know enough by now to know that you shouldn't have been able to do that, and...I think I have a right to know why."

His smile didn't return. "You're right, I suppose...but probably not in the way you mean. I was going to bring this up anyway, after...the connection happened, but at the time I used it to save you, I was sincerely hoping you wouldn't know enough to question me about it. But of course, among the many details Ben so frequently forgets to tell you about, Royal half-forms couldn't be one of them."

My heart thudded. "Kor...you're not...."

His smile slowly returned, cold as ice. "Oh, but I am. In...a matter of speaking."

"But I thought only Sunfilled could become Monarchs."

"Generally, yes, but I am a direct descendant of Tolsyon, the Starkissed Lord at the time of the Moontouched 'departure.' For the Starkissed's aid to the Moontouched, which went deeper than anyone outside my clan knows, the Tree of Flame secretly promised him that if ever the Sunfilled became unworthy, one of his blood could rule instead. So, though I am *not* the Golden Heir...you could say I am...the Tree's hidden reserve. One that no one outside the bloodline and most especially my clan has ever known of, except Ben, and now...you."

Though he had spoken so matter-of-factly, as if talking about the color of his hair, I felt as if Kor had punched the breath from my lungs. "You? In particular? Not just any of your cousins, or...."

Too late, I saw where that could have led.

Kor's smile, cold as it had been, vanished again. "Yes, me. It *was* Solim, at first. Unfortunately, there's a good reason he began to have delusions of grandeur, but that...was what made him unworthy."

"When he tried to kill Ben," I whispered.

Kor shook his head grimly. "No, before that even. It was when he first sought for power. That is the one thing the Tolsyon heir must never do; we are to be held in reserve if the Sunfilled should become unworthy, so it is even more important for us to avoid that sort of taint. To seek status, power, or glory for its own sake is enough for the Tree to revoke our birthright and give it to another. That's what happened to Solim."

"How do you know?" I asked, beginning to be curious in spite of myself. "Either when the Tree chooses you or revokes you...."

Kor smirked. "Knowing you are chosen is simple, really. Other than the sudden rush of power, more than we have any right to have, the Tolsyon heir—if male, that is—can't grow a beard."

I blinked. "Wait, what?"

Kor chuckled and ran his fingers down his smooth jawline. Which...oddly enough, was still as smooth as ever. Shouldn't he have grown at least a five o'clock shadow by now?

Come to think of it...beards seemed to be the norm among the dramá men. Oh, some went clean-shaven, but it was like the ratio here of beards-to-not-beards was the reverse of my Western society. I'd just put Kor's lack of one down to him being...Kor.

As if he were reading my thoughts, he smiled. "This isn't just a vain quirk that I've somehow kept up on our hectic journey. I don't shave. I honestly *can't* grow facial hair anymore. Not since...it happened."

Kor sighed. "And I was just starting to get enough hair to grow a proper one.... Since you always want what you can't have, I've longed for years to try a goatee."

I rolled my eyes. Of course. That would *just* complete the picture. Really, perhaps his mandatory hairlessness was a blessing to us all.

I hesitated, then decided it needed to be said...and that Kor could handle it. "Solim...was clean-shaven. From what I saw in the ice."

Otherwise, it would have been harder to mistake him for Kor.

Kor sobered, eyes darkening. "That...lingering vanity doesn't surprise me. He hates me even more than he hates Ben, you know. More than anyone, for what he thinks I took from him, for how I betrayed him. For all I'm sure he made Ben think that this morning that everything...was about him, I'm certain it was actually about getting revenge on me. If Ben had been sacrificed, near our childhood home, after my greatest moment of triumph, because of my cascade of failures as his leftwing, well...."

I sighed and shook my head. "Ben's right. It wasn't your fault, Kor."

He shrugged nonchalantly. Which told me just how much he truly still blamed himself.

"In any case, that's the answer to your question. Female Tolsyon heirs blend in better, but even they know, without a doubt, when it comes to them. You can't mistake that kind of increase in power."

I narrowed my eyes. "*That's* why you're so powerful. You and Ben keep giving this B.S. about you simply being 'efficient,' but that doesn't cover it."

"No." Kor smirked. "It's true, to some extent. I *am* unusually efficient, but that's like saying Ben's merely tall and strong. The real question is how we got to be that way, and what keeps us going when others like us would have burned out."

My heart sank. "And you had to be that way, because Solim tried to become Ben's leftwing."

Kor sobered. "I don't know how much Yvera told you...."

I swallowed. "She said that you told Ben something that made Ben think twice about choosing Solim, but she couldn't remember what."

For the first time...Kor's cheeks heated, his brown skin getting darker. "Yes, well. Ben probably gave her some forgettable drivel to throw her off, but that's what I truly told him: about what Solim had lost, and unwillingly given me."

I blinked. "You. Told Ben about a cherished, centuries-old Starkissed secret. One about a *Starkissed* like you one day potentially supplanting a *Sunfilled* like Ben. Just like that?"

Kor's flush got darker. "I was *fifteen*. And terrified out of my mind—of myself, and of what my brother must have done to deserve its revocation, but most of all, of what would happen if Ben tried to choose Solim as his leftwing."

Kor hardened, heat cooling to ice. "I knew Solim. I loved him, practically worshiped him. Wanted to be everything I thought he was but knew I couldn't be. But I knew him. I knew that if he had begun to do what was strictly forbidden us—seek for power—that he was more than capable of getting it. That, once begun, he might never stop. And I had no idea how to convince Ben quickly enough of that other than to tell him everything. More than just, 'Oh, Ben, by the way, I've noticed that my brother has started shaving.'"

"And you convinced him," I said quietly. "Saving more than just his life, probably. Perhaps even the Realms."

"I wouldn't quite go that far," Kor said with a weary smirk. "The Tree had revoked Solim already. I knew She would never have confirmed Ben's choice in Solim, and he would never have been made leftwing. What I was worried about was Solim's anger at a public rejection. Of course...if I had known that Ben would choose me *instead*...I might not have had the courage to do what I did to dissuade him."

That man would do anything for power.

Whatever half-truths Solim had fed Svyer, that, at least, had been a blatant lie. A reflection on Solim, not Kor. Korinth, "oathkeeper," the brilliant but bumbling, bespectacled, scrawny young scholar who had just wanted to be left alone to his history books, yet had a centuries-old birthright dumped on him and then forced himself to betray his beloved brother *twice,* accept Ben's offer to be leftwing, and *make* himself the leftwing he thought the Realms needed.

Contrary to what I had always wanted to believe about him, Kor...was yet another of the good people the Tree had placed into positions of power at this time...who didn't want to be there.

And that was what made him worthy to be.

Kor, watching my expression, hardened.

"Don't...look at me like that," he snapped, getting to his feet.

He began packing, movements sharp. "I'm not some noble hero. I'm not even the villain Svyer tried to make you think I am. Inside, I'm still just a desperate, terrified, fifteen-summer boy who seems to be the only one able to see what's coming and know what we have to do to save our skins."

That's what's incredible about you, I thought faintly.

With more than a bit of unease. Not because of mistrust; that had been a losing battle ever since I found out about Solim. Rather, because I was afraid of what would happen if I truly trusted Kor.

I only snapped out of my troubled daze when Kor picked up the only remaining object left, the glowing stone, and held out his hand for mine.

"Ready?"

"Ready for what?" I asked, but with unthinking trust, I put my hand in his.

Always my mistake with him. Because the moment Kor pulled me to my feet, he turned off the glowing stone.

Plunging us into darkness.

"Kor!" I snapped.

Kor chuckled in the dark, not relinquishing my hand. "Wait for it."

I didn't have to wait long. Not a moment after he spoke, the room lightened again.

Because the very walls began to glow.

And I began to feel the pull...from everywhere.

Chapter Eight

GAME

Sarah

WHITE SPIRALING LINES APPEARED on the walls, glowing with a familiar light.

Now that the lines had emerged, illuminating the cavern as never before, I realized how oddly smooth the waves in the dome were, with only the occasional column at the edges to hint at what might have once been a natural cavern. Now, it looked like we were inside a giant conch shell, with the white spiral that traced the crevices as the glow-in-the dark coloring.

"What is it?" I whispered in awe.

"I'm not sure," Kor said, sapphire eyes glowing as he gazed at me. "But for lack of a better word for now, I'm calling it...moonstone."

I abruptly realized I had been unconsciously clenching Kor's hand as I turned around and around to take it all in. I now hastily pulled away.

"What makes you think it's associated with me? Other than the color."

I thought he was right; there could be little doubt with how strongly I now felt the pull from every direction, but how had he known that?

"Because, my dear Sarah," he said with a grin, "it only started glowing when I brought you here."

"Really?" I said, blinking. "What about you? It could just be reacting to anyone's presence."

Kor held his hand to his chest in mock dismay. "What kind of scholar do you take me for? Of course I tested my theory by leaving you a short distance away—heavily protected by wards—and entering by myself. And...nothing happened. Not a glimmer."

I rolled my eyes. "Of course, and that's why you stopped here, so you could show me, and why you left the light on, so you could do your grand reveal."

He winked. "I always said you were clever. But you haven't thought of the *other* reason I might have stopped here. One much more important than allowing you to appreciate this scientific discovery, as marvelous as it is."

"What?" I said in surprise.

"Think."

I thought. Then looked up. "Hang on.... What is a bunch of 'moon-stone'...doing somewhere remotely near where we're looking for a moongate?"

"That's my Sarah," Kor said with a grin, tapping my nose.

I wrinkled my nose. "I'm not *your* anything. Except maybe your friend, but I have doubts about even that sometimes."

He mimed a wounded heart. "After I saved your life at great personal risk not too many deken ago. I'm hurt."

"Well, I then saved yours, and because of that, Ben now thinks I'm dead, so...I think we're even."

I walked away from him and trailed my fingers over a streak of white at arm level. It glowed brighter at my touch, and the pull stronger, but nothing else happened.

"This place...." I said with a frown. "It's *not* a gate, but it's something special. That's for sure."

My eyes began tracing the whorl of the conch repeated on the floor. Even there, the streaks of moonstone lined the stone, but it had been carved and polished flat, perfect for walking....

My eyes traced again, widening. "Kor," I said, grabbing his hand. I took him to the center of the spiral on the floor, then I pulled back at the pulls around me, causing all the lines to flare. Then, keeping that power coiled tight within me, like holding an ever increasingly powerful magnet in my gut, I started leading Kor around the spiral.

"Sarah?" he said intently, squeezing my hand.

"It might not be a gate..." I said slowly. He wasn't the only one who could do a dramatic reveal.

We approached the end of the spiral, which was the passage out of the cavern.

"...but it might just be a path."

Sure enough, the power exploded out of me in a flash, and the opening iced over, forming a filmy curtain just like the ones that were inside my gates. Through it, we could see a different sort of passage entirely, one lined with more moonstone.

"Yes, you clever young woman!" Kor said with savage delight, throwing his arms around me and crushing me in a hug almost worthy of Ben. "I knew you could figure it out!"

"Uh, Kor," I said, cheeks flaming. I was more than a little disturbed by the similarity between Ben's reaction to when I had surged to him and Kor's now.

He ignored me and let go, grabbing my hand again. "Not a second too soon, because that's the first sensor ward I set activating now. Our reprieve is officially at an end. Let's go."

"Wait, *what*?" I spluttered.

But Kor just dragged me through.

"YOU SEE," KOR SAID, "the Moontouched knew they had to get clever."

As we walked down the moonstone-lit passage somewhere *else* deep within the bowels of the blizzard-assaulted mountains, Kor began to explain his theories.

Yes, *theories*, in plural. One being about the moonpath. (Was it going to get old for anyone else coming after us to use the terms we hurriedly made up just by slapping *moon* in front of everything?) The other being about why we had a reprieve to discover it.

Kor believed we were safe enough for now. His sense of direction told us we must have shifted position at least an elden east. I wasn't sure what an elden was, but it seemed far enough that whatever our consumed pursuers were, they would have to tunnel through quite a lot of solid rock to get to us first. Although, given the existence of rock wyrms, that still might have been a concern, which was probably why Kor stayed alert and close to me.

He had also gotten into an annoying habit of holding my hand. What was even more annoying was that it seemed so natural to even me under the circumstances, I didn't seem to notice until minutes after the fact, making it hard to fuss about it.

Kor started with the moonpath.

"They knew they couldn't entirely hide from the Devourer what they were doing when they built the moongates. Ever since its incursions into each world, it's had eyes and ears everywhere. The Moontouched also knew that by now, the Devourer would be on to us and setting up ambushes, so here, on Ekrel, the second-to-last and one of the most consumed-infested worlds, they made things a bit more complicated. To throw it off, they made at least that one moonpath, and I'll be surprised if that's the only one."

"Why?" I asked.

He raised an eyebrow at me. "Do you feel the gate yet?"

I sighed. "No."

"That's why. We're not close enough yet, but we've started on the trail. A trail that only *you* can follow. The Devourer *might* know where the moongate is, unless the Moontouched were clever enough to hide that completely from it, but at the very least, we're sending its forces on a good chase, bouncing around from one moonpath to the next, making our movements hard to follow and its forces divided."

"But if it knew we were coming, why wasn't it immediately on us? We had a chance to heal, even sleep."

"Excellent point. Which brings me to my next theory, and the only reason I risked sleeping at all. I think that has to do with two Flamesends in disguise: the blizzard and Ben."

"What?" I said flatly.

"First, the blizzard. Entirely natural, and as dangerous as it was for us, that made it even more so for consumed. The Devourer doesn't care about the lives of its slaves, but it can't do anything with them if they're dead, can it? Well, technically, it can, but that requires more work. So, it had to adjust whatever ambushes it had planned. Probably had to delay them entirely in the case of the one near our first moonpath."

Kor took a breath. "Second, Ben. I know this is going to be hard for you to hear, Sarah, but he may have saved your life by thinking you were dead."

"What?" I demanded. "How?"

"Because he had to throw such a public fit about it, *again*," Kor said dryly. "A less dangerous one than last time, true, but he made his pain quite clear to everyone in the area. Shouted your name, caused *avalanches* with those roars of his before he finally went under again. You know Ben can't act to save his life—and the Devourer knows that too."

I inhaled sharply, finally understanding. "The Devourer wasn't bothering to look for me...because Ben convinced it that there was no point."

"Exactly," Kor said. "As awful as it was for Ben to go through that...I'm not certain we would have been alive, or at the very least, not so rested, without the time he unintentionally bought us."

I shook my head. "But couldn't it have seen you pulling me off his back?"

Kor flashed me a grin. "No. Because, partly to save your skin, partly to keep my secret, I cast a haze illusion around us that should have been more than good enough to hide us in that blizzard. True, the Devourer might have been tipped off if it were paying attention to my sudden disappearance...but I think it did not. There's an advantage to being smaller and seemingly weaker sometimes, don't you agree?"

"Maybe if you're as powerful as *you* are," I said dryly.

"Give yourself time, Sarah," Kor said, squeezing my hand. "You're meant to be a Queen, after all. You're going to surpass me like the moon does the stars."

That was hard to believe. I mean, in niceness, maybe, but power? Knowledge?

"Of course," Kor said morosely, "my concealment could have easily backfired, since it fooled even Yvera and Ben's elites, who were still searching for your body in the snow where Ben fell by the time I called Yv, and they had no idea where *I'd* gone. You might be interested to know that Yvera was surprisingly relieved, in her own way, to learn you were alright."

I smiled. "Probably just because she hoped Ben might snap out of it."

Kor chuckled. "Oh, no. I am not as well-versed in the many flavors of Yvera's temper as Ben is, but I am fluent enough, and I am certain I detected relief for your own sake. You're hard not to like, after all, and I think you are starting to creep into the good graces of even ice-hearted Yvera."

"Can't be," I said, shaking my head. "She told me just this morning that she was destined to forever hate my guts."

Kor mock gasped. "Why, coming from her, that's practically a proposal. What did you say?"

"Kor," I moaned.

"Anyway," Kor said with a chuckle. "It was their conviction that you were dead and I at least missing that gave me a glimmer of hope that maybe the Devourer thought so too. That is when I made a judgment call that you will perhaps disagree with, given the risk it puts us under. By then, I had explored enough where we had fallen to find the first moonpath. Putting it all together, I decided that this was the best chance we were going to have at finding the moongate, and so I did *not* allow Yvera to come find and bring us back in. I ordered her to gather the elites back to the hold as if they were giving up the search for me...and had one of the more skilled magic workers conjure up a convincing enough body for you, which they prominently displayed as they took it inside."

"And she listened to you?" I said skeptically.

"Well, she didn't have much choice," Kor said innocently. "You see, with the two Royals incapacitated, I was the highest-ranking member of the group. Leftwing beats righting in that scenario, and she knew it. Though she gave me quite a few choice words, some of which even I didn't previously know."

I glared at him. "One would almost think that you had incapacitated *one* of those Royals on purpose."

"You needed rest," Kor said, still innocently, "and night was falling. A decision had to be made, and quickly. Too quickly for me to wake you up and explain all of this to you. Do you disagree with it?"

"Well...no," I said through gritted teeth. "It's just...if we die tonight because of you, I'm going to kill you."

"Fair enough."

"Alright," I said, thinking. "That nearly brings us full circle. You settled us down in the moonpath cave to get some rest—because we were *going* to need it, to find a moongate on our own and survive."

"Not before first setting up *many* protections. Including those sensor wards I mentioned. I would have woken the moment the first was activated, and I set it a long way off."

"But would we really have had time to figure it out before...."

I saw his wide-eyed look of innocence and then groaned. "You'd already figured it out."

Kor grinned. "Mostly. If needed, I could have hurried you along, but as long as we were safe, why not let you figure it out on your own?"

"But we weren't." I frowned. "I only figured it out just in time."

"Or," Kor pointed out, "more likely, it was you figuring it out that alerted the nearby consumed. You used a lot of power, Sarah. That would have been hard to miss."

"Oh, right." That did seem more likely.

"Almost at once, the Devourer would have figured out our ruse. Then the game was officially on, although we now have a lead. Which I intend to keep as long as possible. I, liking my blood where it is, thank you, would prefer to win."

Which explained why he was leading us at such a fast walk, fast enough that my heart rate was up.

"But how would the Moontouched know where to put the first moonpath for us?"

Kor shrugged. "How have they known any of the things that they shouldn't have known about the future?"

Right. Dumb question. Except....

I clenched my teeth. "Did that mean they knew Ben would get hurt? That they *counted* on it?"

Kor frowned. "Counting on it...is a strong way to put it, but I understand your sentiment. It is, after all, one of my greatest sources of mistrust with the Tree Herself, let alone a mortal, fallible clan that can see at least something of the future. However, I think it is just as likely that the Moontouched were prepared for many scenarios by this point—perhaps another reason for all the moonpaths. Perhaps they don't have to lead from one point to the next, in a continuous stream, rather perhaps the next is selected more at random, until we have used all paths before the gate."

That made me feel better...but not completely.

Kor sighed. "I understand, Sarah, like I said, but in my calmest moments, I understand that knowing *what* is going to—or merely what could—happen is not the same thing as *making* it happen, or even wanting it to. I highly doubt they wanted Ben to get hurt, but they prepared us to make the most of the scenario if he, through his own choices, did."

That would have to do for now, because....

"I feel it," I said, heart racing. "A moonpath ahead."

Though it pulled in the darkness, it had a different pull than a gate did. More dispersed somehow.

"Stay close to me," Kor said grimly, clenching my hand. This time, I didn't feel like protesting.

But we got lucky: no consumed on the path, none in the conch-shaped cave.

"Perhaps this strip is entirely self-enclosed and undiscovered by the Devourer," Kor mused after he declared the cave safe.

"That would be nice," I said, making my way to the center. "Certainly gave you the time to explain all that to me. I don't know if you've noticed, but people are more cooperative and trusting when they understand what's going on. Plans tend to go better too."

Kor's lips twitched, but he held out a warning hand when I started pulling power to open the path. "Wait, Sarah. I know it costs us time, but I think it's worth it to set up protections. Just in case there's something waiting for us on the other side."

My heart pounded, and I let the power go. "Right. Good idea."

He turned to the conch opening and frowned thoughtfully. "I think I can save some time and power by just focusing on the passage. That's the only place they would come through, after all."

I shrugged. "Make sense to me."

But he had already gotten to work, tracing the opening with a silver rod—much like the one he'd tried to steal from my hold's storeroom, in fact.

"Is the wand necessary?" I asked curiously. It amused me to see Kor looking so stereotypically wizard-like.

"Flame, no," Kor said with a chuckle. "It concentrates the power a bit, but mostly it saves me from having to touch all the surfaces myself."

"Oh," I said, blinking at such a mundane answer, and one so...Kor-like.

Kor smirked over his shoulder. "I'm not being squeamish, if that's what you're thinking, but I'd rather leave as few traces of me behind as possible when I know a consumed might come looking for them."

"Right," I said. Also a very Kor-like answer, and reemphasizing a mindset I was really going to have to start getting into.

After a few more minutes of work, Kor said he was done. He came over and took my hand again. Probably not strictly necessary. He might not even need to walk the path with me, but why experiment now?

Kor gripped my hand tightly, his eyes intense as he looked down at me. "This is perhaps a bit late to mention, but in the interest of fully informing you of what is going on and what I am thinking...there is a good chance we'll encounter Solim somewhere along the way."

I stared at him. "And you *still* thought it was a good idea to do this on our own?"

"When I understood the nature of the game and the relative advantage we had, yes," Kor said grimly. "We *have* to get to that moongate, Sarah, one way or the other, and the more time we give Solim to prepare for us...."

I swallowed. "Right."

"I *will* keep you safe," Kor said, eyes burning now. "I swear it. But before you open the next path, I need you to promise me you'll surge ahead the moment you feel the moongate."

My heart pounded. I swallowed dryly. "Kor...."

"*The moment*, Sarah. You must promise me. Unlike the case for you and Ben, there are plenty of capable Starkissed who can take my place. You are irreplaceable."

"What will you do if I don't promise?"

He smiled thinly. "I will knock you out again now and trap us here forever, or at least until you come to your senses. Even if that means our window passes."

I shook my head wearily. "I...really hate you."

His smile deepened, eyes increasing in brightness for a moment. "You know, the more times you say that, the more I doubt you."

"Fine," I snapped. "I promise to surge ahead like a coward and leave you behind to face your doom. Happy?"

His eyes burned even brighter. "Not quite."

He grabbed my head between his hands and pressed his lips to mine.

It lasted just a few seconds, just a few heartbeats of his smooth, warm lips moving against mine, just enough for him to ignite a teasing spark of power in my mouth. Just enough for his pull to draw me in, magnifying the pulls all around. Then he withdrew and smirked.

"You know, to remember me by, just in case I meet my doom and all that."

I just shook my head at him. I was too stunned to even be mad. "That...could have been better timed."

"Probably," he agreed, "but seldom is one's doom convenient."

"Enough talk about doom," I snapped, turning away to walk the spiral as I pulled power into me.

Kor captured my hand again as he followed. "I thought you hated me, would be glad to see me go."

"Will you just. *Shut. Up?*"

"I suppose. Since you asked so nicely."

Always has to have the last word, I grumbled.

At a deeper level, I recognized what Kor's chatty bravado really meant, with his sweaty palm in mine being a clue: He was scared. He truly thought we could soon be facing something with the power to kill us.

That made me terrified.

Terror lent me focus and willpower, though, so it was much easier this time to gather and hold the energy I needed, and when we reached the end a few moments later, I released. Then braced myself. Kor stepped around me, putting an arm out to hold me back.

So I didn't get a good look at what suddenly roared and hit the ice curtain and Kor's shield there with a deafening bang.

"Ah, *fantastic*," Kor said dryly. "*Troll.*"

Chapter Nine

STALEMATE

Sarah

"REALLY?" I SAID INCREDULOUSLY as I peered around Kor.

The large, chunky, gray, dumb looking creatures with thick clubs and loincloths that were pounding furiously on Kor's shield were exactly what I had pictured when he said the word.

Trolls.

"They're called that in Drona too?"

"Sarah, as fascinating as the coincidence is, this really isn't the time to explore cognates and etymology," Kor said tensely over the bangs.

"What *is* this the time for?" I said nervously. "What are we going to do?"

"Well, I might be able to maintain that shield for a while, but that obviously gets us nowhere, and gives more time for...nastier things to show up."

Nastier things that started with the letter *S* or *L*.

"So...."

"There's too many," Kor muttered, barely audible over the banging sounds. He peered and ducked this way and that to get a better view. "Two up front, but at least three or four behind. Too many to handle with finesse once I take the shield down."

"Soooo?"

Kor took a deep breath. "Time to stoop to their level, then. Brute force, it is. Torch it, where's Ben when you need him?"

He got down on one knee. "Alright, Sarah, get on my back."

"Why?" I said suspiciously. Drakón seemed to keep telling me to do that and not telling me why.

"Because I need to protect you, and because it's easiest to shield one, smaller area that moves with my own body."

That was...a practical-sounding reason, and he got points for bothering to even explain, so though I internally grumbled, I wrapped my arms around Kor's neck and lifted my legs so he could hoist me up as he stood. Meanwhile, the trolls just continued raging and banging against the shield, as dumbly unexpectant of what was coming next as video-game mobs.

"Not very bright, are they?" I asked, though my stomach was still churning from what we were about to do.

"Not at all," Kor said, backing up. "Fortunately for us. Really, I'd expected something different from Solim. He must be scrambling."

"That's a good thing, right?"

Kor didn't answer.

I hoped that was just because he was busy sending a cannonball of sapphire power toward the trolls and lowering the shield at just the right moment to let it through—and beginning to run.

The cannonball knocked the trolls over like bowling pins. I heard sickening crunches and terrible roars, even more deafening for how they were timed just as we were shooting past them.

Then we were running down the passage, the glowing moonstone streaks keeping pace with us, only warming up when we were within twenty feet and fading twenty or so feet behind. The trolls that weren't incapacitated recovered within moments and began running after us with more roars. Fortunately, Kor ran much faster than they could, and they soon fell far behind.

That was too easy, wasn't it? I asked.

Again, Kor didn't answer.

Then I felt something shifting ahead in the darkness.

Kor—

I know. His inner voice was grim.

Shadows rose up from the floor ahead, moving like thick, animated goop.

Hold on tight. I need my hands.

I wrapped my legs and arms as tightly as I could while keeping the latter off his throat to not restrict his panting breaths.

Kor raised both his hands, wrists touching and palms facing outward, to send a wave of power over the goop, but it just absorbed it, and Kor cursed. He began to slow.

That wouldn't do.

Following those instincts he told me to trust, I thrust out my own hand and sent ice shooting out from the ground and walls, covering and entrapping the substance entirely.

Kor let out a triumphant bark of laughter as he returned his hands to my legs.

Sorry about the slipperiness, I said, realizing I may not have saved us much time.

Don't worry about it, he answered as he crossed the ice nimbly. *It's far easier to give myself friction than it would have been to do what it would take to deal with that stuff otherwise.*

Are you sure you don't want me to get down? I asked in concern as Kor's chest heaved.

I don't. Just...give me a boost, will you?

Oh, of course. I felt sheepish for forgetting the biggest contribution I could make to our odds of survival.

I promptly used the hand over his flameheart to deliver energy straight to the source.

Ah, he groaned. *Better.*

But there was an edge to his mental voice that I couldn't identify.

More?

No! he said, a bit too quickly. Then added, *We might need it later.*

I felt a bit of satisfaction to hear crunches and howls behind us when the trolls hit my ice-covered goop.

The consumed don't work well together, do they?

No. They were never meant to coexist, and the Devourer never cared to make them, which often works to our advantage. For instance, that's also why they're spread out like this.

Flying things began darting at us through the dark, giving me the impression of giant rats with bat wings. Automatically, I tightened my grip on Kor so he could have his hands free again and throw a combination of fire and energy at them. That took care of most of them, but Kor still generated a bubble of energy around us as we ran through that prevented a couple of swoopers from hitting me.

This would be why I was on his back. I pulled my gun out of its holster and shot down the rest behind us as best as I could while Kor held onto me.

Just when I was starting to hope we could handle whatever was coming....

We heard a roar echo down to us.

Let me guess, Kor said. *That thing is right about where the next moonpath is.*

Yup, I said in faint horror.

It was one thing to hit our way past things and keep running. It was another thing entirely to reach the dead end and have to kill or immobilize what was there so that I could walk the spiral.

Lovely. Time for you to get off, I think, but stay close.

Will do.

He paused only long enough to drop me, and we sprinted off again, side by side.

As we approached the opening to the conch cave, a hulking, blue-white shadow waited inside, taking up the entire entrance.

Aaagh, Kor said. *Seriously, where's Ben? Hitting tough, angry things is his job!*

What is it? I said, feeling about ready to puke from fear. I could not believe the audacity of my feet that they continued to run toward that thing, especially when it roared.

Ice bear, Kor said grimly. *Think the Yvera...of bears.*

We were dead.

Alright, Kor said. *Let's start making it mad. Shoot it, shoot it as much as you can, aiming for the eyes if you can manage it.*

I obeyed, focusing the magical intent behind my shots on accuracy and sharpness. The shards of ice pierced through the darkness, one right after the other. I gave them just enough glow so that we could see if they hit their target.

So we saw the bright ice shard that shot straight into the ice bear's dark eye, sending blood and juices flying.

The bear roared, shook its head...stumbled...and collapsed. By the time we were slowing down to approach...it was still.

You.... Kor said, his inner voice faint. By contrast, his chest was heaving loudly for air, and mine wasn't much better. *You just took down an ice bear. Just like that.*

I think...I sent the shard straight into its brain, I said, feeling sick. *I felt...it.*

What I didn't say, because I was a bit too horrified at myself to admit it, was that in my terror, in my desperation to just *end* it...I had instinctively used the anchor of the shard to expand my power out from there and freeze the liquid in its brain. Essentially, making its brain literally explode.

It had been...so easy.

I lost the battle with my stomach and puked. Kor cradled me with one arm and held my hair back with another. Fortunately, I was able to swallow the rest of the bile after just a mouthful. I was glad that Kor didn't say anything, not during and not when I straightened. I didn't need trite assurances now, or pep talks about "it's us or them." I just needed to fully accept, in silence, the horror of what I had done.

And, the worst part...what I now knew I was capable of.

Well, Kor said, approaching the bear warily. *I did not...expect the hardest part to be moving it.*

Because its massive bulk was now taking up the entire entrance.

He took a deep breath and looked back at me. *I'm...going to need another boost.*

"Coming right up," I said with a tremulous attempt at teasing.

I slapped my hand over his heart and gave him a double espresso.

He staggered under it, eyes blazing. *Torch it, Sarah!*

Sorry, I said sheepishly. *You did ask.*

Not for you to empty yourself!

No, I'm good, I said in surprise. *There's plenty more where that came from.*

Kor stared at me. Then shook his head. *And you think you're weak.*

Actually, I wonder, I said thoughtfully as Kor walked up to the bear. *I didn't usually give Ben much, but it seemed to have a greater impact on him than it should have. Like...what was little to me was more potent in him.*

Interesting. I'll want plenty of details later, but right now....

Kor raised his hands and sent a crashing wall of energy into the bear, making it roll back from the entrance.

Is that going to interfere? Kor asked, eyeing the giant corpse as we entered.

I don't know, I said, troubled. *How did it even get in here?*

Same way all the others did, Kor said darkly as he began putting up his protections. This time he circled the entire room, and multiple times. *Feel that in the air?*

Now that he mentioned it...I could feel a *wrongness*. Like a smell, but one I sensed with magic. Also, an itching sensation of exposure, like the prickles on the back of your neck from someone's watching eyes.

Darkrift, Kor explained as he worked. *Unlike a darkgate, it's one that's just temporary; the Devourer can't hold it open for long, and it can't always make them wherever and whenever it wants to, obviously, or we'd be overrun.*

What's the key?

We don't know for certain. Just that it's easier for it to do it at night. We've also discovered a way to make wards that stop them from being created in a certain area as long as we can maintain them. That's what we do to protect our holds, and that's what I'm doing now, here. But we can't cover the whole worlds, so the worlds' natural defense, the Tree, is still our best shield against darkrifts. She's not infallible, though, so sometimes the Devourer gets consumed through. The Devourer itself can't come through without a darkgate, though. A big one.

The kind it would want my blood for, I said soberly.

Kor flinched as he straightened from his work. *Yes. Some people might think me mad for risking you like this but....*

This is what the Tree asked me to do, Kor, I said with surprising calm, and the surprising beginnings of...faith.

Then may She watch over us now, Kor said grimly as he approached me. He stopped by the bear, though, eyeing how much of the spiral it took up: almost half the cavern.

He shook his head. "Oh, what the hellwinds," he said out loud. "Yvera's not going to believe me otherwise."

He reached down and grabbed it near its neck...and it disappeared.

"Kor...." I said hesitantly, feeling my queasiness rise again. "Do you now have a giant, dead bear in your ether storage?"

"You would *never* want to see the entirety of a drakón's hoard," Kor said with a wink. "But especially mine. I'm quite popular with the Zoological Branch of the Conservation Guild, though. Even if they usually wish Ben would leave the corpses in better shape."

I stared at him, the bile rising to my throat. "I...did not need to know that right now. About either of you."

"Consider it a distraction from what's coming," he said, not the least bit apologetic as he joined me in the center of the spiral and took my hand in his.

Fortunately, with the hand that hadn't grabbed the bear. That...mattered for some reason.

Ready? he said grimly.

I nodded slowly. I understood now why we had fallen into talking with our inner voices about anything we wouldn't want to be overhead, even now that we could spare the breath. Something about the remnants of the darkrift in the air set my teeth on edge.

Remember your promise, he repeated.

I remembered. I also remembered my plan to make it unnecessary, which was the only reason I had made the promise.

I just hoped neither my promise nor my backup plan would be needed.

Please, let the way be clear, please let it be clear, I begged as I led Kor through the spiral, pulling power as I went.

As I let it go, Kor stepped in front of me and raised his hand, ready for anything.

When the ice film formed....

Kor's older, psychopathic reflection stood on the other side.

Solim.

My stomach dropped.

No.

"Hello, Korinth," he said with a too-familiar smile, though his voice was deeper than Kor's. Rougher. How could I not have noticed? Even more obviously now, his silky black clothing set him apart from Kor's wintery apparel at once.

Still, the sight of him shook me more than I had expected, beyond the terror it evoked. Even though I knew, I *knew* by now that they were two very different people, the similarity still got surprisingly deep under my skin, perhaps all the deeper for how deep my trust in Kor was becoming.

If Kor was surprised, he didn't show it. Though his hand didn't lower. "Ah, Solim. I was wondering when you'd show up."

His smirk deepened, with a darker edge than Kor's ever had. "You gave us a bit of a run, I'll admit, but it's not difficult to intercept someone when you know what they're looking for."

This was what Kor had been afraid of: not what we would encounter along the way, which had only been meant to slow us down, but what we would inevitably face at the end, so long as the enemy knew where the end was—and could get to it before us.

"I assume that means the moongate is just past you," Kor said.

Can you feel it? he asked me.

No, I said stiffly, gut wrenching.

When I'd made my plan, I'd expected to at least get through the *ice* first! Would it still work?

Did I have any other choice but to try?

Solim smiled darkly. "Presumably, if it's still there from when the Devourer discovered its construction. Of course, *we* can't sense it, and from the horror on your little Moontouched's face, I assume she can't from this distance, either."

Sarah, Kor silently groaned.

Sorry....

"Where does that leave us?" Kor asked coolly, slowly lowering his hand.

Solim's eyes glittered. Darkly. Where Kor's irises were sapphire, his were only black. "At an impasse, I believe."

What?

"So it would seem," Kor agreed.

How? I asked him.

Not now, Kor hissed.

As if reading my mind, as Kor so often seemed to, Solim looked around Kor at me and smiled. "We have guessed that you have a bothersome ability to share power—to fantastic effect."

At my surprise, he chuckled. "It was not hard to figure out, after Koriben's theatrics. How else could his drakáform have become so large? If you can make the Golden Heir do that, then what can you make the *Tolsyon* heir do?"

My heart thudded. Had they also figured out my connection had switched to Kor? Or did they just assume I could give that amount of power to anyone?

Solim didn't say, but continued, "It's quite possible that you could give Korinth enough power to hold out against even me until I shattered this icy connection between us altogether, and what would be the point in doing that?"

"If they could send more consumed to this area we're currently in, they already would have," Kor added flatly, seeming willing to play the explanation game as long as Solim was. "I've warded this area against another darkrift, and the ones in the passage are healing, and when they do, they're harder to pierce through than ever, just as scarred skin is stronger. And dawn is coming, which ends our chance at the moongate but increases our chance of survival if we go back the way we came."

"*Increases*," Solim said, eyes glittering, "but you can't fool me that you'll actually try."

I saw now. The two of them had been playing a game of speed chess with each other the whole time, taking risks, making moves, calling bluffs.

And now we were at a stalemate.

Which meant....

"What's your bargain, Solim?" Kor said calmly.

"Why, you, of course," Solim said, slowly smiling. "In exchange for the moongate."

Kor snorted, but still seemed unsurprised. "You convinced the Devourer that something is better than nothing, did you?"

"It's a pragmatic being," Solim said easily. "It recognized, as I knew it would, that removing you removes one of the main pillars of Sarah Lind's defense. Perhaps the most important one, in fact."

"You flatter me," Kor said with a thin smile. "How is this to work?"

"I think you've already guessed. You swear a blood oath that as soon as you have seen Sarah safely through the moongate, you will come along quietly with me. Then I'll allow you both through so that she may get close enough to her gate."

My heart stopped.

I gaped. "You can't be serious."

Sarah, Kor snapped silently.

Kor, there's no guarantee he won't hurt us once we get to the other side.

I'm *the guarantee, Sarah,* Kor snapped. *He wants me more than anything, but he knows he can't take me if I don't go willingly.*

What did that even mean? Kor was powerful, yes, but more than Solim?

Kor, he's a lish—

"Have you not told her?" Solim said in amusement. "She didn't seem surprised when I mentioned what you were."

"We hadn't gotten to that part," Kor said flatly. "Sarah, I said I've never had a gate, but...I *can* do something that neither Ben nor you can."

"What?" I rasped.

"He can enter the ether," Solim said with a shrug, though the increased darkness in his eyes belied his nonchalance. "The in-between. Thus becoming invisible and incorporeal—out of reach. If he chose, he could abandon you now, and there would be nothing I could do to stop him."

All those times that Kor had appeared out of nowhere. Showed up at such opportune times. Seemed to know things he shouldn't have overheard....

His confidence that if only I could surge to Ben, he would be fine.

Inconvenient, he'd said.

From when he first discovered the moonpath and figured out "the game," he knew it might come to this. And still he'd decided to play it.

Knowing that it meant he might have to sacrifice his bishop to save the queen.

I looked at him in horror.

"No," I breathed, shaking my head.

"So, Korinth," Solim drawled. "Dawn approaches. What's your answer?"

Kor looked at me, eyes hard. *You promised.*

Then, eyes on Solim, he created a ball of sapphire fire in one palm. At first, I felt a rush of hope that he was about to throw it, to resist, to reveal his plan that would save us both, but he just let go of the ball, letting it hover in the air in front of him. Then he pulled a knife out of the ether and raised it over his right palm.

I hadn't seen a blood oath sworn before, but I could guess that this was the start.

He was going to do it. He was truly going to do it.

"Wait!" I gasped.

Sarah! Kor snapped.

I looked at Solim, pleading. "Just...let me say goodbye. Please."

Solim looked at me with dark amusement. "Well, Korinth...you got further with her than I expected you to. Go ahead, girl. I actually want to watch this."

Sarah, Kor said, tense as I pulled him to face me. *What are you doing?*

For once, I am asking you to trust me, I said.

Then I threw my arms around his neck to pull me up and press his lips to mine.

This had better work, I thought.

For so many reasons. I really didn't want this bit of PDA with the man I *wasn't* in love with, in front of our mortal enemy, to be for nothing.

Also...I simply didn't want Kor to die. For any reason—let alone for me.

Perhaps Kor understood, or perhaps he was letting his own instincts guide him. Because after his initial stiff surprise, he pulled me in and returned the kiss with a desperation that stunned me, momentarily breaking my concentration. What he took from me in focus, though, he gave to me with the *pull*.

It pulsed between us, stronger than ever.

Just as it had after my first kiss with Ben, that primary pull magnified my feel for all others. I felt like I was radiating from the magnetism in the moonpath cavern, and that connected me straight to....

The gate.

First miracle down, next one to go.

I lashed Kor tightly to me with my power, although the pull was so strong between us by this point that it might not have been necessary—but I wasn't taking any chances.

Then, gripping Kor physically and magically with all my might, I reached for my gate and pulled us through.

CHAPTER TEN

OFFER

SARAH

ONE BLUR LATER, KOR and I were falling on the floor in the Inner Rim in my hold.

And, of course, Kor fell on top of me, crushing the air from my lungs. It seemed to be my day/night for that sort of thing, but I simply didn't care, because we were *both* here, and we were *both* alive.

"Sarah," Kor gasped, pushing up off me. "Are you alright?"

"Better now," I wheezed. At least Kor wasn't as heavy as Ben, and his hand had still been cradling the back of my head from the kiss, saving my skull from the worst of the hit. I imagined that hand must be smarting something fierce.

I need mats in front of these gates, I thought faintly. *Big, thick, spongy mats.*

Kor stared around us as he sat back on his heels, looking as stunned as if I'd hit him with a mallet. It wasn't an expression I could ever remember seeing on his face, and I was recovered enough to savor it.

"How...did you...." he rasped, his eyes wide when they met mine. "You said you couldn't feel...."

"I...couldn't," I said, slowly sitting up. My head spun, but that could have been from shock and energy depletion as much as oxygen deprivation. "Not until I kissed you. I noticed...that worked with Ben, too."

Kor stilled, expression blanking. "You...kissed me...to find the gate?"

"It's hard to explain."

I trembled with exhaustion and dying adrenaline, so I turned around and sat against the wall, not even caring that it was a gate. It was closed and inactive, so no psychopathic lish was getting through, so whatever.

Kor sat next to me, not looking much better off. "Try."

I rolled my head to look at him. "It's like...amplifying the main connection helps amplify all the others."

He raised an eyebrow. "And...*kissing* amplifies the main one?"

I shrugged weakly. "I don't make the rules, and I haven't had time to test these things. I just did the one thing I knew worked last time. I'd say I was sorry for pulling one on you, but...you know, you pulled one first."

He chuckled tightly. "True. And I suppose you *did* just...save my life."

I glared at him. "About that. What kind of idiotic—"

Kor's face hardened. "It was the gamble I was willing to make, Sarah. Of course I'd hoped it wouldn't come to that, but I liked the consequences of waiting another night even less."

"Well, what if it was a gamble *I* wouldn't have made if I'd known that's what you were planning to do?" I snapped.

He smirked, curling his fingers to run the backs of them down the side of my face. "I'm touched, truly. But see, that is exactly why I didn't tell you."

"I...." I sighed. "I can't really say it anymore, can I? I want to hate you...but I can't."

"You sure about that?" he said with his best attempt at a brilliant smile, given his own clear exhaustion. "I can do something truly obnoxious to bring it all back, I'm sure."

"Not tonight, please," I said wearily. "Or...today, or whatever time it's supposed to be for us anymore."

"It's day, here," Kor said blearily. "But I agree. I think we both deserve some sleep before we have at each other again. Truce?"

He held out his hand.

I rolled my eyes and put my hand in his, and he gripped it without shaking.

"Sure, truce. For whatever that means from my end. You're the one who's always doing the torturing."

He snorted. "You would be surprised."

I didn't know what he meant by that, and I frankly didn't care.

We sat there for a moment, both of us too tired to move.

"One other thing," Kor said finally, turning his head to look at me.

"What?" I asked suspiciously.

"Ben does *not* have to hear the details about this, don't you think? We found the moonpaths, had a good run through them, didn't encounter anything. Agreed?"

Tempting, and surprisingly so. There was only one problem.

"You really think I can lie to him that well?"

Kor moaned. "We have *got* to work on your inscrutability."

"I don't know," I grumbled. "You seem to like me pretty well without it."

Then I froze as I realized how the word "like" could be interpreted.

Fortunately, Kor only smirked. "True enough."

He got to his feet with a groan. "Since you did just save my sorry hide, and since I'm the only one able to, I'll make the calls to let people know we're alive. Go to bed, Sarah. We'll figure out how to get you to Ben when you wake up."

I watched him go in a daze.

What I had said was true—I didn't think I could hate him anymore, no matter how obnoxious he tried to be. Because Eskala was right. Especially after seeing the contrast between brothers, I was starting to learn Kor's tells that revealed his good core, not to mention the fact that he often seemed to hide his true feelings under the exact opposite ones.

Right now, my gut told me his casualness was a bit overdone, that there was something bothering him—something *other* than nearly swearing a blood oath to put himself in his merciless brother's hands.

But that was ridiculous. That was more than enough—more than one mortal mind could take, even Kor's.

Right?

KOR WAS AWAKE AND eating in the kitchen when I wandered into it to go to the restroom. I paused in the archway, and he spotted me.

In many ways, he looked recovered. Normal. He was dressed in fresh, fine sapphire clothing as usual, and his curls were drying from a shower. From his relaxed face and brisk movements, he seemed fully rested.

He looked good, actually. Really good.

Now, where did that come from? I thought, shaking my head.

Must have just been the lingering relief that he was sitting there, safe, instead of a cold, bled-out corpse on some altar like he had been expecting to be by this point.

"Ah, good, you're up," he said in a normal tone, face showing nothing of what had been bothering him earlier. "I was about to wake you. Wash up, then come get something to eat. There are things we need to discuss."

I swallowed. "Any news on Ben?"

He grimaced. "No change there. I don't think he's ever gotten this much sleep in his life, so I guess there's that. Hopefully it's at least somewhat restful...."

He sighed at my pained expression and waved. "Go on, get ready. This can wait."

If Kor said his business could wait, then it probably could, so I headed to the bathroom without another word.

I had taken a shower before going to bed, so after doing just the basics, I came back to the kitchen. I was touched to see that Kor had made me tsha to go along with my "breakfast," and he was grimacing as he valiantly tried to make it through a mug of his own.

"Why are you doing that to yourself?" I teased as I sat down across from him and dug in.

"Because I need *something* right now, and I figured you would disapprove of wine," he said dryly.

I raised an eyebrow. My parents weren't prohibitionists, but they weren't big on alcohol, especially my dad. That whole sober, self-control thing.

"I think we need all our wits about us right now, Kor."

"I have a few wits to spare," he said with a smirk, making me roll my eyes. "Besides, I can outdrink Ben."

"Really?" I said with a smile. "How much does Ben normally drink?"

Given his fears about himself, I thought I knew the answer.

Kor chuckled. "Alright, you have me there. Hardly at all—mostly mild wine on feast days for him, but that's it, but the *one* time I was able to get him roaring drunk, he passed out, and I did not. Because, unlike me, *he* hasn't bothered to master the knack of using our healing energy to purge just the right amount of alcohol."

I sighed. "Of course you can do that."

Kor grinned. "It's trickier than you think. Because what's the point of drinking if you can't get the high? So you have to hold the healing back to get that far and then maintain it, but purge the excess."

"Let me guess: you're a master at it."

He raised his mug of tsha to me. "I'm *the* master, thank you very much. So, for your information, I am refraining now only to indulge your sensitivities, not because I would allow it to impair my judgement in any way this fine afternoon."

"You're too good," I said with a dry smile. "Alright, let's get down to business. I assume we're discussing how to get back to Ben?"

"That's the most important thing, yes." Kor sighed. "The tricky part is, the blizzard still hasn't let up yet, and doesn't look like it will anytime soon. It's too dangerous to fly in, either to get Ben out or for us to fly in from the closest sungate, as before."

I knew better than to think Kor was suggesting we wait out the storm. "That means using the moongate—and hoping that there's some way for us to get safely from it to the hold where Ben is."

"Exactly," Kor said grimly. "Solim *should* be gone by now, and with it still being day there, the Devourer shouldn't be able to tear more darkrifts into the area, if it could even do so with the scars of the old ones there, but Solim could have taken the risk of being trapped to linger, or he could have left all sorts of nasty surprises for us."

"So, you're saying that's what you think we have to do, but it will most likely be dangerous," I said grimly.

"Yes. Then what's your answer?"

"We should do it. What other choice do we have? Even if time wasn't of the essence, Ben is suffering. I don't know if I can reach through to him, especially...given how he's pulled away, but I have to try."

Kor's lips pulled into a humorless smile, and he gazed at me for long enough that I shifted uncomfortably.

"What?"

"I am debating. Part of me wants to tell Ben everything that you did and are going to do for him...and the other part doesn't want him to know any of it."

My cheeks heated. "Right, so what's the plan? To not die, that is."

Kor took a deep breath. "You are going to *crack* the doors open. Just a *crack*, do you understand?"

He held up his thumb and pointer finger with only a half an inch between them. "A crack. Just enough to activate the gate. That's all I need to slip through."

"That?" I asked, staring at his fingers in consternation. "You're not that ski—"

Finally, his look at me sunk in, and I remembered, mouth forming a silent O.

"Really?"

Kor's smile was thin. "I wouldn't even need that much if the gates could be active without opening. Trust me, I've tried. There's nothing but solid rock behind them right now."

"You...can walk through walls," I said faintly.

With surprising simplicity, no cheek whatsoever, Kor said, "Yes. It's not that hard when you can become...nothing."

Outrage filled me. Was nothing sacred with him? Nothing safe? He couldn't just be brilliant, charismatic, and powerful—already the perfect spy. He could become something that you simply couldn't keep out.

"You found out about my secret passages *before* me, didn't you?"

There was some of his normal cheek in his crooked smile. "If by 'before,' you mean our first day here...yes."

I gritted my teeth, but my old standby phrase still rang false in my mind, so I just stewed in silence.

"Oh, don't fuss," Kor said irritably. "I only got to the outer rim. The walls beyond that were astonishingly...resistant. I've never encountered something that has repelled me in that way before. Now I am *dying* to know what lies beyond."

"Well, you can just wait, then," I said petulantly.

His revelation of at least *one* impediment to his reign of informational terror gave me a surge of comfort. Maybe...I would start sleeping in my special room after all. Not that I thought he was a peeping Tom—I just wanted somewhere where I *knew* I could be alone, dang it.

"As much as it pains me to say it, I must agree. Because, as we were discussing, there's no time to waste on personal indulgences."

I wasn't *quite* ready to move on from this injustice to the balance of the universe. "Why would the Tree give you a gift like *that*?"

"Why indeed? To summarize centuries of past Tolsyon heirs' own exploration of this topic, we think it is because *nothing* is precisely what is left for us to have dominion over. The gift itself is a symbol of our lack of crown, until such a time as we are given one. The Golden Heir has the sun, you have the moon...and we have the void."

"Oh," I said. That made...a bit of sense.

He sighed. "You can think of it as my own kind of surging. That's a bit what it felt like when you brought me here. Except *I* have no gate to surge *to*. When I enter that state, I am alone, and thus remain where I am until I move myself under my own power."

That made...even more sense. Dang it.

He grimaced. "You're right to be nervous, though. Even with no gates, it's a dangerous gift in the wrong hands. Why do you think Solim loathes me so much for taking it from him?"

I froze, heart skipping a beat. If the thought of Kor with this gift made me uncomfortable, the thought of *Solim*....

I stared at Kor. "He...he would have been unstoppable."

Kor was grim. "Precisely. Which is exactly why the Tree does not tolerate any abuse of it. I must only use it in the service of the Realms. And...in the preservation of my life. It's the reason...well, one of the reasons that Solim wants to kill me, but it's also the reason he hasn't yet managed it. It hasn't been for a lack of his trying, trust me, but last night...was the closest he ever came."

Because, just as Solim had with Ben, Kor's twisted brother had used someone against him. Someone that even Kor, used to making the hardest of choices for the good of the Realms, could not justify sacrificing: the Moontouched Heir.

I had saved his life...but just as when I'd given him the energy to heal himself in the ice tunnel, his life would never have been in danger if not for me.

When I remained quiet, Kor put his hand to his forehead and sighed. He reached across the table with his other hand and took my own. "Sarah...I swear to you, I try to only use it when I need to. You can trust me. Please...don't be afraid of me, not now."

I blinked. For once, he had misinterpreted me. That in and of itself was comforting, making me truly hope he could *not* read thoughts on top of everything. I was simply as open as a book. Right then, that book had been turned to a sober page, and Kor thought that meant I once again didn't trust him.

Kor's gift made me uncomfortable. A privacy-loving introvert like me could hardly feel otherwise, but that didn't mean I was afraid of him. Not anymore. If the mountain of evidence I had by now wasn't enough, then there was this: twice in twenty-four hours, he had been willing to make the ultimate sacrifice for me.

For the good of the Realms, of course.

I smiled thinly and gave his hand a squeeze. "I'm not afraid of you. I just needed to process that. I...argh. You're going to make me say it, aren't you?"

I took a deep breath. Then said the words with difficulty. "I...trust you."

A smile lit his face. A genuine smile—not a smirk. I had just made him...happy. And he hadn't felt like he'd had to hide it.

My cheeks heated. That kind of smile was doing weird things to my insides, things I shouldn't be feeling right now.

"Don't let that go to your head," I grumbled. "I'm still going to want explanations and common courtesy and...all that stuff."

"Oh, I know," he said, nodding. "I think I know what your boundaries are very well by now. I promise to push them only when I have to."

I glared at him. "You mean when you *think* you have to."

"I am bound by my own perceptions," Kor said innocently. "If I think I have to, I'm hardly going to know if I don't actually have to, am I?"

That made my head hurt. "Alright, that's enough philosophy for today."

"Shame," Kor said with a regretful sigh. "I love philosophy. It's such an undervalued field of study."

I raised an eyebrow. "I thought we didn't have time for 'personal indulgences.' I've already wasted enough on my mini crisis, sorry. Let's get back to your plan."

Ever in the back of my mind was the awareness that right now, Ben was in pain, even in whatever subconscious place he'd dug himself into. After all, he was refusing to wake up, wasn't he? *Some* part of him was making that choice.

Kor grimaced. "Alright. Although it's simple. You open the gate just enough to activate it, and I slip through and investigate. You close the gate immediately after me, just in case. Then, if I determine the coast is clear and I have neutralized any nastiness Solim might have left for us, I'll call you to open it again and come out."

"How?"

"With this, of course," Kor said, bringing a small blue scale to his fingers like a magician materializing a card. He slid it across the table to me.

Ben's scale burned in my pocket. Even now, when it was useless to me with Ben catatonic (this morning I'd tried it, with no answer), I still carried it as the precious treasure it was to me. Also, though the intention had been mostly subconscious until now, I realized I had put it in my pocket as a statement that no matter how many connections I'd once had only with Ben that I'd lost to Kor, I still had this one only with Ben...

...until now.

"I set the spell for you just before you woke up," Kor said with a grin. Which slowly died as I just stared at the scale without moving. "Sarah?"

"Sorry," I said, trying to snap myself out of it.

There was absolutely no reason I could refuse such a necessary, practical gift. It was, after all, a key part of Kor's necessary, practical plan to get me back to Ben. Kor meant nothing more by it than giving me his number, which I should probably have had a long time ago, anyway. For necessary, practical reasons.

I reminded myself sharply of that as I made myself reach out and pick up the scale—and not flinch when I felt the spark of magic imprint me onto it.

"Thanks," I said, smiling wanly. "So...you'll call me on this if it's safe, I come out, and we find our way to Ben. Right?"

That's what I had to focus on. Getting back to Ben. That's what all of this was about. Nothing else—beyond the mission and returning to my family—mattered.

"Right," Kor said, but he was studying me with a sober expression.

"Great," I said, standing up and gathering our empty plates and utensils. "Just let me clean up and grab my gun and stuff, and I'll be ready to go."

"Here, let me handle that," Kor said, standing and taking the dishes from me. "You go get ready and meet me at the gate."

"Really?" I said in surprise.

Kor rolled his eyes. "Just because I let Ben handle cooking *and* cleanup when I can get away with it doesn't mean I'm incapable of it. Go on. The sooner you get ready, the sooner we can go."

I could hardly argue with that, so I hurried away.

Not long after, I met Kor outside the new gate. It was near the kitchen, actually, with the first three moongates having appeared in turn on the other side of the southern entrance arch and the Oshal and Ekrel gates on this western side of it. There was only enough blank space between the kitchen arch and the Ekrel gate for one more.

That was immensely satisfying.

"Only one more gate," I said, grinning as I came up to him as he leaned casually against the Ekrel gate, arms folded, one foot against the wall.

"Yes," Kor said with a smile that echoed my own satisfaction, "and we think we have a good idea of where to find the next one."

"You do?" I said excitedly.

His smile widened. "We do. I have the start of a plan as well, but I'll wait until Ben is awake for the grand reveal."

"Right," I said with a nod.

That kind of good news might just be powerful enough to make even Ben happy right now.

"Alright, ready?" I said, then gave Kor a once over and a frown. "Is that how you're going to dress while going into potential danger?"

He was still wearing his soft-looking, tight, V-neck shirt, stylishly cut pants, and black boots with silver accents. Which was typical of his everyday apparel, but for the first time, it occurred to me that it wasn't entirely practical with how much danger we ran into on a normal day.

He smirked. "What *should* I wear?"

"I don't know. Armor or something?"

Ben rarely wore his armor because he didn't want to appear more intimidating and warlike than he could help. What was Kor's excuse?

His smirk deepened. "Sarah, with all the things you've learned about me in the past day, do you really think I need *armor*?"

I frowned. "Alright, fair point, but you said Ben and I are the only ones who know. Wouldn't you at least wear it sometimes, just for appearances?"

"I do, which is why I even have a set, but a leftwing isn't supposed to be dragged into as much bodily peril as Ben has dragged me, so people expect it less from me. When asked, I say that not wearing it gives me more flexibility, which it does. I don't need armor to weigh me down and hinder me. As for Yvera, well—she has a low enough opinion of my combat acumen that she simply doesn't care about my reasons."

He chuckled. "Plus, she's hilariously ignorant about magic. It's all one big mystery of smoke and mirrors to her. Sometimes I can even *surge* right in *front* of her, and she just thinks that I'm doing what any other magic worker worth his wages could do."

I huffed a laugh in spite of myself. Even though I felt bad for it.

"Alright, point taken. Ready then?"

"Not quite. Before we leave the safety and...privacy of your hold, there's one last thing we need to discuss."

"What?" I asked in surprise.

Kor slowly smiled. A kind of smile that made me nervous. "Allow me to begin with a demonstration."

Then, before I knew what was happening, he pulled me into him against the wall, captured my back with one hand and my head with the other, and pressed his lips to mine.

"Kmor!" I said in consternation, the word slightly muffled against his mouth.

Relax. I won't go far with this, I promise, he said silently, his lips never ceasing to move against mine. *Just let me show you what I mean.*

Relax?! How was I supposed to *relax*?

But then....

Gosh, he was so good at this.

His fingers rubbed tiny circles at the back of my neck, sending tingles shooting from there to clear down my spine. I was pretty sure he was sending me heat through that hand on my back and through his chest; there was no way he could naturally be that muscle-meltingly warm. His incense-like scent enveloped me, drawing me further into the trance. His lips moved deliberately, luxuriously, masterfully. Unlike Ben, who dazzled me from sheer passion and instinct, Kor had clearly had some practice, but somehow, being the beneficiary of it now, I didn't care how many had come before me. His cool-headedness was intriguing—comforting, almost.

His cheeks were so smooth compared to Ben's, a fascinating sensation in and of themselves. In fact, it occurred to me that everything about Kor was smooth where Ben was rough, and (in how Kor normally annoyed the heck out of me) rough where Ben was smooth.

Just as he had suggested, I found myself relaxing, my eyes drifting closed—melting into him, even. Melting into that long, slow, measured dance of a kiss. No matter how a part of me pounded away in my head, screaming that I shouldn't be doing this.

Gradually...the dance came to an end, with a conclusion as graceful as if he'd twirled me. Then we both, knowing it was over, parted enough to open our eyes and look at each other. Kor's eyes were glowing, and I knew from the reflection in his eyes that mine were too.

Melted as I was...I didn't move away.

Still, the screamer in my head finally got ahold of my voice and spoke. "What...the heck...was that?"

Kor slowly smiled. He loosened his hand from my neck to brush against my face. "That, my dear Sarah, was giving you a choice. And a choice is not a choice unless it is enticing."

My heart began to pound. "What?"

I should move now. I should *really* move now.

But I didn't.

His smile softened. "Do you think I have actually *tried* to win you before this? That I don't know exactly how my trite flirtations with you for Ben's sake have disgusted you? I disgusted you on *purpose*. I have *always* made you disgust and hate me on purpose, because that was what I thought was best for you and for Ben. But Eskala told me how upset you were that the Trees have intended you for Ben, as if They were taking away your choice."

I swallowed, heart pounding even faster. Yet I still didn't move.

His nose brushed mine. "Well, here I am as living proof that's not true. You don't have to either reject your birthright or marry Ben. They've given you a third option, and that kiss was to show it to you. It was to show you how things could be so different, so much *easier* between us...if that's what you wanted. If that's what you decided. The Trees are giving you that choice. I may not have the Royal Blood now, but They gave me the potential, and for good reason. If Ben is not satisfactory to you, yet you would like to keep the birthright that belongs rightfully to you so that you may serve the good of all, then I am...amenable to the idea of taking his place at your side."

I flinched, jerking away from him.

Only now, Solim's words came back to me, their meaning finally sinking in. *Well, Korinth...you got further with her than I expected you to.*

No. It...it couldn't be. That was just Solim's lies again. Kor wasn't actually...trying to...just to....

"Sarah?" Kor said uncertainly at the sudden change in me. His hands fell slowly back to his sides, though one of them clenched, as if wishing to reach for me again, but he held himself back. I imagined he could read me now just as well as he always could, and that what he would be reading right now was fear.

"Sorry," I stuttered. "Sorry. I...it's just...I know it was all lies. I know it. I know it. I—I trust you."

I trust him. I trust him. I repeated that in my head like a mantra.

Then why was I so afraid? So much that I was trembling?

Kor stilled. "Sarah, what lies?"

I took a deep, steadying breath, wrapping my arms around myself, but I still shook. "Svyer...you know, when she was giving me the lies Solim gave her...she said that you might try to—to become my consort. She—she said it was for the power, but I know—I *know* now that's not what you want. I know—I know that's not why you just offered. I know you mean well, that you're just—just offering out of duty, like always. Always duty."

Kor just stared at me, unmoving and unspeaking, expressionless.

I took another few breaths. Finally, my heartbeat was slowing. "I—I appreciate that. I really do. So—so thank you. For that. I just.... For both our sakes, I hope...I hope it doesn't need to come to that."

Kor stared at nothing, and when he spoke, he whispered, lips barely moving—perhaps not even intending me to hear. "That's why he had her turn you against me. He...knew. Even then. Even before I...did."

He put his head in his hands and groaned, his fingers curling into his hair. "Of *course* he knew."

I swallowed. "Knew *what*?"

Kor stayed still for a moment. Then he lowered his hands wearily. "That...I would make the offer. Out of duty. As you said. But now that is...clarified...for both of us, you won't hear from me about it again. You have my word."

I tried to conceal my breath of relief, tried not to let my shoulders visibly sink from it.

"In fact," he said, with a tired attempt at a smirk. "I think it's time to end our truce, don't you? Time for me to once again become my lovably obnoxious self."

The way he put it both relieved and troubled me. On the one hand, I desperately wanted things to return to the way they had been, which was surprising considering how much the way things had been had driven me crazy. On the other....

"Kor, you shouldn't have to live...in a way that isn't...true to what you want to be."

"Who says that isn't who I truly am?" he said innocently.

My heart sank. He couldn't fool me anymore.

"Now that's cleared up," he said, energy returning to his voice as he turned around to face the gate. "Time for us to figure out what surprises Solim might have left for us."

I came forward slowly.

"Just a crack, remember," Kor warned. "Just enough to activate. Then immediately close it behind me."

"I remember," I said quietly.

I put my hands on the gate. *Just a crack, please.*

The glowing lines flared, took the power, and ground open. Just a hair.

Then Kor blurred...and was gone. One moment there, one moment not. Just like that.

I gave it a handful of seconds, hoping that was enough time for him to get through. Then I pushed on the doors, and they closed of their own accord, and the lines faded.

Now that I was finally alone, I sunk against that blessedly cool stone, and a final tremor of release went through me.

I could now name the reason I had been so afraid.

I had once snorted at Kor in disbelief that he could actually win me. Well...now, after a kiss like that...and even more important, after a day like yesterday....

I trusted him now. That was precisely the problem, the reason for my fear. Because now that my last defense was gone, I knew that if he truly *tried*, that if he thought we had to marry for the good of all...there would be no stopping him.

Chapter Eleven

PATH

Sarah

I waited perhaps half an hour, or half a deken by my watch, growing more tense by the minute. I had been too overwhelmed with other things to worry about what Kor was going into when I had let him go—which perhaps had been his intention, at least in the timing of his "offer."

Though it wasn't long before worry sunk in and began to grow. Hundreds of horrible scenarios ran through my mind, all the way from cave collapse to Kor bleeding out on an altar—and I knew I was naive when it came to the dangers of the Six Realms and about what Solim was capable of.

But once again, I felt helpless to do anything. Except....

As soon as it occurred to me, I cursed myself. I rushed to the nearest blank section of wall and touched it. I'd learned from my experiment in Eskala's study that glass wasn't necessary, since she hadn't a mirror in sight. I guessed that any surface that my ice could cover would do, but flat was better to avoid distortion of the image, and walls were convenient to avoid bending over or craning my neck.

Show me Kor, please, I begged.

After the ice crept away from my fingers, I pled in a different way, a way powered by emotion, not magic—a wish, not a request. *And please show me he's alright.*

When the image came, I saw...darkness.

No. No, no, no—

Then the moonstone streaks on the wall began to glow, illuminating the passage. I let out one breath of relief. There was nothing there—nothing and no one in sight, and I supposed I should have expected that. After all, he was—

Kor materialized in the center of the image, scowling. "Sarah, you were supposed to wait for my call."

"It's been half a deken, Kor," I snapped. "Excuse *me* for thinking you must be dead by now."

He rolled his eyes. "Thank you for your concern. Perhaps I should have specified that traveling like I do isn't...easy. It's slow going at best. Particularly the more I try to remain enough in this realm to still observe what I need to."

"Yes," I said stiffly. "You should have."

"Well," Kor said grudgingly. "Now that you're 'here,' perhaps it's time for me to test a theory of mine."

"What?" I asked, shifting to surprise.

He only lifted his palm and created a ball of sapphire fire inside of it.

Then cursed. Vividly. He was so livid that his skin was flushing darker.

"That torched *asher*," he snarled, staring at the ball of flame in his palm.

"Kor...." I said hesitantly.

"He knew," Kor raged. "He knew, and he knew *I* didn't know, because I was with you, and I was protecting you."

"What. Did. He. Know?"

"Moonstone," Kor snapped. "There's something about it that suppresses magic—unless you, Sarah Lind, are there and at least unconsciously give permission."

I gaped. "What?"

Kor just continued his rant. "I have found nothing, Sarah. *Nothing.* Not a single trap, not a single curse or enchantment. We *weren't* at an impasse last night. We had the *advantage.* We were *winning.* But Solim wasn't going to tell us that, no. That's why the Devourer could barely make any darkrifts. That's why Solim sent brute, nonmagical creatures against us, and ones he might not have picked if he'd had the time to find better. That's why he met us right at the opening. He wasn't about to let me through so that I could figure out that *he couldn't use magic against you.*"

I blinked. "Oh."

Well...that put last night in a different perspective.

"I could have ended him!" Kor shouted, clenching his fist to dispel the fireball, as if imagining it were Solim's head. "With you, I could have ended that hellfrosted asher, right then and there! But no, instead, I was such an *idiot* to not see what was right in front of me, I nearly...."

Sacrificed himself...for nothing.

"Well...." I said. "That...stinks."

Kor gave a hard laugh. "You have no idea."

He groaned and put a hand to his forehead, taking deep breaths.

"Does...that mean it's safe for me to come out now?"

"Not now," Kor said wearily, lowering his hand. "Just...let me be sure. But if my suspicions are correct, I'll have more good news for you when I call."

"Like what?" I asked, heart pounding with hope.

His lips pulled into a thin smile. "Don't get your hopes too high, alright?"

"Sure," I said, making my face serious.

His smile grew a bit. "I think...that this passage dead ends with a moon-door into Roddan Hold."

"Really?" I exclaimed, nearly jumping for joy.

No crawling our way to the surface and risking our lives wandering through a blizzard? Ben was *this close*?

Just on the other side of my gate, down a passage, through a door.

Why couldn't I go *now*?

My eyes drifted to the side to the gate, and Kor saw.

"Sarah," he said sharply, raising a finger. "Don't you dare. *Wait*. Wait until I'm sure it's safe and I'm at the gate to meet you. Wait until I call. You hear me? You're no good to Ben if you get yourself hurt or taken now."

I sighed, but as always, Kor's argument was irrefutable.

"I'm really tired of being so vulnerable."

Kor sighed. "Sarah, anyone would be vulnerable with the full might and cunning of the Devourer bent on their destruction. Even me. I'm lucky that Solim is the worst of my problems."

He seemed quite bad enough to me.

"Besides," Kor continued, unusually gentle. "You weren't born to this like we were, and it's only been days since you came into it, and most of those days haven't given you the time to learn what you're capable of. Give yourself a break. You won't be the vulnerable one forever. In fact...I bet my finest bottle of Kallin Red that after you've had even a few months of growth and training...I'll be the one hiding behind you."

I raised an eyebrow. "Really?"

He smirked. "Really. I don't risk my hard-earned wine for anything. Now end this call and save your strength. You're going to need it for Ben, after all."

"True," I said with a sigh. "Just...be safe, alright?"

"I think I can manage that," he said with a wink.

Then disappeared.

ANOTHER AGONIZING HALF HOUR later, Kor led me down the passage, turning right at a fork.

He pointed back. "That way leads to the dead end that the last moonpath connected to."

"Where Solim was," I said quietly.

"Yes," Kor confirmed, his eyes glittering dangerously.

He still wasn't entirely over his temper, and I didn't blame him. Once again, even in defeat, Solim had delivered quite a mocking blow to his opponent. At least this time, I had more confidence that Kor could work through it on his own. For all Solim being his own brother, Kor seemed in a better state of mind about him than Ben was.

Or he was simply better at burying the pain of what Solim had done to them.

His words to Eskala came back to me. *My heart is fully iced over.*

Maybe...not in a healthier place after all. Just a temporarily more functional one.

A short time later, we reached the moondoor, the arched outline and white tree on its stone surface already ready and glowing for me, as if in welcome—or perhaps responding to the stretching of my soul. Even though I still couldn't feel what I was searching for, still I reached, even if I was now fumbling in the dark.

Even if the pull currently led in a different direction, inviting me to turn back.

I rushed to the door and pressed my hands against it, heedlessly slipping through as soon as it started swinging, despite Kor's protest.

Who should be there and waiting for me but Yvera, along with another Battleblood I recognized from Ben's elites—a friendly yet tough-looking young man with short-cropped violet hair whose name I knew I'd heard but couldn't remember.

I paused, looking up at Yvera uncertainly. Her eyes were glowing. That couldn't be good.

She put her hands on my shoulders, fingernails digging into them, and leaned down to my level.

"If you ever do something so torched dangerous like that again, I will kill you myself. You understand?"

Before my life could flash before my eyes, I caught the young man's gaze. He was smiling.

Allow me to translate: that means she was worried about you and is glad you're safe now.

When I looked back and noticed the tightness in Yvera's eyes, I realized he might just be right. Would wonders never cease.

"Because of Ben, of course," she said with a sniff as she let go of me and straightened. "As much of a dimtorch as he's being right now, what you have put him through is unacceptable."

"I know," I agreed quickly. "I'm sorry. That's why I'm here. Can you take me to him?"

"What do you think we're here to do?" the young man said with a grin, putting a friendly hand on my shoulder.

He looked up at Kor over me. "We've got her, Kor. You go do your thing."

"Much appreciated, Ordran," Kor said with a smirk and a parting wave to him. He didn't even look at me as he began walking toward the exit of the storage room we were in.

Wait, that...was it? After all we'd been through, after all Kor's fuss about my safety until this point...he was just going to dump me on Yvera and walk away? Without so much as a *See you later, Sarah*?

"What thing?" I asked incredulously.

Kor paused and turned slightly, not fully facing me. "Getting everything in place for finding the next gate, of course. Just in case Ben is in any state to get going soon."

"Oh," I said, deflated. That made perfect sense. As always.

But then...why wasn't he even trying to smirk at me? Why was he...not even looking at me?

"Alright. Good...luck, I guess?"

His lips turned up in the faintest of smiles. The pull from him abruptly surged, nearly staggering me...then waned. As strong and as brief as a tidal wave.

He shook his head and turned, calling over his shoulder, "You take care of Ben, Sarah. Let me take care of the rest."

In moments, he was out of view around the stacks.

Yvera folded her arms and snorted. "What's gotten a bur in *his* tail?"

So, it wasn't just my imagination.

"I have no idea," Ordran said, in a neutral expression worthy of a Starkissed.

He smiled down at me and gently patted me on the shoulder. "Come on, Sarah. Let's get you to Ben."

"Right," I said numbly, looking back the way Kor had gone.

Ben.

PEOPLE STARED AS YVERA and Ordran led me through the halls and courts of that small mountain hold. Fortunately, they appeared to me to be mostly Battleblood, judging from the coloring of the drakón, and though most of them looked less forbidding than I'll-bite-your-head-off-if-you-say-hello Yvera, I gathered they were a stoic lot not prone to demonstrations or mobbing celebrities. For the most part, they just stared for a bit as we approached, and by the time I had reached and begun passing them, their attention had already moved on.

Oh, look, I imagined them thinking. *It's that Moontouched girl all the torched idiots are talking about. Huh. She doesn't look like much. Wonder what the fuss is over.*

Then they would go straight back to whatever they had been doing or wherever they had been going.

After the Starkissed's red-carpet treatment, the Battleblood's attitude was rather...refreshing, actually. I felt almost normal again. I could desperately use some normalcy in my life right about now.

The only one who even tried to approach me was a spindly amón man, his hair white and face wrinkled, tottering forward with a cane. Yvera gave him a glare that should have sent him running, but he just smiled back at her.

"Oh, don't you worry, little Yv. You know I mean your charge no harm."

I blinked at him. Little? Had he just called Yvera *little*? Did he have a death wish?

Yvera, to my surprise, didn't rush to strangle him. In fact, all she did was fold her arms and frown.

"Great Uncle Erdan," she snapped. "I'm on Crown business. We've got to get her to—"

"I won't hold you up long," he said, still smiling. "I just have something I need to give the Moontouched child. A new creation of mine, made just for her."

Yvera stared. Even Ordran looked startled. People who had been studiously ignoring us let their gazes drift back. One young woman paused in lacing up her boot. A potter paused in his work, his wheel slowing to a standstill. Passerby slowed, lingering.

"Really?" Yvera asked incredulously. "*New*? For *her*?"

She cast me a glare, as if swiftly regretting any good feelings toward me that she'd allowed to take root inside her.

"I couldn't have made it otherwise," he said, smile fading to soberness. "A Tree came to me in dreams each night, showed me where to find what I needed and how to make it each day, and that Tree...wasn't our own. She was of Ice."

You could have heard a pin drop in that marketplace. Everyone was frozen, watching. For these stolid, backcountry Battleblood, I gathered that meant something significant.

Erdan turned to the leather satchel at his side and pulled out a thin, flat strip of familiar-looking silver metal about the length of my forearm. In fact, it had white leather straps at each of the ends that would just about fit....

"May I, child?" Erdan said, holding up the strip next to my arm.

Not sure I had any other choice to hurry my extraction from this situation, I numbly raised my forearm in front of me and allowed him to slip on the strip. The length fit perfectly, and the only adjustment he needed to make was to tighten the wrist strap once my hand was through. It reminded me of arm guards for archery, except the metal strip was on the outside of my arm, so that made little sense.

Of course, one wasn't enough, so he pulled out another and attached it to my other arm. By this point, my cheeks were flaming, and people had begun to whisper.

"What do you think—"

"What kind—"

"—look like much."

When he finished and stepped back, I lowered my arm and then turned both of them this way and that to examine my new ornaments. So far, that's all they looked like: some kind of skimpy, decorative gauntlet. But since he was Battleblood, and everyone was in such awe of him, I knew it couldn't just be for decoration.

"Thank you," I said, trying to sound as sincere as I could through my mortification. "If you don't mind me asking, though...what are they?"

He chuckled. "Send some power into them, child."

It was past noon here, so I didn't have much, but with a sigh, I gave what I had.

A silvery white field zapped out from each gauntlet, perfect circles that originated from the circle—moon?—etched into the center of each strip. I started with surprise and broke my concentration, and the circular fields zapped back into the gauntlet as quickly as they had appeared.

"Excellent, excellent," Erdan said in delight, as if he hadn't seen the result of his labors yet.

He might not have. I had felt the sort of drain that made me wonder if this was yet another thing that had imprinted on just me. In fact, I realized why the silver looked so familiar now: it was the exact same shade as my gun.

"Are those...." Yvera said faintly, paling.

"Item-generated mobile shields, of course. The first of a kind." Erdan patted my upper arm fondly. "May they keep you safe, child. You have a hard road ahead, but your Tree is not leaving you to walk it alone, nor as unprepared as you might think."

With that, he tottered away. The crowd that had gathered parted almost reverently for him, and whispers broke out again as soon as he was gone.

Ordran whistled, and he smiled as he put a hand on my shoulder. "That was Erdan Battleblood, by the way—the most brilliant magicsmith of all time. Most of the magic-class weapons we have are of his design. He's retired, though. Hasn't made anything new in ages. Aren't you a lucky girl?"

That...wasn't exactly what I was thinking as Yvera glared violet daggers of jealousy at me. I felt like the metal strips should be branding themselves onto me with the heat radiating from her.

I seemed doomed to forever take one step forward and three steps back with her.

"Come on," I said, cheeks hot as I avoided her gaze. "Let's go."

AFTER FAR LONGER THAN it should have taken, given the small size of that hold, we reached the guest wing. Every single door was occupied, which I guessed was because of the blizzard and the influx of our group.

There was only one golden, Sunfilled gem, though, and I gravitated to it immediately. I wondered how they'd gotten Ben to light it: just smacked his limp hand on the door or something? The image made my lips twitch despite the tension coiling in my gut.

The pull behind weakened, and though there wasn't yet one ahead, I could feel the promise of one. Gravity was shifting around me, recentering, coming back into balance as I approached my sun.

I could hardly stand still long enough for Yvera to push open the door for me.

There Ben lay on the bed, even more deathlike than when he had been in the coma Kor had put him under to recover from his berserker rage. He lay straight on his back, his arms limply resting on top of the covers at his sides, his face utterly empty. Not even loneliness cried out of him now. He looked...dead.

"Ben!" I said in a strangled cry as I rushed to him.

For a moment, I was terrified that everyone had lied to me up to this point to keep me sane while I was in danger, and that he *had* died, and they had only kept him here long enough for me to say goodbye.

"Ben, *no*," I sobbed, heedless of the audience behind me as I clambered up on to his bed and over him.

Then I saw his chest rise and fall, and when I put a hand over his flameheart, I could feel its warmth thrum under my fingers.

He *was* alive.

"Thank God," I said shakily, collapsing onto him. I wrapped my arms around him as far as they would go and held him as tightly as I could.

Ben, come back to me. Come back.

Gravity moved, stirring around us, pulling from all directions as it had on the moonpath.

Kor said I had a choice. That the Trees had given me a *choice*. I finally accepted that They had been more than fair. That maybe, just maybe, They hadn't chosen me and *then* arranged my fate. Rather...perhaps They had chosen me *because* I was the woman who would have wanted to walk this path all along, and this was the man I would have wanted to walk—or fly or run or even hobble—with me.

From the very first moment we met, collapsed together like this, and per-haps...even before.

But certainly, forever after.

Chapter Twelve

LIFE

KORIBEN

Ben, come back to me. Come back.

The familiar voice pierced through the darkness of the void.

Slowly, the darkness retreated as a star formed from its nothingness.

It was the most breathtaking sight I had ever seen, and I was irresistibly drawn to its whispers of hope and light and joy. I longed, as I had never longed before, to reach out and touch it. To take what it offered and let myself *be*.

Be, in all that life offered: be happy, be sad, be angry, be delighted, be hurt, be healed, be sick, be well, be weak, be strong, be afraid, be valiant, be feared, be hated, be loved.

Be.

With that star.

My hand reached reflexively, unbidden. But as soon as I saw my hand in the star's light, I pulled it back in horror.

I had no right to *be*. Let alone to *be* with it, where my *being* had...did...would put that light, that glorious light, at risk of darkening forever. I didn't know why it was bright again, after what I had done, but I couldn't dare reach for it now. Not again.

It should leave me. It should just *go* and let me stop being again. The darkness had been...needed, if comforting was too strong a word. Necessary. This was my prison, but also my fortress. This was where I was safe. This was where everyone else was safe from me.

Where the star was safe from me.

And yet, it didn't leave. It grew brighter and brighter, burning hotter and hotter.

Ben, come back, it pled. *Ben, I choose you. I choose you, you kind, noble man with a fiery heart of gold. I choose my sun.*

She...thought I was her sun?

She...chose *me*?

Even after all I had done to her.

Why?

There was only one way to find out. As much as the darkness started wrapping its arms around me to pull me back, I reached desperately for the star.

Perhaps I would *be*. Not long enough to darken her. Just long enough to find the answer.

My fingers brushed her light.

That was all it took for her to pull me in—up, up, up and in.

Back into the light.

MY LAST THOUGHT, FROM that snow drift of agony where I had collapsed, became my first. I froze with it, muscles clenching in agony.

"Sarah," I gasped.

"I'm here, I'm here, I'm here," she sobbed in relief.

To my utter shock, when I blinked open my crusted eyes, there she was, her forehead pressed against mine, her hands against my face, her legs against my sides.

Flame help me, she was straddling me. Only over my torso, of course, but it was a good thing that all my limbs felt like they were filled with lead.

"I'm here, I'm alright, you're alright, it's fine, everything's fine."

Then she pressed her lips to mine, giving me the salty taste of her tears.

How? I asked, not wanting to break that kiss for anything but still desperately needing to know. *How are you alive? I thought I....*

I....

Thank Flame that I could feel, taste, smell, and see her. That when my disturbingly weak arms wrapped around her, and I sent my fire through her to make certain, that I felt nothing but wellness and wholeness inside of her.

She pulled back, eyes troubled. *Kor pulled me off you just in time. I never fell with you.*

She never....

Of course.

Of course the one who would save her from me...was Kor.

I would owe him until eternity for this. Again.

"Heir Sarah," Ordran said, smiling as he came into my view. "If you wouldn't mind giving the healers some time with Ben now...."

"Oh, right," she said, cheeks heating.

To my intense disappointment, she began scrambling off me.

"Wait, what? Why?"

I had at least part of my answer when I tried rising to reach for her and fell back limply.

"Relax, Ben," Ordran said, putting a hand on my shoulder to keep me down. "Everything is fine. You've just been...asleep for a long time. They just need to make sure you're alright now. Which I'm sure you are."

"What?" I said, blinking. "How long have I been out? And why?"

Woran, the head healer of my elites, came up to me with a roll of his eyes and put his hands on my shoulders to begin his examination.

As I felt his power sink through me, Yvera came to the foot of my bed with folded arms and snorted. "For about twenty-five deken. Because you were being a torched idiot about Sarah."

"Twenty-five...." I said faintly.

And because I was....

Of course. I remembered being in such mental and physical pain I blacked out again, and, it seemed, I had somehow refused to even wake up. Not until the irrefutable proof of my innocence was *sitting* on me.

That...did sound like me.

"Wait...." I said slowly. "Sarah has been trying to wake me up for twenty-five *deken*?"

How much of a deaf, oblivious idiot was I? Not to mention torched unfortunate, if she'd spent the night with me....

Yvera looked away. "Not...exactly. She...just got here."

"What? *From where*?" I tried rising, and Woran sent me a shocker that had me sinking back down with a wince.

"I'm not done yet," he said with a glare.

For a Peacegrowth healer, he could certainly be mulish. Which...he needed to be to deal with as troublesome a patient as me.

"Sarah—" I said, looking for her among the people now crowding my room.

But I couldn't see her anymore. In my mind's eye, her star—thank the *Flame* her star was there again—was outside of it, somewhere down the hall I could get glimpses of through the people and my open door.

"Where'd Sarah go?" I asked in pained bewilderment. Couldn't she understand I needed her here, with me—

No. She wouldn't.

Not after the way I had treated her. Even before I'd thought I'd killed her.

Despite that, she had come from wherever she'd been holed up, probably risking her life to go through a blizzard, to save me from my stupid self. She had...sobbed over me. Kissed me, completely of her own choice. In front of everyone.

I knew she *cared*, wanted me even, but...she didn't...she couldn't....

Shouldn't.

It all came back. The rushing panic. The need to protect her from everything. Most especially from myself.

Only just in time, Woran pulled away, or he would have felt my pulse skyrocketing.

"He's fine," he told the others. "Just needs food and movement."

Oh, I need a lot more than that, I thought, feeling like I was going to be sick.

KOR KNOCKED AT MY door while I was picking at my food, having finally gotten the others to leave. For a few blessed moments, I didn't have to pretend. At least until he showed up.

As soon as I opened the door, he took one look at me from head to toe and then scowled. "I thought I might find you sulking."

"Kor, I really don't—"

He shoved his way into the room and then shoved the door closed behind him.

His sapphire eyes were hard. I gulped.

Not good.

"Sarah and I found the moongate," he said.

"What?"

That was not at all the kind of news I was expecting in Kor's current mood. Hope surged in me, momentarily quelling the panic. Perhaps the past twenty-five deken hadn't been in vain, after all.

He shrugged. "We fell into a hole when I pulled her off you. While we were wandering around underground, we found the moongate, and a passage that led to here. Took us a while, but we finally made it."

I waited a stunned moment, then said, "That's it?"

"Oh, there's a bit more to it. We found this new type of gate we're calling a moonpath. Also, moonstone. *Fascinating* substance that has the potential to revolutionize—"

"Wait," I said, holding up a hand as jealousy, hot and poisonous, choked me. "You're telling me you and Sarah wandered alone together, overnight, for twenty-five deken...and *nothing happened*?"

Kor's lips pulled into a wintry smile. "If anything of the nature you are implying *did* happen, what have you to say about it, Ben? You pushed her away. Torch it, you are *still* pushing her away."

I stiffened. "She left—"

"Did you *ask* her to stay?" Kor demanded. "Did you go find her when she did?"

Torch him. I had nothing to say, not to any of that, so I remained silent.

Kor shook his head. "Look, we don't have time for this. I think we may have found the location of the next moongate, but I am going to need an Heir with his head on straight. We are *this* close, Ben. Don't fail me now. Don't fail *her* now."

I ran a hand through my hair. "I'm *trying*, Kor, but I just don't know how to do this with her."

Kor hardened again. "She wandered all that time thinking only of you, Ben. All she wanted was to get back to *you*. Now that she's found you again, you're just going to keep pushing her away?"

"I don't know...if I can do...anything else," I said with great difficulty. "If I hurt her—"

"You are hurting her *now*, torch you," Kor shouted, eyes blazing bright sapphire. "And I cannot stand another moment seeing her so miserable, so pull yourself together and *make her happy again*, or so help me Ben, I will take her from you."

I froze, flameheart sputtering. "You...."

Kor just shook his head, smile and eyes both ice. "You think you're the only one who loves her?"

I stared, breathless.

I'd known from Kor's behavior toward her that he was *interested*, but he had been interested in plenty of people since I'd known him, so I hadn't thought anything more of it than to see him as an unworthy rival, one likely to lose his interest just as quickly as it had come to him. But I had never seen him like *this*. If he...truly....

He plunged on mercilessly. "You're just the one that the Trees—and Sarah—prefer, but prove yourself unworthy of her, and I will claim her by right. And you know They'll let me."

"No," I said faintly, shaking my head. But it was in horror, not denial.

I remembered what he was. Torch it, I always remembered.

But Kor had to go on. "You know why you thought she was dead? Because when I fell, I was hurt enough that Sarah had to transfer the connection from you to me to save my life."

I felt as if he'd stabbed me in the stomach and turned the knife. "*What*?"

"I had that for one day, Ben. For one day and one night, I had her star in my mind, and her power in my flameheart, and I honestly don't know how I'm going to keep going without either. But she never wanted to give them to me. All she wanted was to get back to you to restore what she thinks of as yours, and so she did."

She had. I felt her, burning brightly. I used that star as my guiding light in riding the tumultuous storm Kor was setting off inside me. I felt like I was drowning in those waves, not sure if I would ever reach her again.

Kor smiled coldly again. "But what I had once, I can have again. If you don't claim your place by her side, if you don't fight for it, if you don't *make her happy*, then for her sake and for the sake of the Realms, I will claim my right as the Tolsyon heir and take it from you."

Who else? I had once asked the Tree, and thought the answer was no one.

Well, that's where I had been wrong a second time. There was at least one other.

The Trees would have given Sarah a choice, and of course that choice would be Kor. Sometimes I wondered why the Tree had been so cruel as to make me Heir instead of him. He was everything a King *should* be. Already.

"I'll leave you to think about that for a quarter deken," Kor said coldly. "Eat your food, make your choice, and come out ready to be the Golden Heir. One way or another."

Then he opened my door again, stepped out, and closed it behind him.

I stood there for dek, unable to think about a single thing at all.

Then, in my mind's eye, I saw my star coming closer. Coming...to my door. Where she knocked tentatively, as if half-hoping I wouldn't hear, afraid of what she would face if I did.

As before, when she had been in danger, when I had thought she was within Solim's grasp, I didn't think.

Sarah was in pain. Because of me. And if I didn't do *something*, right this second...I would lose her.

I didn't think. I acted.

I went to the door and opened it.

Then, before she could say or do a thing, I said, "I have been a torched idiot. Though you probably shouldn't for your own good, can you forgive me?"

Her eyes widened in surprise. That had clearly not been the greeting she had expected, but when the meaning finally sunk in, those warm brown eyes that I loved widened again in pure joy.

She jumped up so suddenly that I almost didn't catch her, and when I raised her up to me, she grabbed my head and kissed me, her lips tingling with her cool power, even at this time of day.

I supposed that meant yes.

Flame, you have to protect her from me. Because I can't live without her.

CHAPTER THIRTEEN

GATES

SARAH

"REALLY?" BEN SAID INCREDULOUSLY. "The *Library*?"

For the sake of privacy, and because that was where we had to go anyway to get anywhere else with the blizzard still raging, we had returned to my hold and were once again all sitting in my kitchen to a meal Ben had just cooked up for us (Kor having declared that the cooking would do Ben mental and physical good, Ben retorting that Kor simply didn't want to eat the plain fare found in remote Roddan Hold).

And I couldn't be happier.

Alright, maybe if my family were here, but while I was thinking in the realm of the immediately possible, I couldn't think of a single thing that would make this moment brighter.

I had just cooked a meal with Ben, which had taken us twice as long as it needed to and we'd burned a couple things because we couldn't seem to keep our hands and mouths off each other, and the pull hummed stronger than ever.

My friends—yes, even Yvera now fell into that category—were gathered safe in my hold and sitting to eat it with us, and I was sitting thigh to thigh with Ben on the bench, and, to be honest, could have been in his lap if that wouldn't have made eating ridiculous. It was already difficult enough as it was eating with just one hand, because of course we were holding hands too.

I was bursting with happiness, and to top it off, we were discussing the final gate, and Kor was surprisingly confident he knew the location.

Even if Ben wasn't. "The Crownhold Library? You're kidding, right?"

"Nope," Kor said coolly. "Think about it, Ben. What other area of Ythra has the Starkissed always had nearly undisputed dominion over?"

With the Starkissed once having been the greatest ally of the former Moontouched Clan....

"I...guess," Ben said hesitantly. "But...it's the *Library*. In *Crownhold*. It's such a public place, in the largest hold in the Realms."

Lovely, I thought, but even now I couldn't quite manage the proper level of sarcasm.

"It's also one of the oldest parts of Crownhold," Kor pointed out, "and has gone through extensive expansions and renovations over the centuries. Why couldn't the Moontouched who resettled there have...slipped in one of their own? Hiding it in plain sight? And where would be one of the *safest* places for them to put the last gate, the gate which we might have otherwise faced the most risk reaching, but in the middle of Crownhold?"

"Alright, fine," Ben said. "I suppose we can look, but how are we supposed to get Sarah in there without half the Realms finding out that she's there the *moment* we come through Crownhold's sungate, and the other half by the time we get to the Library?"

"That's an exaggeration, right?" I said.

Ben just gave me a look.

Geez, these people didn't even have social media, paparazzi, or Google alerts, and they were *that* gossipy?

I still thought he must have been exaggerating. At least slightly.

Kor smiled slowly. "Using you, Sarah, sungates, and daygates, of course."

"What?" I said in confusion.

What were daygates? And weren't all sungates only usable during the day?

Ben just looked at Kor, thinking it through. "You really think Sarah can do that? Help me bring all three of you? She's only helped me surge with *one* other person before, and that was going straight to her. It might not be possible otherwise."

"Technically," Kor said, "she's done it twice now, and the second time was bringing both of us to her own gate last night."

"Really?" Ben said, frowning and casting a glance at me.

I thought Kor had explained things to him. That's what Kor had said he'd done, when he came to me to suggest I go try talking to Ben while Ben was still recovering in his room in Roddan Hold. Although...Ben hadn't been freaking out nearly as much as he would have if Kor had told him *everything*, so I suppose I should have known Kor would leave out important details. Like this one.

"We...were in a hurry?" I said, inwardly wincing at how I had ended my statement like it was a question, making an already poor lie a downright terrible one.

Sarah, Kor silently moaned.

You're the one who brought it up, I snapped back.

Ben's frowned deepened. "Why? Kor said you just found some paths and rocks."

Goodness, Kor had managed to leave out a *lot*.

"It was almost dawn by that point, Ben," Kor said, letting genuine grimness come to his expression. "It was either get to the gate then or wait another night."

Ladies and gentlemen, I present Korinth Starkissed: the master at lying with the truth.

"Oh," Ben said, seeming to accept that.

He thought another moment, sitting back. His thumb rubbed the back of my hand absently. "Still. I don't know, Kor. This is unfamiliar territory, and we have no idea of the dangers. I don't want to risk taking all three of you multi-gate surging across the Six Realms with only two very different experiences under our belt. Especially when we don't know what kind of strain that might put on Sarah."

"Then why not do an experiment?" Kor suggested. "You take all three of us to just *one* sungate, one relatively close by?"

Ben sighed. "I suppose you have one in mind?"

"There's sunlight at Goldek Gate right now."

Right now, we were in my hold, built by my Moontouched ancestors in the newly discovered Seventh Realm—too far from any of Ben's sungates for him to surge us to one of them. For Kor's experiment, we first needed to get back into the Six Realms, and that meant going through one of my discovered moongates with a connecting sister gate in one of the Six Realms. Hence why Kor had named the Romskal sungate that was nearest to my Romskal moongate's location. The sunlight part was crucial because sungates were only active during the day.

Ben looked at me. "What do you think?"

"What's a daygate?" I asked. That was the part that I was stuck on.

"It's a smaller version of a sungate that can only go elden instead of worlds," Ben explained. "Really, that's the only difference, but gates of any type are so costly, it isn't often that daygates are worth it. In fact, most of them are in Crownhold. Since it's so big, the daygates are necessary just for people to get from one section to another."

"Ooh," I said. "So, sungates are like your airports, and daygates are like your public transit."

Ben blinked. "Huh?"

"Ignore me," I said, brushing my Earthren statement away. "So, let me get this straight: Kor's plan is for us to go through one of my gates to get back into the Six Realms, for me to lash all of us together, and for Ben to surge-bounce us through his gates all the way across the Realms...to the closest daygate to the Crownhold Library?"

"*The* Library daygate, to be precise," Kor said with a smirk. "It has its own, of course."

I rolled my eyes. "Of course. Kor...you realize how crazy that sounds, right?"

If he was offended, he didn't show it. "Not much crazier than anything else we've done."

I paused, then admitted, "True."

"And I *did* propose an experiment."

"Why not have me try lashing three people at once?" I said. "Isn't that the natural progression?"

"We *could* do that," Kor said grudgingly. "But that is more time to wait for the one left behind—and by the one, I mean Yvera—to fly to catch up to us."

"Hey," Yvera said irritably. "I need to stay with Ben."

"But I'm smaller, lighter," Kor said with wide-eyed innocence. "In case that matters for this. Besides, I'm not as fast a flyer as you are, nor so tough and capable of being left on my own."

I choked on my juice, which may have contributed to Yvera's suspicious glare at Kor.

"Would we really have to wait, though?" I said when I had recovered, trying to think it through. I needed models, so I pulled my hand out of Ben's and started grabbing fruits from the fruit bowl at random.

"Say this one is Ben, and this one is me."

Ben was a scaly, tough-skinned fruit, kind of like a spherical pineapple without the crown. I was the soft, plumlike orange one.

I cast Ben a belated sheepish glance. "I have no idea what any symbolic significance these could have, so this is in no way personal."

"Oh, no offense taken," Ben said with a grin, propping the side of his head on his hand to watch me adoringly.

Yvera snorted. "Because sava are your favorite."

"Is that what these are called?" I said curiously, tapping the tough-skinned sphere I'd chosen to represent him.

Ben slowly smirked, tapping my orange. "No, these are."

"Oh," I said, cheeks heating. My thought process was momentarily derailed by the look in his faintly glowing eyes.

"Oh, get a *room*, will you, you two?" Yvera snapped, bringing me back into the present.

"Right, right," I said with a small jump. "Where was I going with this?"

"I believe you were selecting this one to represent me?" Kor said with a smirk, holding up the teardrop-shaped blue one with thick, shiny skin. Kind of like a smooth, blue avocado.

I rolled my eyes as I took it. "Why not?"

"If Kor gets to pick, then I do too," Yvera grunted, grabbing the one that was the spiniest of the lot and placing it with the other three on the table.

Of course, I thought, but didn't say out loud. Because, you know, I valued my life.

"The key in this scenario is that I think Ben and I have to stay together. That's because I need to do the lashing, and Ben needs to do the surging, at least to his own gates."

I placed the tough and the orange fruits together.

"But say we took just one of you with us."

Because of Yvera's protest earlier, I picked her, then pushed all three fruits half a foot away from Kor's.

"Kor is still at my gate."

I placed my cup where he was, then grabbed Ben's cup and placed it where the others were. I paused and thought a moment, seeing a hiccup in my plan: timing. My gate had to be active, but so did Ben's. Then I thought of a workable solution, took a deep breath, and plunged on.

"*If* we timed the jump perfectly, so that there's enough daylight for Ben to surge just before night fell, then my gate would hopefully become active soon after. Maybe, just maybe, if the sungate is close enough to the moongate, and I had Ben's help, I could bring both Ben and me *back* to the moongate and the person we left behind."

I pushed our two fruits back to Kor's.

"You think I hadn't thought of this?" Kor said, tapping my cup. "That leaves us at the moongate, at night, when Ben can't surge us back to Yvera. With Yvera stuck at an inactive gate that she can't go through to meet us somewhere else."

I deflated. "Oh, right."

"There's an easy enough solution to that," Ben said to me as he put a hand on my shoulder, casting a quick glare at Kor. "Instead of just you and me surging back to the moongate, we take Yvera back with us. We already did it once by that point. We might be able to do it again, even though this time it's to a moongate, with you surging us. At the very least, it's a test of that aspect. Then we go back into your hold and pick a different moongate to start over."

And people kept saying Ben wasn't intelligent. They just kept trying to put him down, because if he was *smart* on top of all his other advantages over them, what chance did they have?

In case you were wondering, the answer was none. Zip. Zilch. Nadda. There was a good reason he made people who didn't know him nervous. It was a good thing for everyone's sake that the Tree chose and cultivated Her Heirs carefully, and that Ben had a heart of the softest gold.

And that he took the weight of his power seriously. In fact, a bit *too* seriously right now, but I thought that someday, if he gave himself half the chance, he could find the balance his father had.

"But Ben, that's just more time and risk of the Devourer tracking us," Kor protested. "Not to mention risking one of us getting stranded. Crownhold only has so much more daylight left. If we don't get there soon, we'll have to wait until dawn breaks there, and we'll have lost an entire night to search for the moongate."

Ben glared at him. "And whose idea was it for me to cook us dinner? Besides, it's the next logical step for Sarah. This is all dependent on how much is safe for her to handle, after all."

"I've surged with her," Kor said tightly. "*I* think she can do it."

Ben's gold eyes turned hard. "Do you really want to risk her that way?"

Kor's own eyes flashed. "Do you really still doubt her that much?"

Geez, what was up with these two? Ben's flare of temper, I had expected, but Kor was normally more coolheaded—and knew when to stop pushing his luck.

"Guys, stop it!" I cried, pressing my hands to the table. Then I pointed at the leftwing. "Kor, you *know* Ben doesn't doubt me, so cut that ashdust."

I couldn't believe how easily that dramá swear word came to my lips, both in the profanity and fluency aspects. These drakón were really having an influence on me, for good or ill.

I went on with only the slightest pause. "He's just understandably a bit more concerned than the rest of us, because he cares for me."

Kor sat back, face turning hard and unreadable.

I took a deep breath, made my decision, and looked at Ben. He was the one I had to convince.

"Ben...I think Kor has a point. What do we risk by at least seeing if I can just *lash* us together first, before you try to surge us? If I don't feel absolutely confident about the strength of that lashing, then we break it and start with leaving someone behind. If I am as sure as I'll ever be that I can keep all of us together while you surge us...then we try."

Ben took my hand, clenched it, and sighed. Then finally nodded. "Alright. If you're sure...we'll try."

It was *AMAZING* how fast dinner cleanup could go if all four of us, even Yvera, helped—however grudgingly in the latter case.

In a surprisingly short amount of time, we were standing, all geared up, on the sunlit mountainside of the Wirthen Desert, with my moongate fading back into nonexistence behind us. Kor and Yvera were standing in their places at Ben's right and left, if a lot closer than usual, close enough that Ben had his arms around both of their shoulders, and I was on Ben's back.

This time, that had been my idea. I had no idea if closeness or contact between all of us would help, but I figured it wouldn't hurt.

"Ready?" I said, heart pounding. This felt strangely like the start of one of my track races.

"Ready," Ben said grimly.

"Just get on with it," Yvera snapped with a glare over Ben's shoulder at me. She wasn't happy with the closeness of this arrangement. From Kor's stone-faced expression, he didn't look that much happier, even though this surging thing was his idea, and even he had agreed that the closeness was a good precaution.

I closed my eyes to concentrate, and with at least half of the energy that rose up within me, I lashed all of us together. Half, because I didn't know if I would have to remake the lashing for the next jump, but I still wrapped them in that power with all the willpower of my entire being.

Nothing visibly happened, as usual, but I could tell all the drakón felt something from how Kor stiffened, Yvera grunted, and Ben tensed under me.

I paused, feeling the strength of that connection, testing it, debating whether anything could break my grip on them. Then I felt the certainty sink into me, far more than I had thought I would feel. I realized I had never actually thought I would have the confidence to tell Ben to go through with this. Even I had just assumed that I would fail and that we would have to start small.

Ben and Kor may not have doubted me, but I had.

But this felt...right. Like this was what we were meant to do.

Like this was our destiny.

I suddenly realized that at least *some* strength of the lashing came from the connection I already had with these drakón, and they to each other. Nothing like the pull between me and Ben, but something was there, between each of us. Something I hadn't recognized until just then.

I might not have been able to do this with any other three beings in the entire universe. At least not yet.

But with these three...it felt almost easy.

"Well?" Ben asked tightly.

"It will hold," I said, with perfect confidence. "Go."

Ben took a deep breath, tensing, but he had agreed. If I was sure....

He surged, turning us all into blurs that streaked through the darkness of the universe.

Not a heartbeat later, we stumbled out of the arrival side of the flame-filled Goldek sungate, Ben breaking his hold on Kor and Yvera as he staggered, but they were there with us.

We were *all* there.

"Anyone missing anything?" I gasped. "Limbs? Vital organs?"

"No," Yvera snapped.

Still, she had paled, and I didn't blame her. That was her first time surging, after all. The sheer shock of being in one place one moment and the next in another, without going through a gate under your own power, would have been quite enough.

"You did it," Kor breathed, eyes firing up with triumph. "Sarah, you did it! I *knew* you could. You've changed *everything. Again.*"

I didn't have the heart to tell him in that moment that I didn't think I could do this with anyone but the four of us yet, nor did I have the time.

"Sarah, how are you feeling?" Ben said tensely.

I saw why as shocked and staring people began making their way toward us. They probably assumed we had simply walked through one sungate to this one, but the fact that Ben and his wings had *walked* instead of flying through was probably surprising enough, let alone with Ben's arms around them and me on his back.

"Fine, fine!" I said urgently. "I can do it again! I'm sure I can do it all the way!"

I may not even have had to do the lashing again, since it hadn't weakened in the slightest from the transfer, but Ben stumbling and letting go of his wings and them stepping away from him had broken it.

"Alright, then come in, you two," Ben ordered, grabbing his wings again.

"Ben," Yvera whined, but she let him pull her in, as did Kor.

I lashed us all together again with everything I had left and pulled us tight.

"Ready," I said.

"Then here we go."

A HEARTBEAT LATER, WE were stumbling through a much smaller gate, somewhere in a dimly lit, giant room, with a lofty, elaborately carved ceiling that reminded me of a cathedral, if the largest and tallest one I had ever seen, and down below....

Oh, I thought. *Of course.*

Because what else would a dramá library be full of except...archivals.

Giant ones. The grandfathers of the measly twelve-foot, rectangular stone slabs in my little library. Now I realized why I had always felt the L in *library* as a capital when Ben and Kor had mentioned it, just as I had always felt the capital K in *king*. Ben's father was the *King*. And this...was the *Library*.

Instead of shelves, those towering black stone monoliths stood in rows as silent and sober as tombstones, hiding the true depth of the cavernous space from view. We stood on the center aisle, though it hardly deserved that name from how massively wide it was—larger than a four-lane highway, large enough for a small dragon to walk down it. In fact, in the distance, I *saw* the tail of one, a bright blue, before he or she disappeared into the dimness.

The reason for the dim lighting was immediately apparent. The people consulting the archivals appeared to be scrolling through small patches of glowing runes on the stones, running their hands over the stone to bring up new text. That text glowed only faintly against the dark stone, and might have been difficult to see, or at least strained the eyes more, in bright light.

Crystalline lines in the floor connected the shelves to each other in a complicated web that reminded me of....

Goodness gracious, a circuit board. A far more organic one than I had ever seen, to be sure, since the lines didn't bother staying straight but curved and split in patterns as natural and beautiful as a root system, but the purpose of them seemed clear when line after line flared as quick as dim lightning as information shot down one connection to the next.

The dramá...had a computer. Or...many computers? I didn't know enough about Earthren technology to know what technical term was the closest and most accurate, but I thought that what I was witnessing was something like a server farm. Even if *all* these archivals did was *store information*...this blatant of a sign of the advancement of their society, achieved to at least some degree *centuries* before Earthren had, astounded me more than it should have.

I suddenly felt very small—and that wasn't because I was clinging to the back of the largest person I had ever met in the largest indoor space I could ever remember being in, so large that the ends of it were lost to shadow.

Of course, I had only seconds to take all of that in, and some of those seconds were Ben gently dropping me off his back and the three drakón hurrying me away from the center aisle and down a side one, while both trying to shield me from view and not look like that was what they were doing.

So far, so good, since only a few of the Library patrons glanced our way, and none of them seemed interested enough in what they saw to pull them from their research. Clearly not *everyone* wanted to drop whatever they were doing to report in on our location to their network. Of course...Library-goers would probably be just the sort of people to think we weren't worth the bother.

This way, Kor said silently, probably for my benefit since Ben and Yvera didn't hesitate in going the same direction as him as he took point and they formed the back of the drakón triangle around me.

We had planned to go as swiftly and quietly as we could to Kor's office—which, of *course*, was in the Library—and hunker down until nightfall, when I could feel for my gate.

Except....

"Hold on," I whispered, stopping suddenly enough that Ben had to throw a hand out to steady Yvera and keep her from falling on me.

Oops. I should probably have thought of that.

Sarah, Ben said anxiously, eyeing the couple of people who were looking away from their archivals at us.

"Ben," I whispered out loud, because I wasn't confident I knew how to broadcast my inner voice yet, particularly to just the three of them. "I feel something."

A pull. Faint, but there. Originating at some point in the ten o'clock position from us, out in the depths of the library.

But that made no sense whatsoever. I may have the faintest of connections to two other people besides Ben, but I was pretty sure that the *only* other person I could be connected enough to at this point was in a coma in Olsdak. Unless....

"What?" Ben said, whispering out loud as well in his shock.

"Ben," I said, looking at him soberly. I hated to bring this up, but it was important. "Where's Svyer? Did they keep her in Olsdak?"

Ben's face darkened. *They took her to her family, on Ykran.*

I swallowed. "So, nowhere remotely close to here?"

No, he said slowly, clearly thinking hard about why else I would be feeling something *now*.

Then his eyes widened. *I...I feel it too. Or see it, rather.*

"You do?" I breathed, heart pounding.

A gate, he said soberly. *Where one has no right to be.*

He looked and subtly pointed. In the same direction.

I stared at him. "What does that mean? If we *both* feel it?"

He looked back at me, just as baffled. *I don't know.*

Can you surge us there, Ben? Yvera asked tensely, hand on the knife at her side.

Ben looked at me. I shook my head regretfully. "We've broken the lashing. I used all I had left on that second one."

I had a bit more growing back, deep in the soil, but I didn't want to risk our lives on so little.

Right then, Kor said, turning in the direction Ben had pointed with relish. *Looks like we're finding it the old-fashioned way. That's a more dramatic reveal than if we skipped right past its location and straight into Sarah's hold, anyway.*

Right, Ben said dryly, with his hand on my shoulder. *Because all that matters in this situation is the drama.*

Ben, the Moontouched worked hard on these gates, Kor said innocently. *Given our probable safety, we should properly appreciate that for them.*

Ben looked at me, expression grim. *At the slightest hint of danger, you surge to the gate, leaving the rest of us. In fact, the moment I* tell *you to surge, you surge, regardless of how safe it seems to you. Understood?*

Ben, I said with a sinking heart. I was more than disturbed by how close his command was to Kor's from last night. I really hoped that didn't portend the same result.

I'm not budging on this, Sarah. We won't have to hold back if you're gone. We'll be fine. Understood?

Man, being the weakest yet most valuable one was getting *old*. I was half tempted to accept that crown now for the sole reason of finally being able to stand with my drakón with the valiance that my name in their language implied.

The fact that my blood might no longer *be* so valuable to the Devourer if I rejected the crown didn't have the same temptation anymore. I was terrified, but I didn't want to hide any longer. Somewhere along this dangerous road of mine, I had started to not just reach for what I wanted. I had started to think that maybe I could *fight* for the ones I loved. I had started to *want* to, to ache to *be the one* who could protect them.

As Eskala had wanted me to...I had started to dream, and about more than just Ben.

Though that day of my dreams might yet come, that day...was not today.

Understood, I said grudgingly.

Thank you, he said simply, ducking to press a brief, yet still burning kiss to my lips.

Then he got us moving again, this time taking point while Kor and Yvera fell in their usual places behind, and me in the middle.

Ben skirted as far as he could to the edge of the current chamber, then followed the pull—or rather, for him, the light, I guessed—along the wall until we came to a big arch that seemed to lead to another wing.

Ben glanced at Kor.

Don't look at me, Kor said with a raised eyebrow. *Gates are your territory.*

Ben gave him a pointed look and jerked his head at our surroundings. *But we are literally standing in yours, Kor.*

Kor chuckled softly. *True enough. What's our heading now?*

Ben pointed at an angle that seemed to imply going through the arch was a good idea, but I knew from Kor's and my frustrating explorations of Olsdak that going in what seemed to be the right direction wasn't always the right way to get there in the end. Ben seemed to grasp that too, which was why he was asking for Kor's opinion.

Hmm, Kor said, eyes narrowing. *Interesting. That just might be it.*

That was good enough for Ben, who started through the arch, but I was still curious.

What's this way?

The history section, Kor said mildly. *Covenantal history, to be precise. My second home.*

I swallowed. Interesting indeed.

Ben skirted the wall again. Fortunately or not, this room was much smaller, being about the size of a *normal* library, with mid-sized archivals and a normal-sized peaked cathedral ceiling, with columns supporting a second-level balcony that ringed the entire room and contained much smaller archivals, even smaller than the ones in my hold.

This time, the walls were lined with something much more library-esque to me: books. Less familiar but still more so than the archivals were the honeycomb nooks for scrolls. Also interesting to me were the glass panes over all the book and scroll cases. The glass and even the stone of the cases themselves hummed to my sixth sense with magic.

What are these for? I asked Kor, tapping on the glass.

For preserving the books, obviously, Kor said in surprise. *Paper is delicate—surely you know that. Yes, it's a simple, low-energy way to store information, and not to mention that originals from the time before their archivals were made are worth preserving and consulting for their own sake, even with all the information they contained stored in the archival for common use. But paper still is terribly fragile, prone to decay. It has to be protected, cleansed, strengthened.*

Ah, I said sheepishly. *Makes sense.*

The dramá truly had mastered storing information securely, in a way easily accessible to the masses, long before we had.

The pull was getting stronger with each step now as Ben approached the leftmost end of the room. I knew it wasn't just my imagination when Ben looked back at me for confirmation, and I nodded. We were getting close.

As Ben turned the corner and began leading us along the left, shorter wall of this rectangular wing of the Library, I saw something interesting ahead. Another arch in the middle of this left wall, but a much smaller one. Through it, though, the light of a warm fire spilled outward—even more obvious because of the dimness of the room we were in.

Kor, Ben said slowly. *Isn't this the—*

Ben had stopped in front of the threshold. And froze.

My heart iced over and leaped into my throat, suffocating me.

No, no. It couldn't be. Kor couldn't have betrayed us now. Not like this.

Then Ben gasped out loud. "*Avva?*"

Papa. That was the closest word in English that my mind had always given me for what Ben always, without exception, called the King.

Papa.

"Hello, Koriben," a warm, deep voice said. A voice I knew better than I should have, for only having heard it once before, because it sounded so much like Ben's. Or what Ben's older, deeper, wiser voice might sound like one day.

The King's voice radiated pride and joy and all-consuming love, even with just those two words.

Ben rushed through the arch, out of sight. But it wasn't the rushing I had seen him do to go into battle.

I heard the soft thump of two big bodies colliding, and I knew exactly what it meant. My heart, even though it had sunk safely back into my chest, nearly burst from happiness for them, and tears stung my eyes. Yvera had rushed forward as well, eyes brighter than I had ever seen them.

She loves him too, I realized in surprise. Though it shouldn't have come as such. How could someone *not* love *this* King? And Yvera had known him her whole life....

I hesitated, stopping.

"Come on," Kor said with a soft smile, putting a gentle hand on my back.

I looked at him sadly. *I'll just be intruding.*

No, you most certainly will not, Kor said, smile growing. *You are the guest of honor.*

Before I could protest again, I heard the King say warmly, "Now, where is my Sarah?"

My....

I didn't know a heart could feel like this. I didn't know a *body* could contain this. The tears spilled over, uncontainable.

Without thinking—because I couldn't have moved my feet if I'd had to *think* in that moment—I slowly turned the corner and walked into the room...and saw him, in the flesh, for the first time.

The Golden King. Illuminated in all his glory by the warm flames behind him.

He was holding out his arms to me. *To me.* With tears streaming down his cheeks and into his golden beard, the streams illuminated in the fire's light like streaks of flame.

"Sarah," he said simply.

That one word contained everything that couldn't be said. It contained worlds.

He reached for me, and I didn't just reach back.

I ran.

He scooped me up with a joyous laugh, marred only by the thickness of tears, and crushed me to him.

"Sarah, my Sarah," he whispered.

Only to me, he said, *Sarah, my beautiful, precious daughter. Home to me at last.*

I was, I realized. Both of those things.

He didn't replace my birth father. He didn't replace my home with my birth family. He simply *was* my other father—and, with Ben, my other home. They were mine, and I was theirs. Forever.

I hugged him with all my might and silently whispered, *I am. I am. I am.*

He held me even tighter for one moment. *You cannot know how much it means to me to hear you say that.*

After a slight pause, he said, *His mother's single greatest regret was that she could not be here in the flesh for this moment, but I can feel her with us now.*

To my shock, I could too. I felt a touch on my shoulder that was as comforting as it was ephemeral, and a kiss on the back of my head that filled me with warmth and overwhelming love from head to toe.

Slowly, with obvious reluctance, the King loosened his grip and set me down. Fortunately, Ben put his hand on my shoulder to steady me, otherwise I might have fallen over, I was so dazed. I looked up at Ben, and I thought I could have died from the final surge of joy I felt to see Ben's eyes glowing with pride and happiness. He had wanted this moment too, perhaps even before I did.

"Sarah," Ben said quietly. "Allow me to introduce you, in person this time, to the Golden King of the Six Realms, King Kavarian. My father."

Ben looked at his father, a watery glint in even his eyes now. "King Kavarian. Avva. This is the Moontouched Heir, Sarah Lind, declared Heir to the Crown of Ice."

The King took my hands in his and kissed the backs of both of them. It wasn't a facetious gesture. It had all the solemnity of a sacred act.

When he lowered—but didn't relinquish—my hands, he said, "Heir Sarah Lind of the Moontouched clan, it is an honor beyond words to finally meet you and formally welcome you to my Realms. You, and all of yours, will always be welcome here, so long as the Golden Crown shall stand worthy of our Tree of Flame, and may that be until the stars fall from the heavens."

I tried to hide my trembling under the weight of this moment, but I wasn't sure how successful I was, since Ben tightened his grip on my shoulder. "Thank you," I rasped.

What else should I say? I asked Ben frantically.

That's enough for him, he said with a laugh in his voice.

Clearly, because the King let go, but only to place his hand on my back and turn me to face the two others standing behind him, on either side of the flaming brazier and statue in the middle of that small, round room. At that signal, they came forward.

"Eskala!" I exclaimed in delight. Only too late did I realize that was breaking with ceremony, but she and the King only chuckled.

"Hello, dear," Eskala said, pulling me into a brief but warm hug. "It is good to see you again—especially safe and well."

"You have already met my incomparable leftwing," the King said with a smile at me and a wink—a *wink*—at Eskala. "Then allow me to introduce my stalwart rightwing, Alyish Battleblood, who is three-quarters of the reason the Six Realms are still standing."

He gestured to a dark-skinned and scarred yet somehow warm-looking drakón man who was nearly as tall as he was, with fuzzy violet hair shaved close to his head and sharp, clean-shaven cheeks.

"You exaggerate, Kavarian," the man said dryly, his voice a deep bass. He smiled crookedly at me. "And he downplays his and his Heir's roles too much."

"Koriben is the other quarter, of course," the King said with a widening smile.

"Avva," Ben said with a sigh. He had a pained look in his eyes as he gazed at his father, the meaning of which I couldn't guess at. He wasn't embarrassed, but rather saddened, by his father's praise.

"It is good to meet you," I told Alyish. Then looked at the King. "All of you. But...if you don't mind me asking...why are you *here*? *Now*?"

The King smiled. "For the same reason you are. To witness the opening of the final moongate, and the ushering in of a new era."

"You *knew*," Ben said to Kor, but the accusation lacked heat. "You made it seem like you didn't know *where* in the Library, but you *knew*."

"Well, it was rather obvious, once we narrowed down the general area," Kor said as he gestured at the statue with a smirk. "If you had even stopped to *think* about likely locations within the Library, you might have come to the same conclusion. In fact, you were, just before you spotted your father, remember?"

Ben just flushed.

I decided it was high time I took in my surroundings, so I did.

The circular room was small, enough so that there wasn't a whole lot of space with five drakón and two amón crowded into it. Kor and Yvera had had to step behind the statue to make room for the rest of us to be arranged around the front. The room was carved smooth from the mountain sandstone, but its only objects were two ornately carved, curved benches to the left and to the right, and what was in the center.

A large brazier burned bright and warm in the very center, though it was the only source of light in the entire room. Just behind it was a golden statue that flickered mesmerizingly in the fire's light: A beautiful Woman with billowing hair that curled around Her as if blowing in the wind. For some reason, the artist made the hair look more...granular than strand-like; everything else was so masterfully done that the granularity couldn't be a flaw. Also of note: she was nude except for tastefully placed curls of flame around Her body. I was kind of surprised the drakón had bothered with even that much covering, but then, considering who this probably was, maybe even they drew the line somewhere.

Lest there be any doubt of who She was, a golden Tree was just behind her, so close She touched and even in some places melded with it; the Tree's branches and flame-shaped leaves took up the entire ceiling. With all of that gold reflecting the light of the fire behind and above it, it was actually bright in the room, at least compared to the darkness outside.

The final detail was in the Tree's outstretched hands over the fire: a bowl filled with a red liquid that steamed slightly, filling the room with its sweetness—that was how I knew it was wine and not...something else. Although *blood* was no doubt what it represented.

Then I put it together: our location, this monument, this *moment*.

"Oh," I said. "It represents the Covenants somehow, doesn't it?"

Alyish looked at me in surprise, but Kor only chuckled, and Ben, Eskala, and the King smiled.

"The Shrine of the Covenants," the King said softly, looking at the Woman and Tree with loving reverence.

I noticed he still hadn't relinquished his hand at my back, but his touch was so warm, comforting, and anchoring, everything I needed in this moment, I wasn't going to ask him to remove it. I was definitely starting to get used to—and like—dramá touchiness. At least with the ones I trusted.

"What better place for the final moongate than a symbol of how it all began?" Eskala said with a smile at me. She then smirked at Kor. "What my protégé *doesn't* say is that, although we thought we all were so clever by narrowing the location down to Crownhold, then guessing at the Library, it was Kavarian who actually discovered its exact location."

"How?" I asked, looking at him.

"In the same way you did," the King said, smiling down at me. "The moment you found the Ekrel moongate, I saw a new gate appear in my mind, and I knew what that must mean."

"Did you?" I asked Ben.

He shrugged sheepishly. "Maybe? To be honest, I wasn't paying attention."

Only then I remembered that he would have been unconscious at the time it first appeared, besides.

"You were far away," the King said gently to him. "I had the advantage of being relatively right next to it."

To me, he explained, "That makes a difference in how we see gates. The further away they are from us, the harder it is to distinguish them from each other, unless we are focusing on them or are charting our course through them."

I nodded. "Like a map of stars in your head, Ben said."

"Yes," the King said, with a warm smile as he looked between me and his son.

"But isn't it supposed to be a *moon*gate?" Yvera asked, arms folded. "How come Ben and the King can feel it?"

The King's answer was quiet as he looked beyond the Tree. "Perhaps it is not a moongate that *we* feel...but something else."

He smiled down at me, nodding his head toward the back of the room. His eyes glittered like a loving parent's did on Christmas morning. "Why don't you and Koriben go find out?"

"Not...you, Avva?" Ben said hesitantly. Although his hand tightened on my shoulder at the same time.

"Not me," the King said firmly, and he finally removed his hand from my back. "The Trees gave this task to Sarah and to you, and Sarah and you will finish it. I and my wings are only here to welcome Sarah and to witness."

"And to make sure nothing goes amiss," Alyish said with a dry smile, hand resting on the sword at his side. "We have had elites guarding and securing this place—with might and magic—from the moment we identified it. Half the patrons in this room right now are disguised elites, the ones that aren't are being kindly encouraged to leave, and other elites have been filtering in since you entered."

"We kept an eye on you from the moment you arrived," Eskala said with a wink, "but we didn't want to spoil the surprise."

Ben looked at his father in alarm.

"I think the Trees chose this as the location of the final gate for a reason," the King said quietly. "This place is now as guarded as much as mortal and immortal means allow, perhaps more so in this moment than any other place in the Six Realms. We don't think anything will happen, but we've done everything in our power to make certain of that."

I could feel that now. The weight of all that preparation, that readiness.

Outside me, I could feel it in the hum of magic and quiet shuffle outside this room, though I didn't dare look back to see how many were now there, watching. I could feel it inside me, in the darkest place inside—dark not from evil but simply because it was the stillness and rest of night, the blackness of rich soil that gave life to all else, the void from which my power sprung. There, in that darkness, a Presence was with me.

Waiting for me.

"Thank you," Ben told his father tightly, clenching my shoulder again.

He took a deep breath and looked at me. "Ready?"

He must have felt how I was trembling. I tried to bravely smile up at him all the more for it. "Ready."

As I'll ever be.

"Go on," he whispered, letting go. "I'll follow."

I breathed deeply as I looked at the face of the golden Woman. She stared back at me with blank, uncarved eyes, but they flickered with warmth from the fire all the same. It could have been a trick of the light, but Her lips almost seemed to pull into a smile.

Impulsively, I bowed to Her, with my hand over my heart.

Then rising, I walked around Her and Her Tree. Kor backed up against the wall to make room for me without a word, his expression unusually sober. I half expected him to touch me in support as I passed, but he didn't move except to watch me go. Yvera did the same as Ben passed her on the other side.

I stopped in front of the curved wall directly behind the Tree. Then, following an impulse, I placed my hand on the wall.

Two glowing white crescents slowly appeared on either side of my hand. They touched at their very pointed tips, so only my expectation to find a moon *something* told me they were probably supposed to be crescent moons, connected to form a circle with an oval in the center. Almost like a sideways...or slitted...eye.

Nothing else happened. Something felt unfinished, undone.

Then, without a word, Ben reached over my shoulder and placed his hand over mine.

Power poured from both of us, both to a degree that staggered us. I had to slap my other hand against the wall, and from the brush of Ben at my back, it felt like he came dangerously close to falling into me.

It's sunset, I realized faintly.

One of those moments when we were at equilibrium, even if I was not yet of equal power to him—when he began his true decline, and I began my true rise. A moment of change.

Waving rays of golden sunlight appeared around my white moons. A golden line split through the center, all the way from floor to ceiling, and Ben pulled me back just in time to keep me from falling as the newly created doors parted inward.

Chapter Fourteen

FIRST

Koriben

The passage beyond was dark at first, but slowly, white and gold streaks in the roughly carved walls increased in luminosity until the passage was brightly lit.

"Huh," Sarah said, blinking.

"What?" I asked her.

"Moonstone. It's the stuff Kor and I found. But...the gold is new."

She looked up at me blankly.

"Don't look at me," I said with a helpless shrug.

She shrugged back and went in.

The passage was short, ending in another, but much more roughly carved, circular room about the size of the shrine room. Again, white and gold streaks lined the walls, but that wasn't the room's key feature.

A familiar-looking, freestanding stone arch stood in the center of the room. Though its fire wasn't currently lit, I knew what it was meant to be. I could see it in my mind's eye and had ever since Sarah had pointed it out to me after our arrival.

"Let me guess," Sarah said faintly. "That's...a daygate."

"Yup," I said. "Banked for the night, though."

I frowned, feeling it again. "If...it ever was lit...."

I reached out and touched the stone of the arch. Sure enough, it hummed with all the potential power I needed, yet I knew it had never been finished. Which only made sense, when I thought about it.

"Stand back," I told Sarah, since she had been peering curiously through the empty space inside. "I need to finish this."

"Finish it?" she asked, but she backed up.

"They did almost all the work for us already, but they left it to me to activate. Because only a Golden Heir or Monarch can do that."

"Oh. How are you going to do that?"

I smiled wanly. "How do you think?"

I pulled one of my knives—my ceremonial one, with the gold and alabaster hilt—from the ether and unsheathed it.

How...appropriate. Symbolic, certainly. A Golden Queen had failed the Moontouched, allowing the blood of its Lady to be spilled in this very hold.

Now a Golden Heir would spill his blood—however little it was in comparison—to bring the Moontouched Queen home.

"Ben," Sarah said, eyes going wide with horror. "Tell me you're not...."

I snorted. "Flame no. Maybe the first gate took lives to power, but not the ones after. Do you think we'd have as many sun- and daygates as we have if one of us Royals had *to die* for them every time? I'm just spilling a few drops, Sarah. That's all."

She sagged, propping herself up on her legs. Then looked up to glare at me, her normally warm brown eyes flashing silver with soulflare, a contrast that gave me chills every time. "Don't *scare* me like that. *Ever*."

"Sorry," I said sheepishly. She was so smart and intuitive most of the time that I kept assuming she understood the way things worked.

I mean, seriously—growing up with *no* knowledge of Trees and of our symbology in particular, she took one look at the shrine outside and said what it represented. She was amazing, plain and simple. But...I probably shouldn't leave anything potentially dangerous in doubt, not on an evening like this one.

I raised the dagger in my left hand over my right.

"Just a few drops," I reminded Sarah when she tensed.

She nodded stiffly, still clearly not happy, but she would allow it. I was reminded of her reluctance to let me paint her ears in my blood so that she could understand me, back when we first met. That...seemed like lifetimes ago, yet still she disliked the necessity of me using a bit of blood for her.

I inwardly shook my head. This? This was nothing compared to the life price the first makers of the first gate paid. This was nothing compared to the loss of the Lady Moontouched's life and all her clan lost thereafter when we made the Moontouched flee to Earth and hide themselves among us. This was nothing compared to what I would do to make things right, to restore the Covenants, to save my dying father.

To make Sarah *safe* and *happy*.

Just a few drops.

I cut a line across my right palm without flinching.

Flame, watch over her, I prayed as I felt Her Power rise within me. *I'm still counting on You.*

That faith—that if this was meant, They would keep her safe—was the only way I was staying sane right now.

Then I held my bleeding hand inside the empty arch, letting the golden drops fall to the stone floor.

I had only done this twice before—once for a daygate for a new expansion of Crownhold, once for a new Ykran sungate—but surprisingly, I remembered the words. That was convenient, and it saved me the embarrassment of going and getting them from Avva.

"By the power invested in me by the Tree of Flame, as the Golden Heir, I now invoke the First Covenant, and swear by my blood that I and my people shall uphold its terms, for as long as the Flame Above and Below may give us Their light."

I'd expected a drain, and a big one, taking most of my remaining reserves as night fell, but that was nothing compared to what came next.

Power dragged from me with the force of a vortex, and through me, from Sarah behind me.

In fact, it took all the power we had...and then some.

My head *hurt*.

I groaned, wincing against the pain.

"Easy, Koriben. Give yourself a moment longer."

At the sound of Avva's voice, memory came rushing back, and I bolted upright, despite the lance of agony that shot through my brain.

"Sarah!" I gasped.

"Torch it, Ben!" Yvera snapped, hovering just behind me. "Lie back down."

"Where is she?" I asked, even as I winced.

"M'fine, Ben," Sarah mumbled at nearly the same time from somewhere nearby.

Kor chuckled tensely. "Liar."

That's when I finally spotted them around Avva, who was down on one knee next to me where I'd collapsed in front of the gate. Kor was holding Sarah in his arms, who lay there limply, eyes half closed, looking too pale. A healer from Avva's elites was examining her.

"What's wrong?" I demanded.

"Just a bruised head, which I have already taken care of, and burnout, and hers is no worse than yours," Avva said soothingly, putting a hand on my shoulder. "But the renewal of the First Covenant was bound to take a lot from both of you."

I stared at him. "The First...."

I...was a torched idiot.

Who, with Sarah's even more unconscious help, had quite unintentionally, in that moment, perhaps double-handedly saved the sungates, the lifeblood of my people, from failure.

Could it...really be that easy? Just a bit of blood, some words, some power? Yes, it had knocked both of us out. But if we were already awake, instead of out for a day or more, then the price still seemed so....

Avva smiled kindly at the stupefaction on my face. "What did you *think* the Trees had asked you and Sarah to do these seven days, son?"

What...indeed.

His voice from just a few dek ago came back to me. *The Trees gave this task to Sarah and to you. And Sarah and you will finish it.*

What had the last seven days of exertion, pain, danger, and blood been but a price? A proving? Each day and night giving everything we had to gain each moongate, one on each of the Six Realms. *Earning* them. Every one.

And all the while keeping the Moontouched Heir They had given us safe. Honoring her. Listening to her. Making her one of us. Until I had quite unconsciously sworn the Covenant again, with my own blood freely given, thinking only of her.

Proving that the dramá were, in fact, worthy of the First Covenant, the Covenant of the Gates—of the beginning of the change that had saved the draká, and all that it gave them and still gave us in return.

For the first time, I realized that the gate Sarah and I had just made now burned to my left, even though it had no right to with night having fallen. And the knife I had dropped lay clean of blood, and the scar in my hand healed—the final signs of the Tree's acceptance.

I just stared at Avva.

And then, feeling the world spin again, said, "I think...I need to lie back down for a dek."

Avva chuckled as he caught me and gently helped me back down. "Good idea."

I COULD TELL AVVA longed to bring Sarah and me back to the King's Wing to recover. I could see it in the wistful way he looked at us, thinking of a peaceful evening of just being together—especially of talking to Sarah, asking her all the questions he had no doubt saved up, hearing all her stories, and taking care of her as much as she would let him. But though Avva was my father always, he had to first be my King, and as such, he knew there wasn't time for such luxuries.

So he and his people guarded us while Sarah and I recovered by the gate until both of us could walk under our own power. I got up, perhaps sooner than I should have, to stumble over to where Kor held Sarah. I didn't even have to ask; the moment I sat down on the floor next to them, Sarah reached for me, and Kor gave her to me, both of them without a word.

Thank you, I said silently to Kor. Because I owed him. But still grudgingly.

I didn't enjoy that as much as you seem to think, Kor responded dryly. *Holding her and having her are two different things. And one without the other is pain, not pleasure.*

I...could imagine. All too well.

I knew it wasn't my imagination that after Sarah snuggled into my chest and my arms wrapped around her that both of us recovered much faster. After all, I could feel her feeding energy to my flameheart, drop by exquisite drop.

Stop that, I snapped at her right after she began.

I can spare that much, she insisted. *It's coming back much faster than that, and I'm keeping most of it for myself, don't you worry.*

That was hard to believe, even with the honesty in her voice. Each drop sent my flameheart blazing.

Not long after that, Sarah pushed away from me, and Kor helped her stand up. I then got to my feet, and considering how I'd stumbled not a few dek before, was surprisingly steady. So was Sarah, color fully restored, eyes sharp and ready.

"So...." she said, gesturing at the fiery gate. "We go through that now?"

"Seems so," I said.

"I still don't get it," Yvera said irritably. "That's a *sun*gate."

"No, actually, dear rightwing," Kor said from his position behind the gate, where he and Eskala and several others were examining it from that angle. I had seen quite a few people round the flame-filled arch and stare, so even I knew by now that there was something unexpected on the other side, even though I hadn't had the strength to go look.

Kor finished, his voice as close as it ever got to reverent. "It is something new."

Avva just smiled when I looked at him, waiting for me to see for myself. I took Sarah's hand and walked with her around to see the back of the gate.

Which was a solid, opaque, white-blue wall of ice.

"What?" Sarah said, gaping. She reached out to touch the ice. I half expected it to give under her fingers as her icy curtains in her gates did, but it held solid. I had a theory growing in my mind about why.

"But that's impossible!" Sarah said, ducking her head around the other side to stare at the fire.

Kor just chuckled and shook his head at her.

She held her hand out in front of it. "It's hot! It might not burn us to go through, but it *should* be melting it!"

"And yet it is not," Kor said, looking at the gate. "A gate of stone, ice, and fire—now all one. For the very first time."

Yvera just stared.

"But...Kor...." Sarah looked back at him, flabbergasted. "What are we going to *call* it?"

I laughed, scooped her up, and captured her gaping mouth with mine.

When I pulled away, I could see the glow of my eyes in her own. "I'm sure you'll think of something. Something as brilliant and miraculous as you are."

Her cheeks warmed. "So, no pressure."

Behind me, Kor said smugly, "Well, you can ask for help, of course."

She grinned as I set her down. "As long as I give you the credit?"

"Oh, I have no intention of claiming credit. Royals always get the credit for a leftwing's brilliance. We give it to them on purpose."

"Sadly, they do," Avva said with a morose shake of his head. And a look at Eskala. "One of the greatest injustices of life."

"Why?" Sarah demanded.

"Because, dear," Eskala said, putting an arm around her. "People need someone to believe in. To look to. And that someone is not us. We must remain in the shadows and be something they need but cannot love."

Sarah didn't look any happier than I felt to be the someone pushed onto the stage.

"Enough talk, I think, don't you agree?" Alyish said briskly. "It's time for you four to be going. Even if our luck is meant to hold tonight, you still have work to do, and the time is short to do it."

"True," I said, a flicker of dread entering even the brightness of this moment. The First Covenant might be renewed, the last gate of the six might be unlocked, but there were still formidable mountains to pass over.

I put a hand on Sarah's shoulder. "Ready?"

"Ready," she said with a nod, a spark of anticipation lighting in her eyes.

This time, she took my hand and led me back around to the front. Though she had to break her grip when Avva crushed me in a hug. No one could hug like Avva could.

"We'll be back," I said, wetness stinging my eyes. Even now, though, I didn't let the tears spill. "Soon."

With hope, I told him silently.

For our people. But most especially for him.

"I know you will," Avva said, pulling from me. "Flame go with you."

He turned at once to Sarah, who reached for him at the same time, and he pulled her into an embrace that made her give a quiet *oof,* but she buried herself in it all the same.

As he slowly lowered her, eyes burning, he said, "May Flame watch over you, and Ice go with you."

Then he kissed her on the forehead and, with great reluctance, let her go.

This won't be the last time, I told him, pained at the look in his eyes.

No, he mused, but still too sober. *Not the last, I think.*

He smiled at me with eyes that were too deep and clenched my shoulder for a moment.

"Go," he said simply.

Sarah put her hand in mine. That gentle, tugging tie was probably the only reason my feet moved from that spot, from Avva's touch. And through the gate of Flame and Ice.

As we walked into Sarah's hold, all six moongates—all of them lined up on the southern end of the Rim, three on each side of the southern arch—flared as we entered, burning brightly before dimming to their normal nighttime glow.

Was it a bit...odd that almost everywhere we had gone, the days and nights were at least somewhat in sync? Had a good degree of overlap, if not near perfect? We never had to go anywhere that was the complete reverse, though with six worlds to search, surely we should have.

Kor had probably already figured that out by now, torch him. It was probably one factor his analysts had considered when narrowing down locations. I would just not mention it, and if it came up, pretend I'd realized that much sooner than after the final...gate.

Whatever we were going to call that thing that seemed to be as much mine as hers.

Dozens of Sarah's little light helpers raced toward her and whirled around her in celebratory welcome, making her laugh. She walked forward to give them space to greet her properly. I just stood there and stared in enchantment at how they illuminated her, made her clothes move as if in the wind, made the locks that had escaped her simple braid dance.

So Kor had to run into me as he came out, causing us both to stumble.

"Ben!" he snapped.

"Sorry," I said sheepishly. I should have known better.

Rule number one of walking through a gate: get out of the way as soon as possible. The magic that worked the gates never spliced two people together...but since there was only so much space it had to work with, it wasn't above shoving them at each other.

Yvera nimbly sidestepped me, as if she knew that's right where I'd be when she walked through. But then, I couldn't remember a single time she'd ever been ungraceful. In words and actions, yes, but in pure movement? Nothing came to mind.

Of course, she might have erased the memory with a solid punch to my head or something.

"Fascinating," Kor said, recovering from his irritation as he backed up to look at the gate we'd come through. I did so too, and saw to my surprise that, from this side, it looked exactly as all Sarah's other gates did, complete with a curtain of ice, an only somewhat blurred view of what lay beyond, and stone double doors on this side that were slowly closing. Just before they shut completely, I saw Avva standing there, staring vaguely into what would have only been flames for him, not knowing I could see. I knew that, because he was no longer trying to hide his dual agonies of sorrow and longing that cut at me like daggers across the chest.

This won't be the last time, I told him again, even though, with the doors now shut and sealed with light, I was certain he couldn't hear.

Dazed, I realized only then that Sarah was talking to her lights.

"Where is it?" she asked excitedly.

The lights raced to the northern end of the Rim, and Sarah raced after them.

"Sarah," I laughed tiredly, following.

She seemed remarkably fast for having just collapsed from burnout. In fact, I noted with satisfaction that she was faster than she had been a couple of days ago.

She was getting stronger, and quickly—almost with drakón swiftness. Good.

Although something inside me sorrowed to notice those soft lines of hers hardening. And something feared.

At the very northern tip of the Rim was another gate. Since the Rim there was a pointed *tip*, this was the only moongate so far that was partially set out from the wall as it covered the gap. It was about half as large again as all the other gates, and a giant white tree, like on the outer side of all the moongates we found, was its only adornment.

Sarah stopped in front of it, panting. I realized she wasn't just waiting for us to catch up, because even after we did and her breath slowed, she just continued to stare at it, standing still.

"Sarah?" I asked quietly, putting a hand on her shoulder.

She started, then looked up at me bashfully. "Sorry. It's just...I can't believe this is it. I'm...I'm nervous. Isn't that silly?"

"Why would that be silly?" I said gently.

"I'm going home," she said faintly. "But...I suppose...that's exactly it. I *should* be going home. But I'm not sure that's where home is anymore. And that makes me nervous...and sad."

I simply held out my arms, and she jumped into them. I pulled her up and held her tightly, felt her wet cheek on my neck.

"Thank you," she said thickly. "You did it, didn't you? You promised me you'd get me home, and you did it. And now I'm crying because...I don't even know why."

I just held her tighter for a moment. Then, throat tight, I said, "I promised I would take you home. But not that I would leave you there if it didn't feel right. Wherever you want to go after that, if it takes a lifetime to find your new home, I'll help you find it."

"Really?" she said with a wet laugh, pulling away enough to meet my eyes and brush her nose against mine. "A lifetime? Eternal servitude is a bit much, don't you think?"

I smiled. I tried to keep my eyes on hers, but they were drifting treacherously to her lips. "I promised, didn't I?"

Thank the Flame she wanted the same thing right now, because she kissed me, salty lips moving against mine.

Until Yvera cleared her throat. Loudly.

Yv, I snapped. *She's having a moment.*

You don't need to be enjoying her "moment" quite so much. In front of us.

True, unfortunately. In fact, now that I thought about it, this was being cruel to *both* my wings. But Sarah didn't know that.

Yet she was the one who slowly pulled away with a sigh. "Time to go."

I reluctantly set her down.

"Unless...anybody needs anything?" Sarah asked, looking around almost hopefully.

"Sarah, we got ready to go before we left for Ythra," I said with a smile. "Which, thanks to your lashing, was less than a deken ago. I have all your stuff. You have the gun? Whistle? Scale?"

"Yes," she sighed. Then held up her arms with a grimace. "And these new things Yvera's uncle made me, underneath this."

She meant her coat.

Those shields were a miraculous innovation, perhaps one of Erdan's finest achievements, and I'd been thrilled to hear that the first of their kind had been given to help protect her. Shields of various types could already be generated from objects, but they were usually large, heavy, set in stone, or all of the above. We drakón could create mobile shields ourselves with pure magic, but they took time and skill to master and were costly in power and attention to maintain. But with Erdan's creation, Sarah, without even knowing what she was doing, with just a spark of power, had reportedly made discs the size of dinner plates before they so surprised her that she dismissed them.

If these shields could be run on so little power and with so little training, then perhaps we could get them into the hands of amón everywhere, giving them one of the most effective ways found yet to shield *themselves*.

Of course, sadly, mass production might not be possible; magic-class weapons tended to not be, and Sarah's bands were of a metal even Kor couldn't identify. Where Erdan had gotten the ore, we didn't know and didn't have time to ask. But even so, the proof of concept was nothing less than revolutionary.

Sarah...was decidedly less enthused, but I thought that it was just because she was too inexperienced with their use to see their potential, and too new to realize how, once again, she had been a catalyst to change everything.

I just prayed to the Flame that it would be a long, long time, if ever, that she had to use them. But I knew better.

"Then I think we're as ready as we'll ever be," I told her.

"Right," she said. Taking a deep breath, she turned and walked to the doors. "Let's go."

Chapter Fifteen

HOME

SARAH

THE DOORS OPENED...TO WOODS. That was all I could make out through the wave of the ice curtain and the darkness, anyway. I wasn't sure *where* and *when* I had expected to end up on Earth, but I guessed...this wasn't it.

"It's night," I said, looking at Ben anxiously. "Is that going to be a problem?"

He frowned. "You tell me. It's your world."

I blinked.

Oh. Oh, *right*. Earth. Earth, where the nastiest things you usually met at night were of the human variety, and I had a feeling that my drakón could handle any of those that might be in these woods with ease.

Unless the Devourer had infested Earth and was waiting to ambush us, that is. If it had, its invasion would have been of a much more insidious variety, because the kinds of monsters that the dramá fought every night and took for granted were only the things of stories in my world. If they were there, after all...they were keeping to the shadows, and in much smaller numbers.

I took a deep breath and looked out. And thought. I needed more information, and a way to get it without needlessly risking us.

I looked back at Kor.

He raised an eyebrow at me and inclined his head subtly toward Yvera.

Really? How could he have stood working side by side with Yvera all these years and not been able to use his greatest weapon except *occasionally*, when Yvera might think it was just smoke and mirrors?

Wait.... That gave me an idea.

"Kor," I said slowly. "Why don't you do that thing we figured out I could make you do last night? You know, when you disappear into the ether?"

Yvera blinked and frowned. "Wait, what?"

But the worrying reaction that I *should* have been thinking about was Ben's. He started, then as understanding dawned on his face at what Kor must have told me, his face hardened, and he glared at Kor.

Kor...glared at me.

Well, I had already sealed my doom, so I might as well figure out if it was safe to die on my home soil.

"Yeah," I said to Yvera. "We figured out I can help him surge...to nowhere. So it's like he just becomes invisible and insubstantial. Nothing can touch him."

Yvera's eyes widened, then narrowed. "You can make him do *what*?"

I am going to kill you, Kor sent me silently. *Very, very slowly. You will beg for death before I'm finished.*

Huh. Was this what it felt like to be Kor?

It was kind of fun, actually. In a sort of everyone-wants-to-murder-me-any-way-soooo-let's-see-what-I-can-do-next sort of way.

You'll thank me later, I returned with a grin.

Then out loud, I said, "So, Kor, seems like a good time to do that thing that you can do *only with my help* to make sure there's not a night ambush outside."

Kor darted a glance at Ben, but Ben had cooled to just hardness now, and with a small huff, he nodded. Kor looked back at me, eyes burning.

Slowly, he repeated. *And you won't see me coming, now, will you?*

Then he vanished, making goosebumps crawl up my spine.

"Oh, come *on*," Yvera shouted, stamping her foot and gesturing with both hands at the space he used to occupy. "Really? *Kor*?"

How much did he tell you? Ben asked me silently, inner voice tight.

Everything, I think...? I replied sheepishly. *But then again, this is Kor, so probably...not.*

Ben clenched his jaw and ran a hand through his hair. Only too late, I saw why this might upset him so much. Was Ben guessing that Kor had...given me an option?

Look, Ben, I said miserably. *I'll give you all the details that he told me, later, but right now.... Like I told you before, I don't want Kor. I told him no.*

Ben slowly let go of some tension, though it never entirely left. *Thank you...for telling me that. I know I'm being ridiculous. But it's...Kor.*

Enough said. So I just went up and hugged him.

"Oh, what the hellwinds is going on now?" Yvera said, gesturing to us.

"Now *I'm* having a moment, Yv," Ben said dryly.

"Why? Because Kor can suddenly become untouchable? *You're not a rightwing.*"

"He's not displacing you, Yv. Besides, he can only do it with *Sarah's help.* Isn't that right?" Ben said, looking down at me with a grin slowly growing on his face.

Ah, yes. The *good* part of what I had just done was finally occurring to him. Kor's secret weapon was no longer his to claim...at least in front of Yvera. And that was probably quite bad enough in Kor's mind.

"Then what can Sarah make *me* do?" Yvera said, eyes growing intent.

"Wait, what?" I said in growing alarm, pulling away from Ben.

"You made Ben's drakáform huge, you made Kor untouchable. You think I can't see a pattern here?"

I looked at Ben frantically for help, but his grin just kept growing. *You started this.*

"Er, Yvera," I said slowly, brain scrambling. "Are you really sure you want *my* help to—"

Kor appeared right next to me, making me jump and let out a yip of fear. I supposed I deserved that, so I nobly refrained from punching him.

"Coast is clear," he said flatly. "By far, the most 'threatening' thing I sense nearby is a herd of some kind of skinny cattle."

"Skinny...cattle?" I said, squinting at him.

"Must be a peaceful area," he continued, ignoring me. "There are signs of settlements nearby with surprisingly few protections."

"Oh, settlements," I said. "Huh. That could be good—might help us figure out where we are. Just hope they speak English."

That was pretty much the only useful Earthren language I knew, because of course I'd taken useless things in high school like Latin. Given my partial Latina heritage, my Spanish was abysmal—to the eternal shame of Abuela Valentin.

Although I supposed I could understand whatever *they* were telling me because....

"Wait...." I said, freezing.

"What?" Ben asked intently. "What's wrong?"

"Ben," I said slowly. "How long did you say the magic you did on my ears would last?"

He blinked. "A sevenday.... You know what...it should have faded by now, shouldn't it? I haven't heard of one lasting more than nine, and even then, it was only traces...."

He looked at Kor.

Kor raised an eyebrow. "This is only *just* occurring to you two?"

He put his head in his hands and moaned. "Am I the only one who *pays attention*?"

"What's your theory, Kor?" Ben snapped.

Kor lifted his head. "Whatever this—"

He waved vaguely between Ben and me. "—is, it's either extending the life of Ben's enchantment, or it's giving her the ability altogether. *Or* she could be developing it on her own. She has Royal Blood of the Covenants, after all, *and* just took part in the renewal of the First Covenant, the Covenant of the Gates. That's how the draká got the gift of interpretation, after all."

"It is?" I asked blankly.

"Yes," Kor said, in the tone that implied this should have been one of the most crucial details Ben would have included when he had told me about the beginnings of their history. "How *else* were the draká expected to communicate peacefully with whomever they should meet once they stepped through a gate?"

As usual, that...made a lot of sense. But, as usual, the way Kor had to say it was entirely aggravating.

"I think someone really has to explain these Covenants of yours in detail to me some time," I said.

"You think?" Kor said dryly. "I agree, but unfortunately, we don't know the original wording. The words that Ben just said are the closest record we have of the First Covenant, and they just say we agree to abide by the *terms*. We know vaguely what the terms are, of course, because we have to follow them. But we don't have any original record of them from the Tree's own mouth."

"Why?"

"In brief," Ben said grimly, eyeing the open door. "Because we broke the Covenants. Then the Tree destroyed the records after the Moontouched left."

I sighed. "Of course. But you'd think the Tree would restore at least something of the first one now that it's been renewed...somehow."

I was still wrapping my brain around that one.

"And who knows?" Kor said, raising his hands. "Maybe She has. Maybe a new archival has appeared in the Library."

I blinked. "That's a thing?"

"No! But it just might be now. But we'll never find out if we just stand here talking about it, will we?"

Boy, he was mad at me.

I took a deep breath. "Right, right. Sorry. I should just...get us going now, shouldn't I?"

"I think so," Ben said, putting a hand on my shoulder.

I patted that hand and gave him a smile, then slipped out of it to walk forward...through the ice....

And onto Earth.

The moment I passed through the icy curtain and stepped into the clear, I realized this was no dense, remote forest. Kor was right—the lights of probably some kind of suburban neighborhood were in the distance. The "cattle" he'd described gave me a start when they darted off deeper into the woods, and I let out a breath when I realized what they were.

"What?" Ben said sharply, having come through not a second behind me.

"*Deer*," I said. "Kor saw *deer*. Which are as basically as harmless as...well...."

I tried to think of a creature I'd seen in the Six Realms that was harmless. That I knew the name of, anyway. Lots of little critters, here and there, of course. Placid herd animals. But anything I'd bothered to get the name of had tried to kill me.

"Um.... They're harmless, OK?"

I began striding toward the lights I saw in the distance. Fortunately, the moon was bright and looking full, if not already there. Although that only helped in the breaks in the dense deciduous canopy above and undergrowth below. As proof of how much a little perspective of deadliness can change you, I tromped through that foliage with nary a care about what ticks I might pick up.

Although it occurred to me that I should warn my drakón.

"Check yourself over later," I called over my shoulder. "There are these small bugs on the leaves and branches that can attach themselves to you and suck your blood. They could give you diseases, too."

"Really?" Ben said sharply.

At the same time, Yvera cried, "Eeeeew!" And shuddered.

"Nothing you can't heal me of, I'm sure," I told Ben confidently, inwardly trying not to laugh at the sight of Yvera's elaborate attempts to not let anything touch her.

She hates *bugs*, Ben told me silently.

So I gather.

And so I, the weak, helpless amón, confidently strode forward into the dark, while the fiercest drakón I had ever seen muttered her displeasure and flinched away from leaves.

Something started to feel familiar. Certainly these woods were like the forests of the East Coast I'd mostly grown up on. We weren't in the Amazon, that was for sure.

But when I saw the creek...my heart began to pound.

And there...hanging on a branch, as if left for me to find...was Abby's macaroni-and-bead necklace. The one I had been wading to find when it all began. I picked the necklace off the branch and held it in my trembling hand.

"No," I whispered. "It can't be...."

It couldn't be *that* easy, could it? For once in these past however-many crazy days of my life, could it be *that* easy?

I began to run.

"Sarah!" Ben called after me in frustration.

It's OK, Ben, I said as I ran into the large, open space ahead. *It's....*

There it was. My neighborhood park, where I had spent countless hours watching and playing with younger siblings—and that was only in the year that we'd lived here. And across the street....

My neighborhood, the sign lit with the glow from electricity-powered light-bulb spotlights. Streets paved in asphalt. Streetlights. Trimmed bushes in mulched beds. Weedy grass with brown spots.

It all looked so....

Dull.

Had it...all just been a dream?

No....

"Sarah?"

I jumped. I didn't know why. It was as if I had momentarily entered a nightmare, except the nightmare was terribly confusing because it was everything that *should* be safe, familiar, inviting. Except it wouldn't have had that voice. That warm hand resting itself on my shoulder.

And all the *other* incredible, wondrous, and beautiful things I had seen and even *done*. Yes, I'd nearly died more times than I had kept track of. But I felt only relief and a longing to go back the way we'd come as I whipped around and hugged my dragon with all my might.

Just to know he was still there. With me. Here.

"Are you alright?" Ben asked uneasily.

"Odd," Kor said as he stepped out of the woods. "How are those things powered? I don't feel *any* spark from them."

He pointed to the streetlights.

"Electricity," I said thickly. Dang it, I was crying again. That wasn't a promising beginning to my homecoming.

"Uuugh," Yvera said as she stumbled out of the woods, rubbing herself down.

I decided it was time I stopped having my fun and had mercy on her.

"Yv, you *probably* haven't gotten any," I said, still holding onto Ben. "I'd say that armor of yours is tick-proof."

"Unless they've crawled into the cracks," Kor said with a smirk.

"I...will kill you," Yvera said in a fierce whisper, pointing a finger at him.

A car drove by on the main street at a sedate forty miles per hour, and normalcy must already have been sinking into me again, because I thought absolutely nothing of it.

But my drakón did.

Ben shoved me behind him—and I mean *shoved*—Yvera drew her claymore, and Kor threw up a shield in front of us. Fortunately, the car was already passed and *probably* didn't see the sapphire glow in their rearview mirror.

It would have been hilarious, really.

If I wasn't suddenly so afraid of prison.

"Guys," I hissed. "It's just a *car*. Yvera, put that thing away. You're going to get the cops called on us."

Speaking of which, I should take my big, intimidating drakón *out* of the dark park. So, I squared my shoulders and started walking again.

"Sarah, what's a *kar*?" Ben demanded.

"Yv, I mean it," I said, looking back and pointing at the claymore. "You're going to get us in *big* trouble if anybody sees you with that."

And then, to my surprise, she put it back in the ether, though she gave me a death glare as she did so.

"I'm a *Battleblood*," she muttered. "What's a Battleblood without—"

I stopped, turned around, and put my hands together, praying for patience. "That doesn't *mean* anything here. Here, the only people who go around openly carrying weapons are either the police or—*it's just a car!*"

I shouted that last bit as another passed by and all three tensed again. Just in case, I held out my hands wide in front of them, although that was stupid, because what could all five-feet-six-inches, one-twenty-pound me do to hold back three drakón?

And yet...they stayed back, doing nothing more extreme than shifting positions. Although Ben was giving me quite the glare now.

"Sarah," he repeated, tone getting dangerous. "What is a kar?"

"Some kind of transport," Kor said, eyes sharp as he watched the last one disappear. "There's an amá inside, directing it."

"Exactly what Kor said." I gestured to him while looking at Ben. "It's...it's like a really fast, metal wagon. You are going to see *thousands* of them. Almost everyone here, in this area at least, has at least one or two. It's how we get around."

"You have one?" Kor said, eyes lighting up.

"Technically, I share one with my sister, but you are *not* allowed to disassemble it to figure out how it works," I said fiercely, pointing at him. "I don't care if it's a beat-up, decade-old Corolla, it's the only one she and I've got, so hands off."

"Sarah," Ben said, approaching me as one would a wild animal. "Sarah, calm down. It's alright."

I took deep breaths. "Right. Right. Sorry. This is...harder than I expected."

A lot harder, and in not just an emotional way. Or, at least, not the just emotions of confusion or nostalgia or loss or displacement. No, the emotion I found pounding in my heart right now was...fear.

I thought for a few long moments about how to explain this to them. On how to put to words the terror I had felt when I saw how they would have *inevitably* responded to the most normal sight in my world. Why hadn't I thought to prepare them better?

Perhaps because it had always felt like this moment would never come.

"Look," I said finally. "This is...a very, very different world. I know you are used to hopping worlds, but this isn't just another planet. It isn't one of the Six Realms. It's another *world*. It works very, very differently. Ben's not in charge here, nor is his dad. And the people who *are* in charge...run things very differently. If they find out what you three are...."

There it was. The hard core of fear growing inside of me.

"The good ones...will just be scared. Even if you get the chance to talk a few of them out of being scared, there's just too much...it's like a massive machine that's too big to stop once you get it going, and fear of you *will* get it going. And if the bad ones find out...."

I stared at Ben, heart pounding.

"Sarah, what are you afraid of?" Ben said quietly, putting a hand on my shoulder.

I shook my head, tears stinging my eyes again. "I don't want to lose you," I said thickly. "And not just you."

I looked at Kor, then Yvera. "*Any* of you. But there are dangers here that, to my knowledge, have *nothing* to do with the Devourer. And yet, they still can and will *kill* you if they find out about you. Or...even worse...find a way to use you."

The thought of Ben as some despot's *slave*....

I felt like I was going to be sick.

I pointed behind them, back into the forest. "There is only *one* gate we know of, in this entire world, and it's back there, and it's only mine. Which means, once we leave this area, I can't pull us out. If you come with me now, there's no way out. There's no escape. There's no backup plan. And you'll be fighting a *whole* different battle."

"What kind?" Ben said.

How could he be so freaking *calm* about this?

I looked up at him. I couldn't believe I was asking him to do this. My sun?

I swallowed. "Hiding who you are. *Everything* that you, you remarkable, breathtaking drakón are. I know you guys think you know what it means to hide, but you don't. When you tried to keep me out of public sight, that...that was different. The key in this world is to *blend in*. To not look or act different than anyone else. To be *average*. And you all are starting off at a massive disadvantage there. Not only are you *drakón*, you are used to standing out among *drakón*. That's what kept you safe before. But it *won't* keep you safe here. Trust me. I, of all people, know by now what you three are capable of, and it won't."

Kor's face as he watched me was unreadable. Ben was grim, clearly thinking hard. But Yvera looked incredulous, and that worried me. A lot. Because all it took was for Yvera to stab or punch someone that looked at her the wrong way....

I took a shaking breath. "Let me try to explain it this way. Think of it as like this giant...monster. An *enormous* monster. One that, trust me, *you cannot defeat*. It is just too big, too complex, too scattered...too everything. It's like a monster that if you cut off one head, you create three more, and once it gets your scent, it will just keep coming and coming and coming, endlessly, and one of those times it comes for you, it *will* kill or capture and enslave you for what you are. The *only way* for you three to not just survive but help me find the Tree is to *not let it notice you*. Don't attract its attention. Don't let it get your scent. Because if it does, it will come after you, and it will never stop."

"What *is* this monster, in your metaphor?" Ben asked firmly. "Sarah, *what* are you afraid of?"

My shoulders sunk. My head hung.

"Humans," I whispered.

I blinked through my tears up at my sun. "*We* are the true monsters, Ben. And...there are too many of us for me to save you from them. They have weapons that can kill even you. And...when they get scared enough, they use them. Even the good ones. And...a lot of the ones with those kinds of weapons aren't good. They're not like your father. They're like...Solim."

Ben kneeled down and looked me in the eye, studying me closely.

I shook my head at him through my blurred vision. My nose was running into my mouth by now, but I didn't care. "I can't lose you, Ben. But I'm afraid if I don't hide you well enough from my own kind...I will."

The very faintest of smiles appeared on his face. "Can you understand, even the slightest bit, what I have felt ever since I found you?"

I gave a choked laugh. "That was different. You weren't protecting me from your own *people*."

"You're wrong. Although I'm glad to hear that your interactions were so positive that you think that highly of us. But you're wrong. There are dramá that couldn't care less if the Moontouched came back, Sarah. In fact, there are some radicals who would prevent it. There are a few who, not even being consumed at all, would kill you if they got the chance."

I stared at him.

He shook his head, eyes soft. "We're not perfect, Sarah. We have our true monsters too."

"But you have one advantage," I said quietly. "Leaders as good as you."

"I suppose there is that," Ben agreed with a slight smile. "Avva *is* pretty much perfect."

I laughed wetly and threw my arms around him. "I meant *you*, silly. You're just as good as him, in your own way."

"Flattery aside," Ben said, clearing his throat. He pulled me away to meet my eyes again. "I understand what you mean. I understand that hiding is necessary while we're here. So, what do you need us to do?"

I took big, deep breaths. Just hearing him say he understood, not to mention that he had heard my admission of the darkness of my humanity without flinching, was doing wonders for my stability. "I'm so sorry to ask this. You shouldn't have to hide who you are."

Ben snorted. "And what is precisely what I have asked *you* to do from the moment you came to my Realms?"

"That's different," I insisted. "I didn't even know *what* I was most of that time."

"And in some ways, that made it even worse. But, for the sake of getting us out of the open, right now, let's focus: what do you need us to do?"

I took a deep breath and nodded.

Focus.

"*No* weapons. Visible ones, anyway. No attacking anyone or anything unless it is excruciatingly clear it's attacking you. This is a safe area, really. No animal predators, no consumed monsters, and a low crime rate. So you should probably wait for me to say whether something is dangerous before doing anything...drastic. And most of all, *no magic*."

I looked at Kor. "*Any* magic. *Anywhere* that *anyone* can see it. *Anytime*. Magic isn't a thing here. People don't have it, people don't use it. Nothing is going to scream 'Look at me, I'm weird and potentially dangerous' like using magic."

I looked back at Ben. "And...I'm stating the obvious just in case: absolutely do not, under any circumstance except clear peril of your life, change into dragons. I take what I said about magic back. Changing into what you can become will bring down the hellwinds like nothing else."

"Alright," Ben said with a nod. "I think that sounds doable, if this place is as safe as you say. Does that mean you know where we are?"

"Yes," I said soberly. "We're—"

I saw flashing lights reflected off the playground equipment and forest. And froze.

"Sarah," Ben said quietly, rising. "One of those kar things is coming. Toward us."

No, no, no!

I *knew* I should have gotten my drakón out of the park. Or, at least, I *had* known that until other concerns became more urgent.

Now, confronted with the fulfillment of my dread *already*, my mind was frozen with indecision. Not to mention my Earthren instincts from before came roaring back, back when getting in trouble with authority was pretty much my biggest fear. Sense flew out the window. All memories of gates and the pull I still could feel through the woods were gone. It was just all too much at once.

I was simply frozen.

I think Ben saw and understood that. Though he seemed to heed my caution about not doing anything "drastic," he stepped behind me, putting himself between me and the source of the flashing lights in a distinctly forbidding way. Kor and Yvera closed ranks just behind either side of him to do the same, almost circling me.

No, no, I moaned to myself. *Guys, that's the opposite of helpful.*

Frantically, I tried thinking of believable excuses for why three tall, strangely dressed and colored, dangerous-looking people were pinning in a relatively small, helpless looking young woman, but all I was drawing were blanks.

I heard the police car pull up in the parking lot, the car door creak open, boots step out.

"Excuse me, sir, but I believe that's my sister right behind you."

I gasped.

Michael?

Oh no.

This situation just got ten times worse. Because *Michael* would know I had been missing. And who else would these people be but my kidnappers?

If my brother didn't have a gun pointed at Ben *right now*, then I was a dragon.

Pure protective instinct kicked in, thawing the freeze.

"Michael!" I cried, spinning around to face the parking lot and pushing in between Kor and Ben to rush in front of them with my hands up. "Michael, this is *not* how it looks."

But Michael didn't have a gun up. In fact...his hands were on his hips, and he was grinning from ear to ear.

"Hey, sis. I was hoping you'd show up on my shift."

I froze again. "Er.... This isn't...how it...looks?"

"Sarah, *is* this your brother?" Ben asked quietly, in a tone that told me he was ready to spring into action if the answer was no. I was kind of surprised he'd even spoken out loud, but maybe he was giving Michael the benefit of the doubt. Or at least one warning.

Michael's eyes darted to Ben at the sound of his voice, but it was just the natural look of someone looking when another person spoke. There was no suspicion, no hostility. No...OK, there was *something* of the older-brother protectiveness I was expecting. I might have thought he'd had his brain swapped by aliens if there wasn't. But it was more the you-better-treat-my-sister-right look rather than I-am-going-to-shoot-you-for-what-you-did-to-her look.

"Oh, it isn't, is it?" Michael said, returning his gaze to me, grinning widening. He held open his arms. "Because it looks to me like my sister finally found a way back to planet Earth. Welcome home, Sarah."

CHAPTER SIXTEEN

BROTHER

KORIBEN

I WAS ALMOST CERTAIN by this point that the young man who had gotten out of the car was Sarah's brother. Even if they hadn't called each other by name, the family resemblance in their light brown skin, dark hair, and dark eyes was striking.

So I didn't panic *quite* as much as I might have when he grabbed her and pulled her into a hug. Something still wasn't right to me about Sarah's stiffness, though. Was she not happy to see him? Were they not on good terms? What should I be *doing*?

Sarah— I began.

But just then, Sarah spoke to him. "So...you're not mad at them?"

Mad at us? Why would this Michael be mad at us? He didn't even know us yet. And we'd just brought him his sister, hadn't we?

Michael pulled away from her. "Well, I might have been, except for your messages. At least one of these three was often in them. Especially *this* big guy, who I recognized from a mile away."

He pointed at me with a grin. While Sarah remained stiff and unmoving in shock, Michael came up to me boldly and offered his arm. I took and clasped it in what I thought was a friendly manner, but he started in surprise, as if that hadn't been what he was intending. But he quickly recovered his smile.

"The name, as Sarah shouted, is Michael. I'm her older brother."

Something about that struck me as familiar, and when I remembered, I smiled in return, a surprising amount of good feeling rising already. "So *you're* the one who taught Sarah how to shoot a gun."

He started at that. "Come again? Speak any English?"

I grimaced, only now remembering he wouldn't be able to understand me.

Sarah had recovered enough by that point to insert herself between us. "Michael, what do you mean by *messages*?"

"Sarah, you're being rude," Michael joked. "Aren't you going to introduce me to these people?"

"Once I know why you're taking this all so calmly! How long have I been gone? *What messages*?"

Michael's smile finally faded. "Wait. You mean *you* didn't send them?"

"*No*," Sarah said emphatically. "I thought all of you would be frantic when I came back. Michael, it's been...."

Sarah looked at me in a daze. "How many days, Ben?"

"Ten," Michael and I said, almost at the same time. In different languages.

"Ten," Sarah repeated in her own tongue. "Ten days, for both of us. Ten days in which I *didn't* send you any messages. Not that I wouldn't have *wanted* to. But I didn't think I *could*."

Michael frowned. "Wait. If *you* didn't send the ice pictures, then who did?"

He looked questioningly at me and my wings. I just echoed his frown and shook my head as the only answer he might understand.

"They didn't either, trust me," Sarah said dismissively. "Now, what are you talking about?"

He put his hands on his hips again, frowning in thought. Not for the first time, I noticed the gun at his hip, but my eye was drawn to it now. It was similar enough to Sarah's that I could recognize its function, but I saw now why Sarah had puzzled over her own gun so much if *this* dark, hard, angular thing was what was typical in her world.

The gun troubled me. Sarah had said that no one openly carried weapons except certain kinds of people, but she hadn't had a chance to specify who. But it *seemed* like she trusted this man. The more time went on, the less she seemed frozen and the more just baffled.

"It would happen every day at sunset," Michael said after a pause. "To every single one of us. Well, not Tommie, separately from us, as far as we're aware. But even Laura and Abby. Every day at sunset, for the past ten days, wherever we were, whatever we were doing, we would all see a small sheet of ice appear on the closest flat surface. And in that ice, we'd see things. Still images, like photos. They were all of you. Seemed to be some kind of montage of your day. Like you were sending us postcards or vacation photos or something."

I was only just barely following at this point, but Sarah seemed to be doing a much better job, although her eyes were widening with horror again.

"What did you guys *see*?"

"Good stuff," Michael said in surprise. "Normal stuff. Eating. Sleeping. Talking with these guys."

He waved at me.

"Stuff that let us know you were as happy and as safe as could be expected, even though we had to piece together over time why you weren't *here*, obviously. Don't get me wrong, we were in a *panic* at first when you didn't come home. That was actually how we knew you were gone: at sunset, we all saw you in the ice in some kind of large stone hall, walking and talking with the blue guy. Rachel felt awful at first, believe it or not."

"She did, did she?" Sarah said, a tired smile growing on her face.

"She got over it pretty quickly," Michael said with a grin. "The fastest of us adults, anyway. The littles were never that worried, in fact. Abby said she had a dream that a tree lady came and told her that you were needed for a special 'quest' but that you would be back safe when you were done."

Sarah and I stilled, so much that sharp-eyed Michael took notice. His joking smile faded. "Wait. What did I say?"

"Ben," Sarah said, looking up at me with wide eyes. "The Tree of Ice. She sent my family *messages*."

"That's what it sounds like," I agreed.

"The *what now*?" Michael said.

"The Tree of Ice," Sarah repeated to her brother, this time in her own language, this *English*.

At what point in the past ten days had she begun saying the term exclusively in Drona? I couldn't remember, but it had been days at least. She had begun to use a lot of our words, actually....

She continued. "That's who sent the messages. It's got to be."

"You're kidding, right?" Michael said. "An actual *tree* took you away? On a *quest*?"

Sarah folded her arms. "You're taking an ice-picture montage of me appearing at sunset every day in stride, but not a Tree?"

"Oh, believe me, it weirded the *crap* out of me at first. But...you know...it's amazing what you get used to," he said sheepishly, hand on his neck.

He lowered his hand and sighed. "Plus...the more time went on...the more it was all we had to go on. It was all we had to keep *going*. We couldn't tell anyone else, not the searchers or cops or anything—because, *crazy*, right?—so we just banded together about it. If we can't get together for dinner, we have nightly video calls right after it ends to compare notes, just in case someone saw something or noticed something that someone else didn't."

He smiled faintly. "It was like you were sending us clues every day to this giant puzzle of where you must be and why. The littles actually think you're cooler than Carmen Sandiego now, thinking that you were just off on some adventure in some magical place. And the rest of us, well, the more days that passed with more pictures...the more it felt like maybe, just maybe, you *were* alright. Safe. Happy. Trying to find your way back. And then...I guess I became a believer."

He grinned at me, then looked back at her. "Except I didn't realize that I was until I saw that guy, talking to you, in the park. Just as the last picture tonight showed us you would. That's why I drove this way tonight, hoping I'd find you. And...here you were."

Sarah gaped—and then was abruptly irritated. "If you recognized Ben and knew he wasn't a threat, then what was with the flashing lights?"

She gestured to the car, which was still strobing in a painfully bright blue and red pattern. I could *not* understand why that was useful. Did the lights somehow power the wagon? Then why didn't the other cars have them?

"Oh, well, I had to play it up just a little," Michael said with a grin at her. "Some payback for how you worried *me*, you know."

He...had worried her on purpose? The lights meant something worrisome? Danger?

Suddenly, I understood a bit more why Sarah had frozen like that. And I felt a lot of my goodwill toward him dissipate.

"Jerk," Sarah said, but it was without heat. She then sighed. "Yeah...I suppose I deserve that much."

"So, are you going to finally introduce me to these people?" Michael said pointedly. "We only had pictures to go by, remember, so we have running bets as to what their names are. I think you can imagine what some of them are."

Sarah groaned, but the worst of the storm seemed to have passed. She took a deep breath, then finally managing a somewhat genuine smile, she turned to face us both.

"Ben, Kor, Yvera, this, as you've gathered from his own introduction, is my brother Michael. He's a...well, he's kind of like a...Strongshield. That's the red ones, right?"

I chuckled. "Yes, their drakón are red."

"He's what we call a cop, or police officer. In case that didn't translate well, he's, like...a local guard. Who enforces the law, not defends against...things."

"Ah, I think the term you're looking for is *lawkeeper*," Kor said. "And those tend to be Strongshield, but not always."

"Right, sorry. Probably shouldn't stereotype."

"That explains the weapon, then?" I asked, nodding toward his gun. I felt better about it now. Of course a lawkeeper should be armed.

"Exactly," Sarah said, then dryly added, "And the flashing lights. Speaking of which, can you cut those out, Michael?"

"Do you really think we'll attract *less* attention if a cop is talking to four people in a park in the middle of the night *without* them?" he said dryly.

"Maybe," Sarah muttered. "People at least wouldn't come *looking*."

"It's three A.M., Sarah. I'm probably doing you a favor by keeping away types that shouldn't be poking their noses into our business at three."

I alerted at that implication of danger, but neither he nor Sarah seemed concerned.

"That late, huh?" she said in surprise, reflexively looking at her watch. I wasn't sure why, since didn't it show Ythra's time? Then she grimaced, remembering.

"So that's the new gadget," Michael said, leaning in curiously. "It *looked* like a smartwatch, but something like that seemed out of place with everything else."

"They made it custom for me," Sarah said. "Long story. Anyway, I wasn't done with introductions."

"Oh, right," he said, pulling back, though his eyes drifted back to the watch.

Sarah took another deep breath and smiled at me, gesturing. "Michael, this is Koriben Sunfilled, or just Ben. He's...well, maybe I should go into the details of what he is when everyone is there, so I only have to explain myself once. It gets...a bit complicated."

She introduced Kor and Yvera in the same way, with Michael's amusement growing with each name. "Well, that wasn't what we were expecting at *all*. No offense."

I nodded in what I hoped was a friendly, respectful way. Even if I was still irritated with him for scaring Sarah, I needed to be in his good graces. "It is an honor to meet you, Michael."

Sarah translated for me.

Michael frowned at that. "Wait, how come he seems to have no trouble understanding you, but he can't speak English back to us?"

Technically, I *had* picked up on a few English words by now. Even I could hardly help that after ten days of listening to Sarah. *Yes, no, hello, thank you*, that sort of thing. But nothing I felt comfortable trying to use without sounding like a dumb barbarian—not nearly as many words as Sarah had seemed to not just know but mix in with her own with a fluency that belatedly astounded me. She was something special.

"They can *understand* all languages, but they can't *speak* all of them," she explained to her brother. "Just...for now, just trust me that it's the way the magic works, alright?"

"Magic," her brother repeated, and Sarah winced.

She anxiously watched him process that but didn't say anything further. I remembered what she had said about magic not being done here, and I too waited a bit tensely for his reaction. If the Tree had sent him to us tonight, then it must have been for a reason. Michael must have been a key, one we needed for at least one door we needed to unlock.

Michael stood back, folding his arms. Looking at us drakón. Then looking at her.

"Well...I'm seeing pictures in ice every sunset. In *July*. Or at least, I was until you showed up. Who am I to deny the existence of magic?"

Sarah let out a breath of relief. "I know it's a lot to take in. So thank you, Michael. Especially...since this doesn't even scratch the surface."

"Long story, huh?" Michael said, smiling crookedly at her.

"You have *no* idea," Sarah said with a weary smile.

"Yeah," Michael said with a sigh, throwing an arm around her shoulders. "We figured it would be."

SARAH AND MICHAEL DEBATED for a bit about what to do next. Sarah wanted her brother to come home with her right away, but Michael protested.

"Sarah, don't get me wrong, I am beyond *happy* and *relieved* to see you're back, but since you seem alright, I've got to get back to work. I'm on duty right now."

Perhaps Sarah's comparison of him to a Strongshield was apt after all.

When Sarah opened her mouth again, he pressed on. "We're shorthanded tonight with some people sick and out, and I already took a lot of time off recently looking for *you*. Now that I've seen you're OK and given you a hug, I have to go. I'll come by as soon as my shift is over and you can tell me your long story then, promise."

The Sarah I had found ten days ago might have stopped there, and for a moment, I saw her waver. Then her face firmed. "Michael, I wouldn't ask if it wasn't important. I'm not just *back*. There are things I have to tell you and things we have to do *now*."

"At three—" Michael began incredulously.

"Yes, at three A.M.," Sarah said grimly. "We don't have much time. Every hour counts now. The fate of *worlds* is at stake, Michael."

He stared at her. "You're kidding, right?"

Sarah shook her head slowly, brown eyes glowing silver for one moment. A moment that had her brother flinching back, as if he had never seen soulflare before. And, I supposed, he probably hadn't.

"I am dead serious. The fate of *worlds* depends on us right now. And we have only hours now to save them."

"Sarah," Michael said slowly. For the first time, he glared at me and my wings with open hostility and suspicion, and his hands drifted to his gun.

Knowing a bit of how lethal they could be, all three of us tensed, and I could feel power building in Kor, readying a shield.

"What did they do to you?" he asked quietly.

Sarah slowly and deliberately stepped between her brother and me. And raised her hand up to a flexed position at the wrist, her palm facing him in a halting gesture. As if to reinforce her unspoken command, that hand began to glow with white, frosted light.

"*They* did nothing," Sarah said. "*They* are the reason I'm still alive. And if you lift that gun to shoot any of them, so help me, Michael, I will freeze it beyond functioning. And even *if* you outshoot me, your bullet will never reach them. Isn't that right, Kor?"

"Correct," Kor said flatly.

"See, Michael," Sarah said steadily, "they can do *magic*. *I* can do magic. You can't touch them with anything that you have on your person, and I won't let you even try. So cool it right now before it has to come to that. *They* aren't the enemy. *They* are here to protect us. But they need our help, and they need it now. Or all our worlds, including Earth, are doomed."

Michael just continued to stare at her, particularly her glowing hand, jaw gaping. But at least his hand moved away from his gun. "Sarah, can you even *hear* yourself? Even if anything you say is remotely true—and that's crazy enough as it is—you're not some kind of hero or savior. You're *Sarah*. My little, timid, can't-hurt-a-fly sister."

Fury pulsed hot through me.

"How *dare* you," I said hotly, and I would have taken a step forward, but Kor threw out a hand to warn me back.

Let me handle this, Ben, Sarah said to me.

"What does it look like I'm doing now, Michael?" Sarah said flatly.

He snorted. "That glow trick? That doesn't look like much—"

Sarah pointed her finger downward and sent a spear of ice slamming into the ground near his foot, making him jump back. He stared, wide-eyed, at the glowing shard of ice that steamed in the warm night air.

"That—that's asphalt," he stammered. "That *thing* broke through asphalt."

Sarah raised her hand back up to the halting gesture. "Oh, did it? I guess it did. Imagine that."

Michael glared at her. "Who are you, and what have you done to my sister?"

Sarah's voice softened, and she slowly lowered her hand. But it didn't stop glowing. In fact, she curled it into a determined fist. "I'm still your sister, Michael. But, even though I know the last ten days have been rough on you, most of the time, they have been hell itself for me. I am so *glad* that the Tree sent you pictures of me being safe and happy, because there would have been nothing you could have done to help me in the moments I wasn't. But that isn't the full picture, not even half of it."

The rest of her skin began to glow, and I could only imagine what her eyes looked like. Even her hair stirred in some unfelt wind. "I wasn't safe. Not always. And as you know well, being in danger, having something to fight for and protect, does things to you. You tried to explain that to me, but I never understood, not before. I'm still your sister. I'm still Sarah. But now I'm more *sera* than I have ever been before. I am now something you can scarcely imagine."

My flameheart trembled from the force of my pain for her and pride in her. She should *not* have had to go through what she had to become this thing that had us now staring in awe.

And yet how magnificent she was.

Sarah sighed, and her glow faded, her hair settling back down. "So, Michael. I know what it means to you to bail on your team like this, I know what your job means to you, but I'm asking you once again to make that sacrifice. I wouldn't if it wasn't absolutely necessary. I wouldn't ask it if I hadn't made sacrifice after sacrifice already to help the people behind me and get back to you, and I wouldn't ask it if I didn't *need* my brother *now* to help me save the worlds. But I do."

Silence fell for a few seconds, with Michael looking from the melting, glowing shard, to Sarah, to us, and back again. Finally, his eyes rested on Sarah, face grim.

"You're *serious*, aren't you? Not just about magic, not just about having a long story. You honestly think you're needed to save the world."

"Not just me," she said simply. "All of us. You, Mom, Dad, Rachel...."

Michael hardened. "Even the *littles*?"

Sarah winced. "They won't have to take the same risks I will. Hopefully none of you will. Just me. But I need you all to come with me to find the Tree of Ice. Then hopefully She can send you back home, safe and sound, as if you just went on vacation."

"And then what are *you* going to do?" Michael demanded.

My gut twisted. Had she decided? Either of her choices could lead to equal parts hope and heartbreak for me, so I didn't even know what to want anymore.

Sarah took a deep breath. "I...will hopefully be safe too. But I'll need to go back with Ben and the others. At least for a bit. They'll...need my help with something."

My flameheart both surged...and sputtered, joy and pain and hope and fear mingling in equal, excruciating measure.

"Something dangerous?" Michael said, glaring at me again.

Sarah hesitated. "Maybe."

"What the f—"

"Michael, please," Sarah begged. I heard tears in her voice now. "I don't want to ask this of you. I don't want to go into danger. I don't want to do *any* of this. I am scared out of my mind right now. But I *have to*. Because if I don't, I'll lose you all anyway. The Devourer will come, and it will consume us all, and *I will lose you anyway*."

I couldn't hold back any longer, and Kor didn't make me. I came forward and stood with Sarah, putting my hand on her shoulder and clenching it tightly.

Michael, very rightly, glared furiously at me. He didn't need an inner voice to say, *This is all your fault, isn't it?*

It was rude to speak to a stranger with an inner voice unless one was in drakáform, when amá speech simply wasn't possible. But Sarah wasn't *entirely* right that we drakón could only understand and not make ourselves understood. Inner voices, after all, spoke a universal tongue. The only reason I didn't use my inner voice with her back when we first met was because she was terrified of me already, and I thought it better to try to get her to understand me the normal way. Or...what I had thought would be the more normal way.

Yet from how hard it had been to get Sarah, already wanting to trust me, to paint her ears with my blood, I didn't think that was going to happen soon with Michael. Besides, this was a message that needed to pass just between the two of us.

Yes, it is *my fault,* I told him silently. *And because I love her too, you don't know how much this is* killing *me right now. But I have* no choice. *Not if I'm going to be able to save her from what's coming for her.*

He started, eyes widening at me. Sarah looked up at me questioningly, guessing I must have said something. But I just kept my gaze on Michael. Sarah may have been through a lot, but she still had a lot more to learn, and one of those things was to never take your eye off your enemy.

Not that Michael was my enemy. But neither did he seem like he wished to be my friend. No matter how much I understood why, even agreed with the sentiment, he still had a gun within easy reach. I wasn't about to let him draw it and upset Sarah with what might result.

If he draws it, target just the gun, I told Kor silently. *We don't want to hurt him.*

Agreed, Kor answered. *You'll shield yourself and Sarah?*

Yes.

In that scenario, Kor might have a better angle than me to get the gun out of Michael's hands if I were blocking my way with a shield, which was why I was leaving the gun to him. And I trusted him to be more...delicate about disarming him than Yvera. Speaking of whom....

Yv, if he does anything, leave it to Kor. You are not, under any circumstances, to hurt him. Understood?

I figured, Yvera grumbled. *When are you going to finally let me* kill *something?*

When there's an enemy to kill.

Which hopefully wouldn't be *any* time soon, although I didn't want to further aggravate her by saying that.

Fortunately, our quick preparations didn't seem necessary.

"They're not the bad guys, Michael," Sarah said quietly. "They're the super-heroes. But they can't do this alone."

Whatever *that* meant.

It seemed to mean something to Michael, though, because he let out a breath. He rubbed his neck, looked at all of us for a moment, particularly me, and then back to his sister.

"Alright.... Maybe you're right, at least about the part where I'd better come hear what this is all about. Let me...make some calls."

He trudged back to his car and flapped his hand in the direction beyond. "You go home, start waking up Mom and Dad and whoever else you want. I'll be along."

"Thank you, Michael," Sarah said. "Really."

"Yeah, yeah," he said as he climbed back into his car and shut the door. The car didn't move, though. He simply stayed inside it and began talking, seemingly to the car itself. Did he have a scale in there?

No, that couldn't be right. Sarah hadn't even known what call scales were, or how to use them. Then how was he communicating?

"Come on," Sarah said wearily, shoulders drooping. "Let's go. It's not far."

Chapter Seventeen

MEETING

Koriben

WE FOLLOWED SARAH ACROSS the grass of that small field, but all three of us kept a wary eye on both the car and the lawkeeper inside. Fortunately, both remained where they were.

Sarah had us wait for a moment at the concrete edge of the wide road as she looked both ways—for cars, she said.

"So they're dangerous after all?" I asked, frustrated at how the rules kept seeming to change.

"Not in the sense that they want to kill you," she said as she led us across the road. "They don't. But they have the road. And if they don't see you, or if they can't stop in time, well, intentions don't matter when something that heavy hits you when it's going that speed. It's like...like just trying to be careful on a landing circle, or when going through a sungate. It's just common sense."

Ah.... I supposed it was. And...I was feeling a lot more empathy for how lost she must have felt trying to figure out my Realms.

"Well, I thought that conversation went well, don't you?" Kor said, catching up with Sarah to give her a smirk.

"If I'd had time to think about this, I would have known Michael would have been the hardest one," Sarah said tiredly. "So, in a way, yes. It did. Hopefully the worst is over."

"Perhaps that's why the Tree had him meet us first," I suggested quietly, casting one last glance back at that car before we made the bend onto a road with rows of very similar-looking structures on each side.

"Perhaps it is," Sarah mused, looking at me. "She really is smart, isn't She?"

"That's an understatement," I said with a thin smile.

"Dad will...be the next hardest," Sarah said, almost speaking to herself. "Mom will follow Dad's lead; I'm not saying that's right or wrong, that's just the way she is. So, Dad is the one who matters most. He's protective, too, because he's my dad. But he's logical. Cool-headed. More like Kor. He'll take convincing, but he'll want the whole story upfront. Plus, he doesn't own a gun."

"Is that the main weapon here?"

"Yeah. I mean, we have kitchen knives...but I don't think anyone would think to use them, and I don't think it's going to get *that* tense again. Like I said...I think the hardest bit is over."

She stopped in front of one structure. And took a deep breath. "Although this is going to be hard enough."

She looked back at me with a brave attempt at a smile. "Well, for what it's worth...welcome to my house."

"What's a house?" I asked, blinking.

She blinked back. "Oh. That didn't translate? It's that thing."

She pointed to the structure we stopped in front of. "It's...like a really small hold, meant for only one family. I live in there. Or...I did once."

Her voice became lost as she looked back at the "house" and said those last words.

I said it before I could think better of it. The panic was just too sudden and strong. "You live in *that?*"

That flimsy, two-story structure of wood, a bit of visible cement, and I didn't know what else looked like it could blow over in the *wind*. Let alone last a *night*.

"Hey, I know it's not a palace, but it's a decent size," Sarah snapped. "It has to be to fit seven kids. It's one of the nicest we've ever had, actually. Mom and Dad worked hard to give us this much space and yard."

"No, Sarah, that's not what I meant," I said quickly. "I'm sure it's very nice...and comfortable and.... It's just...so...*vulnerable*."

As in, utterly and completely indefensible. Not to mention very flammable. Those glass panes everywhere, that flimsy wood door.... There wasn't even a defensive *wall*.

Sarah finally registered the worry in my expression. "Oh. Right. Sorry. I understand what you're saying now."

She looked again at the house, as if with fresh eyes. "Yeah.... It's not a fortress, is it?"

"No," I said tightly.

Please, please say you're not going to go back there permanently, I thought.

Especially if I wasn't there to protect her.

"See, the thing is Ben, most people don't *need* fortresses here. Look." She gestured around us. "All of those are houses, each with their own families, pets, and cars. This is how most of us live here. Not...all together in some mountain or underground."

"Interesting," Kor said, eyes intent as he studied everything around. As he had been doing this whole time. He didn't seem surprised, so he might have already even come to that very conclusion.

"We don't get attacked by monsters at night," she continued soothingly to me, taking my hand. "Most of these structures are perfectly fine to protect us from the elements and whatever small dangers there are out there."

"And what about the big dangers?" I said. "Your metaphorical monster?"

Her face darkened. "Remember how I told you that there isn't much you can do against them? The key is to *blend in.* And hope they never come to call."

I took deep breaths to calm myself. Sarah sighed and hugged me, which helped marginally.

"Most people in this place...at least in this country...never have to worry about the big dangers," she said. "I grew up *safe*, Ben. I promise. Here, as long as you are an ordinary, law-abiding citizen, you are generally safe."

Generally. She was no doubt hoping I wasn't catching on to her caveats, but I caught every one.

A lot of things about her were making more sense now, if this was the way she was raised—thinking that the best way to survive was to become an invisible, tame oramose hiding in the prairie.... Because there wasn't anything you could do against the gorhawk. You just relied on numbers, on your small size, your camouflaged fur, and your hundreds of burrows. Most of your life, you could go about as normal, thinking you were safe. You knew the gorhawk existed, somewhere, but because you played by the rules, because it only picked off one or two of your colony of hundreds per day, you must be "safe."

Sarah had grown up thinking the only way to defend yourself...was to make yourself not a threat.

Even if that made you vulnerable.

And maybe that worked for most of the hundreds. But as soon as you stood out, as soon as the gorhawk began to target only *you*....

"I think...I understand," I said, pushing her away to meet my eyes. "But you're not normal anymore, Sarah. Nor will your family be. Do you...understand what I'm saying? Do you understand why I'm still worried? About you, and your family?"

Her eyes widened, and she looked at the house. "Oh," she whispered. "That...won't be enough anymore. Will it?"

"No," I said sadly. "It won't. At least...not for much longer. We don't know if the Devourer has penetrated this world yet. But even if it hasn't *yet*...."

"It will come for us eventually," she said. Louder now, though. Her voice gaining strength and her face firming. "I understand."

She looked back at me, eyes calm. "That's what you meant, isn't it? You told me once that my family would come to live in my hold, but we never got around to talking about why. This is why. Earth...or at least, this house...isn't safe for us anymore."

I let out a deep breath of relief that she *understood*. "No, it isn't."

"That's what it was made for," Sarah said to herself. "The Tree even said it. To keep me and my family safe. Because, even back then, they knew it would come to this."

I just clenched her shoulders in comfort.

"Right," she said with a sigh. "I get it. They're not going to like it, but...I'm not going to give them a choice. I'll get them to move, even if I have to burn the house down myself."

She said the last with a wry smile.

"Why, Sarah," Kor said with a grin. "That sounded almost *ruthless* of you. Not to mention cunning."

She raised an eyebrow. "To protect my family? I'll do anything."

She turned and began walking up the wide cement path to the house. "Come on. Before Michael gets here and wonders what took us so long."

She led us under the awning and to the ridiculously flimsy-looking door. Not to mention small. I was going to have to duck through that thing.

Then she hesitated, as if having forgotten something.

"Oh, er, Ben, do you have my purse still by chance? That small bag that I came to the Realms with?"

"I think so. Didn't we put it with your other stuff?"

"Right," she said with a sigh. "I guess you're going to have to bring it all—"

Just then, a light came on inside. Sarah froze, but I was fairly certain by this point that didn't mean danger. Sure enough, a few moments later, the door opened, and in the doorway stood a woman that looked so much like an older, darker version of Sarah it momentarily stunned me.

She gasped, then grabbed her daughter into a tight embrace and began sobbing her name and kissing her cheeks, eventually saying, "I knew it! I knew it was a sign! I knew you would come back!"

A fit, clean-shaven man with short, dark blond hair touched with gray and an angular face came down the hall and to the doorway. For an amón, he was tall at just over six feet, which explained where Sarah got her height, since the mother was shorter than the daughter. He didn't look nearly as much like Sarah as her mother did, but there was something about his bearing, or perhaps the serious, intelligent look in his eyes, that made the connection unmistakable. Especially when he met my gaze, his pale blue eyes sharp and evaluating.

Those were a father's eyes if I ever saw them.

"Mom," Sarah said faintly. "Dad. What are you doing *awake*?"

"We were hoping tonight was the night," her father said, smiling thinly. "After the image of you in the park with these three. So, of course we couldn't sleep."

"I told you, Jake," the woman said, turning to beam at her mate through watery eyes. She still didn't relinquish her hold on Sarah. "I *told* you."

"So you did," Jake said calmly. "Now, are you going to let me hug Sarah or not?"

Sarah went to him without waiting for her mother to let go, and he wrapped his arms around her. The tightness of his grip betrayed his otherwise placid exterior. He wasn't so unmoved as he let on.

"Welcome home," he told her simply.

"Thanks, Dad," she said wetly, eyes squeezed shut.

"Now," he said a moment later, pulling away. "All of you had better come inside. I have a feeling there are some things you and your new...friends...need to explain."

His sharp eyes flicked to mine. I suddenly realized that Sarah's brother may have been the one with the gun...but he wasn't the most dangerous one.

"You do?" Sarah said, startled.

"Yes," he said grimly. "And I'm guessing it's a bit more than about where you've been and why. Isn't it?"

Sarah stared at him. Then a thin smile crept onto her lips. "Figures you would catch on to that."

He's smart, Sarah told me silently. *Like, really smart.*

So I gather.

Like his daughter.

"It's not hard if you pay attention," Jake said wryly. "Come on in, all of you. Sarah, lead them into the living room. Who do you need your mom and I to wake up for this?"

"Michael's already coming. We met him on the way while he was on patrol. So that leaves Rachel, David...." Sarah took a deep breath. "And Lizzy. Let's let the littles sleep as long as they can. Plus...I don't want to give them any more nightmares than I have to."

"What do you mean, honey?" her mother asked, eyes widening. Her brown eyes—even more open and expressive than Sarah's—darted between her husband, her daughter, and me and my wings. But unlike Michael's, they didn't narrow in suspicion or anger. "You were safe. That's what your messages were about. You couldn't come to us, but you were safe."

Sarah looked at her father. His lips thinned, and he shook his head slightly. Sarah nodded just as subtly, unsurprised. Even I could read what that meant. Whatever Jake had suspected about Sarah's actual situation, he hadn't told his hope-filled wife—or if he had tried, she hadn't believed it. I could see perhaps one reason: she seemed to be a tender, deep-feeling woman, one who had been clearly determined to think the best of the situation. Perhaps that had been the only way she could cope, and Jake had decided he could not take that from her.

"We'll do that," he said, putting a hand on his wife's shoulder. "Come on, honey. Let's wake up the kids. Those, at least."

"Why not all of them?" she asked, bewildered, but she followed him up the stairs that I could see from the doorstep. "They'll all be so excited she's home...."

I missed Jake's murmured reply, because Sarah took my hand and began leading me inside, and I had to focus on ducking and listening to her. "Come on, this way to the living room. That's...a gathering place, by the way."

The inside of Sarah's home was strange, but nice. Fairly simple, but clean, orderly, practical—exactly what I would have expected. Still, it was full of bizarre objects whose purpose I couldn't guess at and lit with delicate glass globes that looked (like a lot of things in this place) terribly fragile, with white-hot elements inside them. (Surely that wasn't *safe*?) The walls were some kind of painted plaster, and, from seeing the edges in the doorways, incredibly thin. I wondered how they could even bear the weight they must have been supporting. Astonishingly lifelike portraits of her and what must have been the rest of her family lined one wall we passed, and Sarah had to tug me to get me moving again, since I had unconsciously stopped to study them.

As he followed me, Kor took it all in with eyes that glowed with his greed for information. Yvera....

"Yv, close the door, please," I told her over my shoulder.

As much good as that toothpick of a door did us, it was still something. Besides, all the other doors of all the other houses were closed, so I figured that was what was expected. We had to blend in.

It seemed my instincts were correct, because Sarah paused and looked back. "Oh, right. I just assumed, so I didn't think to mention. Please, Yvera?"

Yvera huffed, but she closed it behind her and strolled after us.

My rightwing was getting dangerously bored. I might have to send her to patrol around this flimsy structure, no matter its current safety, just for something to do.

But for now, she should probably be here for this. I could feel the momentousness of this occasion sinking in. This was when the Golden Crown formally met with the Moontouched *clan* for the first time and presented our request for aid. And that moment should have the Golden Heir and both his wings present.

Hopefully Yvera managed not to smash any of these very breakable things until then.

Sarah led us into one of the larger rooms I'd caught glimpses of. It had a couple long couches, some bookcases, and a low table in the center, but it's main feature, or at least the one that everything else appeared to revolve around, seemed to be a large, flat, shiny black rectangle of some sort attached to the middle of the far wall. Sarah paused for a moment at the threshold, thinking. Then she took a deep breath and led me to stand in front of that black rectangle.

"Here is probably best," she said. "They're going to want the couches, and we're going to need to be the center of attention."

She looked grimly determined when she said that.

"Where do you want Kor and Yvera?" I asked.

Sarah looked around. "Well, having *all* of us stand here would probably be a bit much.... Kor, Yv, would you mind standing in the corners here and there?"

She pointed to either side of us. "You can always sit down on something if you get tired of standing."

"Don't worry about us," Kor said with a chuckle, patting her shoulder as he passed her. "We can stand for as long as it takes, I'm sure."

"I'm not sure I'd want to sit on these things anyway," Yvera said, eyeing one spindly chair with a dubious look.

Sarah winced. "Yeah, probably better not with that one. That's Great-Grandma Lind's rocking chair."

Michael strolled in. I noticed that he no longer wore his gun. "What, you guys haven't even started yet?"

"Mom and Dad are still waking up the others," Sarah said. "Oh, sorry, Michael. I didn't even think—do you want Laura to be here?"

"This is that big of a deal, is it?" he said with a crooked smile as he plopped onto one couch.

Sarah raised an eyebrow. "Haven't I convinced you of that already?"

"Yes, well, there's end-of-the-world news, and there's wak-ing-my-wife-at-three-thirty-in-the-morning news, which is the worst pos-sible kind. Is it *that* kind of news?"

"It's that kind," she said grimly. "This is going to involve her, too. And she's going to be even more mad at you, and me, if she's left out of this."

He sighed. "I was afraid you were going to say that. Here, let me call her."

To my surprise, he pulled out a rectangular object with a glassy surface that glowed with vibrant light at his touch. After tapping and manipulat-ing the glowing colors on it for a bit, he put the thing to his ear and leaned back, his expression bracing.

"Heeey, hon," he said after a moment. "So, good news first: Sarah is back."

I faintly heard a voice exclaim from inside the object.

"Yes, yes. It's great. Thing is, though—"

I was distracted from their conversation by a shout from the hallway.

"Sarah!"

A girl of about eleven or twelve summers ran toward her sister and smacked into her hard enough that I threw out my hand to keep them both from toppling.

"Lizzy," Sarah said, tearing up again as she wrapped her arms around the girl. "I'm so happy to see you. I missed you so much."

"I missed you *more*," the girl declared with a pout as she pulled away. "Why didn't you take me with you? Whatever you were doing, it looked like fun."

Sarah's smile became forced. "Some parts *were* fun, true. But most weren't. You wouldn't have liked it at all."

"You sure?" Lizzy said suspiciously. "That party you went to looked cool."

Both Sarah's eyebrows rose. "Oh. You. Um. Saw that."

Her eyes darted to mine, and her cheeks heated. "What did you *see*?"

"Your dress was *amazing*," Lizzy enthused. "Do you still have it? Can I see it?"

"Ah, there you are," another sister said with a yawn as she came in. This one looked older than Sarah. Whereas Sarah was slight, this one was all curves, and from the sultry way she moved, she knew it. Alarm horns immediately started blaring in my head. From her catlike walk to her tight, sleeveless shirt and nearly nonexistent breeches, I knew this was exactly the sort of girl I had spent my entire life avoiding. At all costs.

She came over and gave Sarah a quick hug. Her proximity made me shuffle a step to the side uncomfortably.

"Took your time getting here, didn't you?" the young woman teased as she pulled away.

"So glad to see you too, Rachel," Sarah said with a tired smile.

Rachel shrugged. "You were fine, weren't you? And seemed to be enjoying yourself to me."

She smirked and nodded meaningfully in my direction while keeping Sarah's gaze. I stiffened, worried she would start turning her attention to me, but fortunately, her eyes brushed right past me and searched the room...until they fell on Kor.

Her grin suddenly widened, showing white teeth. "*Bingo*."

She sauntered right up to Kor and winked at him. "Hellooo, handsome. What took you so long getting here?"

"Rachel...." Sarah said, horror slowly dawning on her face.

Kor looked at Rachel in a way I didn't ever think I'd seen before: speechless shock, so severe his eyes were soulflaring. Before I could worry too much about his health, a grin of incredulous delight replaced it. "Flame Above. How is it that *you* could be related to Sarah?"

"Ooo, I didn't understand most of that, but it sounded amazing," she said with a flirtatious grin, leaning against the wall next to him. "Hi, I'm Rachel. Yes, one of Sarah's many sisters. And you are...?"

"Kor, don't you dare," Sarah said fiercely, pointing at him.

"I haven't done a single thing, Sarah," Kor said innocently.

"What?" Rachel said with a pout at her sister. "*You're* the only one who gets a superhot boyfriend out of this? How is that fair?"

What was a boy....

Then I noticed Sarah's cheeks, which were on fire now.

Oh.

Torch it, now I was blushing too.

"Just—just now is not the time for this, alright?" Sarah pleaded with her sister.

"Sarah, Sarah. I believe that is called hypocrisy."

"Hey sis." A gangly boy, almost a man judging from his height and the scruff on his face, blinked blearily as he came into the room. He smiled at her and pulled her into a hug. "Good to see you back in one piece."

"Hey, David," Sarah said with a strained smile, clearly trying to focus on him, but her eyes kept drifting in alarm to Rachel and Kor in the corner.

I sighed. I was going to have to have a word with my leftwing at some point about Rachel, regardless of—or perhaps *because of*—his feelings for Sarah. Fortunately, language appeared to be a barrier at the moment, though seemingly not a formidable one in Rachel's mind as she continued with unflagging enthusiasm to make some sort of conversation with him.

Fortunately for the state of affairs between our peoples, Sarah's parents walked in next, holding hands.

"Oh, good, you're here, Michael," Jake said placidly. "Is that Laura on?"

He looked at the rectangular device, which Michael had set up on top of the low table against a stack of books to face Sarah and me, and on its glass surface was an irritated young woman with freckled skin and curly, light orange hair.

"Yes, I'm here," she said. Something was off about her voice. It didn't sound natural, and it echoed strangely. "Awake, unfortunately, and ready to receive this doomsday news."

"Hi, Laura," Sarah said with a sheepish wave. "I'm sorry, honest. But you'd have been madder at me if you weren't included, promise."

"Probably. Good to see you're OK, Sarah. You gave us quite the scare."

"I know. I didn't mean to, but I'm still sorry."

"Then it looks like we're all assembled except the littles, Sarah," Jake said as he and his wife sat on the shorter couch, with room for just the two of them. David and Lizzy had already sat down on the longer one next to Michael. "Go ahead."

Sarah took a deep breath. I could tell this was difficult for her, but she soldiered on. "First off, I think...introductions. Ben, in case you missed names or need the reminder...."

She listed them all again, pointing to each in turn. I *had* indeed needed the reminder, and I was anxious thinking about how I was going to remember all of their names. It was a good thing I'd had so much time to prepare myself for the size of Sarah's family. The number of such similar-looking, or at least so closely connected, people was dizzying—and this wasn't even *all* of them.

The only name that was new, though, was Sarah's mother, Maria. She beamed at me when Sarah pointed her out, and the reason for such benevolence became clear as she looked dotingly between the two of us with that look that only *mothers* got. My cheeks heated again.

Just...what exactly had the Tree of Ice shown her family about Sarah and me?

"Everyone," Sarah said once she'd finished with them. She gestured to me. "This is Koriben Sunfilled, or Ben for short."

She pointed to Yvera. "This is Yvera Battleblood."

And then Kor. "Korinth Starkissed, or just Kor."

"Ooo, I like it," Rachel said to Kor in a conspiratorial whisper.

"Rachel," Jake said sternly. "Not now. Pay attention."

"Yes, Rachel," Sarah begged. "*Please* just trying taking *this* seriously, for once in your life."

"Fine," she huffed, folding her arms.

Sarah thought for a moment, then looked at me. "This is going to be a *lot* harder if they can't understand you."

"Probably," I agreed.

"Even *if* I tried to explain all by myself, so many of the terms I'd use are in your language. I'd have to keep stopping to interpret them."

She sighed and looked at her family. "Alright. I know this is a strange way to begin, but...please just trust me on this one. These guys can't speak English, but they can understand it because of a magic that's in their blood."

"Magic?" David snorted. "Seriously?"

Michael, who was completely slouched against the couch, rolled his head to look at his brother sitting next to him. "Seriously, man. She shot an *ice spear* at my *foot*."

"Sarah!" Maria gasped.

"It wasn't *at* your foot," Sarah said awkwardly. "It was...right next to it."

"Wait, wait, you can do *magic*?" David said, gaping at Sarah.

"Guys, is this really such a surprise?" Lizzy said. "The ice messages? That's what you call *magic*."

"Lizzy is correct," Jake said calmly, and as he spoke, he had a visible stilling effect on his family. "We've had this discussion before. The only logical conclusion to the appearances of the ice pictures and what we saw in them is the existence of magic. Can we accept this premise and move on?"

Silence, which Sarah seemed to take as confirmation. "There. First thing down: yes, magic exists. Second: as I was saying, these people have a magic in their blood that lets them understand all languages. But in order for us to get anywhere else in my explanation, you're going to need that ability too. And they can share it with you, at least temporarily, like they did with me. But...now, don't get grossed out about this, OK? This is perfectly normal for them. The magic is in their blood...so they need to put that blood on your ears."

They all stared at her.

Then most of them broke out in various exclamations of surprise, disgust, or refusal. All except Jake, who slowly stood and raised a hand.

"Everyone."

And everyone fell silent. He didn't even have to shout. He just exuded calm and authority. Flame, he made me jealous. Could we make *him* Heir? Instead of me, I meant.

Jake addressed me directly for the first time. "This is normal procedure?"

I nodded firmly.

Technically, we rarely had occasion to use the spell, since even amón had enough of the Blood to understand tongues. Before Sarah, I had only done it to negotiate with a sentient, freed consumed descendant that seemed willing to abide by the terms of peaceful cohabitation in the Six Realms.

Sarah added, "And they heal *really* fast, too. Like, within seconds, if they need to. So it's not a big deal for them that way, either. And the blood disappears after the spell is done, so no ick afterward."

For the first time, I realized what an advantage we had in having Sarah as not just an interpreter but also an ambassador. All the painful experiences she had gone through, all the explanations I had botched, all the things she had learned would save us time and error now, when time was of the essence, and we couldn't afford mistakes.

"Very well. Do me first," Jake said simply, walking up to me.

I knew what the look in his eyes meant. He was doing this on his daughter's word. But he would not ask or perhaps even allow the rest of his family to do the same until he had experienced it for himself and knew it was safe.

I nodded to him, showing I understood, and rolled up the sleeve of my right arm. I had just began to shift my left hand when Sarah put her hand on my arm and said, "Oh, wait one sec, Ben!"

She turned to her father, but she spoke to the room. "He can...pull things out of thin air, basically. He's about to bring out a knife, but that is *just* so he can get the blood he needs from himself. *That's it.*"

I stilled. Yes, it was a very good thing I had Sarah.

"Wait, he can pull *weapons* out of the *air*?" Michael said, straightening up from his slouch.

"Michael, for hopefully the last time, I'm telling you: *these are the good guys.*"

He scowled at me and stood, folding his arms. But at a look from his father, he let out a breath and nodded. "Go ahead. But I'm watching you. All of you."

He cast a glare at each of my wings as well.

He makes me want to kill him just to show him how easy *it would be to,* Yvera sent to just me.

Yv, if you do that.... I said dangerously. I didn't think she was serious...but I wasn't taking that chance.

She rolled her eyes. *I won't, don't worry.*

No breaking bones or hurting him in any other way either.

Fine.

I shifted my hand quickly, hoping no one would notice the change, and my ceremonial knife appeared in my hand. I had decided this was a worthy enough occasion. Then slowly, mindful of Michael's hard gaze, I brought it to my arm and sliced carefully. I wanted enough blood to do this but no more than that to avoid alarming them.

Still, gasps went around at the sight of my blood.

"Oh, yeah," Sarah said sheepishly. "And...as you can see, it's golden. For him, anyway. And unusually warm."

With Jake's visible permission and the turn of his head, I began to apply my blood to his ears. He started, perhaps at the heat, despite his daughter's warning. Or perhaps it was from the magic I was already beginning to work on them. After all, it was this act that was the most important part of the spell, not the result.

I heard Rachel say to Kor, "Oh, so you're hot and blue on the inside and the outside, huh?"

"Yes," he answered. I could *hear* the smirk in his voice.

She gasped. "That was English!"

Well, yeah, even *I* knew that much by now.

"I learned from Sarah," Kor said in English.

Torch it. Did Kor *always* have to show me up? I tried hard to focus on my task and tune him out.

"There," I said when I was finished. As I drew back, the gold stain faded into Jake's skin. "How does that feel?"

Without his expression changing a bit, Jake reached up and touched his ear, feeling the dry, normal skin there. "Like I can understand you."

I smiled thinly. "That's the general idea."

"It worked, then," he said, his eyes scrutinizing me.

He looked at Sarah. "He did this for you? Ten days ago?"

She nodded. "Although...it might not last that long for you."

"It normally lasts a sevenday," I explained. It was a relief to no longer have to hold my tongue. "Sarah, as you're well aware...is something special."

And you called me *a flatterer,* Sarah muttered to me.

"Alright," Jake said slowly, looking at the healing cut on my arm. "That seems...acceptable. You may do this for any other member of my family that gives their permission, but only those."

"Ooo, me next!" Rachel said, raising her hand. Then she elbowed Kor. "But only if this guy does it."

"Rachel," Sarah moaned.

"Sarah," Kor said innocently. "You don't expect Ben to have to bleed for everyone, do you?"

I would have volunteered to help Rachel, for Sarah's sake...but I would honestly have rather touched an enraged ice bear. Old habits die hard. Plus, I was *still* not betrothed, and Rachel's type could sense such things like an irkan could smell blood.

"Was that a yes?" Rachel asked Kor, confident in the answer.

Sarah groaned. "Don't make me regret this, Kor."

She turned to the rest of the room. "Is anyone else interested?"

"I'll do it," Michael said with a hard face, coming forward.

"Let me guess," Sarah said dryly. "To keep a better...ear on them."

Michael couldn't keep his lips from twitching. "You could say that."

My first cut had already healed by then, and I'd used most of the blood besides, so I retrieved my knife again and cut another. Michael watched both the retrieval and the stowing afterward with sharp, narrowed eyes, and I knew that he saw the slight change in my hand when his eyes widened. But to my surprise, he simply shot me another glare and turned his head for me to begin.

In the end, all the Linds in the room accepted our ministration, even tenderhearted Maria, although she flinched away and squeezed her eyes shut when Kor made his cut for her, and he was unusually gentle in tending to her.

Before I could stop him, David walked up to Yvera and shyly asked her if she would do the same for him, even calling her by name. I froze in the middle of painting Michael's second ear, wondering if I needed to throw myself between her and the boy. Sarah looked just as alarmed; her hand drifted to her gun behind her.

But to our shock, Yvera just scowled at him, and when he didn't move, but rather kept looking at her hopefully, she grunted and began taking off her vambrace. "Fine. I suppose it's something to *do*."

"Thanks," David said, grinning in relief. No doubt because he couldn't understand what she had just said.

In that way, my wings and I were soon done. Lizzy was the last and most timid overall, although she insisted on me for some reason. But once she sat back down and everyone resettled, Sarah spoke again.

"Thank you, everyone. I know that was…a lot to ask. But it will make things a lot simpler, trust me. And not just in explaining things. These people need our help…and we need theirs."

"What do you mean?" Michael demanded.

"Michael," Jake said, his tone and eyes warning. "Listen. Then judge."

I guessed this might be an old argument between father and son.

Sarah looked up at me. "Do you want to explain, or shall I?"

"Go ahead," I said. "This is your world, and your family. You'll know how to say it best."

And you'll probably explain it much better to anyone *than I did to you,* I added to her with silent amusement.

You did fine, she told me.

She took a deep breath and looked back at her family. "It starts...with the Trees. The Tree of Flame watches over what they call the Six Realms. Really, they're six *worlds*—six planets. That's where these three are from. Their Tree, the Tree of Flame, guides them, chooses their top leaders, and keeps them safe from the greatest enemy there is out there: the Devourer."

"You mentioned that word before," Michael said, eyes narrowed. "Except I didn't understand what you meant because you said it in *their* language."

"See, that's exactly why we needed this translation magic," Sarah said with a sigh. "I'm so used to calling things what they call them that even I would slip up a lot like that otherwise. I've never had to think of the English equivalents because I've always just understood what they meant and used that."

"What *is* 'the Devourer'?" Jake asked intently.

Sarah looked soberly at me. "I think you had better take this one."

All their eyes turned to me. I sighed, and not just from the pressure. "It...is a force. A force with intelligence, ruthless and cunning. It consumes life, wherever and whenever it can, and the more it consumes, the more it grows, the more it wants. It is the true enemy of all that is living. It has left entire worlds barren, with nothing left but rock and ash. That is what it has tried to do to my Realms, and it has taken everything we have and are to stop it. Even that would not have been enough...except for our Tree."

"A Tree is a world's only *true* protection from the Devourer," Sarah explained. "She acts as like an immune system for the planet She is on. As long as She is healthy and strong, She can keep the worst of what the Devourer is at bay. It can still slip in some of its minions here and there, but it can't enter and consume the world itself."

"She?" Lizzy asked, glancing at Jake. "As in, the 'tree lady' Abby dreamed about?"

"The Trees always use female avatars, apparently," Sarah said with a shrug. "I haven't actually met one yet in person, but Ben and the others have, and that's what they say."

"So Abby dreamed about something real?" Maria said, troubled. "This...fire tree?"

"Actually," Sarah said hesitantly, looking at me. "It's more likely that Abby dreamed about *our* Tree. Earth's Tree: the Tree of Ice."

"The ice messages," Jake said with a nod.

"Those were most likely sent from Her," Sarah agreed. "*Not* from me. I never even knew about them. I'm grateful that She sent them to comfort you, but I had nothing to do with it."

"So, what?" Michael demanded. "This Tree thing *took* you and gave us messages as *compensation*?"

I stiffened, but Sarah put a hand on my arm. "Not compensation. Comfort. She isn't unfeeling. But...She does what She has to do to protect Her children. Us. *All* of us. All of humanity."

"And how was taking you protecting all of humanity?" Michael demanded.

"Can't you see, Michael?" Jake said calmly. "The Devourer is coming for Earth."

Silence fell as everyone, including me, Sarah, and my wings, stared at Jake Lind.

His eyes fell on Sarah, and for the first time that I had seen, a sadness entered them. "Abby wasn't the only one to have a dream of a Tree."

"What?" Maria said, dismayed. "Honey, you never said...."

"Because it was only a few nights ago," he said, putting his hand comfortingly on her thigh. "And it wasn't...a happy dream. I didn't want it to be true, and I wanted you to cling to hope and happiness as long as you could, especially with Sarah still gone. But now that she's here, I'm beginning to understand what it means...and why this Tree gave it to me."

He looked back at Sarah. "I saw it. I saw this Devourer consume Earth, even though I didn't know what it was at the time or what it was doing. Then this Tree appeared to me in the form of a woman made of ice and told me that She couldn't stop it. She couldn't save my family. Not alone. She would need our help...but most especially, She would need Sarah."

A pause of one breath.

"For *what*?" Michael demanded.

"She said Sarah would know," Jake said, his gaze still not leaving his daughter.

She swallowed. "I...do. I still don't know why *me*. Or why us. But I know for what. Her...voice came to me. To Ben and me."

She glanced up at me. Then, taking a deep breath, she straightened her shoulders, firmed her stance, and lifted her head.

As she spoke, she looked at her family, one by one. "She needs us to find Her, here, on Earth. Then when we all come to Her, She will...give us power, basically. Make us something different, something magical."

"What, you mean, like them?" David asked, pointing to me.

Sarah shook her head. "Something new. Something...like me."

Then she held out her hand...and a shard of ice crystalized in the air above her palm, slowly turning in the light of those glass-contained fires like a precious jewel. As she did so, her eyes glowed silver, and those mesmerizing, glowing white patterns danced across her exposed skin.

Her family all gaped...except, of course, Jake. Who just continued to gaze at her with that deep look of sadness I now recognized, for I had seen it far too many times in my own father's eyes.

It was the sorrow of knowing there was nothing you could do to save your beloved child from their fate.

Not without consigning them to one that was far worse.

Sarah sighed and released all the magic, allowing her glow to die and the shard to fall into her palm. She placed it in a bowl on the table, where it continued to glow with an inner light.

"Except not even that is enough for me anymore. When we go to her, She will have to give me more. She will have to give me the power I need to help Ben and his people fight back the Devourer when it launches its next attack on the Six Realms in two days."

"You can't be serious," Michael said. "You're going to let some magical tree turn you into a...who-knows-what, so you can go and help *this* guy?"

He pointed at me. "Why is it our business what that hungry monster does over there when it sounds like we have big enough problems right here?"

"Because they are my *friends*, Michael," Sarah snapped. "Because they're *people*, too. Who deserve to *live*, too. But if you need a selfish motive, then here it is. Dad's right: if the Realms fall...Earth is next. So our best bet to buy us the time we need to save our own skins is to first save theirs."

"I'm not being selfish," Michael said through a clenched jaw. "I want to know *why* the person who has to save their asses is my little *sister*."

"I don't know why!" Sarah shouted at him, the sound exploding from her. Her eyes began to glow again. "All I know is the Tree picked *me*. And if there is one thing I have learned over these past ten days, it's that when the Tree picks someone...*that's* who it has to be. For the good of all. So I sure as *hell* am not going to risk the lives of the people I love by shirking my duty to protect them *now*."

I placed my hand on her shoulder—more for my sake than for hers. She seemed to be holding her own. But I didn't know how to contain or even describe what I felt in that moment.

She breathed heavily for a moment, then slowly softened, the glow dying. "Because I'm *your* sister, Michael. Could you expect anything less of me?"

He looked down, face taut with emotion. "It's...*my* job to protect *you*."

The last of her anger and soulflare died. She crossed the room and hugged him, and he pulled her in tight.

"You did," Sarah whispered. "Part of the reason I'm still alive right now is because of you. And a huge part of how you can do that again is by coming with me to the Tree."

"Right," Michael snorted. But he didn't let go. "So she can turn me into an ice person like you."

"Admit it," Sarah teased wearily as she slowly pulled away. "You're tempted. Just the *slightest*, teeny-weeny bit."

"I think it sounds *awesome*," David said, eyes brightening.

Michael snorted. "You would."

"Ah, c'mon, Mike. You know you want superpowers too."

"I don't know exactly what you'll get," Sarah said sheepishly. "I shouldn't oversell what the Tree is offering, because I don't know exactly what that is. Just that you all are supposed to become Moontouched, like me. Or...maybe already are, but just need that part of yourselves woken up. Actually, I'm a bit fuzzy on that."

Sarah cast glances at Kor and me.

Kor shrugged. "That's as good a guess as any at this point. You all are Moon-touched descendants, that much must be true."

"Moontouched? What's that?" Rachel asked.

"It's one of their original seven clans," Sarah said with a tired sigh, waving at me. "Except some disbanded, and some left and went to Earth, and that's where we get it from. Long story."

"Wait, you're telling me that we're related to *them*?" Michael said.

"Way back. Like, centuries back. Like I said, long story that we don't really need to get into tonight."

"Then what *do* we need to do, Sarah?" Jake asked quietly.

Resolution settled onto her soft features. "Decide if you're coming with me."

"That's it?" Michael said flatly. "That's all the explanation we get? We just have to now...decide?"

"Michael," Jake said quietly. "You had *ten days* to pick up on the clues that the Tree was sending us that life as we knew it had changed forever when Sarah left. I think we have heard enough now to make our choice, because if we only have two days before the Devourer strikes Ben's home worlds, then every hour is of the essence. Anything more, Sarah can explain along the way."

"There's one more thing," Sarah said, pain and guilt lancing across her face. "That will have bearing on your decision, that is. I'm not asking you to come with me *just* because I need your help. I'm also asking you because...I'm not certain how safe it is for us to live here anymore."

"What do you mean?" Michael asked intently.

"The Devourer is hunting me, Michael," Sarah said, a trace of despondency entering her voice. "It knows I have the potential to stop it, so it is trying to stop me first. I don't think *it* has managed to enter Earth. We'd know if it had. But it might have been able to send its minions. And if so, they will be searching for me...and for my family...now."

Silence.

Broken by Michael's forceful curses.

"Sarah," Lizzy said, voice trembling. "I'm...I'm scared."

Sarah's face crumpled. "Oh, Lizzy...."

She ran to her sister, and Lizzy stood and reached for her at the same time. As they both embraced and wept, Sarah said, "Lizzy, Lizzy, it's OK, it's alright. I won't let anything happen to you. I promise. I promise."

I felt as low as the ashes that there was nothing I could have done to prevent this, and that there was nothing I could do to give this family the safety they deserved now.

"That's why the tree lady gave us your castle."

Everyone, even Sarah and Lizzy, turned to look at the entrance to the living room. A little girl stood there, holding a stuffed purple draká under one arm. She yawned sleepily and rubbed her eyes.

"She came again, in my dream. She said to get up and tell everyone that it was time to get ready to go. She kept the bad guys away from us for as long as she could. But they'll be here when the sun comes up."

Chapter Eighteen

FLIGHT

Sarah

LESS THAN TWO HOURS later, Ben and I were crammed (uncomfortably, in his case) in the back seat of Dad's sedan as our two-car convoy made its way to the Philadelphia airport. Dad had offered the passenger seat to Ben for more legroom, but he had declined in favor of sitting with me.

Although I wasn't sure whether Ben's reasoning was more about him protecting me or me protecting him. I saw the way he avoided looking out the windows as we sped down the highway. And how his hand clenched the side door grip so tightly I was worried he was going to break it.

You're going to make yourself carsick, Ben, I told him gently.

If that's what this is, I think I already am, he said queasily, clenching my hand more tightly. I was trying to hold out as long as I could before asking him to loosen up, but I was going numb.

How he had no trouble with neck-breaking speeds and acrobatics while he was a dragon but was getting sick over a simple car ride, I had no idea, but I felt too sorry for him to point that out or even feel amused.

Try looking straight ahead, I encouraged.

That's not much less terrifying. How do you people survive *these things?*

I...began hoping we didn't come across any major collisions.

Dad is a very safe, responsible driver, I soothed. *We'll be fine.*

Not to mention the fact that we weren't traveling over fifty anymore, having hit the morning rush going into Philly. Which apparently began before six A.M. Ironic that the reason *I* was feeling a bit queasy was because we weren't moving *faster*. But at least we had gotten miles away from home by the time the sky began to golden.

To say the last hour and a half had been a flurry of planning and preparation would have been the understatement of my life, but Dad rallied and directed us in the chaos with the aplomb that would have been worthy of a four-star general. He got the answers he needed from me and Ben with rapid-fire questions and then began issuing orders left and right, giving each person a task that got us moving and doing within minutes while he planned our best course of action.

He, Ben, Kor, and I pored over maps on his study computer for an agonizing half hour as we debated the best way to get to not just Greenland but where I remembered that glowing white dot to be inside it. Of course the dot would be inside the Northeast Greenland National Park, one of the remotest and most scarcely inhabited destinations on the planet.

Dad took in stride the information that my drakón could turn into *dragons* capable of flying us, but we eventually ruled out that option as taking too much time and risking too much exposure. Three enormous dragons flying over the northeastern coast of North America could hardly escape notice. Besides, even the narrowest stretch of water we could identify between mainland Canada and Greenland was still hundreds of miles across, and once we conveyed the distances and possible conditions in terms Ben could understand, he said he didn't want to risk us humans over that much cold, open water unless there was no other option.

Which meant flying.... In a plane, that is.

Ben took some convincing. We wasted precious minutes showing him pictures of airplanes and giving him the statistics about air travel safety before he reluctantly agreed that seemed to be our best option.

It was a good thing we had gotten him committed to this course before we got him in a car.

As if it was a sign, though, there just so happened to be a flight this morning from Philadelphia to the Nuuk Airport, connecting through Iceland, with just enough seats.

That's where we hit a snag that not even Dad was thinking fast enough to foresee until he was trying to buy the tickets: passports. Fortunately, we had just gone on a family vacation to Canada just last month, so all the Linds had the necessary documentation. Unfortunately...my drakón most certainly didn't. So either they had to stay behind while we legal Earth citizens found the Tree, or we weren't flying by plane. And guess which option Ben wouldn't even consider?

While Dad tried to explain to Ben and Kor why a lack of some glossy bound papers was an insurmountable obstacle, I stood back in exhausted despair, unable to believe it had come to so simple an end as this. We didn't have *time* to fly the drakón way. But we simply couldn't fly the other. Even if we knew of a handy plane to steal, none of us knew how to fly it.

Then a thought came from nowhere. *Check the mail.*

At first, I dismissed the thought as being brain neuron's misfiring. It was bound to happen with how weary and worn I was by now.

Then it came again. *Check the mail.*

And *this* time, I recognized where that voice came from: the quiet dimness deep inside.

Numbly, I left the study and walked to the mail organizer by the front door. It must have been a very junk-heavy day, and the flyers and grocery ads were still stuffed in there. In fact, the more I sorted through it, the more I realized there must have been at least several days' worth in there. Odd, that. Mom and Dad were both tidy, organized people. They normally didn't let the mail stack up this long. I guess that just went to show how tired and distracted they'd become since I...left.

Then my fingers came across a largish, stiff, cardboard envelope. I pulled it out...and stared at the sender's address.

Nuuk, Greenland.

Moving my fingers purely on autopilot now, I cracked open the envelope, reached inside...and pulled out three U.S. passports.

By now, when I opened the first one, I was fairly certain I knew what I would find, even though I could scarcely believe it.

There was Ben.

Technically, Benjamin Gold. Born three years before me on July 1, and, according to the inserted white card with further biographic information printed on it, with an address in a nearby town. Seven feet, five inches.

I flipped open the second. There was a picture of Yvera. Even though that stiff passport photo could never have possibly been taken, they had somehow managed to get every detail of her picture-perfect, right down to that scowl. Every detail...but her hair and eyes. Which were now black and hazel accordingly.

Vera Battaglia.

When I opened the third, I saw Kor. Except his hair, instead of dark sapphire, was now simply black. They'd left his eyes blue, but they didn't seem so intense.

Connor Starr.

I walked back into the study and handed Kor his passport. "Think you can make yourself look like this for a day?"

Kor took the booklet from me and stared at the impossible, never-taken photo. Then looked up at me with narrowed eyes. "Where did you get this?"

Beyond the photo, he knew by now something of the significance of what he was holding.

We now had Dad's and Ben's attention. With one hand, I gave Ben his passport, and with the other I handed Dad the envelope.

"It was in the mail. For me. From Greenland."

Dad stared at the address, then at the open passport in Ben's hand. "Well...I guess that means we're on the right track."

And without another word, he gathered the three passports and went back to his computer to buy the tickets.

Dad said nothing about the cost. When I apologized to him about it, he brushed me off.

"Emergency savings does us no good if the world comes to an end, Sarah."

"Whatever the price you pay, I can repay you," Ben said firmly. "Maybe not in your world's money. But in anything else of value to you, I can get you."

"He really can," I said when Dad cast me a wry look. "He's...important. Back where he's from."

"Oh, I gathered that much myself," Dad said to me dryly.

To Ben, he said, "That's kind of you to offer, Ben, but the only thing of real value to me is my family, and I intend to take them with me. Everything else...can be left behind."

And so we took surprisingly little with us. Dad was forceful about that. He told the rest of my family to pack light and only the essentials: snacks, medication, toiletries, a couple changes of clothing, and our cold weather gear. Even when Ben told him quietly that he could store in the ether whatever they wanted to bring with them, no matter the size or amount.

"We simply don't have time to decide what to keep and what to bring," Dad answered him grimly.

But Dad did hand him our heavy bags full of cold gear. Not having checked luggage would make our lives easier, after all.

For the sake of the others, Dad told them we could always come back for treasured keepsakes and gadgets. But I could see when he met my eyes that he knew the truth: we were never coming back.

When we pulled out of our driveway, I didn't even look behind me as our house disappeared from view. It was just another move, after all. If the most flurried and traumatic yet.

At least the Tree had given Abby one bit of good news that I currently sheltered in my heart like a burning candle against the whirlwind of terror: if we were interpreting Abby's childlike, English terminology correctly, the Tree said She would provide another moongate at Her location that would connect back to my hold. Which meant that not *all* of us had to brave the Greenlandic adventure and any perils we might face along the way in order to be present for the final gathering in front of the Tree.

That meant one of my most urgent tasks, done early in our preparations to minimize their risk and stress, was surging all the littles—the twins Jonah and Noah, Abby, and even Lizzy this time—and Mom into my hold (my "castle") and getting them settled, so that they, at least *would be safe*. Then I stepped out of the moongate, closed the doors behind me, and surged across a distance to Ben for the first time. *He* had wanted to meet me in the woods with Yvera and run me back, just in case I couldn't do it, but I insisted I had to at least try first. I wasn't going to let any of my drakón, but especially him, leave the rest of my family vulnerable.

Plus, the look on Michael's face when I rematerialized out of thin air and smacked into Ben was priceless.

We repeated the process again with Laura and Tommie when she arrived at our house with him and their essentials in tow. Laura wanted to come to Greenland, but Michael threw a fit about that. As fiery and stubborn as Laura normally was, she seemed to see that her husband had been pushed to his limit that night, so she reluctantly let me take her to safety with their son. Besides, that meant Mom had at least one other adult and twelve-year-old Lizzy to help her take care of the littles in their new, strange home.

So, scared as I was, sitting in that car, wishing that the slowdowns would melt away so that Dad could put the pedal to the metal, at least I could function. Because whatever was coming to my house, it wouldn't find anything of value to me to destroy. And whatever might chase *us* in this race against time, it wouldn't be able to touch the most vulnerable of my family. They, at least, were already as safe as mortal and immortal means could manage.

That would have to be enough.

For now, intentionally or not, the rest of us blended in with the herd.

We fit the remaining expeditioners into two cars: Dad was driving his sedan with David in the passenger seat and me and Ben in the back, and Michael was driving the passenger van with Rachel, Kor, and Yvera. We could have perhaps fit everyone in the van, but it would have been a tight squeeze with our two larger drakón, and Dad thought we should divide up. I didn't ask him why, and Ben grimly agreed—so long as he stayed with me. The only thing that comforted me about Rachel enthusiastically sharing a bench with Kor in the van was that Michael was in the car and could probably rein her in. Enough, anyway. I hoped.

I wasn't worried about Kor, obviously. I knew he could handle even the formidable Rachel. That...was exactly my worry. Because the more time those two spent together, the more I could see in his eyes that some *handling* was just what he had in mind.

Just an hour before our international departure, we arrived at the airport long-term parking. Dad paid for a week's worth for each car. When I asked him why he bothered, he said grimly, "Just in case. We don't want our cars to be found *too* soon. If we can at all help it."

Ah. It was the same reason Dad had made everyone leave their cellphones at home, in case they could be tracked.

Because that was the most terrifying aspect of all, and I contemplated it again as we rushed into the airport: *We didn't know who the enemy was anymore.* We didn't know what had shown up at my house, because we sure as heck weren't going to stick around to find out. It could have been just a hoard of brute monsters.

But how would brute monsters know how to find us so quickly? From long before I had even shown up again. From what Abby told us, the Tree had been holding them *back*, and she implied for days. Which meant they had known where my family lived for days now.

Maybe even ten days.

Which meant two potential scenarios.

One, the Devourer knew where the moongate near my house was, just as it had known about all the others, and had merely watched and waited until it spotted people that looked like me. Then it had simply sent its mythical horde after me as soon as it broke through the Tree's protections, per normal.

Or, even more terrifying (if that were possible), scenario two: the Devourer and its most intelligent consumed had gotten more use out of my driver's license than just my picture. As soon as we started talking about passports, I made the connection: my license...also had my address. And consumed that knew how to navigate my world enough to find that address...was a dark thing to contemplate.

The Devourer may not have entered Earth itself...but we had good reason to suspect now that it had penetrated my world, nonetheless.

The only question was...how deeply?

I didn't dare try to explain the depth of my fear to Ben. I didn't tell him how I had to keep myself from flinching at the sight of a security guard or force myself to smile as innocently as I could for the desk attendant as we checked in, sweating bullets all the while.

Ben, and his wings for that matter, had quite enough problems as it was simply dealing with the *normalcy* of my world, and I was frequently distracted from my inner turmoil by the need to help them and keep them looking at least somewhat ordinary.

At least Kor's illusions on him and Yvera, and a bit of work on Ben's gold eyes to tone them down, kept the unnaturally colored drakón trio from looking like rock band escapees. Dad's clothes had fit Kor well enough, and Rachel's baggiest shirt, hoodie, and sweatpants fit Yvera, even though the sweats now looked like capris on her. (Getting her to wear *that* instead of her armor had taken a direct order from Ben.) And for Ben, well...good thing simple was his usual style, because after a few minutes of him dumping out his wardrobe for me, I put together a set of nongold clothing and shoes that could look passably Earthren, if a bit on the medieval cowboy side.

When he came back out of our laundry room after putting it all on for me, I thought, *All he needs is the hat.*

At the completed picture in my head, I began giggling hysterically, turning Ben bright red before I finally managed to somewhat explain the inner workings of my frenzied mind to him and apologize.

I was long past hysterical giggling now as I herded my drakón through the airport and tried desperately to keep them from breaking anything or committing a grievous faux pas. Michael impatiently did his own thing, but Dad and David were a huge help with Ben and particularly Yvera, who surprisingly deferred to Dad's calm authority, seemingly unconsciously, and for some reason couldn't scare away David, though it wasn't for a lack of trying.

Rachel, only too happy to help her new "friend," was usually all Kor needed, who was observant enough and a good enough actor to be nearly self-sufficient. With him, I was mostly worried about the danger of his eyes soulflaring from the hunger in his expression as he took in every electric sign, escalator, elevator, kiosk, motorized cart, and...you get the picture.

He was probably thinking of all the patents he could submit just with what he'd *seen*, let alone without understanding how it *worked*. I might have quite unintentionally changed dramá technology forever.

Even with the others of my family helping, I took on the most responsibility for my drakón. After all, I knew best what to expect from each of them, and I was the only one who could tell them with an inner voice what to do without looking like that was what I was doing.

Security...was a harrowing experience. Because of *course*, on top of all the rapid-fire instructions I had to give them about the regular procedures—to take off their shoes, put their stuff on the conveyor belt, step through the machine—Ben was "randomly selected" for a pat down, and I had to mentally shout at him that this wasn't the prelude to an attack, this was *normal*, that he should just do whatever they said and we would be fine. And of course Kor's bag (David's school backpack, part of the disguise) was flagged for inspection, and the pocket knife inside confiscated.

"Ah, man," David sighed after we reconvened. "That was my nicest one."

"David," Dad said, eyes hard as he led us toward our gate. "Why was that in your *school* bag to begin with?"

"Because it's *useful*," David said sheepishly. "That's all, honest."

And because this was David—his happy-go-lucky, everyone's-friend son—Dad only sighed and seemed to accept that.

"If you had wanted to keep it, you should have just asked me to 'hold' it," Kor said with a smirk.

"Oh, no, I meant it's just useful for everyday use. I totally forgot it was in there." David sighed again. "But yeah, that would have been smart."

I stared at his now blasé acceptance of the fact that my drakón could store stuff in the ether. But that easygoing, adaptable worldview was so David, too.

In the end, we arrived at our gate just as the last passengers were boarding and practically walked on, which would have made even a normal trip beyond stressful. On the other hand, I didn't think I could have stood around waiting another jittery hour. Besides, once we were walking down the ramp and I could breathe a tad easier, I realized that cutting it this close had another advantage: that was that much less time for any pursuers to stop us.

Hopefully they weren't the kind that could order a plane to land mid-flight. Or...shoot it down.

As frightening as that last possibility was, I didn't think it likely. There were at least two passengers on board that the Devourer would want taken alive if possible: Ben...and me. Now, if my family had taken a trip without me while I was gone, if the Devourer had a chance to wipe out most of the nascent Moontouched clan in one shot....

I didn't let myself think about that.

Especially since my jaw was dropping to realize Dad had bought Ben and me first-class seats. I checked our tickets three times, but the seat numbers matched up.

"Dad," I said in protest, gesturing to the two first-class seats as he continued to lead the others back.

"They only had two," Dad called over his shoulder. "I figured Ben could use the room."

Which was a fact, especially with the nine-plus-hour flight we had ahead of us—just to Reykjavik. Ben would have been in agony in those tiny seats back there that looked like they didn't have enough leg room for *me*. And I supposed, considering Dad was just throwing away everything at this point, it wasn't that much of a surprise that he'd made the splurge.

The shock that lingered, though, was that Dad had put *me* with Ben.

It made sense from a logical, objective standpoint. Ben needed an Earthren with him, I was the Earthren he was most familiar with, and Dad was ever logical.

And yet...he was a dad. And in this, of all times, I had expected his dad instincts to be screaming at him that he shouldn't be sitting his daughter far out of his sight next to a handsome near-stranger (to him, at least) whom she was obviously attracted to, for over nine hours.

Maybe the way he was justifying this in his head was that there was only so much we could get up to buckled to our seats, in public. Still, that wasn't the look in his eyes when he turned his head away from me. The look wasn't encouraging, but nor was it *that* kind of worry. It was simply…normal. As if he'd already accepted that this was the way things were. He'd put us together as naturally as he would have put together Michael and Laura.

Why?

"Sarah?" Ben said uncertainly, eyeing the attendants who were eyeing us.

"Nothing," I sighed, climbing into the window seat. I figured I'd also give Ben the benefit of the aisle. And…easier access to the bathroom, in case he got airsick too. Wouldn't that be the saddest irony?

Which made me think about telling him about the facilities, preemptively.

"That's the bathroom," I said, pointing. At his look of confusion, I added hastily in Drona, "Or…privy."

Thank goodness I remembered the word. Just to be sure that meant what I thought it did, I continued in English, "No shower or anything, just the toilet."

Then *silently*, I explained about how the toilet would probably function, the occupancy lights, the norms of not congregating, and so on. Meanwhile, he figured out his buckle on his own by watching me. I supposed he already had some idea about that from the car.

I was definitely glad that I was sitting with Ben for the start of the plane's motion and especially the safety demonstration. He gripped my hand the whole time through it and kept shooting me questioning glares, and I had to keep reassuring him that, as they said, water landings were *rare* and seldom were flotation devices and oxygen masks needed.

Of course, that required an explanation of what "cabin pressure" was and why oxygen masks were a thing, so it was a good thing that by the time Ben chokingly said, *We're going* that *high?*, the plane was already taking off. I had deliberately closed the window slat, but other people had theirs open, and Ben watched our ascension with visible panic.

Ben, we talked about this.

He glared at me. Fortunately, no one else could see his eyes from this angle, because they were glowing molten gold.

Sarah, the only reason I agreed to this...madness was because I thought that if the worst happened, I could fly you out of it.

Oh. I should have known what had been behind the grim look in his eyes when he finally gave in.

And my family? I retorted.

His eyes flicked away. *I...would have tried to save them, too. I didn't expect us to get separated like this!*

I sighed. Of course he hadn't. He hadn't known what to expect at all, and still didn't, poor guy. That was the whole problem.

"Ben," I whispered, because the business types across the aisle from us were casting sidelong looks, and they needed to at least see my lips moving. "Do you think that I would have risked your life and the lives of my family if I wasn't *sure* this was the safest possible way to travel?"

"Safest doesn't mean *safe*," he answered, eyes still burning when they met mine again.

"Life isn't safe," I said flatly. "No means of travel is safe."

Silently, I added, *I'm sure sungates have their risks. And so does riding a drakón.*

Too late, I realized what a nerve that would hit for him. Only when he flinched back did the memory of our snow crash and my near-death return.

"Ben," I said, stricken. "I'm sorry, that's not what I...."

"Isn't it?" he said tightly.

I clenched my teeth. *Not in that way. Ben, surely it means something to you that I wasn't even thinking of that day when I said that. That was entirely not your fault, and you have saved my life far more times by carrying me than you have risked it.*

When he said nothing, I pressed on, mouthing the words for lip movement as I silently said them. *What would have happened to me if you hadn't carried me out of that jungle on Ykran?*

He flinched again, although less so.

You didn't even have a saddle for me then, but still you thought the risk to me was worth it. Because what was the alternative?

He sighed and settled back. He only took my hand again and held it, but he seemed resigned to where this was going, and that gave me some relief. Still, I finished what I'd started.

I don't have an alternative, Ben. You were a part of the discussions. Even if you had decided flying over the sea was worth the risk, we don't have that time. We don't have gates, so this is the only *way we are going to reach the Tree of Ice in time.... And, fortunately, this way has a proven track record of being as safe as can be expected.*

As long as missiles didn't shoot you down, or hijackers didn't take over. Possibilities I deliberately didn't mention.

"Fine," he said out loud with a sigh, clenching my hand. "You've made your point. Doesn't mean I can entirely make myself comfortable with this."

"I'll take being you being merely uncomfortable over having a panic attack," I teased.

"I wasn't.... Argh, come here, you," he said, capturing the back of my head and kissing me, soft and yet demanding.

As much as I wanted to melt into that literally burning kiss—it had been far too long since the last time—our neighbors were staring, while trying hard to not look like that was what they were doing. But surely at least one of them should have been typing away at their laptop by now. Dad couldn't have given me better, more disapproving chaperones than if he'd tried. He might as well have sat me across from nuns.

Sorry, Ben, I mentally sighed as I pulled away. *I want to. But not now.*

He sighed too. *I...figured. I just couldn't help it for a few seconds.*

He brushed my hair behind my ear, eyes now soft, vulnerable. *I can't lose you, Sarah.*

I swallowed thickly. I mouthed, *I know how you feel. Now more than ever.*

Is this what he had felt, for ten *days*? This deep-seated, all-consuming panic, this crushing need to protect him from the dangers that only I could protect him from because only I knew what they were, and even if I had the time and words to explain, I desperately didn't want to have to.

How had he not gone insane?

Fortunately for both of our mental states, we reached cruising altitude and the in-flight service began. I ordered tea for both Ben and me because I thought it might be soothing and I was eager for him to try it. Decaf, though, since I had a feeling that as soon as both of us could relax enough, we should try to get some sleep. As much as I regretted the waste of even one hour with him like this, we needed to rest while we could.

Sure enough, Ben loved the tea and wondered if there was more he could take with him. I laughed and said silently that if I ever made my way back to Earth, it would be easy enough to get him more. And practically as soon as I showed him how to recline his seat and we settled in (sharing a warm, fluffy blanket he had pretended to pull out of his backpack—traveling with a drakón definitely had its perks), we were out. The last thing I remember was contentedly resting my head against his warm arm.

To my shock, I slept solidly for most of that flight. I only woke up when the pilot announced over the intercom that we would be coming into Reykjavik in an hour.

By then, I'd somehow curled myself around Ben as much as my (admittedly, greatly loosened) seatbelt and armrest had allowed. It was a good thing that our blanket partially concealed how I'd gotten my legs over his, though it couldn't hide that I'd used his chest as a pillow and had one arm splayed over him like he was some giant teddy bear. Astonishingly, I wasn't sore from my contorted, C-shaped, unevenly elevated position. At all....

Probably Ben's doing.

I was almost sure of it when I cracked open my eyelids and craned my neck up at him. He was smiling down at me, the softest look of adoration that I had ever seen and would ever see on anyone's face.

It utterly scrambled what few functioning neurons I had firing as I stirred from my slumber of death.

"Hey," I said brilliantly, blinking.

He grinned. "Hey," he replied in English.

OK, time for me to remove my legs.... Though I did so slowly, with a great exertion of self-control required, and the pull hummed all the while.

He sighed, said he had to use the privy, and got up. Which was no doubt true, seeing as I'd pinned him down for nine or so hours, but I knew enough about drakón to know their eyes didn't flare simply because they needed to use the restroom. It was a good thing our neighbors were now studiously ignoring us.

I got up and did the same as soon as he came out, and when I got back, he pulled some food "out of his backpack," since we had missed the in-flight meal. As we ate, I asked him how he had slept, and he shrugged.

"Well enough."

The way he wouldn't meet my eyes made me suspicious that he'd done more than erase any soreness, since, thanks to Kor, I knew healing magic could also induce slumber. But I didn't question him about it because I agreed with his logic that if he hadn't been able to sleep well, I might as well so that I could give him more energy later.

As much as I wanted to use our remaining time just talking, I knew I had to use it to prepare Ben for what was coming next. I began with describing customs and border crossings, concepts I knew would be utterly alien to him. I didn't delve into the details, and especially not the whys, although Ben was flabbergasted; I made us focus our time on instructing him on what to expect, do, and say. I hoped that Dad was subtly preparing the other two drakón as well. I'd meant to go back there to explain things to them as well, but now Ben was all I had time for, at least on this flight, and I hoped that would be enough.

I made him get out his passport, intending to have him study it, but he reminded me that he couldn't read what it said. So, suppressing another surge of panic, I repeated the details on it and the white card to him, over and over again, until he was sure he had them memorized.

Then I questioned him, acting as a border guard. I made him whisper the answers at least twice to make sure he could form the words in English. He had an accent you could cut with a knife, but hopefully the border guard wouldn't care. After all, I had no idea how strict Greenland was even going to be on their border crossing. It wasn't exactly a top destination for terrorists and criminals...was it?

What's your name?

Benjamin Gold.

Where do you live?

He listed off the address.

What do you do for a living?

I'd made up an occupation for him that seemed both to fit his appearance and made sense in the area where he lived. I couldn't say *cowboy* if he was supposed to live in urban Pennsylvania, now, could I?

I'm a fitness coach.

Why are you here?

Tourism.

How long are you staying?

Just a week.

I assumed those answers would be more than enough, but better safe than sorry. I'd learned the quick and hard way from Ben's "random" selection that he would face the most scrutiny of all of us. The last thing I wanted was for him to somehow get separated enough from me that I would have difficulty feeding him answers. Particularly answers in a language that anyone on Earth could even understand.

That took us until we landed. Considering Ben's panic from the takeoff, he handled the landing with surprising calm. But then, maybe he thought we were finally reaching an altitude at which it was safe for him to bust open a door and fly off if needed.

The hustle to our next flight was easier. Our next gate was close by, and the drakón knew better what to do and what not to do. We even had time to stop for a restroom break, because of course David hadn't bothered to go before our landing, and I was able to show Ben the Earthren innovation of a water fountain. I remembered the huge ornamental fountain on Oshal and knew they had plumbing, so I knew the concept wasn't much of a stretch to him. But he seemed amused that the fountain was activated by pushing a large plastic button, which he kept doing over and over until I told him he should stop if he didn't want to look five years old. That's when I remembered that the public drinking fountains I'd usually seen in the holds I'd been in were small alcoves set into the stone with a constantly running stream coming from the top, perhaps in some circulating system, and no doubt meant for filling containers and not drinking from directly.

Our next plane was understandably much smaller and not as nice, so even though Dad had put Ben and me in first-class again, that didn't mean a lot. Fortunately, Ben only had to endure it for under four hours, and I gave him the aisle seat again.

At least at first, but then I realized I had better take advantage of this time to prepare Kor and Yvera, so as soon as the seatbelt light went off, I reluctantly left Ben and asked him to give my vacant seat to his wings' seatmates (Dad and David respectively) in turn so that I could sit with Kor and Yvera to go over everything.

Yvera, of course, was the hardest to coach. It took me looking her right in her disturbingly illusioned hazel eyes and telling her just the sorts of horrible things that could happen to Ben if she exposed him before she would remotely comply, but even then, she refused to do more than repeat the information back to me until she said she had it and then sent me packing.

Kor, of course, was by far the easiest. Though customs and border protection were still foreign concepts to him, he grasped them swiftly and had brought out his passport to examine it before I had even finished my preface explanation. He had his part memorized with only a couple repetitions, spoke the English words with remarkably slight of an accent (at least with him whispering) and even added his own innovations with small words he knew. And I was pretty sure his acting could have fooled an interrogator, let alone a bored border guard.

When I got back to my seat with Ben, he and Dad had their heads together and were whispering, but they stopped as soon as they saw me coming. I knew they weren't trading embarrassing stories about me because, first, this was Dad, and second, their expressions were far too serious.

"What are you two up to?" I asked hesitantly.

"I'm just getting to know Ben," Dad said, getting up from the aisle seat. Ben had moved over to the window seat to more easily accommodate the transitions. Dad smiled tiredly at me as he passed, but that was all.

I raised an eyebrow at Ben.

"He was, actually," Ben said, and his expression was honest.

"Oh," I said, feeling silly now. "Well, do you want the aisle again?"

I pointed to that seat.

"Actually, I think I like the window, for now," he said, looking out.

"It's not so bad now, is it?" I teased, sitting down and buckling up again.

Well, this way, I can watch for something coming. Sort of.

I sighed. Of course.

"Why don't we occupy ourselves a bit more pleasantly?"

He looked at me with a raised eyebrow, and I rolled my eyes. "I mean by talking, Ben. It's not fair that Dad is the only one on this trip who's had a chance to get to know you."

"Ah, right," he said sheepishly. "That's a good idea. What...do you want to talk about?"

I thought of Eskala's question (*What do you dream about, Sarah?*), and I found myself wanting to ask Ben the same thing. But I was also scared that he wouldn't know the answer at all, like I hadn't, or that he wouldn't yet have formed a place for me in his dreams. I knew he cared, loved me even, even though he hadn't said it in so many words yet.

But had *he* had a chance to dream yet? Set aside my fear of the hurt I would feel if I set him scrambling for an answer, was it even fair to him to talk about dreams right now, when we were still rushing through danger and didn't know if either of us would survive everything in the end? Would that just sadden him? Worry him? I'd made my choice, but had he? Had he had enough time to be *sure*?

What finally decided me was that this wasn't the place for what would probably be an emotionally intense discussion. Even the best possible conclusion would probably result in more PDA than was acceptable. Which, in my culture, in these close quarters, was any.

"Sarah?" Ben asked hesitantly at my pause.

I kept my serious expression and asked, "What...is your favorite color? And don't say gold."

He blinked. Then chuckled. "Well, no one has ever asked me that one before."

"Really?" I asked in surprise.

He snorted in amusement. "Do you think anyone cares what the Heir's favorite anything is? I'm there to serve them, not the other way around. Anyone who tries to pretend otherwise, I automatically know they're trying to get something from me."

That made me sad, as many things about his life growing up as the Heir did.

"What about your dad? And Yvera?"

"They already know those kinds of things about me. Although, color.... Hmm. That's not one that's come up, I guess. Is this an important question for your people?"

Belatedly, I realized that for a people for whom color was such a mandated part of their lives, determined in more than just a racial sense by the magic in their blood and the clan they chose, that things like favorite colors might not occur as much to them. I remembered Svyer bemoaning her lack of dress options. And I thought this was the most nongold I'd ever seen on Ben other than the night of the Moonfair.

Man, he'd looked so hot in black. Not to mention that cape....

Trying to not let myself get derailed, I said, "It's pretty much the standard get-to-know-you question, which was why it was the first thing that came to my mind."

Or nearly the first.

"Hmm," he said, looking at me. "I've never had to think about it."

"Well, go ahead," I encouraged. "*I* care."

Then he started going red.

"What?" I asked, confused. That was hardly a surprising admission, was it?

"Er, brown," he blurted, looking away.

I blinked. "OK. Like, what type of brown? Earth brown, sandy brown—"

He took a deep breath and then cupped my face in both hands. Before I could worry—or hope—he was going to kiss me, he simply looked into my eyes. "*This* brown."

"Oh," I breathed, heart pounding.

He sighed as he let me go. "I'm...going to miss it."

My heart accelerated again. "Wait, what?"

He looked back at me in sudden worry. "Oh. Sorry. I just assumed you'd decided.... But you still have a choice, Sarah. Don't let me...."

"No, no, go back to the part about you missing it. Why would you have to miss it?"

He blinked at me. "If you...."

He took a breath, and even with the fact that no one here could understand him, he switched to his inner voice.

If you decide to become Queen.... Surely you've realized by now that you might...change.

And just like that, my panic dissipated. In a way, he'd done me a favor. That implication of my choice hadn't occurred to me yet, and if it had been under any other circumstance, I might have felt a sharp pang of loss. After all, I could wake up tomorrow looking at a near stranger in the mirror. But in the face of what I'd just feared....

Eh, a bit of hair and eye-coloring felt like nothing.

"Oh, that," I said, letting out a breath of relief. "Right. *Right.* White."

Silver for your eyes, actually, judging from how they already soulflare. We'll see what happens to your hair, I guess. He looked away. *That is, if that's what you decide. And if that's even the way it would work for you.*

Seems logical, I mused. *After all, like you said, I already soulflare like you do.*

What an interesting word, *soulflare.* Apt, I supposed.

I thought of mentioning to him that my choice was made, but we were supposed to be avoiding the heavy, and somehow we'd gotten into it anyway.

He must have been thinking the same thing, because he cleared his throat and looked at me with a grin. "So, what's *your* favorite color?"

"Gold," I said automatically. Even though if you had asked me eleven days ago, it would have been sunflower yellow. Similar, but the difference was telling.

Especially when my cheeks started heating at my slip. And Ben's grin widened into a beam. He dazzled me, my sun.

We continued trading those light questions, but somehow every time kept dipping into the heavier. All the while, we danced around the *one* question, but if Ben wanted to ask it as much as I did, then he must have come to the same conclusions as I had. Now, sitting in this plane, surrounded by people, as we flew over the northern Atlantic hoping to find a Tree of Ice...was not the time.

CHAPTER NINETEEN

BLOW

KORIBEN

FLAME ABOVE AND BELOW, I thought when we finally got up out of our seats. I had never been so glad to stand in my life. More than just the cramped quarters, the forced immobility had killed me. I'd never had to stay so still for so long in my memory, not even as a student. Although as Sarah and I waited in the tight aisle for our turn to get out of the belly of this artificial bird, I still couldn't stretch as much as I wanted to, and I had to duck my head besides.

And yet, conversely, part of me had never wanted those peaceful hours I'd had with Sarah to end. Not when so much uncertainty lay ahead. Even given the emotional pain those hours had of forcing myself to keep to casual talk, to keep from touching her, and most of all to keep from asking her....

No. That might overly influence her decision regarding her birthright. Only after she had made *that* choice, and truly made that choice, in front of the Tree, regardless of what she might be thinking now...

...could we talk about after.

I didn't let myself think right now about whether the Trees would still allow a union with her if she declined what the Tree of Ice offered her. I most *certainly* did not let myself think about being forced to....

No, I put up a wall there. Locked the gates and threw away the key. I had to focus right now, after all.

And on far more mundane but, according to Sarah, dangerous things. Like answering questions about what was in the bag on my shoulder and what I was doing on their soil. The humans I talked to didn't seem so threatening to me, nor did they seem to care much about my well-rehearsed answers, but Sarah had been so serious about this part that I took this seriously, too. And I was ever mindful of her warning that the greatest danger was in attracting attention, because it was the gorhawk you had to worry about, not your fellow oramose.

Besides, Sarah's beaming hug afterward made that bit of effort worth it.

In a blur, we were passing out of the larger structure and out again into the open, where Jake began arranging for a few cars to take us away. I distracted myself from that stomach-churning prospect by studying my surroundings curiously. Sarah did too, although probably for her own reasons. Her sigh was one of relief.

"Greenland. We made it."

This "land of green" had little that was green about it; the Pennsylvania where Sarah had lived had had much more. From my vantage, I saw mostly rocky hills with a bit of green turf sprinkled here and there and dusty roads. I had to admit that it had its own kind of beauty, though. It looked so open and free, which was a true breath of fresh air compared to the claustrophobic conditions in the plane.

And always, of course, I kept an eye out for danger and stayed next to Sarah. For all our frantic hurry this morning, things seemed to be going too well so far. So far, the Trees had kept us ahead of our enemies, but that could change at any moment, and with little warning.

I longed to transform *now*, but I knew better than to ask Sarah about that. We were still among her kind, and changing into our drakáforms in front of them had been her most ardent prohibition. But Flame, I could use the air under my wings right now, could use the fire in my belly and the armor of my scales, and if I could, that counted double for Yvera. It was an act of true loyalty that was keeping her by my side and not tearing into that open sky, which she stared at with a ferocious hunger.

It was a good thing we had that break, because all too soon, we were climbing into those tiny, enclosed metal wagons of death. And this time, Sarah and I were the only ones of our group in the car, since apparently no one could sit in the seat next to the man operating the contraption. When Sarah gave him the code that signified the location she wanted him to take us to (one of these "addresses," similar to the one she had me memorize), the man looked at her strangely, but the first car was taking off, so he shrugged and followed.

The man drove the car much more slowly than Sarah's father had, and there were far fewer cars around. And perhaps knowing what to expect now, it wasn't *quite* so terrifying. Still, my stomach churned. If I never got in another car again, it would be too soon.

The cars came to a blessed stop not a quarter deken later and allowed us to get out. Jake paid them all, and they drove off, still giving us strange looks. I wondered if I should be concerned about that. It seemed to me that they found our behavior odd, and wasn't that a problem?

"Well," Sarah said, looking at our destination: a spindly pile of wood and metal scraps that had probably once been meant as a storage shed of some sort. "Let's hope this is what we think it is and not some sort of trap."

"What *do* we hope it is?" I asked warily, sniffing the air.

Sarah held up the sticky paper that she'd torn from the package that had contained our booklets. "This is the address that the passports came from. It could be a clue from the Tree, so Dad and I thought it was at least worth checking."

"For?"

"Ideally, a moonpath. That would make things...simpler."

"Otherwise, it's just you three, carrying us to the northeast across hundreds of miles of frozen waste," Jake said placidly. "Not ideal, in timing for you or in safety for the humans."

"Like I said," Sarah offered to her father, but it was with a grimace. "They could probably keep us warm enough. And they have plenty of food, even aside from the stuff we gave them to carry from home."

"Let's see what we find," Jake said simply. But he waited, looking at her.

"Oh. Right. I'm in charge. Um...Ben, I delegate this part to you. Considering the potential trap and all of that."

"Lovely," I said. But I was glad she entrusted this to me. "Yv, you first. Kor, you stay with them. I'll take up the rear."

"*Finally*," Yvera said with relish, striding forward. She paused, then looked back at Sarah with narrowed eyes.

"Yes," Sarah said with an eye roll. "Since there's nobody and nothing in sight, you can bring out weapons."

"Excellent," Yvera said, bringing out a long knife and a shield—the corporal, nonmagical kind. I was a bit surprised at her restraint, but then, that shack wouldn't allow for much freedom of movement.

"Then can I have my gun now?" Michael said irritably.

"Oh, right, sure," Sarah said. "In fact, Ben, it's probably a good time to give me mine, too."

I brought out both of their weapons in their holsters and handed them over.

Once she had her gun in place, I handed Sarah her shield bands pointedly. She said she hadn't wanted to wear them at the airport; something about things that detected metal. Now she sighed at the sight of them, but she took off her coat to put them on.

"Ooo, what are those?" Rachel asked. "They're pretty."

"They're not meant to be pretty. They're shields."

"Those?" Michael said with a snort.

Sarah glared at him as she tied the last strap. Suddenly, dual silver fields of magic burst from the circular centers of each of the bands, large enough to cover her from head to toe on each side. Though they originated from the bands, they weren't directly connected to them now; an entire half a foot of empty air separated them. Which was good. That meant that their utility wasn't reliant on the strength of Sarah's arms; if they were hit with a blow, they might hold themselves without transferring the kinetic impact to her. That's what I'd been hoping for.

Sarah started a bit, then firmed up her face, as if pretending she knew this was what would happen all along. She nodded proudly to her older brother, who had jumped back and now stared.

My lips pulled into a smile.

"Shields," Sarah repeated, then dismissed them.

Then, despite the cool weather, she handed her coat back to me.

"At least for a bit," she explained when I gave her a look of concern. "Until we know whether it's safe."

"We can probably adjust the straps to be on the outside of the sleeves—"

"I'll be fine for a bit, Ben," she insisted.

I sighed and relented, putting her coat away.

"Ready?" Yvera said dryly, her eyes having never left the shack. "Because if this *is* a trap, it's waiting patiently."

"Ready," Sarah said sheepishly. Then looked at me.

I nodded to Yvera, and she started forward again, the rest of us following.

She paused in front of the building, and all three of us drakón strained all our senses to detect whether anything was inside. Then looked at each other.

I don't smell anything but damp stone, rust, dirt, and wood, I sent to just my wings.

Yvera narrowed her eyes. *Nothing warm, certainly.*

Nothing magical, either, Kor said, then added dryly, *Not that that means as much as it once did.*

Alright—Yv, Kor, you go inside. I'll stay with the others.

My wings nodded and slipped inside the door of the shack, one swiftly after the other. Kor came out less than a dek later, shrugging. "It's clear as far as we can tell. If it's a trap, it's cleverly set to spring for someone other than us."

Meaning Sarah. Her eyes met mine, showing we had come to the same conclusion.

Sarah frowned. "It might not *be* a trap. After all, the most likely person to send us the passports was the Tree...or someone following Her instructions. But if it is, and not even Kor can detect it, then there's only one way to find out."

I sighed. "I was afraid you'd say that."

"Yv," I called, knowing she should be able to hear me from here, especially through all the cracks in those walls. "Come out and stay with Sarah's family."

Lowering my voice to a normal volume, I looked at my leftwing. "Kor, go back inside and be ready. I'll bring Sarah."

Kor nodded and disappeared inside, leaving the doorway vacant for Yvera to come out a moment later, though she cast me a glare as she came to stand next to the Linds. I knew what that glare meant. It was her job to protect *me*, and I could be putting myself in this trap to protect Sarah.

We each have our duties, Yv, I told her with a mental sigh. I was just lucky that mine toward Sarah was the one that trumped them all.

"Let me go first," I told Sarah, and she nodded.

I walked up to the shack slowly, senses straining, magic at the ready, burning in my blood. Just before the threshold, I reached out and took Sarah's hand, and I could feel her cool magic underneath the surface as well. Her hand was sweaty, belying her outward calm. Ever my *sera*.

I led her inside.

And nothing...happened.

We stood there for moment upon moment as our eyes adjusted to the relative dimness, waiting. And yet the only sound was the whistling of the wind through the boards and the creaking of the loosely bound wood. It truly seemed as if the greatest danger to Sarah was this precarious pile of sticks and corrugated metal panels collapsing on top of her.

Which, trust me, I was still worrying about.

Finally, Sarah let out a breath. "Well, that was anticlimactic. But I'll take it."

She turned and leaned outside the doorway without letting go of my hand. "Looks like it's safe to come in."

"Are you sure?" I said dryly, looking up at the peaked roof dubiously.

"Oh, it's stood this long, it will stand a bit longer, Ben," Sarah said dismissively. She finally let go of me to walk around the shack. "Honestly. You'd think a hold collapse would be much more dangerous than this."

Kor, who had been standing in one of the far corners from us, smirked at me.

"We take extreme care to prevent that," I protested, but I came into the center of the room to make way for her family to filter inside. "Seems to me as if no one took care with *any* of this."

I knew it wasn't just me when Rachel, Michael, and even her father cast wary looks around. David just examined everything with interest. As far as I could tell, he considered all this some sort of exciting adventure.

"Maybe that's precisely the point," Sarah said, stooping to brush at the dirty cement floor. "Hiding in plain sight, remember? Making this place seem so worthless, so innocuous.... Ah!"

Her brushing had revealed a pattern etched into the floor, hence her eager exclamation.

"Ben, do you have a broom or anything?"

I rapidly went through my ether storage at a speed of thought and feeling that should have been impossible, but somehow, drakón could do it with our hoards. Otherwise, they would become unmanageable almost instantly. "Er...no. I don't think so, actually."

She blinked up at me. "You have an entire dragon's hoard, and you don't have a broom?"

"It's not like I have to clean up in there," I protested. "I usually keep my cleaning tools where I need them."

For...when I had the time to use them.

"Here, Sarah," Kor said as he handed her a wooden-handled brush with long, sturdy but soft bristles—the kind used in scholarly excavations.

Sarah's eyes lit up, and she grabbed the brush. "Perfect. Thanks, Kor."

I glared at him, and he smirked back.

With the brush, Sarah revealed the pattern etched into the floor that had previously been covered in sandy dirt. The outline looked familiar, but Sarah and her father, who was bending over it with his hands braced on his thighs, came to it first.

"Greenland," Sarah said, looking up at him.

He smiled thinly. "That's what it looks like. Goodness knows I've stared at enough maps of it today to recognize it."

Which would also be why the shape had even been remotely familiar to me.

"We're here, right?" Sarah said thoughtfully, putting her finger next to the dot that would be in the southwestern coast.

"Yes, that would be Nuuk. Although, judging from the lack of anything around, we're outside the city proper right now."

"And we need to be somewhere around here."

She put her finger in the northeast quadrant.

And then the outline glowed faintly with white light.

Sarah gasped, and I guessed it was from more than just the glow. I saw why when she lifted her finger. Underneath where her finger had been was now the faintest dot of light, far fainter than the glowing outline, so dim it would not have shown up without the darkness of the shack.

"That's it," Sarah breathed, looking at the dot.

"That?" Michael demanded. "That's all we're getting from this stop? Just a dot on a map, which probably doesn't do us any good anyway, since we don't have anything to take a picture of it anymore, and we aren't exactly going to be flying high enough to compare, anyway?"

"That's not all we got, Michael," Sarah said softly, still staring at the dot. She put her entire hand over it and closed her eyes in concentration.

When she opened them, they were glowing silver with excitement.

"Ben, I can *feel* something. When I touch it, I can feel something there, far, far in the distance."

She pointed to the northeast.

My flameheart pulsed faster. "Can you surge us there?"

She shook her head. "Maybe eventually. But it's too weak right now—inactive."

My flameheart lowered. "Because it's day."

It was...*still* day. The oddity of that hadn't occurred to me until that moment.

Sarah must have thought of the same thing, because her eyes widened again. This time in worry. She looked at Jake.

"Dad, we're in *Greenland*. In the middle of *summer*."

I knew by now that was far to the north of their world. I realized the problem, and my flameheart began pulsing more rapidly again. I found Sekinek in my mind and reviewed His path in my memory, and realized with dread that He should have sunk past the horizon a long time ago. That dread dispelled the awe that I had felt that I now had that legendary, almost mythological sun now feeding into my flameheart.

"Near the Land of the Midnight Sun," Jake agreed grimly.

"Is it even going to set?" she asked anxiously.

"It's past the solstice," Jake said slowly. "That was a month ago. But...I don't know, Sarah. And I'm afraid we have no way to find out, unless we leave and go ask someone."

Michael folded his arms and snorted. "Great. So, let me guess, that means we didn't get anything out of this after all."

Sarah's face hardened into resolve. "No. The Tree sent us *here* for a reason." She jabbed the dot that represented our location.

"And She sent us *when* for a reason. She wouldn't have brought all of this together here and now if it were impossible. There has to be a way...."

Sarah's eyes fell on me, brightening with an idea. She motioned for me to join her. "Ben, come here. Come touch this with me."

"Like the door at the back of the shrine?" I asked, kneeling beside her.

"Maybe," she said excitedly.

She laid her hand over the dot to the northeast, and I laid mine on top of hers. I felt a stir of power inside me, and the glowing outline of the land increased in luminosity, but Sarah's shoulders sank.

"It's...not enough. It's stronger, definitely. I'm sure now that with your help, I could surge all of us there—if the door were open. But...it's not."

"Then it *will* open," I said, meeting her gaze. "I trust Her. And I trust you. It will open, and you will get us there."

She smiled slightly at me. *Thank you.*

Out loud to everyone, she said, "That seems to be our best option. We might lose a few hours if we wait to see if there will be any night, but if there is, we could gain so much more."

"Perhaps we do not need Sekinek to entirely set," Kor pointed out.

"Seki what now?" Rachel asked.

"That's what they call our sun," Sarah said with a sigh as she climbed to her feet.

"You've named our sun?" Rachel asked Kor blankly.

"You haven't?" Kor returned, raising an eyebrow.

"Well, it only makes sense, Rachel," Sarah said. "They have six suns in their own Realms to keep track of. Besides, suns are their source of power and safety. They're important to them."

She was right, of course, although I'd never heard someone put it that way.

Reverently, I said to her, "Flame Above *and* Below."

The Tree to guard and tend us down below, and above....

Sarah blinked, making the connection in her mind. "Wait, you revere the sun as much as the Tree?"

I smiled. "Who do you think is Her other half? The Sunfather watches over us just as much as the Flamemother does. If...from a greater distance."

"Ironic then," Kor said, "that right now, Sekinek is not entirely our ally. But neither might He be our foe. If He can lower enough to put this land in twilight, then it might actually be the perfect time of balance between yours and Ben's powers, and the gate might open."

"Oh," Sarah said thoughtfully. "Good point. That just might work."

"You realize what we risk by waiting, though," Kor cautioned. "More than just potentially losing a few hours. If we are being pursued, then that might just be all the time our enemies need to catch up."

"Sounds about right," Sarah said with a sigh. "I knew this was too easy."

She looked down at the outline on the floor, whose glow had by now faded. Although the dot where the Tree must be did not. As dim as it was, it still shone while all the other lights had gone out. And...was it just me, or had it become brighter?

Sarah was looking at that dot too, thinking hard. She looked up at me, face resolved. I knew what her answer would be before she said it.

"Ben, I think this is what we're meant to do."

With a lowering flameheart, I nodded slowly. "I think so, too."

"Right, everyone," Sarah said, putting her hands together. "This is not a trap. This...is where we make our stand."

WE BEGAN PREPARING IMMEDIATELY.

Yvera scouted the area—on foot, because Sarah insisted drakáforms were still too dangerous.

"We're close enough to Nuuk that someone is bound to spot you when you take off."

When Yvera protested, Sarah kindly cut her off. "I'm sorry, Yv. But I'm not going to ruin everything now by bringing a nervous mob of humans down on us. You'll get a chance to fly again soon, I promise. I have a feeling this part of our mission ends tonight...one way or another."

I hated it when she said things like that.

But it got Yvera to comply, especially when Sarah allowed her to change out of the Earthren clothing and back into her armor. As soon as she was dressed properly, she took off at a run across those rocky hills that almost turned her into a blur.

Meanwhile, Kor and I laid wards of protection in wide circles around that shack: fields of defense and offense that would activate in a time of danger. Not knowing what we would face, we made them so strong and all-encompassing that we waited to finish them until Yvera returned so that they would not attack her.

I left Kor to do something about strengthening the shack—if only because we didn't want it collapsing on top of our way out—while I ducked inside to check on Sarah.

While we had worked outside, she had been preparing her family for what might be coming. She also mentioned to me that she might try calling the rest of her family in her hold with her ice-image magic to see how they were faring. So I wasn't surprised to see her kneeling and Michael hunched around another cleared section of floor that glowed with vibrant colors that would not otherwise have been there.

What I did not expect to see was Jake holding and comforting a pale, sobbing Rachel, or for David to be standing back, looking dazed.

That's when I noticed the paleness and abject horror on Sarah's face, previously hidden from my first glance in the reflected glow.

My flameheart sputtered.

Flame, no. What have you done to her?

"What is it?" I demanded, striding over.

Sarah didn't even look away from the scene in front of her. "See for yourself," she whispered.

Michael stood back, face hard, to make room for me.

I kneeled carefully next to Sarah, putting my hand gently on her back, and looked.

I saw ashen ruins. Tongues of flames still licked, embers still burned, but the fires were mostly out, leaving only jagged edges of the structures sticking out of the ground like black bones, the skeleton of some great beast long since slain and flesh burned to the ground. Even outside of the structures, the ground was ashen, and husks of crumpled metal sat on scorched concrete.

It was the metal husks on their concrete pads that finally made me recognize what this was, a moment before Sarah whispered the word.

"Home."

She leaned into me weakly. "That's my house, Ben. Or...what's left of it."

I was still for a moment. Then a consuming fire of my own grew within me.

She turned into me, and I put my arms around her. I felt the wetness as she began to quietly cry. The image faded and the ice retreated as she stopped concentrating.

Silently, she said to me, *When I said that I would burn it down to save my family....*

This is not your fault, I told her, carefully keeping the bonfire growing inside of me from leaking into my voice. *You saved your family, remember?*

Yes, she whispered. *But not the others.*

What do you mean? I asked in alarm.

That...wasn't just my house, Ben. It was at least the other two, on either side. Maybe more. I couldn't see from that angle. I...didn't want to see more.

I stilled again as I realized what that meant. But even then, there was more.

"You realize what this means, right?" Michael muttered to Jake. "They're going to know from our flight info that at least half of us didn't die in that. We're going to be branded as arsonists and murderers at best, terrorists at worst. If a manhunt isn't on for us now, it will be soon. I'm surprised we even made it out of—"

"Michael, not now," Jake said tightly as Rachel's sobs increased in volume, loud enough that Kor heard and came inside.

I didn't understand all the implications of what Michael had said. But I understood enough.

And then I saw red.

The Devourer had not just hurt Sarah with the loss of her home, and not just the loss of potentially many other lives, though the latter was probably the only reason Sarah cried into me now. It had blamed its horrific act on Sarah and made her the blackest of traitors in the minds of her own people.

I carefully controlled my breathing, reeling back the red. It didn't serve me—or, most importantly, Sarah—now.

That was not your fault, I repeated to her.

They wouldn't have died if not for me, she said dully.

They would die anyway if the Devourer consumed them.

I should have saved them too....

Sarah, there is no mortal—or immortal—way we could have saved them all. All we can do is keep going to save who we can. If we stop now, then the Devourer wins, and we lose everyone.

Her next words nearly extinguished my flameheart. *Why do I deserve to live, Ben?*

It was the question I asked myself nearly every day.

Except hearing it from *her*....

I crushed her to me. I wanted to physically and mentally shout at her that it was because I loved her. But I knew that made no sense in the grand scheme of things and would not comfort her now.

It's not a matter of deserving anything, I said finally. *Everyone deserves to live. And no one deserves to have their lives taken like that. But* you *did not take them. The Devourer did this because it knew it would hurt you. That is the only reason. It would have done the same to anyone the Tree had chosen, anywhere. This is not your fault.*

She shifted to look up at me, so I turned my head to look down at her. Her eyes were wet and silver.

I think...I might be able to accept that, someday. Do you think...you'll ever be able to accept that Svyer isn't yours?

I inhaled sharply. I would have looked away, but she reached up and captured my face with her hand. Even that gentle touch held me in place.

Svyer wasn't your fault, Ben, she whispered.

I closed my eyes, unable to meet those too wise, too clear silvers any longer. Unable to bear how they saw right into the darkest parts of me, as always. And loved me anyway.

Even though she shouldn't.

She pressed on. *The Devourer hurt her to hurt you. And it would have done the same to any Golden Heir.*

Yes.

But why did it have to be *me*?

Why did *I* have to be the one to keep living?

I expected no answer. I had never gotten one before, and I never thought I would. I thought it would forever remain an unknowable mystery, one of those things that I had to just someday accept on faith, even though every day it seemed more impossible to do so as I sunk further and further into despair.

But then, in the depths of my flameheart, a voice whispered.

Because she needs you.

I stilled, even as Sarah curled back into me for more comfort.

The voice was not finished.

And We need you both. Or all are lost.

CHAPTER TWENTY

STAND

SARAH

FOR BETTER OR FOR worse, I didn't have long to mourn.

Time passed in a pained blur as Ben held me, but eventually, Kor came up to us. "Sekinek is below the horizon, Ben. Has been for a while now."

"I know," he sighed. "Is Yvera back?"

"Yes. We need to complete the wards now."

The tears had stopped by then, fading into numbness. I was able to pull away with surprising ease. Not calm, but...stillness. What was inside of me now was hardening into something new.

And that something needed *action*.

"I'll come with you," I told Ben as he stood.

"Sarah...."

"I need to be doing *something*, Ben."

He sighed but nodded and pulled me to my feet. He understood what I felt—perhaps more than anyone else in the Seven Realms and Earth could. So, we walked hand in hand outside.

As Kor had said, the sun was now out of sight. But that didn't mean it was dark. The sky was pale and dusky, but still surprisingly bright, and it continued its darkening progression at a snail's pace as Kor and Ben worked and Yvera kept a lookout.

At first I just watched Ben and Kor, knowing that even Ben would refuse to take energy from me now. After all, it wasn't as if I had more than he did at this point. So I just tried to learn, in case I would be able to do the same someday.

Similar to how Kor had traced lines of sapphire power over the moon-path openings, Kor and Ben had traced overlapping circles, diamonds, and triangles in sapphire and gold on the ground. The lines faded out of view when they weren't actively working on them, which was good for avoiding notice; this much was bad enough if any planes were to spot them from the air. At least we were on a slight rise, so the ground wouldn't be easily visible from the road that was lower and a few hundred feet away.

They had done most of the work already and were just tracing the last lines along a gap they had made in each one, perhaps to let Yvera through. Each ward flared as it was finished and faded from sight.

"There," Ben said when he'd finished his last one, the innermost circle, since they had understandably worked their way backward to finish them. "We're as ready as we're going to be, I suppose."

Following a curious impulse, I crouched and put one hand to the ground. To my surprise, I could *feel* the wards, even though I couldn't see them, through both the ground and through my connections, however faint in Kor's case, to both of them.

Then, just to see if I could, I sent power through the ground.

All the wards flared brightly at once, hotter than ever. Ben stumbled back, Kor stared.

"Sarah! What did you do?" Ben demanded.

I shrugged. "I thought they could use a boost, so I tried to give them one. And it worked."

Just for the fun of it, I reached down again and sent another surge, nearly blinding us with the brightness of the momentary light.

That...had probably not been the smartest move. In terms of conceal-ment, that is. If some pilot or satellite hadn't already reported the strange patterns around this shack, they probably had now.

Ben stared, but Kor finally unfroze and chuckled, shaking his head. "Of course. You can strengthen more than just us. You can strengthen our magic *itself*."

"Well, *now* we're as ready as we're going to be," Ben muttered. "Sarah, don't spend more now. Save your strength for what's coming. After all, we can't reach the Tree without you."

I sighed. "You're right."

He looked at Kor and pointed at the shack. "How do you think that *thing* will hold up now?"

Ben was clearly prejudiced against any structure that wasn't literally rock solid. Of course...I knew better than ever now why that was the case. Grief and guilt threatened to drag me under again, but I pulled myself back.

"As well as I can make it," Kor said with a smirk. "Are you sure you don't want Sarah—"

"No, that will do," Ben said firmly.

"And just in time," Yvera said, pointing to the west.

There, clouds gathered, blocking out the dusky sky—dark, boiling, menacing. And moving far too swiftly to be natural.

I...knew those clouds.

"Tell me that's not...." I said, mouth dry and heart pounding.

Ben came next to me and gripped my shoulder. His wings came to stand on either side of him. None of them spoke, which was how I knew. So, we just watched the oncoming storm together.

Yvera finally broke the silence. "He's not even trying to be subtle, is he?"

"Well, he hasn't revealed himself yet, even through ghost lightning, so in a way, he is," Kor answered grimly. "If the Devourer holds sway in this world, it seems to be in secret. It isn't going to let Solim spoil that secret...just yet."

"Time to go inside, Sarah," Ben said grimly.

"Ben—"

He gave me a hard look. "You have to let us know when the gate is open, don't you? Because the *moment* it is, we need to leave."

He looked up at the clear part of the sky, which had darkened enough to reveal a few stars. "Which hopefully is *soon*."

I let out a resigned breath. Then nodded. I held up my arms, and he understood what I wanted—and probably wanted it just as much. He pulled me up and gave me a blazing kiss, hot and demanding. Only seconds later, though, he broke it and lowered me back down.

"Go," he said simply. "And keep your family inside, if you can. There's nothing they can do, so they don't need to see this. We'll do our duty out here."

"Come when I call," I said, swallowing thickly.

"I will," he promised. "We all will."

I made my steps quick, even though my feet felt like they were filled with lead, because those clouds were over halfway toward us.

Dad and Michael were talking when I came back in, their discussion intense for all that it was whispered. Which explained why even Dad hadn't noticed that danger was coming. Poor Rachel was sitting on the ground with her arms wrapped around her legs, staring at nothing. David had his arm around her, and he didn't look in much better shape.

I felt a fury grow inside me that I had never felt before. Neither of my siblings had deserved this rough awakening to the reality of evil.

But then again, neither had I, nor Ben, nor anyone who had suffered because of the Devourer's never-ending hunger and Solim's cruelty. There was even the possibility that Solim had been the one to destroy my home and the lives of uncounted others this very morning. That sounded like what I knew of him.

Suddenly, I understood Kor's rage when he'd realized how close he had come to ending one of the greatest threats to all the Realms. Those clouds that I could still see through the doorway, far from making me want to hide, now made me want to burst out there and be the one to end him myself.

But I couldn't.

What I could do...was this.

And in the end, perhaps the greatest revenge against Solim was to keep living. To keep trying to save the ones I could.

I walked to the center of the room and got down on one knee next to the map there.

"Brace yourselves," I told my family calmly. "There's a storm coming."

The Tree dot was glowing brighter now, but I knew even before I put my finger over it that it wasn't quite enough.

"A storm?" Michael asked. "What kind of storm?"

He walked to the doorway and looked out. And stilled. Dad joined him.

"The worst kind," I said grimly.

"Let me guess," Dad said. "Those clouds aren't natural."

"Nope. You still need a bad guy, Michael? Well, he's coming right for us now."

"The Devourer?" Dad asked quietly.

"No. But the next worst thing. *That* is what happens when a powerful drakón goes to the dark side."

"And what are your 'good' ones doing now?" Michael snapped.

"Getting ready to defend us, if you'd bother to look. They would give their lives, every one of them, to buy us the time we needed to get away."

Even Yvera. I was sure of that now.

"Is there anything we can do?"

To my surprise, the one to speak was Rachel. When I turned to look at her, her eyes were focusing again. Hardening.

Even the softer Linds were made of tougher stuff than they looked.

"Unfortunately, no," I said, grimacing. "My job is to stay here and wait for the moment the moongate opens so I can pull us through. Theirs is to guard us. I hate to say it, but...we'll probably help them most by staying in here, close together. Easier for them to shield us that way, makes us less of a target."

"Is there anything we can do to help *you*?" Dad said, kneeling next to me.

I frowned in thought. "Hmm. Maybe. I wonder—"

Just then, hurricane-force winds hit the shack, sending it quaking. If Kor hadn't magically reinforced it, I was certain it would have collapsed then and there.

I felt a surge of magic around our perimeter, perhaps one of the wards activating. The wind decreased but didn't entirely fade. Darkness fell over us, making the already dim light in the shack almost nonexistent. Ben shouted something that was lost to the wind, and I had to mentally anchor myself to the ground to keep myself from running out to him.

Then lightning flashed, lighting up the shack eerily for a split second in cold white light. Even if I hadn't felt another ward flare to life and then suddenly die, I would have known the lightning had aimed for us. I smelled the burned ozone in the air, and thunder cracked above our heads in an ear-splitting roar. And hidden inside that slightly more natural roar, I heard another, one that any other Earthren might have mistaken as part of the thunder.

But I knew better.

"Alright, everyone in!" I yelled hastily, slapping my hand over the Tree dot. "I have no idea if this will do anything, but it is sure as hell worth a shot at this point."

Lightning flashed, another ward caved, and the burning smell grew stronger as my family swiftly gathered around me without so much as a question, not even from Michael. As if we were playing some bizarre game of blindfolded Twister, they all fumbled and shuffled until their hands found mine. I don't know who was last, but I knew the moment they completed the stack, because the gate...

...opened.

"*BEN!*" I shouted with mind and voice, broadcasting it everywhere so Kor and Yvera would hear too.

Lightning flashed again, illuminating Kor and then Yvera as they dashed through the door. A field of gold illuminated the cracks in the ceiling above, explaining why Ben was waiting until the last moment.

I sent just to him, *Ben, I swear, if you die on me....*

"*In, in, put your hand in,*" I shouted to his wings over the thunder.

Kor threw up a blue orb for light as Yvera bent over, bracing a hand on David's back as she reached for our stack of hands. Then, as another flash hit, Kor did the same, and for some reason, his orb went out. The gold "sunlight" above disappeared, and in the darkness, I could have choked on the burned smell that seemed to fill my soul.

BEN!

A warm, familiar hand on my shoulder, and a surge of strength that sent the outline of Greenland shining, illuminating his hand on top of all the others.

He threw up a golden bowl of light around us just as the shack shattered into a thousand pieces.

Go, Sarah!

I pulled, and we went.

WE COLLAPSED IN ONE big, painful, lumpy heap on a cold, smooth floor in a different sort of darkness.

Grunts, yelps, and curses rang out all around as people untangled themselves. I was one of the ones at the bottom of the stack, so I had to wait breathlessly for the others to get clear. Kor, again, threw up a ball of cold sapphire light, which helped.

And showed that Ben was once again partially on top of me, this time with his front on my back, with my front being pressed against the floor. At least it was only half of him, so now with the others off, I could somewhat breathe. The reason why he didn't immediately get off too became clear when he suddenly raised his head with a jerk, as if he'd momentarily gone unconscious.

You OK? I asked urgently, craning my neck over my shoulder to look at him.

Yes, he groaned, meeting my eyes in a daze.

With terror for him out of the way, humor jutted its way in. *We have got to stop meeting like this.*

What? he asked blearily. And then his eyes widened, and he immediately rolled off me. *Sorry! Sorry!*

I only laughed. With what little breath I'd regained, that is.

"Anything broken?" I called out as I slowly pushed myself up and turned to sit on my rear. As the vertigo faded, I braced myself further with my arms behind me.

All I got was groans back, so I assumed that was a no. I saw everyone except Ben was at least sitting up or standing by now, so I took that as another good sign.

Light was increasing all around us as white streaks in the stone walls began to glow. Except these weren't the rough moonstone walls of the passages Kor and I had gone through, or even the carved conch-curves of the moonpath domes.

These walls were as smooth and polished as marble. They revealed an enormous circular room, with a ring of mighty columns carved in the shape of trees, complete with roots and branches that stretched from one to the next on the floor and ceiling, respectively. The dome straight above us was a map of the night sky every bit as breathtaking as a planetarium night show, with the background somehow remaining dark even despite the glow of its stars and of the moonstone all around.

I faced an enormous arch whose end was lost to shadow, but when I slowly stood and turned, at the opposite end, I saw a moongate, half the size of the arch, although larger than my six regular gates. The white tree on it beckoned.

Dad came up to me, looking where I looked. "I...am assuming that's a moongate."

"Yup," I said, choking up. Maybe it was the adrenaline that was still shaking its way out of my system. I gave Dad a watery smile. "Want to go see what Mom and the littles are up to?"

He put an arm around my shoulders. "That's a definite yes."

I looked back at Ben, worried about leaving him, but he was finally sitting up too, looking uninjured, if exhausted.

"Go on," he said, giving me a tired smile. "Don't worry about me. Go see your family. I'll catch up."

Heedless of the eyes of this half of my family on me, I went to him, grabbed his face, and gave him a quick kiss. *I'm very glad you're not dead,* I said as I pulled away.

His eyes glowed gold. *I'm very glad you aren't either.*

Still not quite believing my nerve, I swerved around and marched to the moongate, strictly avoiding anyone's gaze.

I stopped in front of the gate and took several deep breaths. Then I put my hands on the doors and asked them to open. They took what they needed from me, and I stepped back. They slowly swung open, revealing...

...the northern end of my hold, facing south. I blinked, but when I passed through the curtain and backed up, the gate I saw was the one from before, the one that had led to the woods outside my house.

The house that was no more...and the gate that was no more. Because what would be the point?

I truly was never going back.

I trembled. But I tried to remind myself of Kor's words. *Knowing what is going to happen is not the same thing as making it happen.*

"Sarah!" Abby squealed.

I turned to see my baby sister running to me with outstretched arms. Safe, happy...and, judging from her pajamas and the lateness of the hour, having stayed up long past her bedtime.

The tears spilled freely as I caught her up and hugged her to me. Then the twins came racing and crashed into me with a force that made me *oof* dramatically. Then Lizzy, who still technically came running but at a more sedate, grownup-like jog. She wrapped her arms around me as well, this time from behind, since my front was taken.

This...was the kind of greeting we should have had before. Not me snatching them half asleep in the dark of the morning and dumping them in this strange, new place.

This...was being welcomed home.

APPARENTLY THE LITTLES HAD their sleep schedules all messed up now, having crashed sometime in the middle of the day for a stress-induced nap—even the nine-year-old twins. So they had resisted bedtime until our ice-call to check in, and since Mom had gathered from us that we would ideally be seeing them soon, she hadn't had the heart to force the issue on them after that.

Which was just as well, because it was time for all of us to go meet a Tree.

Mom fussed a little about them being in their pajamas, but I brushed off her concerns as I walked hand in hand with Abby back through the ice curtain.

"Mom, if the Tree can't have compassion for the fact that we've all just been through hell today, then I'm not sure I want to serve Her. But I'm betting She will."

Besides, I knew time was more important at this point than appearances.

My drakón stood in the center of the rotunda, waiting for us. I was more than relieved to see Ben now standing straight and tall, smiling warmly as I approached.

Since there hadn't been proper introductions before, I stopped in front of Ben and looked at my sister. "Abby, Noah, Jonah," I said, smiling. "This is Ben."

Ben kneeled down on one knee with a gentle smile. He silently asked for the English words from me, and I quickly gave them to him. "Hello, Abby. It's good to meet you."

"I dreamed about you, too," Abby said with a grin. "You're the dragon King."

Ben's smile faded, and chills went down my spine.

"Uh, Abby," I said hastily. "I think you must have dreamed about Ben's *dad*. They look pretty similar."

"No—" Abby began in a pout, but she was drowned out by Rachel's exclamation.

"What the freakin' hell? *Ben* is a *prince*?"

I groaned. I didn't know why I'd kept putting this detail off, since the revelation was inevitable, but I had.

"He's not a prince," I said, turning to her. "He's the Heir. It's different."

"Oh, excuse me, he's the freakin' *crown* prince. How could you possibly have not mentioned this?"

"Because...it didn't matter!"

"How can it possibly not matter that *your boyfr—*"

"Rachel," Dad said sternly. "Now is not the time."

"Actually, Dad," I said with a groan, putting a hand to my forehead. "Now...is probably a good time to explain a couple things. I didn't earlier because I didn't want to freak you all out more than I had to in one sitting. But it...has to do with what's coming next."

Michael snorted. "You mean the part where this magical tree all changes us into something else and you get a power boost?"

"Sort of," I said, not quite meeting his eyes. "See...Trees—I think I mentioned that They pick leaders, right?"

Dad smiled thinly. "*Very* briefly."

"Well...the top leader they pick is called a King or a Queen. But it's not like what you think a king or queen is here. They're...servants. They *really* are. They protect their people. Serve them. Love them. Would give their lives for them. The Tree wouldn't have anything less. Ben's dad is the King of his people, and he's...."

I shook my head, without words. "He's something else."

I smiled at Ben briefly, but his answering smile was strained. I hoped Abby's mistaken comment hadn't shaken him too badly.

I looked back at my family. "Then the Tree picks an Heir, the person who will become the next Monarch. That's Ben for his people right now, but it's not because he's the King's son. The Tree doesn't care about that. She just picks who is worthy, so that could have been anyone from his clan. Again, the Heir isn't some spoiled person who gets waited on and goes to a bunch of parties. From the moment he became Heir, Ben had to work harder than you can imagine to serve and protect his people. In fact, he's the one who often has to brave the greatest dangers of them all."

I grinned at him. "That's how he got saddled with protecting me."

This time, his answering grin was more genuine. "And I don't regret a dek of it."

"Speak for yourself," Yvera muttered.

"Oh, you know you like her too," Kor said, looking across Ben at her to give her a wink.

Which reminded me of their roles. While I was explaining things (and because a premonition was growing in my gut), I might as well finish.

"The Monarch and Heir don't serve alone, though. They, in turn, pick two helpers. And, because they're a dragon people, they call them rightwings and leftwings."

I gestured to Yvera. "Yvera is Ben's rightwing. That means she's his primary bodyguard and is in charge of Ben's elites. She'll also be a military leader of some kind when Ben becomes King someday."

"Head of the Warflight, thank you," she said with a sniff.

"Right, sorry," I said soothingly.

I gestured to Kor. "Kor is Ben's leftwing. That means he's...everything else."

Kor chuckled. "How eloquent."

"Well, it's true, isn't it?" I said in exasperation. "Counselor, researcher, diplomat, spymaster—"

"You're a spy?" David asked excitedly.

Kor winced. "Why is *that* what everyone always focuses on?"

"Because spies are hot," Rachel said with a smirk and a hand on one hip.

Kor's eyes grew speculative as they rested on her. "Are they...."

"Moving on," I said quickly. "The Monarch has a rightwing and leftwing, the Heir has a rightwing and leftwing. There. Think you guys have got that?"

Michael demanded, "Sarah, why are you telling us all of this now?"

I took a deep breath. "Because.... That's all the people that the Tree of Flame, *their* Tree, has chosen. For the Six Realms. For the Seventh Realm, our Realm, the Tree of Ice...told us She intends to do the same thing. At least...She told us that She intends to make me...Queen."

They all stared at me. All, that is...except Dad and Abby. Abby just beamed at me proudly, clenching my hand and swinging it between us. Dad's eyes, when they met mine...were sad.

He already knew. The Tree had told him, or he had figured it out enough on his own. So he was the first to understand what a burden, not a distinction, this calling was.

Michael broke the silence. "The queen of *what*?"

"Hon," Laura said, quietly, but with a warning edge to her voice as she put her hand on his shoulder.

The twins were looking bored, though, and were peeking around, looking as if they'd rather be chasing each other around this space, and the only thing holding them in place was Mom's determined grip on each.

"That's what I said," I answered wearily. "What indeed. Certainly not you all. You're not subjects. You're my *family*. So, yes, you could say it's an empty title in that sense. But not in the sense that it's *supposed* to mean. I understand that now. Making me Queen means I am supposed to serve you. Protect you. Love you. And that's why it's a title that comes with literal power—magical power—that I need to protect you, and that Ben's people desperately need for both of us to protect them from what's coming in...."

I looked at Ben. He looked back, pained. "Today. This is the day of the Dark Solstice."

"Right," I said numbly. "Today...."

"Are you even hearing this?" Michael demanded, looking at Dad.

"Yes," Dad said calmly. "The question is, are you?"

He clenched his jaw. "You can't possibly be intending to allow Sarah to—"

"May I remind you that Sarah is not just a legal adult but that she has always been the most serious, mature, and self-aware of all of you," Dad said flatly. "I love each of you equally for your individual strengths. But if I could trust anyone to make this kind of decision for themselves, fully knowing the consequences, and doing it for all the right reasons...it would be Sarah."

I stood there, stunned. I was fairly certain that was the highest compliment my reticent father had ever given me.

He looked at me, face pained. "And I think this Tree knows that too."

Michael looked at Mom. "Mom...."

Her eyes were shining with tears, but she just shook her head. "It's her choice."

I swallowed slowly. Then looked at my brother. "They're right. I've made my choice, Michael. You can't stop me. I just hope...you'll still stand with me.... Will you?"

Michael looked at me, and the fear for me that I knew had been eating at him all along finally came to the surface. He wasn't normally this much of a jerk, really.

He swallowed. "I...I don't want to lose you, sis."

I came forward and hugged him. He hugged back tightly. He couldn't quite give a drakón bone-crushing hug, but he could give a good one all the same.

"This should be my burden," he said thickly. "Not yours."

"Then help me bear it," I whispered.

His arms slowly loosened. He held me by my arms while he looked me in the eye for a long moment. Then he closed his eyes briefly and let go slowly, nodding.

"Alright."

"Thanks, big brother," I said with a wan smile.

"Go on," he said with a flap of his hand. "Let's get on with this."

He smirked at Noah and Jonah. "Before the twins explode."

Noah smirked back. "Yeah, before we explode."

I walked backward for a few slow steps, looking at all my family, taking them all in. They were the reason I was doing this, after all. Them...and my sun right behind me. And his wings. And all the good people I had met who didn't deserve the fate that others had met today.

And...for me. For that little girl who was once strapped to an altar, thinking there was absolutely nothing she could do to save herself. For the strong, powerful, valiant woman I was becoming. For the dreams I was ready to fight for.

I turned around. Smiled as bravely as I could at my drakón. Then went around them and walked toward the dark unknown.

Where my power...and my Tree...had always waited for me.

CHAPTER TWENTY-ONE

CROWNED

SARAH

THE ARCH DID NOT remain dark for long, of course. As I approached, the moonstone inside it glowed, and now we could see that the lofty passage beyond stretched only maybe fifty feet before it came to an enormous gate. This time the tree on it was made of what seemed to me to be the same silver metal that was in my arm guards and gun. It shimmered with almost liquid movement in the moonstone's light.

I paused in front of the double doors for a moment. Not out of trepidation, because for each step I'd taken since the rotunda, that had slowly left me.

No....

I paused to take in the stillness, to find that quiet place deep inside me. I realized after a moment that I, who had never really felt a connection to a higher power all my life, despite Mom's best efforts....

Was pausing in reverence.

Ben really was rubbing off on me.

With that thought, I raised my hands and gently placed them on the doors.

The wordless pulse I sent to them wasn't a request. It was a question.

And in answer, the doors began to swing inward.

By now, I was well practiced in the backing up that was necessary to give them room, although my family—not so much. I bumped into Michael, who stumbled back with us both in a wordless protest.

Inside...

...was a Tree.

She rested on a high rise that made only the bottom of Her trunk visible from this vantage point, but the tangle of Her thousands of roots that dipped in and out of the dark soil—some as big as Ben—were fully in view. As were the frosted stone steps that led up the rise to Her.

I walked into the room. That grand, cavernous room was as big as a basketball stadium, if reversed in elevation. The gradual slope of the rise took up almost the entire floor, with only a crescent of paved path and columns of ice circling around the perimeter closest to us.

The room was, of course, freezing. I could tell that from the way my breath fogged the air, from the frost that lay like a coat of magic over everything, and, when I looked up, from the blue ceiling of thick, thick ice. Yet I wasn't cold, even though I still hadn't put my coat back on. That meant I could see for myself that no goosebumps crawled up my arms. I didn't shiver. My eyes didn't sting, my throat didn't hurt.

In fact...the cold felt *good*. Invigorating. Life-giving. Every further step became stronger, surer.

Which was good, because it was going to be a bit of a climb, and I got started.

The Tree towered above us, perhaps a hundred feet thick and more than a hundred high. She wasn't entirely made of ice; that surprised me a bit, though perhaps it shouldn't have. Her trunk, roots, and branches still looked like normal tree trunks, roots, and branches, if larger than life and completely covered in frost. Only the leaves appeared to be made of ice. They glowed, providing the primary source of light in that room—although given how many thousands of them there had to be, they were quite enough to have made me at first think that the domed ice ceiling had been open to the sky.

To say that She was awe-inspiring...would be an understatement. I had never felt so small in my entire life. And yet, it wasn't in a way that was discouraging. It was simply an acknowledgement that I, as a mortal being, was only a tiny speck in this vast and wondrous universe, and yet how needed and beautiful and *loved* a speck I was *all the same*. Instead of feeling worthless and alone, I felt of more worth than ever, and more connected than ever to life across the cosmos, that precious life that Trees everywhere guarded with all the love in Their immortal souls.

Then I recognized the emotion that I was feeling in this moment, so strong it was like a heatless fire burning in my heart and blood: love.

My Tree...loved me.

More than I could have imagined anyone, anywhere, loving anything.

Of course She did.

She...was my Mother.

Tears spilled down my cheeks, the streaks frosting over quickly in the frigid air. But still I was not cold.

At last, I reached the last step and came to the round stone circle there, set into the earth and surrounded by a retaining wall of more stone, and there She stood—Her avatar, at least. Waiting for me. Smiling.

A Woman of ice, wearing a simple sleeveless gown of the same that draped down Her and spilled into multifaceted folds to the floor, concealing Her feet, if this avatar even had any. Her eyes glowed white and featureless, their shapes made even more indistinct for how they constantly emitted wisps of cool vapors.

She held out Her perfect, crystalline hands to me. Hands that glittered like diamonds.

"*Sarah, my daughter,*" She said.

Her voice was like the crunch of frost, the howl of a winter storm, the crack of deep ice, and the silence of deeply falling snow—all at once. And yet, it was full of love. Her white eyes burned heatless fires with it.

She must have known—of course She knew—why I hesitated at the top step, why my eyes drifted wistfully to those arms.

Her smile turned sad. "*Though I long to hold you, I must not. Not today. For though you are My child, you are mortal. Were I to touch you, you would have to return to Me.*"

I...could figure out what that meant.

"I...see," I said. So, I merely bowed to Her and approached, making room for my family behind me to come up and start filing around that large circle. Each of them stared, but none of them said a word. Not even the twins.

Except Abby, of course, who escaped Lizzy's grip before Lizzy knew what she was about and ignored Lizzy's desperate plea to come back. Abby trotted right up to me, where I stood across a small, circular well from the Tree, and beamed at me before beaming at the Tree.

"*Hello, Abby, My daughter,*" the Tree said, smile widening.

"I told them everything you told me to," she said proudly.

"*You did,*" the Tree agreed. "*You did very well.*"

Abby grinned the biggest grin, pulled me down to kiss my cheek, and trotted back to a stunned Lizzy.

Last of all came my drakón: first Kor, who went to stand at the left side of the steps, then Yvera, who stood on the right, then Ben, who remained at the top center.

The Tree's eyes lifted to meet his, Her face sober. "*Welcome, Heir of Flame,*" She said in Drona, "*to the Realm of Ice.*"

"Thank you for allowing me to be here, O Lady of Ice," he said quietly.

Her lips finally pulled into a small smile. "*You have proven yourself worthy. And so, though you are the first chosen of Flame to be admitted into My presence...you shall not be the last.*"

Ben blinked, as if he didn't quite know what to make of that. Which meant I most certainly didn't.

When I looked back at the Tree, Her eyes were on me.

"*There is no time now to waste. So, let us begin.*"

I nodded. I was...ready.

"*Sarah, My daughter. I have chosen you from My children to receive My power and become My Queen. Should you accept what I offer you now, you will become My Right Hand, sworn to do My will in the service of My children and to give your life, if called for, in their defense. Do you accept this, of your own will and desire?*"

Now I finally understood at least part of the reason for those past eleven days, as dangerous and painful as they had been. They had not just made me into the kind of person who even *could* say yes now. They had taught me, in ways words could never have described, just what it meant to be an Heir...and Queen.

I paused, but only again in stillness, in reverence. To show I understood the full gravity of this moment and this choice.

"I do."

"*Then accept what I offer, and become,*" the Tree said simply.

She held out Her hand, and a ball of ice appeared in it, burning with an inner light. She waved Her hand, and it floated across the dark well to me. I held out my hands, and the ball lighted in them. I was reminded briefly of the Moonstar, especially when gravity once again took over and my hands dipped under the weight. It felt remarkably...substantial, for all that it was only the size of one of my fists.

"*Place it inside your heart,*" the Tree murmured.

I stared up at Her, breathless as understanding dawned.

She smiled sadly. "*You must have a new heart, as did the Seven draká of old, and the Seven humans who swore with them. Once again, you must become something...new.*"

"This...this *is* the Second Covenant," I whispered.

"*Indeed. In its simplicity, it is to do the will of your Tree in order to receive of Her power, to become new creatures capable of saving Her children. The Covenant of Power...and Change.*"

Kor is probably freaking out *right now,* I thought numbly. If he hadn't seen it coming all along, that is. I didn't dare break with ceremony to look back to check. Besides, knowing him, he was probably perfectly calm and respectful on the outside, no matter what was going on within.

I made myself refocus and forget everything and everyone outside this smaller ring with me and the Tree...and the orb of glowing ice in my hands.

Slowly, hands trembling but not with cold, I placed the orb over my heart.

It sunk in immediately, as smoothly as if it had instantly melted, except it left not a trace behind.

And then I was in frigid agony.

I bent over from the pain, bracing myself against my legs as I gasped. Dimly, as if from a distance, I heard murmurs breaking out around, heard Ben cry out, heard the Tree say something back, felt a surge of magic.

But that all felt like a hundred miles away. Darkness filled my vision, sight left me, and my inner self became my entire world.

Ice *literally* encased my heart and began making it into something...new.

And true change...is never easy.

WAKE, DAUGHTER. TIME IS short, and the King of Flame needs you. Wake.

I blinked my eyes open.

To see Dad holding me tightly while crouching on the ground, with tears in his eyes. Which widened when mine met his.

"I'm fine, Dad," I whispered.

And I was. There wasn't a trace of hoarseness in my voice. My body felt...*alive*, in a way it never had before, not even when Svyer healed me or my power began to awake. And the reason for that became immediately clear.

Inside my chest...a heart of ice pulsed. Not with muscle, for it was now truly living *ice*. Filled...with light. And that light surged through my blood and my body with every impossible beat.

Dad stared into my eyes....

And I knew without him telling me that they would now be silver. Not just when they soulflared, but always. Until the day I died and returned to our Tree.

With dazed, almost childlike curiosity, I lifted a strand of my hair.

White. As pure as snow.

Dad closed his eyes slowly, held me tighter for one moment...and then slowly let me go.

Of course, no sooner did I sit up than Mom grabbed me, crying much more profusely than Dad had, but still somehow keeping from the loud, noisy sobs I had been expecting.

"*Mi hija*, my baby," she groaned.

"I knew this would happen, Mom," I whispered to her, tears stinging my own eyes. At least that functionality seemed like normal, though the liquid didn't seem as hot as before. "I made the choice, knowing. And I'd make it again."

"That doesn't mean you aren't my baby," Mom said, nose and eyes wet as she pulled away and cupped my face. I stared into her eyes. Those browns, that hair, that beautiful skin—all of that I got from her. And now that similarity, except the skin—which had always been lighter than hers because of Dad—was gone.

Mom's eyes burned, as if she knew what I was thinking. "And you will *always* be my baby."

I gave her a weary smile. "You're going to have to let me grow up sometime."

She smiled back, lips trembling slightly. "Oh, you can still be a woman and be my baby. That's how motherhood works."

I hugged her again, but briefly. The Tree's warning still echoed in my mind. *The King of Flame needs you.*

Had the attack already begun?

I didn't dare ask. There were still things we had to do.

So, I pulled away from her and haltingly stood.

But because I couldn't help it, I looked for Ben. He stood right where he had been before at the top of the steps. But from the rigidness of his posture, the clench of his fists, and the tightness of his jaw, I could tell that wasn't his preference. Not by far.

When I met his eyes, they were in agony. *This isn't my place. I can't interfere.* I nodded to show I understood.

Then I looked back at my Tree, who also stood where She had been before. *"Are you ready to proceed?"*

"There's more?" Mom asked, eyes widening.

"Sarah is now my Queen. But now I must choose my Heir. And then they must in turn choose their wings."

Mom's eyes flashed with unusual force. I could tell that she wanted to spit out that the Tree had asked quite enough of her family already, so I took her hand and gave it a squeeze.

"Mom. She wouldn't ask if it wasn't necessary—and necessary to save *us*, too. That's why I did this, after all."

Her shoulders sank, and her head bowed. She pulled me in for one more tight hug and then finally, reluctantly, let go and stepped back. Though she curled into Dad as soon as she did so.

The Tree gave us a moment.

Then She turned her head slowly to....

"*Rachel, My daughter. Come forward.*"

I did my very best not to stare at the Tree in dismay.

Rachel? Was my *Heir*?

I mean, I understood the Tree's options were limited, but....

Her?

Rachel, for once in her life, looked like she didn't know what to do. Frozen in indecision, her eyes darted between the Tree...and me.

After too long of a pause, I finally sighed and inclined my head, indicating for her to come stand next to me. She moved, but stiffly, each step taking a painstaking moment. Finally, she was at my side, and looking at the Tree with the most terror I had ever seen on her face.

For the first time...I felt a bit of pity for my sister. I'd gone through hell the past eleven days, but at least they had prepared me for this.

"*Rachel, My daughter. I have chosen you from My children to receive My Power and become My Heir. Should you accept what I offer you now, you will one day become Queen and My Right Hand, sworn to do My will in the service of My children and to give your life, if called for, in their defense. Do you accept this, of your own will and desire?*"

Rachel looked at me, panic-stricken, as if I had the answer.

"It's your choice," I whispered back to her. "You *can* refuse. She won't force you. This is a big thing, and if you accept it, you're going to have to give it your whole heart."

Quite literally.

Rachel stilled. Then that firmness I had seen in her eyes from before, when she had asked me if there was anything she could do, returned. Still with clear fear, but this time with resolve, she looked back at the Tree.

With a tremulous voice, she answered, "I do."

The Tree held out Her hand. "*Then accept what I offer, and become.*"

Another glowing orb of ice formed above Her hand and floated to Rachel. Rachel reached and took it with trembling hands. Then, hesitantly, eyes darting once again to me, she put the orb over her heart.

This time, when she stiffened, I was the one to hold her, and with surprising strength, I held her steady when she went limp and lowered her to the ground myself—although Dad had been hovering at the ready.

"*The pain will not be as severe for her, and it will pass more quickly,*" the Tree murmured to us. "*Even though she did not have as much time as Sarah for her Blood to awaken, she does not yet need to receive so much.*"

She gave us another moment, then sighed, the sound like the whisper of sliding snow. "*Every second now matters. Sarah, give your sister to your mother. We must continue.*"

I handed Rachel's limp body to Mom and stood.

"*It is time to choose your wings. Who among these will you have to be your rightwing?*"

The answer came right away. After all, it was what I had been suspecting would be the case ever since I had to explain these roles to my family. And what I'd known in my heart from when I first came home.

"Michael," I said solemnly, looking to the side at him with a sad smile.

Always my protector. Dad had been too, but in his own way, and he had a different role in my mind.

"*Michael, my son,*" the Tree said solemnly, giving him a start out of the shock he'd been in at my mention of his name. "*Come forward.*"

He came forward hesitantly. As soon as he reached where I was subtly pointing to my right, he whispered out of the corner of his mouth, "What does a rightwing do again?"

"Protect me," I whispered back with a smirk. "Protect *all* of us. Should come naturally to you."

"Oh," he said, blinking.

"*I confirm the worthiness of my Queen's choice,*" the Tree said solemnly. "*Michael, my son. Do you swear to protect and serve your Queen and your people with all your might and power, to defend those who cannot defend themselves, and to strive for peace whenever it is possible? And to give your life, if called to do so?*"

Michael hesitated, glancing at me, then back at his wife and son.

Laura held Tommie close, but her eyes were resolute and her chin high. She nodded to him.

Then Michael firmed and looked back at the Tree. "I do."

Once again, the Tree held out Her hand and formed an orb of light and ice. "*Then accept what I offer, and become.*"

This time, when Michael put the ice inside of him, he didn't collapse. He hissed, squeezed his eyes shut, and clenched my shoulder, but even though Dad once again stood ready, he remained standing.

I knew that was because the change *he* was undergoing didn't need to be as severe. But still that bothered me, just a little.

Even so, Michael's hair turned white before my very eyes, the color spreading from his roots to his tips within seconds. And when he gradually stilled and blinked open his eyes...the irises were silver.

I glanced back at Rachel, who had woken up by now, and Mom was helping her to her feet. The same thing had happened to her.

"Well, look at us," Rachel said shakily, with a tremulous smile. "Starting a trend. White is officially *in*."

"Rachel," I sighed. Of course she would joke about appearances at a time like this. But the better part of me knew it was her way of dealing with what was, to her, a much more significant loss.

But, knowing what would happen because she had watched me...she had paid the price anyway.

When I looked back at the Tree, She asked, "*Who among these will you have to be your leftwing?*"

"Dad," I said, looking at him.

He, like Michael, had been acting in his role from the moment I came home. All my life, in fact.

If he was surprised, he didn't show it. He was already nearby, so it only took a few steps for him to come to my left.

"*I confirm the worthiness of my Queen's choice,*" the Tree said. "*Jacob, my son. Do you swear to counsel and serve your Queen and your people with all of your mind and power, to never take advantage of another, and to always respect their rights and choices?*"

If Kor took a similar oath, he has a funny way of keeping it, I thought.

Of course, that was my most cynical side speaking. My better half knew that he had done his best, in the spirit of every letter.

He was not his brother.

"I do," Dad said without hesitation.

My heart ached when Dad curled from the pain of transformation, but other than grabbing me for balance, he held firm to not put any unnecessary weight on me. And once again, before my eyes, I watched his sandy blond hair, already flecked with gray, turn completely white, and his eyes open to silver.

"It is done," the Tree declared. "My Queen and her wings have been chosen. Now, make way for My Heir."

For the first time, I stepped aside, and Dad and Michael followed me. Whether or not they had to, they stayed at my right and left.

I still think I made the right choices, I sent to Ben. *But man, these two are going to butt heads sometimes.*

What? Ben said in mock surprise. *My wings never do that.*

I had to work hard for a moment to keep my face properly solemn.

The Tree went through the same process with Rachel, who by now had recovered much of her usual irreverent spunk. When the Tree asked her who she wanted to be her rightwing, she winked at David as she said his name.

My iceheart trembled. *No.*

It was one thing to ask my older brother to protect me. I could hardly have *stopped* him, so I might as well give him the power to protect *himself*.

But *David*....

My sweet, unflappable little brother. My gangly ray of sunshine.

It's alright, Sarah, it's alright, Ben told me hurriedly, so my heart-stricken panic must have been visible. *He'll be fine, we'll keep him safe and train him until he's older and stronger. He'll be fine, Sarah. We'll protect him. He'll be fine.*

But...the Heir is supposed to go into danger, I said faintly as I watched my pale but determined brother take his oath and receive his orb.

I am, Ben said grimly. *Because I am the Heir of Flame, and I was raised to be.*

His eyes rested meaningfully on Rachel's back. *I think things are going to work a bit differently for your Heir.*

That...made enough sense that I felt like I could finally breathe again.

When the Tree asked Rachel for her choice of leftwing, she hesitated a moment. Then, face unusually sober, she looked at Laura.

"Laura?" she said, the name a question.

Laura blinked in surprise, and so did everyone else, including me. Rachel and Laura weren't exactly enemies, but the truce between their very different natures was an uneasy one. To keep the peace, they generally avoided interacting with each other whenever possible.

The even greater shock than Rachel's offer...was Laura's acceptance. She silently handed Tommie over to Mom and took her place at Rachel's left. Michael watched his wife's oath and transformation with grim stoicism, but he knew better than to question her on this—because he liked his head right where it was on his shoulders.

"*It is done,*" the Tree said. "*My Heir and her wings have been chosen. Now, make way for my Queen and the Heir of Flame. The wings will remain behind.*"

I stared at Her, and so did Ben. When I glanced at him, he looked just as much at a loss as I was.

And then, as Ben and I made our slow ways forward to stand in front of Her, side by side, my iceheart pulsed rapidly. It was almost as if....

No, no—it couldn't be. We hadn't even *talked* about this. We hadn't—

"*Sarah, My Moontouched Queen,*" the Tree of Ice said softly. "*A grievous wrong was done to your clan many years ago, one that the Queen of Flame could have prevented, had she been heeding her Tree. Though she did not wield the knife, she failed in her duty and in her oaths in countless ways before the final act. In that failure, she and her people broke the Covenants. This Heir of Flame redeemed the Golden Crown by renewing the First Covenant, with your help and for your sake. Now you have sworn the Second, but for the redemption to be symbolically complete and the new order between the children of Ice and Flame established, there is one more thing that must be done."*

I stood frozen, unable to look up and meet Ben's eyes. I had been ready to have my body and destiny altered forever by accepting the burden of being Queen. But I hadn't been prepared for *this* to happen *today*. It was too much. Too much in eleven days. I wasn't ready. I knew what I wanted, what I dreamed, but it was too much—

The Tree of Ice smiled. *"One item from each of the clans was given to you on your journeys through My Sister's Realms. Bring them forward now."*

I stared, heart pulses skipping beats. No matter the sobriety of the occasion, I couldn't help saying in complete stupefaction, "Wait...what?"

"You may begin with the coat," the Tree prompted, still smiling.

Slowly, Ben brought out my coat and handed it to me. Finally, I could dart my eyes up to meet his to ask him what the heck was going on. His eyes were still just as lost as mine, though.

That...made me feel better, and not just because bewilderment likes company. If *Ben* didn't know where the Tree was going with this, then this *wasn't* the roundabout start to a dramá marriage ceremony.

Or, at least...not a traditional one.

But that flicker of sense was what I needed to refocus on the Tree with some semblance of calm.

"Here it is," I said, holding out the coat.

"A gift from the Peacegrowth clan," the Tree said, smile fading to solemnity. *"For My Queen and My children. I accept the offering in the spirit it was unknowingly yet purely given. You may release it to Me."*

She gestured to the well between us.

I stared down it, truly seeing it for the first time. Although I couldn't see very far; not a couple yards down, the rest was lost to darkness.

"You mean...you want me to give it up?" I said, feeling a pang. "Forever?"

Svyer had given me this coat. And Svyer was....

"*Something precious must be taken for something even more precious to be given,*" the Tree said with a sad smile.

Ben tensed, as if in sudden understanding.

What is it? I asked him urgently.

But he wouldn't meet my gaze now. He just stared stiffly ahead at nothing.

"*This is the last act to renew the Second Covenant and restore the peace between Our children, daughter,*" the Tree said gently. "*These things have value to you because they were gifts indeed. They clothed you, aided you, gave you joy, and even saved your life. In their gifting, they showed the purity of enough hearts of the children of Flame to have the Covenant restored to them. Your giving them up in turn signifies your will, as the Queen of Ice, that it may be so.*"

I...wanted that for them. And besides, it wasn't fair that they should have sacrificed so much to bring me to this point that I should not sacrifice in turn.

If not for Ben alone....

Though it hurt deeply to raise Svyer's coat over that well and to release my fingers...I did. The coat fluttered down into the darkness and was lost without a sound. No splash, no thump. Nothing.

Though I felt a surge of...something. Something stirring in the air. Akin to pressure building before a storm, but...better.

"*A gift from the Brightflare clan,*" the Tree prompted with a small smile, looking at my whistle.

Slowly, I lifted the cord above my head and held it over the well.

"*For My Queen and My children,*" the Tree said solemnly. "*I accept the offering in the spirit it was unknowingly yet purely given.*"

I opened my fingers and allowed the whistle to drop into the depths. And the pressure increased.

"*A gift from the Strongshield clan.*"

With a deep sigh, I unclasped the watch on my wrist and dropped it into the well once the Tree repeated Her acceptance.

Sorry, Alya, I thought regretfully as I watched her ingenious prototype disappear. But again, the stirrings of something powerful increased. Was it just me, or were the leaves above shining even brighter?

"*A gift from the Starkissed clan.*"

My mind blanked, so the Tree smiled slightly and prompted, "*The beads that young Yira gave you.*"

Oh, those.

"Uh, Ben. I'm going to need you to get out my bags."

"All of them?" he said in surprise, glancing at the Tree.

"Yeah...." I said sheepishly. "I don't remember which one I stuffed them in."

I looked at the Tree apologetically as Ben began pulling out my bags and setting them on the ground next to me. "Sorry about this. Give me a moment."

"*Do what you must,*" the Tree said with a smile.

Fortunately, the beads were in the first pocket I looked in. I walked back over and, after the Tree's acceptance, released them quite willingly to the well. They were a sweet gift but the least personally meaningful to me. Which was one reason why they were the only gift so far that hadn't been on my person today. I just wished I never had to explain to poor Yira what I had done with them.

Or...perhaps she would think it a worthwhile sacrifice. Maybe this was even what she had intended when she had given them to me. After all, Abby hadn't been the only child or even adult now to dream of a Tree asking them to help me.

"*A gift from the Battleblood clan.*"

When my mind blanked again, the Tree inclined her head to my arm shields.

"Does she...." Ben began to plead before he could seem to help himself. Then he shut his mouth and pressed his lips firmly closed.

The Tree's eyes softened in compassion on him, then looked back at me. "*Only one shield is needed for this. You may keep the other, for you will have need of it soon.*"

Lovely.

Ben, too, didn't seem to know whether to be relieved or grim.

I decided to give up the right band, since that was most likely the hand I would be shooting with anyway, and after the Tree's acceptance, I released it to the well.

"*A gift from the Sunfilled clan.*"

Now I *really* blanked. After all, other than the King, the only Sunfilled I had even *met* was....

Then my hand drifted to my pocket, and my eyes widened.

"No," I said in a small voice. "Do I...I mean, isn't there any other...."

The Tree just gazed at me sadly.

"Sarah?" Ben asked uncertainly.

I numbly pulled out his scale.

Ben let out a breath of relief and shook his head. "Sarah, I can give you another one, easily."

I knew I was being silly, especially with what came next. "But this was one of your *first.*"

He smiled crookedly. "And I shed a couple of others at the same time."

Oh.

Now I felt even more foolishly sentimental. And yet, foolish or not, this gift was by far the hardest for me to hold over the well. After all, it wasn't about the scale. It was about the spirit in which it had been given. It was about him. It was about the moment that I knew I loved him.

He could give me another scale. But neither of us could ever turn back the sands of time to have that moment again.

The Tree spoke Her acceptance slowly and soberly, Her cold-fire eyes soft as they rested on me.

"*For my Queen and my children. I accept the offering in the spirit it was unknowingly yet purely given.*"

Tears stung my eyes as I let that scale go.

The moment it disappeared into the darkness, the air in that ice cavern stirred, the leaves glowed bright enough to blind us for one moment, and the Tree declared, "*It is done.*"

When the light faded and the spots cleared from our eyes and we could look at Her once more, the Tree smiled, those ice lips somehow warm.

"*All that was past has been forgiven. The First and Second Covenants have been fully restored. Heir of Flame, you and the other children of Flame are now welcomed in full fellowship with the children of Ice. And as a token of that fellowship....*"

She raised Her palm high.

One of the bright leaves began drifting down in an elegant spiral all the many hundreds of feet down until it finally rested, like a fallen star, in the Tree's uplifted hand. A string of fluid ice formed from the bright leaf and spilled over the Tree's palm.

For the first time, the Tree crossed around the well and came to me. Slowly, with excruciating care to not touch me, She let the necklace fall over my head.

I stared in wonder at the leaf of ice that now rested on my chest, shimmering with light. It was like it had been carved from a diamond and given an inner white fire in every line.

"*A token of peace, for the Queen of Ice to give to the King of Flame,*" the Tree said quietly, voice as hushed and solemn as falling snow.

"Please," Ben said in a choked voice. I looked at him in alarm at the sudden change in him. His eyes were on the Tree, begging, his voice agonized. "Please, O Lady. Tell me that is...."

The Tree smiled sadly. "*The promised blessing. Yes.*"

I blinked. Promised?

Ben trembled, sagged even, breathing heavily, bracing himself on his legs. "Thank you," he gasped. "Just...thank you."

"Ben," I said in alarm, wrapping my arms around one of his. I looked back at the Tree. "I don't understand. What promise? What does this mean?"

"*The Heir will show you,*" the Tree said soberly.

She looked back at him, face saddening. "*Take her now, and go. The time she has to give it to him is running short.*"

Ben's head shot back up to look at Her, face crumpling. "*What?*"

"*You must hurry,*" the Tree said. "Run. *Now.*"

Ben looked down at me, the most desperate look I had ever seen in his eyes. "Sarah, will you come with me? *Will you give it to him?*"

"Well, yes, obviously, but—"

He didn't wait for the rest. He scooped me up in his arms. When Kor and Yvera started forward, he shook his head at them. "No time. Just get Sarah's family back into their hold, and I'll come for you."

"Ben, what—"

Again, he did not wait. He looked at my family, gaze scanning them as he spoke. "I swear by my life's blood that I will bring your daughter and sister back to you. But right now, I need to take her to my father. Right *now.*"

Then he was racing down the steps with reckless abandon, considering how frosted they were. But his footing never slipped, and within seconds, he was running with me through the gate, down the passage, and into the rotunda.

I had only seen him race like this when lives were in danger.

Suddenly, I understood, and my iceheart pulsed rapidly.

Ben.... I said in dawning horror.

Avva is dying, *Sarah,* Ben said in agony as we burst through my open gate and into my hold. He raced us around the Inner Rim.

No, no—he can't be. He was fine just—just a couple days ago.

He stayed strong for your sake. He didn't want to worry you. And I think the Flame gave him strength, for the renewal of the Covenant. But he's been weakening for over a year now. And now....

Ben shuddered, even as he ran. *It—it comes suddenly for us, sometimes. How the flameheart gives out in the end.*

No.

NO.

Not *him.*

Not the *King.*

Not Ben's *father.*

When we reached the Ythra gate, I slapped my hand against it, shoving power into it, begging it to open, and swiftly.

Fortunately, it did. Ben had to stumble back to get clear quickly enough for how the doors threw themselves open. Ben wasn't arguing with their enthusiasm. The moment he could fit, he plunged us through.

And the moment that we stumbled into the circular room, Ben said, *Lash us, Sarah.*

I did, immediately. *GO.*

Ben took us.

CHAPTER TWENTY-TWO

RESTORED

KORIBEN

THANK THE FLAME ABOVE and Below that Avva was conscious enough to let me through his personal gate. I stumbled through with Sarah still in my arms and raced with her past his startled elites and counselors and to his bedroom, shoving aside healers as I went.

"Avva!" I cried out before I even saw him.

And there he was.

It was as bad as I had feared. He was lying on his bed. Still conscious, propped up in an elevated position, but lying pale and limp, only managing the weakest of smiles as I burst into his room.

"Ben," he rasped.

That was when I truly knew he was dying. Because now he couldn't even form my full name.

"Avva," I gasped, dry sobbing as I *would not allow myself to cry*. "I have her, I have her, and she has the cure. *She has it*. Just hold on, please, please."

As I spoke, I stumbled to him, and Eskala, who had been holding his hand, swiftly moved aside. I set Sarah on her feet, and she jerked the chain off her head.

"Here," she said tremulously as tears ran down her face. She didn't look far from sobbing herself as Avva turned his head on his pillow and smiled softly at her.

With trembling fingers, she put the leaf over his heart and then pressed her right hand over it, grabbing Avva's own right with her other and covering his hand with hers.

"A token of peace," she whispered. "From the Queen of Ice to the King of Flame."

Then she kissed the back of his hand.

"Please, Avva," she said, finally sobbing now as she rested her forehead there. "*Live.*"

Avva's eyes drifted closed.

I fell to my knees.

No.

"No!" Sarah wailed, throwing herself on top of him.

Then....

Avva's eyelids moved. Blinked open again.

And this time they were glowing with golden light.

I trembled, not quite daring to hope now.

Avva slowly looked down at Sarah, who was still sobbing over him, not having seen his eyes open again.

"My dear Sarah.... I don't believe there's a need for that anymore."

She looked up at him, blinking through her tears.

Then she hiccupped.

"Oh. It...worked?"

Avva smiled, and this time it was with some of his old fire. "I do believe it did."

If I'd had the luxury, I would have been stunned numb and unmoving for the rest of the day and night, only beginning to come out of the shock and functioning again by the next morning.

But I didn't.

And I supposed that was just as well, because then I would have missed out on the ferocity of the joy I felt at seeing Avva not just alive but *restored*.

After only a deken of food and recovery, and long before dawn even broke, he was already up and about handling the final arrangements for our defense of our Tree and Realms, and before another deken was even over, he was the man and King he hadn't been in over a year.

And not a moment too soon. Because this day, of all days, was when the Seven Realms needed him most.

The moment I knew I could not just hope but believe, I grabbed Sarah, pulled her up, and gave her a kiss unlike any I'd given her before, not caring how many people were watching. And there were quite a few, even more gathered in Avva's quarters in the flurry of preparations, now that it seemed as if Avva would be taking command of them again.

I half expected Sarah to scold me when I pulled away, but she appeared too stunned. Her now constantly silver eyes blazed.

"*Thank you,*" I said in a choked voice.

She probably still did not fully understand what she had done. In saving Avva, she had not just saved him, or even me. She had saved the Seven Realms, and her birth world as well—as much as it had now forsaken her.

With burning cheeks, she said, "I love him too. I know not nearly as much as you do, but—"

I cut her off with another kiss, unable to help myself as my love for her seemed to crush my entire being. All too soon, though, someone tried to get my attention, and I had to reluctantly set her down and become the Heir once more.

Even though I still moved and worked, it was still always in a daze, as if not quite able to wake from a dream. I still could not believe it.

We had done it.

We had done the impossible. Moontouched Earthren found. Gates opened. Covenants restored. Sarah crowned. Avva *alive.*

Of course...now we had to survive until tomorrow.

SARAH WAS STILL MY primary responsibility. After all, we hadn't gained back the King of Flame only to risk the newly gained Queen of Ice. So, not long after Avva began recovering, he ordered me to take Sarah back to her hold.

"Spend time with your family," he said gently when she protested. "Sleep, if you can, for a few deken. Eat. Rest. We will need you all too soon. The eclipse will start at noon, and we will need you in place and as prepared as you can be before then."

Sarah had nothing to say to that, so she lashed to me, and I surged her straight to our gate in the Library.

"I still haven't thought of what to call it," Sarah said with a sigh as I set her down in the hidden chamber behind the shrine.

Strictly speaking, carrying her probably wasn't necessary for the surging. But...she hadn't protested when I'd picked her up. So I would probably keep doing it until she told me to stop.

"I'm sure Kor will have ideas by now," I said dryly.

"Speaking of Kor," she mused. "He's probably going to have to be the one to call me when you are ready for me, isn't he?"

"What?" I asked, startled.

"I don't have your scale anymore," she said sadly. "Remember?"

Torch it. That was right. And...I shouldn't stop now to enchant another one for her. I had to get back. But....

The implications of what she'd said finally sunk in.

"And you have one of *Kor's*?"

"Because you were...asleep," Sarah said self-consciously. "And Yvera was with you. He was all I had."

Of course he had been, torch it. But I hid my irritation because, first, it was unjustified, and second, it wasn't Sarah's fault, and third, it was mine more than it was Kor's.

But Flame, it rubbed me the wrong way that the only scale she had right now was Kor's. Even more so now for how she was right: that was the only way I'd have to contact her to tell her to come out.

"I'll get you another one as soon as I can," I sighed. "Promise. I just...can't right this dek."

"I get it. You need to get back." She hugged me and let go. "And I need to give you your wings back."

"Oh, don't think you're saying goodbye like that," I said with a grin.

That was the only warning I gave her before I scooped her up again. And this time, with just the two of us, completely alone....

I crushed my lips to hers and gently, ever so gently, pressed her against the wall. She gasped, but when I pulled back in alarm, she pulled me back to her mouth as her arms wrapped tightly around my neck and, using the wall as leverage, her legs curled around my waist. Then I sunk into that kiss and to her. I took it as slowly and deliberately as I could, even now aware of how duty pulled. This was more than we'd ever had, but though it only seemed to fill me with a hunger for even more, I knew this wasn't—couldn't be—the time.

Besides, there were some things we needed to talk about first, and this wasn't the time for that either.

So, though it seemed like tearing off my own scales, I reluctantly pulled away and set her down.

She staggered, dazed, and I grabbed her shoulder to steady her.

"I...think you broke my brain."

I chuckled, even though I wasn't far from feeling the same. "I'm flattered that my very inexpert skills are satisfactory."

"Well, I can't exactly be an expert judge, since you were my first, but I still think—"

"Wait," I said, growing still. I clenched her shoulder more tightly and leaned in. "That was your *first* kiss? With me? At the *Moonfair*?"

"Yes," she said, cheeks growing hot. Her eyes darted toward the gate. "Shouldn't I be—"

"*How*?"

How could someone as lovely as Sarah....

Not that I was *complaining*, mind you. For my own sake.

Her warmth increased. "It's pretty simple. No one...that I ever thought worthwhile...ever thought the same about me.... Until you."

"Well," I said, not knowing what else to say. Nothing that wouldn't come off as glowing with totally unfair satisfaction. She should have had whomever she wanted, all her life.

"I suppose...that makes two of us. About you, I mean."

She grinned. "What, none of those other Moondaughters were in the least bit tempting?"

I shuddered. "Are you kidding? *No*. Despite the Moonstar's vaunted matchmaking powers—*no*. I honestly think it was just picking at *random* before. There's a reason I hate that fair so much."

Sarah may not have been my first kiss, but that hadn't been by choice.

Her smile grew smug.

I gritted my teeth as I straightened and let go of her. "And now I have one more reason to hate it. That should *not* have been your first. I'm going to kill Kor. I really am this time. I can find another leftwing to help me save the worlds today."

"There's no need to go to such extremes," Sarah said, still grinning, though her cheeks were heating again. "I thought it was a pretty good first kiss."

I raised an eyebrow. "You were terrified. And it was in public. And it wasn't your choice."

She smirked. "Oh, it was my choice alright. I mean, public wasn't my *preference*. But you were definitely my choice."

I stilled, but she didn't seem to notice. Which meant there probably wasn't any significance to what she'd said.

She continued with a smile and a shrug. "Every girl dreams of a dramatic first kiss. And that...was dramatic."

I gave her a suspicious look. "Are you sure you're not just saying that to spare my leftwing's life?"

She laughed. "I'm honestly not. *That* was the best part of the entire night, and of most of the past eleven days. In fact, it was so powerful, I thought I could...."

Then her voice trailed off. Her face became still, her eyes distant.

"Sarah?" I said uncertainly.

She shook herself. "Nothing. Or, at least, something to talk about later. Right now, you have to get going, and I have to try to take a nap, right?"

"Right," I said heavily. Although how I was going to focus while worlds apart from my star, I didn't know.

She clenched my hand, smiled in a sad way that told me she felt the same, and slowly let go as she moved through the gate of fire.

I swallowed. "Be ready."

"I will," she said just before her head disappeared.

Her fingers finally fell out of my hand, leaving them cold.

Chapter Twenty-Three

SHOW

Sarah

"What's the point of making me your rightwing and going through *this* if I can't protect you now?" Michael demanded, gesturing to his snow-white hair.

I was still getting used to that. And I was sure from the way that all the others kept staring at me, including him, that everyone was still doing the same. Heck, every time my hair fell into my eyes, *I* started. There was a reason I'd asked my lights to put it into a tight French braid for me.

You know, other than the fact that it completed the whole I'm-going-into-battle getup.

Right then, I was waiting in front of the Ythra moongate for Kor's next call to say he and the others were outside and waiting to pick me up. His first call had said to be ready in about half a deken, but without my watch, I was now back to guessing how long that was. I had already said goodbye to the rest of my family, but Mom and Dad were lingering for moral support. And I suppose Michael was too, but he *wasn't* helping. Any of us. I could see Mom getting more worried by the minute, so *I* at least was trying to keep my voice low.

"Michael, can you do *any* magic yet?"

"No," he said sullenly. "But I've got a gun, and—"

"With how many bullets? This is an invasion, remember? Armies, not one-off bad guys."

He gritted his teeth. "Just give me one like yours."

I sighed. "You're welcome to check the training room armory, if you'd like, but I'm pretty sure this was the only one I saw. And no, I can't let you use mine instead. It's imprinted on me."

At his look, I explained, "That means if *you* try to shoot it, it will only burn your hand."

"Well, that...is both good and really annoying at the same time."

I took a deep breath. "Michael, I understand how you're feeling right now. I would be terrified for me too. But right now...you're more likely to endanger me than help me. The Devourer is a coward, and so is its favorite henchman. They like to use the vulnerable against us."

"And you're *not* vulnerable?"

"Not as much as I used to be," I said grimly. "But you still have a point there, I agree. Trust me, if Ben had *any* other choice, he wouldn't be letting me set foot outside of this hold until everything was over."

"And why *doesn't* he have a choice?"

"The Tree said I had to help. That's why."

"That's *it*?"

I sighed. He had a lot to learn about Trees. As I had, and still was. I was probably the most ignorant Monarch since the first.

"That's enough for them. And for me. But for you, remember what I've already told you. Their power comes from the sun, and today is their winter solstice over their primary Tree *and* a solar eclipse. Think about that. They're going to need me."

Before he could open his mouth to protest again, I pressed on. "They will do *everything* they can to keep me safe, Michael. Ben and his dad aren't going to take chances with me. I'm probably going to be the most heavily guarded person on that battlefield."

"More than their own king and prince?" Michael said in disbelief.

A spiny tentacle of fear lashed through the bars of the cage where I'd been carefully keeping it under lock and key. I gritted my teeth and shoved it back inside.

"*Especially* them. They are their people's greatest protectors. I tried to explain it to you before, but I'm saying it again now: they're *not* like Earth royals. They're going to be on the front lines. Especially...Ben."

Another tentacle lashed out, but I was ready for it this time, and I cut it off and kicked the stump back inside.

"Because he's young?"

I huffed. "No, that's not it. I wish you could see his dad. Actually, I'm sure you'll meet him soon. For now, just trust me. He's aged *really* well."

"Then what is?"

I swallowed. "It's...it's because Ben's Blood is less valuable to the enemy."

Please let that be enough to keep him safe. Please, please.

I was chopping off fear tentacles right and left now.

"How?"

I drew the expository line there. I probably shouldn't have even mentioned Blood, since it came too close to talking about why the Devourer wanted *me* so badly—me, the most vulnerable Monarch ever. Because, though Ben's Heir Blood was valuable to the Devourer, it wasn't *quite* powerful enough to let the Devourer enter a Tree-protected world. Unlike the *King's* Blood. Or...mine.

Not that that wouldn't be Michael's concern eventually, as my rightwing. But it didn't need to be today, when he was too new to do anything about it.

"Michael," I said quietly, looking him in the eye. "Do you want to help me?"

"What do you think I'm standing here trying to do?"

"Then *train. Hard.* Harder than you've ever trained in your life. The moment I'm gone, go to that training room, and figure out what you can do now. That way, the next time something like this happens...you can go with me. And I can hide behind you."

Not that I intended to do any such thing. I said *can*, not *will*. But I threw that in, hoping it would help him feel better. His macho sensibilities had taken quite the beating today.

His shoulders slowly sank, and he nodded. "I hate feeling helpless," he muttered sullenly.

I smiled thinly. "Welcome to the club, brother. How do you think *I've* felt spending the last eleven days around drakón? And not just any drakón—the best-of-the-best drakón."

Michael gave a tired smirk. "Are you sure you're not just prejudiced?"

"Oh, I'm sure. The Heir and his—"

I felt it. A tug that was almost like Kor calling my name, without using the word. I pulled Kor's scale out of the small pouch at my side and answered it with an intentional touch. Michael leaned in curiously. He did like his gadgets. Hopefully he would get enough of them in this new life to satisfy him.

Kor's face appeared on his scale. "Ready and waiting, O Queen of loveliness."

From his wide-eyed, overly flirtatious look, I was certain he'd said that just to get under Ben's skin. At the edge of the scale, I could see a glimpse of gold standing next to Kor, shifting in irritation.

"Call me that again and I'll send a shard through your heart," I said calmly, then ended the call with another tap.

"Sarah!" Mom gasped. Even Michael was gaping.

"Oh, you guys don't know Kor like I do," I said, wagging a finger with one hand and putting his scale away with the other.

Michael chuckled. "Oh, I don't doubt he deserves it. It's just so funny to hear death threats coming from *you*."

I blinked, then realized he was right. Then grinned ruefully. "My drakón are a bad influence. I have a whole new set of swears, too."

Mom looked stunned. Dad smiled, and Michael laughed.

"Maybe I'll warm up to these guys, then. *Someday*."

Michael gave me a quick, tight hug. "Come back," he growled in my ear. "Or else."

He needed to work on his death threats. Yvera could have done much better.

"I will."

Then I hugged Mom, then Dad.

"I love you, Sarah," he said as I pulled away.

I blinked away tears. Dad didn't say those words often. At least, not in that way. And right now, his silver eyes were glowing.

"I love you too, Dad."

"Come back," he said simply, smiling thinly. "I'll get to work as well. Surely there's something here to help me learn what I'm supposed to be doing as your 'leftwing.'"

"Check the library. Er...that's the room full of big dark stones. Tap on them to activate them, and see what comes up. Maybe nothing, but...I'm thinking there'll be something for you."

Then, before I could think too much about what I was doing, I took one last look at the three of them...then turned around and opened my gate. Through the gap, I could see my drakón waiting outside, but I didn't wait for the doors to fully open. Not taking any chances with my family today, I slipped through as soon as they were wide enough and magically pulled them closed behind me.

When I turned around again to face my drakón, Kor whistled. Yvera blinked. Ben stared.

"Sarah, where did you get that?" he said, looking stunned.

He was referring to the armor that now encased my body from head to toe. The pieces were made of a shiny, clear substance laid thickly over white backing to make the whole thing appear white when looking at it from straight on. The clear substance reminded me of epoxy resin, as if each piece had been perfectly and smoothly formed in a resin mold. But if it was resin, it was a kind that was faintly cold to the touch—not ice, obviously, because that wouldn't be hard enough even while it lasted and would melt in any case, or require far too much energy for me to keep cold than was worth it, and this armor didn't drain anything from me at all.

As further proof that the clear substance wasn't ice, as far as I could tell, it was as hard as a diamond. Trust me, I had banged a piece of it as hard as I could against every hard surface in my special bedroom trying to damage it, and I hadn't been able to make so much as a scratch. I'd even nearly stabbed myself with the artisan knife I'd taken from one of the alcoves as the sharp point slid right off.

I...was more careful in my experimentation after that.

The most impossible thing, though, was how *light* it was. It felt like I was wearing hardly anything. And the pieces fit so smoothly together that, though I was a little more encumbered than normal, it wasn't by much. I could still touch my toes and tap opposing shoulder blades, for instance.

And, of course, the whole assemblage fit me like a glove. So snugly, in fact, that I was very glad for the tasteful silver tabard with a white tree emblazoned on it that ended in an elegant V at mid-thigh in the front and back, which was tied tight around my waist with my new side gun holster and pouch for little essentials (like Kor's scale) on the other side. For now, a white ornamental skirt flared dramatically around the back and sides of me. I assumed it was for show, since my lights had pointedly shown me over and over how it could be removed with just a tug when the action started happening. I'd nearly refused it as being a bit much, despite how dang good it looked in the mirror (especially when I twirled), but my lights had been insistent.

And, of course, to top it all off, my lights had insisted on braiding diamond pins into my hair again. For...protection. I assumed. That's what Kor had said they were for the last time, right?

The protection I *knew* was real was strapped over my left forearm: my shield band. Since I couldn't sleep, I'd used the time after my lights had dressed me to experiment with the armor, get used to moving and drawing my gun with it, and to practice generating the shield, and I now felt fairly confident I could form and hold it under stress.

The way all my family had stared when I'd come out of my special bedroom was bad enough, but in a way, I was glad for the getup just for their sakes. The cooler and more competent I looked, hopefully the more confident they would feel in sending their daughter and sister off to battle. The littles, at least, were already convinced I was unstoppable. For only them, this ridiculousness had seemed worth it.

And then...I came out to my drakón.

I blushed and shifted self-consciously.

"My lights," I said, answering Ben's stunned question. "They insisted. It's too much, isn't it? I *told* them it was—"

"Sarah," Kor said sternly. "Why do you think even *I'm* in armor right now?"

I blinked, realizing that, for the first time, he was. Yvera's scale-armor, I didn't even notice anymore; she might even sleep in it for all I knew. Ben's glorious golden set, I'd taken for granted, even before I got out. But Kor was right. Even he was in a set of blue scale-armor—doing his clan proud, of course, in the stylishness of its ornamentation. And they were *all* wearing tabards in their clan colors, with their symbols on the front: an eye with a star for a pupil for Kor, an upright sword in front of a blazing fire for Yvera, and a three-pronged crown superimposed over a sun for Ben.

Suddenly, taking them all in, I didn't feel quite so overdressed.

Actually...for the very first time...I felt like I was part of the team.

The skirt though....

"Sarah," Kor said, reminding me he had asked a question.

"You only wear armor for show," I said.

"Exactly. *You're* not here to do much actual fighting. We hope. Not that we should shelter you forever, but because you simply haven't been given a fair chance to learn to fight, or to grow into your power. That means it is perfectly alright, even *ideal* right now, for your armor to be...."

"For *show*," I said slowly, finally making the connection.

"Not that I think that stuff is useless," Kor said, peering at the clear plates in fascination. "I highly doubt the Tree would prepare something that wouldn't actually do you some good. But keep in mind the *greatest* reason we need you right now, Sarah."

"Which...is?" I said blankly.

I thought we hadn't figured that part out yet. Although, after Ben's reminder of our first kiss earlier that day, I had an inkling. When he'd kissed me that first time, I'd felt his pull so strongly, I thought I could sink *into* him.

What if...I actually could?

Ben finally came up to me, put his hands on my shoulders, and bent down with burning eyes. "To give them *hope*. People are scared right now. Most of them know now what is coming for us today during the Dark Solstice. And as much as I...dislike Kor's methods, I have to admit, they have been effective. Right when they needed something to believe in...he gave them you."

"Oh," I breathed. "I'm...not just the Queen of Ice, am I? I mean, that's big enough. But I'm also...the Moondaughter."

"*The* Moondaughter in many people's minds now," Ben said grimly. "Whether you like it or not, you have become a beacon of hope, the sign that we're going to survive this. *That* is what you're here to be."

And you are already doing a wondrous job on me, he said silently, pressing his lips to mine.

All too briefly, unfortunately, because his wings were watching, and his people were waiting. After only a few seconds, he pulled away and straightened. "Ready?"

I nodded. "Gather in."

Now we really did feel like a team to me as we all huddled closely. I lashed us all together, then nodded to Ben from where I was pressed against his side.

"Go."

AT FIRST, I THOUGHT we stumbled out into some kind of massive sandstone fort. That's the first impression I got from the tall ochre walls going right and left, which had battlements and guard towers (shaped into spikes) and banners waving in the warm currents.

Then I saw how *far* the walls had to go to get around this enormous space—far enough that they grew into tiny blurs in the distance that shimmered in the hot air between us.

And nothing was in the middle of this "fort." The walls appeared to be guarding nothing except an enormous, cracked hole in the ground in the center of it that spiderwebbed outward from all sides. Something *boiling* hot must have been down *there*, because the air above it blurred. A geyser? Lava?

I was suddenly very glad for the coolness of my bodysuit and armor plates against my skin.

This is winter *for you guys?* I sent to Ben. The sun wasn't even at its peak yet, and already it was beating down in waves of heat, warming up the stone all around.

We're at the equator now, in the—

Ben was interrupted by one guard approaching, this one in gold armor just like him. Another Sunfilled. In fact...Sunfilled seemed to be everywhere I looked. On the battlements, on the ground—oh look, two golden dragons just soared past overhead. After seeing Ben as the only one for so long, this many was dizzying.

"Heir Koriben," she greeted, saluting him with her hand over her heart.

Then, to my surprise, she removed her hand, only to salute again to me, this time with a deep nod. "Queen Sarah of Ice, allow me to welcome you to the Temple of Flame. The King of Flame is expecting you. May I lead you to him?"

I wasn't sure I would ever get used to someone addressing me as *Queen.* Perhaps I wasn't meant to.

"Uh, of course," I said, only just scrambling in time to look at least somewhat sure of myself.

"Excellent. Follow me."

She turned and began leading us along the wall, away from the daygate we had just come through, and I thought about what she had said. The Temple of Flame. That was right. The attack was supposed to start at....

I looked to the side and stared at the massive hole, and the heat radiating out of it.

Ben, I said. *Is that....*

He followed my gaze. *The Tree of Flame. Yes. She's inside, and right now we are on the...roof, basically, of Her Temple.*

My perspective shifted, now placing us high in the air instead of on the ground. That also made the walls; craggy, pointed guard towers; and battlements make more sense. This wasn't a fort guarding nothing. It was the roof of a *temple* containing their Tree.

A temple that had to be highly defensible, of course.

I wondered if I, as the Queen of Ice, was now permitted into Her presence, given that Ben had been given the reverse permission. If so, I would no doubt meet Her one day. Perhaps even today, if that's where they decided to keep me.

Although, with the heat radiation I was seeing coming from that hole...I wasn't sure that was a good idea. My magic was already instinctively activating to keep me cool enough in this baking desert. I finally understood *why* the cold was so dangerous to the drakón: their natures *required* them to be warmer than humans to stay alive, therefore when they weren't, more power was required to keep them at a healthy temperature. The cold literally drained them.

And man, was I feeling the reverse now, especially as noon approached. Badly enough that I stumbled, and Ben caught me with a worried glance. He must have seen something in my expression that made him realize what was wrong, because he groaned quietly as he led me on, keeping a hand on me.

We'll get you inside soon, Sarah. We're almost there.

We were approaching the three most massive tower-spikes. Their appearance combined with all the other spikes in my mind to form a picture.

Oh, I said to Ben. *It looks like a crown, doesn't it? From a distance?*

Yes, he said, casting me a strained smile. *The Tree is our ultimate Sovereign, after all. We—Avva and I—are just Her servants, Her Right and Left Hands.*

I now had an inkling where rightwings and leftwings came from. And...why the capital K, Q, and H. It wasn't because of us at all—of course not. It was because of our Trees.

But you keep talking about this place called "Crownhold." Does it also....

I trailed off as we entered the largest spike and the guards on either side of it saluted us. Then I needed to save my attention for the stairs we climbed, and Ben was looking too distracted from his anxiety for me and something else to bother with an explanation without the full question. From the way his hands kept twitching toward me, I knew he'd rather just carry me, but people were watching. Not that that had stopped him early this morning, but I gathered it kind of ruined the hope-giving effect I was supposed to be having if I couldn't even climb stairs under my own power.

Being inside *did* help. The interior was blessedly darker and cooler. I guessed the latter was because of magic or simply because the sun hadn't yet managed to bake all the way through the massively thick sandstone walls. I knew just how thick they were from the arrowslits, which were the principal source of light right now.

I had to give it to drakón: when they built, they built not just to withstand the test of time but also the sieges of the Devourer. They couldn't afford to do any less.

Finally, we reached the top of the stairs.

And entered command central.

Bizarrely, I felt as if I had somehow switched metaphorical universes and entered a sci-fi battle bridge, but there were enough semblances of the drakón technology I knew to anchor me back. After all, all the gold-uniformed communication and observation officers were using *scales,* set into honeycomb nooks in the walls, and the central table displaying what must have been a map of the surrounding area was a raised firepit and the map made of flames. Kor had already shown me solaruses (Solariums? That would be Latin declension, though, and the dramá word wasn't actually Latin-based, despite what the English interpretation in my head implied.), so it was not much of a stretch for me to see holographic displays of planets and runes hovering in the air over other, smaller tables, and people consulting and manipulating them.

Of particular note was the table with the large sun and large brown planet I was coming to recognize as Ythra, with its moon gradually rounding in its orbit to come between Ythra...and their beloved sun.

Still, I might not have spotted that table and given it the attention it deserved if it wasn't for the King standing next to it.

It was a good thing this wasn't our first meeting, or his glory might have stunned me into immobility.

He was in full gold scale-armor now, which I might have expected, but he also had on a billowing, metallic gold cape that surely must not have been practical and would come off the moment the fighting began. An enormous, surely ceremonial gold-hilted sword hung at his side. And when he turned to smile at me, I saw that atop his long gold hair (now braided back for practicality), he was wearing a gold crown—a simple band save for three spikes in the center.

Kaldrir, shining beside him, appeared a pale moon compared to the King's glory.

I knew the King well enough by now to know that his current attire would not have been his preference. No matter how much more confident or how much less self-conscious he was than me, flagrant displays simply weren't his style. There was probably a good reason this was the first time I had ever seen him in a crown, which he hadn't even worn on his deathbed.

In a leap of intuition, I guessed that simple and warm was his normal style for a similar if far more mentally stable reason than Ben's: He didn't want to be feared. Not because the King thought himself a monster as Ben did, but because he yearned for his people to know that he intended to rule as much as he could not with his might but with his love and courage and sacrifice. And communicating that to them when he couldn't help but be so innately large and powerful required a greater degree of simplicity, humility, and gentleness than anyone else would have had to bring to bear.

Life and the Tree had sculpted the ultimate paradox of a leader into one being: mighty and gentle, large and soft, scorching and warm, loving and awe-inspiring. It was scarcely a wonder that any decent soul who met him would love him. Fall to their knees in front of him, simply because he would never, ever force them to. Even though he could.

Of course, even he knew there were times for displays. Moments when, with the trust of his people safely won, it was time to throw off the shadows and be *glorious*. Not for his own sake—for theirs. Always for theirs.

To give them *hope*.

And right now, I was dazzled enough to feel it myself.

And not feeling a *bit* overdressed any longer.

"Ah, Queen Sarah," the King said warmly, coming to greet me.

It took all my self-control not to stumble. If it was odd to hear anyone else call me a Queen, then it was triply so for *him* to do so. I could not possibly be the equal in rank to this breathtaking sun.

The King didn't embrace me; perhaps the formality of the situation and our surroundings prevented that. But he took both my hands in his and kissed them.

"On behalf of the Golden Crown, I thank you for coming to the aid of the Six Realms. We will not forget your sacrifice for us this day."

Working extremely hard to keep a tremble out of my voice, I said, "I am honored to fight alongside you."

The King's warm smile in response didn't help my neurons to keep functioning.

"The honor," he said simply, "is ours."

He let go of my hands and stepped back. He smiled at his son and patted him on the shoulder. More quietly, he said, "Well, with you two here, I had better get started."

Silently, but not just to me, he added, *After all, I don't want to give Sarah too much time to fret.*

With a wink at me, he strode to the opening to our left that led out into the sunlight. Alyish and some others followed him.

I blinked. "Wait. Start *what*?"

And then, the moment the King stepped into the sunlight: deafening roars. Not of a human crowd, although I thought I detected some amón enthusiasm, too.

The roars of dozens, no, perhaps hundreds of dragons trumpeting *at once*.

Numbly, I turned my head slowly to look out the thick glass windows on either side of the opening the King had walked through. Those slanted windows were one of the primary reasons I had first thought this was a battle bridge. From my current vantage, I couldn't see much of the ground below through them. But if the gathered dragons I could see in the far distance were any indication of the rest of the view....

Just then, the King's voice rang out, no doubt magically magnified a hundredfold of what it should be. One of the gold-uniformed soldiers closed the door at the opening, muffling the sound, perhaps to allow the people inside to continue working. But though I couldn't understand the words now, the meaning of the King's resounding voice as it carried on finally sunk in.

I choked. And started shaking my head in pure horror. "*No*. No, no, no—"

Sarah, Kor hissed, discreetly stepping in front of me. *People are* watching, *remember?*

That's precisely the problem!

And this was bad enough. My drakón couldn't *possibly* be expecting me to step *out there*.

Sarah, you don't have to do this, Ben said urgently. *Avva is prepared for his speech to go either way. He's given you a choice.*

At the last minute! Again!

But I knew why. Because...what good would it have done me to start freaking out sooner?

And I knew why he was asking me to do this. It was the same reason that he was wearing his crown and that surely impractical cape and sword now. It was the reason *I* was now dressed like *this*, even though—or especially because—I would probably see little action.

It was the same reason everyone except Ben had asked me to reveal myself at the Moonfair.

It was the reason I was here.

To give them some sign that there would be light, even in their darkness.

To give them *hope*.

I couldn't deny them that. These weren't my people. But I was a Queen nonetheless, and I had made an oath that made my life no longer mine. And these *were* the people of ones I loved. That was why I had chosen to be here: to protect them.

And if being a living symbol of light on their darkest of days was the best—and perhaps only—way I could truly help them....

Then so be it.

Unfortunately, that resolution to sacrifice myself didn't make my ice-heart pulse any more slowly. At least my palms weren't sweating.

Funny, that.... I wasn't sweaty at all. One would think that I would be purely from the heat outside and the climb inside, but....

I was brought back on track from my momentary derailment by another round of roars, and I flinched. A *normal* crowd would have been bad enough. Did it have to be filled with freakin' *dragons*?

"Do...do I have to say anything?" I whispered out loud, still not confident in my selected projection abilities.

Ben shook his head firmly. *Not if you don't want to. Like I said, Avva is prepared for anything you decide.*

Although if you do *want to say a few words,* Kor said with a smirk, *I've prepared a little something for you. And I can send the words to you as you go along.*

His offer to use his services as both speechwriter and living teleprompter was terribly tempting. But that...didn't feel right. A polished performance, as impressive as it might be right now, didn't feel *me*. And I didn't think I could pull off anything but *me* without looking as if I didn't care. Someday, I might be as authentically confident and collected as the King was. But that wasn't today.

Eskala's words came to me once again. *It's a hard, hard thing to do, to rule with vulnerability. But the alternative is even harder.*

"No, but thank you, Kor," I whispered. "*If* I say anything...I think it has to come from me.... But let me know if I start saying anything horribly offensive, alright?"

His smirk faded to a proud smile. *Alright, will do.*

Another roar. My time was limited, so I might as well prepare. "Who is even *out* there?"

As much of the Warflight as we dare risk, Ben said grimly, looking out. *We'll be very surprised if the Devourer only attacks here. So Alyish had to make some hard choices in how to distribute our forces across the Realms.*

I swallowed. "And Eskala?"

I didn't see her anywhere, when you'd think this would be exactly where she'd be, if she were here.

At Crownhold. In...case.

I didn't ask what that meant.

Besides, at that moment, the door opened, letting in the boom of the King's voice, and the soldier there looked at us questioningly.

I took as deep as a breath as my armor allowed...then looked at Ben and nodded grimly.

He clenched my shoulder briefly, eyes so deep with gratitude that they burned slightly. Then he strode to the opening with his wings following, and I trailed behind them all to form the end of our team diamond.

Another roar broke out as Ben stepped into the sun, even more deafening for how it echoed in the passage I was still in. The King paused in his speech to allow them to work out their exuberance.

Wait for his signal, Ben said without looking back as he and his wings continued forward. He took his place by his father, but at a surprising distance, almost double one of their widths. Kor and Yvera parted and took their places at the ends of the curve that was this large sandstone balcony, standing at aesthetically pleasing, symmetrical distances from Alyish and whoever was standing in for the King's leftwing right now.

Once the roars died, the King said softly, "And now, allow me to present the newly crowned White Queen of the Seventh Realm and leader of her restored clan: Queen Sarah Moontouched."

I took that as "his signal."

Taking a shaky breath, iceheart pulsing its way out of my chest, limbs trembling, I stepped from the shadows and into the sunlight.

The roars, the heat, the sunlight all hit me like hammers. I don't even remember how I made my way across that balcony. I knew I didn't float on a cloud there, that was for sure, so the memory must be so blurred from the difficulty that my mind just let it go. The next thing I remember was standing between Ben and the King, with the King putting a hand to my back—no doubt to appear to be presenting me, but secretly to keep me from falling over.

And boy, did I need that support more than ever when my eyes finally beheld what was down there to greet me.

Dragons.

So. Many. Dragons.

So many, of every size and shade, that the dunes of the desert that lay beyond were primarily visible by the undulation of their own bodies as they stood on them.

Oh, there were amón down there, sprinkled among them like colorful confetti, some on their backs, some standing below in their shadows.

But for the first time, I understood what a warflight was.

It was an armada.

Of dragons.

The most terrifying thing about the more-than-terrifying sight of all of them was the thought that then popped into my head: *If this is our army and we're still worried....*

Then the worlds must truly be coming to an end.

Do you wish to speak? the King asked me gently.

I knew from his tone that he would rather not ask this of me now. That he was almost hopeful for my own sake that I would refuse so that he could whisk me back inside, where it was dark and cool and not mind-numbingly horrifying. But because he was their King and because I was a Queen, his equal (in his mind) for whom he could not take away the choice, even with the best of intentions...he had to ask.

That concern gave me the final bit of courage I needed to nod mechanically.

Then do. They will hear you.

I wanted to jokingly ask if they would hear even if I whispered. But there wasn't time for that, and I didn't know where I was finding the brainpower for a joke anyway. Probably hysteria that I shouldn't encourage.

I opened my mouth.

I do not know how I found the words. They were simple, true. And spoken in a voice that was audibly tense and close to trembling. And painfully few. But it was a miracle that my mind and my throat formed any at all.

"Thank you all, for more than you know. For welcoming me so warmly. For protecting me when I could not protect myself. For sheltering me when I was so far from home. Even now, though, I am still new, still learning, still growing. I cannot do much to help you now, and you do not know how much that hurts me. You do not know how afraid I am now.... But the thing I am afraid of most is losing all of you. You, you magnificent people with hearts of flame, who I have come to love. And so, I'm here today for you. What little I can do, I will. I am with you to the end, whatever it may be."

I took a deep, shaking breath. What had the King said to me once? Reversed, that farewell blessing seemed as good a conclusion as any.

"Flame go with you, and Ice watch over you."

We're going to need Them, I thought queasily, feeling like I was about to throw up.

A pause of silence, with the only sound being the whistle of the desert wind flapping the banners overhead.

Did I say something wrong? I asked Ben frantically.

Then, in unison, the dragons all let out a roar that shook the world.

CHAPTER TWENTY-FOUR

GOODBYE

KORIBEN

As the Warflight trumpeted their acceptance of her speech, Sarah's eyes glazed over and her body wobbled dangerously, and Avva saw that too.

Koriben, get her inside, now. I'll smooth things over.

Right, I agreed with grim relief. I replaced his hand on her back and began steering and supporting her (hopefully subtly) back into the command chamber, leaving Avva to make our sudden withdrawal seem deliberate.

And just in time, because Sarah collapsed into me almost as soon as we were in shadow. I scooped her up and carried her the rest of the way inside, striding quickly through the command chamber, down a short hall, and into a side room meant for rest and meditation. I figured this was as good a use of it as any.

Only when I collapsed onto one of the large cushions—trembling myself from what we had both had to go through, and I hadn't had to *speak*—did I allow myself to fully examine Sarah. I'd glanced at her before, of course, but I'd had to keep most of my focus on getting her out of sight.

"How is she?" Kor asked quietly.

Yvera, I could see, was waiting outside, perhaps to discourage anyone else from coming to use the room.

"She'll be alright," I said after a few moments of my power sinking into her. I *hated* seeing her so pale and limp like this, with her eyes closed as if in death—an impression made all the starker by her bone-white hair—but I knew it was just a faint. I could feel her miraculous new iceheart pulse its magic through her, stronger now for the relative dark and cool.

"It was all too much, I think. Asking her to do this, after everything today and yesterday, in that heat, and at nearly *noon*."

Which was doing wonders for us drakón, wonders that I wished I could share with her the same way she could share with me—beyond what I was doing now to heal her.

I hoped she didn't wake up feeling like she was weak for collapsing like this. Hellwinds, if I'd had to do *that* in a *blizzard*, after what she had already been through, I would have fainted before I'd even gotten a word out.

"Well, she knows how to make a sacrifice worth something," Kor said with an admiring shake of his head. "She couldn't have done a better job if I'd planned it that way."

It was true. Whatever pretty speech Kor had written for her, it probably hadn't included anything about fear. That had been a risky move. People were used to thinking their Monarchs had to be strong, fearless. But that was their expectations of *us*, I realized. Sarah could be something new. Something that was awe-inspiring precisely because of how...mortal she was.

Human, even.

At the very least, her raw honesty—which dramá also valued—seemed to have had the right effect.

"Ben," Yvera said as she ducked her head into the room. Her expression made me blink. It was the closest she ever came to being gentle. "Sarah's elites are here for her."

More accurately, some of Avva's elites that he was lending her for today. But I knew what that meant. It was time for me to once again entrust Sarah to someone else's protection. Because I was the Heir, and I and my wings and my elites had to get out there.

I had known this moment was coming all along.

I...I just....

I hadn't...expected...to not be able to say goodbye.

I blinked rapidly and swallowed. "Give...me a dek."

Yvera nodded and pulled out. Kor put a hand on my shoulder, then left without a word.

I sat there alone in that small, dimly lit room, holding my star. Trying my absolute best not to think about the possibility of never seeing her in the flesh again.

Because of my returning to the Flame, that is. Any other...possibility that led to our permanent separation was beyond even the realm of unthinkable.

I touched my forehead to hers and closed my eyes, breathing her in. Her cool, clear scent was stronger than ever since her investment and transformation. It seemed to fill not just my lungs but every part of me. I willed it to, trying to get as much of her into me as possible to sustain me through what was coming. Her star seemed to burn even brighter in my mind as I did so.

I opened my eyes, trying to memorize every single line of her.

"I love you," I whispered.

And despaired that I had waited until *that* moment to tell her, when she couldn't even hear.

I kissed her forehead slowly, feeling her cool skin against mine.

Took one last breath of her.

Then gently stood and carried her out.

And gave her into the arms of another.

"Take care of her," I told Tyri tightly.

"We will, Heir Koriben," she said with a small smile. "Our lives, our blood for hers."

I swallowed. "Flame, I hope it does not come to that."

Then I tore myself away without another glance and strode back down the hall, with my wings right behind me.

ONLY A FEW DEK later, we were soaring.

Normally, flying over the Temple of Flame was a fierce joy, unrivaled by any other I'd felt before meeting Sarah. The heat of the sun and desert, the hot currents, and the closeness of my Tree beating with each pulse of my flameheart made it all too *easy*. The feeling of raw power, unhindered by anything nearby to break or come to harm, the *freedom* of that cloudless sky....

Now I hardly felt any of it and was only glad that flying wasn't much of an effort, because I was having difficulty focusing to begin with. My star had begun to move again, and I was pretty sure it was under her own power now.

I had been *that close*. Missing her by only moments.

But they were necessary moments, as I knew from when I made myself focus on our moon, Edori, as she made her jealous way between Ythra and Kaldrir.

The eclipse had begun.

I, like all the others soaring in large circles over the Temple, scanned the ground, searching for any sign of a darkrift. That's how it would have to begin, since darkgates took a bit of work on this side as well.

First, the Devourer had to make enough tears in the Tree's defenses to get enough of its consumed through to buy its magic-wielders the time they needed to widen and combine those tears into a semi-permanent gate. Still easily collapsed with a bit of fire, like cauterizing a wound, and that area itself would technically thereafter be stronger for the scar. But the barrier *around* it would be stretched, like skin or fabric grown taught from being bunched, and if the Tree wasn't given time to regrow it, then it was easier to break.

It wasn't the first darkrift we were worried about. Or even the first hundred. It was the hundreds, perhaps thousands there would be after that, tearing in ever-increasing numbers until we were overwhelmed.

That was why the Devourer had timed its second invasion for this hour on this day. One less versed in strategy might think it foolish to launch its attack with us fully charged with the light and fire of noon. But it was not the start of its invasion that mattered most...but its end. Starting at our peak meant the only direction we could go was down. And that descent would grow ever more deadly and rapid the closer we came to the ground.

And since the Devourer knew we would be forewarned whatever time it chose, it might as well make it one that stroke fear into our hearts. The eclipse wasn't so terrible in and of itself, with all the energy we had stored. It was merely a symbol of what was to come.

It was a mocking promise.

There, due west, Yvera said to all, sharp-eyed as always.

She was the first to spot the darkrift—a tear in reality with only darkness beyond—on a sand dune only an eld to the west of the Temple. But we were not the closest. Besides, the Temple's three layers of shields activated in the rift's presence and that of the consumed pouring through.

The trolls that surged out of the darkrift before it closed stood no chance of breaking through even one of those layers of gold, which had been established centuries ago and meticulously maintained with each subsequent generation—and ritualistically reinforced by Avva, me, and most of the Sunfilled clan, plus many others, at dawn that morning.

Before they could even reach the first shield, a Battleblood swooped in and torched them, burning them to ash and bone and scorching the sand all around.

Like I said, it wasn't the first consumed we were worried about. But the first rift had been boldly close to the shields, probably as close as the Devourer could make one to the Tree right now. It was as much of a rude gesture in our faces as anything could be.

I can touch you, it said. *Watch me.*

So I did, as darkrifts began tearing everywhere through the fabric of my beloved world. Soon too many for us to call out to each other. We simply reacted, diving or climbing—since many rifts opened in mid-air to allow flyers through—as needed to the closest darkrifts to us.

I spotted one a bit lower to my right and banked, but of course, Yvera was there first, violet flames bursting through her mouth as she tore through the rift. If anything got through, I didn't see what it was before it was gone.

Then one opened up directly in front of me, making it mine. I opened my mouth and let the flame that had been building in my belly finally out. The golden inferno once again obliterated both the rift and anything else.

Flame, that felt good.

The start of a battle wasn't actually the worst part.

The third-worst part was right before, with the dread that built and built and built being worse than nearly anything. But when the fight actually began, with the power and adrenaline surging through your blood, with your first few enemies giving away like ash before you—that was release, that was relief.

The second-worst part of a battle was when people started dying. And with so many darkrifts, it was only a matter of perhaps dek now until some consumed got a spear through an eye or damaged a wing enough to send the drakón into a freefall.

The very worst part was hours away, and it was something I had not yet experienced myself. But as Edori crept across Kaldrir, I knew with a grimness deep in my flameheart that it could be coming.

It was the part when we became too exhausted, battered, and scattered to keep fighting for our Tree and Realms....

And surrendered to our doom.

CHAPTER TWENTY-FIVE

TOLL

SARAH

I WATCHED THE START of the battle numbly, staring at the fire map as Tyri, the Sunfilled who had first greeted me and who was the head of my temporary elites, explained what was going on, and the strategies of both sides. I listened to her dutifully. As dazed as I was, I hungered to understand, so I asked questions and listened hard to those answers as well.

Always, I watched Ben.

Even though the flames were just normal flame colors, obscuring the clans each drakón belonged to, I knew who he was. Even if he wasn't bigger than all the others, the only one with two sets of horns, and always with two familiar dragons at his flanks, I knew that shape too well by now.

He was *my* dragon.

To say that I was disappointed to wake up to discover that I had not just fainted but had missed his departure...would be an understatement. I felt as if my iceheart was breaking, preemptively. I wanted to reach out and grab that diving, twisting, swerving dragon and pull him back to me, holding him against me, where it was safe, where he could never come to harm.

But I couldn't, and not just because trying to capture that merely magical representation of him would probably only give me a burned hand for my trouble.

He was the Heir. He had sworn as I had now sworn.

Our lives for our Trees. Our lives for our Realms.

He was in his place now. And I...was in mine.

Actually, I was a bit surprised at first that they were keeping me in the middle of the "safe" action instead of locking me away in some small room deep within the bowels of this place. But then, even though that would probably be the *safest* option, it wouldn't be accomplishing the point of me being here. If *safe* had been the only priority, they would never have let me come.

So, here I was. Here to be seen. Here to be as in the thick of things as was acceptably safe. Here to be "helping."

And here, some of the time, was the King. He would check in occasionally, especially to consult with Alyish on the progress of the battle, but most of the time he was out being as helpful as it was safe for *him* to be, considering the value of his Blood to the enemy as well. The last thing we needed in this moment was for the Devourer to have enough Monarch blood to open a darkgate large enough for it to come through itself. So, for the good of all, neither of us could be risked in direct combat—not even the King.

The difference between the two of us—beyond the obvious size, strength, and experience—was power, power he could feed into those translucent gold shields that surrounded the Temple of Flame. And it was with the relationship he had already established with his people, so to keep morale up, he went everywhere he could within the confines of those shields that both protected and trapped us now. Or so I guessed. I only was gathering bits and pieces of what he was doing when he went away as time went on. Once we heard he had even gone down to commune with the Tree, and everyone around me shared grim, knowing looks at the news.

I couldn't bear to ask what was behind them.

And so the minutes melted into hours and slowly dragged on. I watched the eclipse progress not through the windows—which weren't a whole lot of good at this angle—but through the solarus's holographic representation, and it was taking its sweet time getting to totality. The wait was torture for *me*, and I wasn't the one feeling my strength fade away from not just exertion but the loss of sunlight. I knew without being told that if it took much longer, the drakón would not have the strength they needed to get through the night.

Because clearly this would not be a quick battle. I understood with dawning horror as Tyri explained the battle strategies that this was a war of attrition—a siege, but one in which the defenders were trapped outside while those they defended were relatively safe within...for as long as the defenders could hold out.

That was the next piece of horror that fell into place: Ben and I were separated now, with chilling totality. Now those ancient shields were activated, there was no letting *anything* through them, not even the defenders. Not even *gates* would function anymore across those shields—because to allow the kind of magic of gates to go through them was to open the potential to darkrifts and darkgates as well. With shields this powerful, it was all or nothing, and in the defense of their Tree and thus their entire Realms, the dramá had, in the preparations they had begun centuries ago for this day, chosen *nothing*.

The defenders had posts in other sandstone plateaus where reinforcements waited to relieve the current flights, and where the relieved flights could go for rest and replenishment. They even had a sungate out there, so they could go through to get some sunlight, or to call for even more backup, if any could be spared from the similar conflicts that were now raging, if to a much lesser extreme, in the other Realms. But other than that, and the coordination and information we could give them from in here through scales and the inner voices of drakón standing on lookout points around the Temple, they were on their own.

I was now trapped in here. And Ben was now trapped fighting for our lives out there. It was just as I had told Michael, except even worse: Ben, as the true Heir he was, was leading from the front lines. I just hadn't expected the lines between us to be so literal. Or *solid*. True, if all else failed, Ben *might* be able to surge to me through those shields. But the connection I felt with him now was faint. Even if he could bring himself to abandon his people now to come to me, I didn't think he would be able to.

Why did I have to be so *weak* that I wasn't even able to say goodbye?

FINALLY, I HEARD THE words I had been both dreading and hoping for.

"Pull Koriben out," Alyish said grimly as he watched the flame map. "He's getting sloppy."

So it wasn't just me. Ben had let a flock of some harpy things near his wings. Though I couldn't see much detail from this magnification—which encompassed the Temple of Flame, miles of the dunes around, and some of the outposts—I thought they'd done some damage. His wingbeats, particularly from his left wing, had seemed a tad more belabored to me after that. Kor had been replaced maybe an hour ago, as had most of the first flights, but Ben and Yvera had kept on. Yvera had been the one to torch the harpies for daring to get near her Heir.

After watching how many times Yvera had saved Ben's scaly hide in this past couple of agonizing hours alone, I not only forgave her for everything, I could have kissed her myself.

The gold uniformed amón who seemed to be Alyish's primary messenger grimaced but passed the message on. I understood what the grimace was about when we got Ben's reply.

"Heir Koriben respectfully declines," another messenger said after a few minutes when she came up to us. "He insists he can last until after the total eclipse. To leave now would be a disheartening blow to the current defenders when they need him most."

"Torch that boy, do I have to get his father in here?" Alyish muttered, running a hand over the fuzzy violet stubble on his head. But his complaint was muted enough that he obviously didn't intend for anyone to hear except the select few right around the flame table. Which, as perhaps one of the best representations yet of the bizarre turn my life had taken, included me.

Can Ben defy an order from Alyish? I asked Tyri silently.

It's complicated. He's not of higher rank, but he's by far the highest ranked person leading the defense outside the Temple. In practice, he shouldn't. Alyish is the head of the Warflight, and the King has put him over the defense of the Tree today, even if it's from a distance.

No one seems surprised, though.

Tyri smiled thinly. *No, no one is. I would have been surprised—and worried—if Ben had pulled back now. I think Alyish is relieved to know Ben's still got enough fire to be stubborn about it.*

These dramá had a funny idea of military discipline. I didn't know whether to be worried or relieved myself. All I knew was that I felt sick from the growing knot of tension inside me.

"Tell him," Alyish said impatiently, "that if he torches up again, he can consider that an order from the King."

The runner nodded and went off to relay the latest message.

Before, I'd at least tried to get the complete picture of the battle. Now my entire focus was on Ben...and the eclipse. At least Ben was indeed more careful after that, and Yvera somehow more ferocious than ever in defending him, even risking her own wings and head—which appeared to be the main parts the consumed went for—in the process.

"What's that?" Alyish demanded sharply, pointing to the ground. "Tell me that's not—"

"Darkgate," a runner said with a gasp as she came up to him. "They've got a darkgate. South by southeast, three eld off."

A new dome had sprung up where Alyish was pointing. The fire couldn't give us enough detail to really tell what was inside, but consumed were rushing through it, as if it were some pustule of infection that had developed on the ground and was now oozing out enemies. Ben and his wings had already spotted it, and with a contingent of others, were diving for it, billowing flame.

"Keep the Third and Fifth Flights off, don't let them get distracted," Alyish shouted to the room at large, in the hearing of all the scales connected to all the drakón on the walls to communicate orders through the speed of thought. "We don't want another forming while—hellfrost!"

Just as Ben and his flight cleansed that pustule, another sprung up on the opposite side of the Temple, and another. The response to the infections was not as fast as it might have once been. Because the drakón were weary, and the eclipse was entire. With a twist of dread, I could see the relative darkness fall outside the windows.

I didn't want to know the answer, but I had to. *Are those domes the darkgates themselves, or....*

No, Tyri said grimly. *The darkgate is inside. The dome is their own shield to protect it. Not as strong, because it can still let consumed through, otherwise there would be little point. But a barrier, nonetheless.*

"All flights, stay in their quadrants," Alyish roared. "Now only Koriben is mobile, do you understand?"

And even Ben could not be everywhere. Nor could even he keep this up for much longer.

FOUR MORE DARKGATES WERE formed by the time the minutes of total eclipse had passed. Once the drakón began regaining their sunlight, they rallied and destroyed them, but not before waves of consumed creatures had poured through, including some who were getting to work on the first of the three shields, and setting up new domes to do so. They sent flashes of magic at the shield, some powerful enough I felt them from here, that crashed into the barrier and made it thunder. Now the drakón were stretched thinner than ever trying to keep any *new* darkgates from forming while dealing with the consumed attacking the shields.

I saw now, with terrible clarity, how this could end. How Ben had always known this could end.

Drakón, fully transformed and powered by the sun, were nearly unstoppable in a battle against a single opponent. Even hundreds of opponents. After all, the Devourer had probably lost thousands of consumed by now, and as far as I could keep track, only a dozen or so drakón were put out of action and a few dead. But the Devourer didn't care how many thousands it took. And the drakón could only last so long, even during the *day*.

When night came....

The question, in the end, would come down to how many consumed the Devourer had. Not how many it would risk, because I had a gut feeling it was gambling everything on today. It had waited a millennium for this, to defeat and consume perhaps its most formidable obstacle in the universe. The power that it could gain and the lish that it could add to its ranks would no doubt make up for the loss of this far inferior army. With that many lish alone...it could go on to consume the galaxy. Including Earth.

Including my Realm. My family.

So how many consumed did the Devourer have? And was it more or less than what the drakón could handle?

Considering the Devourer had chosen to invade...it thought it had enough.

Now I understood why everyone had been so afraid. Why the Trees and the smartest minds kept insisting that something new was needed. Because they knew the Devourer had learned from last time. It had mastered the old game. It knew that it couldn't *beat* the united might of the drakón. But it could *outlast* them.

Unless something changed.

But the only thing that had changed in this whole hell of a situation was *me*. And yet, if I tried to do anything to help by stepping out of that shield, the Devourer could end things then and there. The *one clue* I had finally figured out today at something new I could offer them was now out of reach. Other than that, I had nothing. The gun at my side was useless in a conflict of this scale, just as I'd told Michael his gun would be. I could maybe help strengthen the shields, but not significantly right now, not ones this big, not more than the King already was doing. Not, at least, until nightfall.

And by then, it might be too late.

Strengthening those shields *might* save the Tree.

But it wouldn't save Ben.

As the full horror of our situation now finally sunk into me, as I raged at my helplessness...Alyish wearily called Ben out of the fight. And this time, Ben obeyed.

I didn't know whether to be relieved or cry from despair. Even with him retreating to safety to rest...

...it felt like the first somber toll of his death.

CHAPTER TWENTY-SIX

TIME

SARAH

TIME WAS A CRUEL thing.

It had sped on and on like a whirlwind for the past eleven days of my life, and yet somehow each had felt like a lifetime.

Now each fear-laden, tense minute dragged like molasses dripping down the walls, and yet, before I knew it, the hours until nightfall abruptly were gone.

The sun began to set, and Ben, of course, was back out there, and had been for a while. And the situation was far, far worse.

There were now too many darkgates for them to destroy. It was like a sick game of whack-a-mole. No sooner did they get one down than two new ones sprung up. And through each one, a hundred or more consumed poured out before they could shut it down. Some drakón were just flying around to torch the masses in vast swaths, but for each swath they took out, another replaced it.

There was a reason we had not seen the King in some time. All his energy and attention were needed to maintain the remaining two shields, because by dint of magic and crude banging, the consumed had taken down the first shield and rushed to the next. Other drakón were constantly circling the shield, burning whoever came close, but again, they just kept pouring in like fleshy water into a breach, climbing heedlessly over ashes and corpses of the ones who had come before them.

Even if we survived, that beautiful desert would be a scorched waste of death after this.

But that was not the concern on anyone's minds right now. I could see the real question in every line of stress on everyone's face.

How many more?

And this was even without a lish in the fray. Though Alyish had the scouts keep their eyes peeled, no one had seen so much as the tip of Solim's dark tail yet. He would no doubt be a part of this battle, but it seemed the Devourer wouldn't play its trump card until the end.

I watched the light out the windows, made hazy by all the smoke, gradually turn golden, then red, then dark blue. Such a natural, inevitable thing, that sunset. Bringing such terrible doom.

Because night....

Meant the end of the drakón defenders. The end of their sungate. And the beginning of the *true* siege.

CHAPTER TWENTY-SEVEN
NIGHTFALL

KORIBEN

I WAS SO NUMB with exhaustion, with the constant blur of fire, land, sky, and death, that I almost didn't notice Kaldrir finally abandon us as the last of His life-sustaining rays sunk below the horizon.

Almost.

And yet the change in everyone else around me was too severe not to. Even before Alyish broadcasted the order to retreat far and wide, drakón were disengaging, forced to slip away as they felt their energy plummet to dangerous levels. Even before the sun was gone, each one of us had begun to gauge how long we could hold on to drakáform and time our retreat accordingly. The weaker ones had already left us, and after the order came out, everyone began flying as one toward the largest stronghold, atop the sandstone plateau to the east.

The place where, together, we would make our night stand...and try to live to see the dawn.

Knowing how much longer I could hold out than the others, I shook myself out of my stupor as best as I could, rallying what felt like the last fires in my flameheart to circle broadly around the rest of them, fiercely guarding their retreat with flame and claw. Yvera stuck as closely to my right flank as ever, along with Ordran to my left, though even they were saving their energy now to simply keep up with me as my living shields.

Despite our best efforts, some drakón miscalculated, or couldn't disengage quickly enough, or were ambushed along the way. As I turned and began making another arc to the south, far at the other end of our retreating formation, I saw Barom, a former classmate of mine and an unusually easygoing Brightflare, give out suddenly, shrinking against the twilight sky as he lost form. Panic shooting through my veins, I pounded my wings toward him, but whole clouds of creatures descended on me, blocking my way.

Even as I poured out flame and slashed and flew with a recklessness that had Yvera screaming at me in my head, I knew I couldn't get to him in time.

I didn't even see him fall.

When I reached the end of the arc and could not find him, red crept to the edges of my vision and I roared my rage, swerving back so swiftly, Ordran struggled to make the turn with me as I began tearing back through the consumed pursuing the remaining stragglers.

Though the monsters were giving up the chase to turn as one. Toward me.

BEN, Yvera shouted at me, her roar punctuating my name. *We HAVE to go. They're coming for you, and even you can't hold on much longer!*

She knew my limits, perhaps better than anyone. And she knew, better than anyone, what my answering growl meant.

The day had been too much. Too many friends gone, Barom only being the latest. Never had I lost so many, and never in one day. It was like Ilyam all over again, except far, far worse.

Too much exhaustion, too much mind-numbing bloodshed, too much despair, too much darkness. I was losing myself. I was looking at the gathering storm, not with fear...but satisfaction.

I was ignoring the messenger shouting in my head Alyish's personal order for me to retreat as if it were a fly buzzing in my ear. And I was angling straight for the thick of them.

In a burst of effort, Yvera pounded her wings to veer into me, knocking me off course. I roared in irritation, but as my head swerved to catch sight of her, Ordran shouted at me, *Ben, if we don't go back now, Yvera will die!*

He had said the perfect words at the perfect moment, just as I saw her. Like a key turning in a lock, he gave me just enough clarity to see Yvera's heaving breaths, labored wingbeats, lowered head. To see how little flame she could spit out at a swarm of valper descending on us.

My lethal rightwing, my indomitable foster sister, was fading fast...and could die.

For *me*.

Fear shot through me like an icy blast, chilling away my despairing rage. I swerved at once toward East Fort.

Come on, I growled at them both, narrowing my eyes at the flying horde that now lay between us and the plateau. *And stay close.*

Ben, Yvera groaned, but I could hear the shaky relief in her voice. *Don't tell me you're going to—*

But I was. I would not risk taking us around them, not when seconds could make the difference between life and death for her and Ordran.

So I opened my mouth, gathered all the flame I had left, and barreled into the thick of the consumed like a battering ram, burning our way through with a golden inferno.

I WAS DISMAYED BY what I saw when we reached East Fort, the largest of the fortified rings of sandstone that lay in each cardinal direction on the plateaus circling the Temple of Flame.

There, another siege was well underway, in proportion just as devastating as the one against the Temple. Though it was only a few dek after sunset, an army of consumed already had the fort surrounded, now that no one was able to fly out and destroy the darkgates forming all around, and none of the defenders on the ramparts had enough spark to entirely keep that army from pounding away against the wards layered over the outer wall. The bigger consumed—trolls armed with clubs, ahglen with their stone fists, and so on—were no doubt wearing away those wards with each blow they had to absorb.

At a glance, I could see no physical damage to the walls yet, but that was the only good news I gleaned as I burned and slashed our way through the second army of flyers swarming over the fort.

We got a blessed reprieve when we passed through East Fort's permashield dome. Unlike the Temple shields, it was weak enough to allow us through but strong enough to keep the consumed at bay. Although I felt a blessed rush of power course through the shield the moment we passed under it that indicated an increase in its impenetrability.

We were the last ones in, and now the metaphorical gates had been slammed shut behind us.

Now we would just have to see how long they would hold.

The moment I touched down in the center of the fort, my drakáform slipped from me like water through a sieve. I couldn't ever remember falling out of it so quickly, so rapidly it truly felt like a *fall* as my essence imploded. Then again, I couldn't remember ever being so exhausted, so numb and trembling that I collapsed onto all fours and then onto my side, heaving for air, sweat already soaking my newly formed skin, hair, and armor as my eyes drifted closed, and I hovered just at the edge of unconsciousness.

I may have started out on our way back with more spark than either of my wings, but I had given it all, every last flicker, to get us here.

My collapse must have been alarming enough that Yvera shouted my name across the space between us, though she sounded little better.

But she's alive, I thought.

For now, a dark voice inside whispered.

Armor clattered and boots pounded across the stone court toward us. Everyone had had to hold back as we landed, but now all three of us were out of our drakáforms, healers and elite rushed across the now-empty space.

"Heir Koriben, are you alright?" Woran asked urgently as he dropped to his knees at my side, but I felt his healing hands latch onto me to find the answer for himself.

"Fine," I said through my pants, forcing my eyes to flicker open, though my vision was blurry. "Just...burned out."

The transformation back, even as sudden and forceful as it was, had still healed any cuts, bruises, and pulled muscles I had, which was one reason I was so utterly spent now. Although my drakáwings were going to complain mightily to me for how I'd abused them the next time I brought them out.

Not unlike my metaphorical wings, in fact.

Ben, you noble idiot, Kor silently cursed at me. His inner voice came closer with each word, his hurry belying the harshness of his tone. He had been worried about me.

Hmm, if he was using *that* adjective, as upset as he was with me, he must not have noticed my lapse into suicidal rage. Perhaps it had been too brief or indiscernible from a distance.

My mind flitted to the two people I'd been trying my hardest not to think about since noon, and I wondered if they knew. I was lucky I was too weary to even wince, or Woran would have misinterpreted my resurging guilt as a pain from an unseen wound.

Good to hear you're alive too, Kor, I sent back, letting my eyes drift closed again.

Of course I am, he snapped. *That was the idea, wasn't it?*

For all his formidable power and intellect, and for all the danger I'd put him through, Kor hadn't trained for battle as extensively as Yvera and I had. That was both his preference and traditional expectation: leftwings were *meant* to be the noncombatant member of the trio, the one able to focus the most time and effort on governance, scholarship, intelligence.

In addition, Kor's relatively small size put him at an even greater disadvantage than normal in his drakáform. He had begun the fight at noon at my side more for the symbolism than anything, and that was only because he was drakón. If he'd been amón like Eskala, no one would have expected even that much of him. I'd sent him away as soon as the fighting intensified, and he, exhausted by then from simply trying to keep up with me, had left without protest, knowing his time would come—and all too soon.

What lethality he *could* bring to bear was mainly in his amáform, when he had full access to his power and could use stealth or finesse. Given those narrow parameters, Kor *was* deadly—contrary to what he allowed most everyone, even Yvera, to believe. Tonight...all the Realms might just find out how much.

"He's right," Woran confirmed out loud a moment later, referring to my self-diagnosis of burnout. "Severe, though. It's a wonder he's even conscious."

He then ordered someone else, "Sundew, now. And you, prop him up."

Whoever it was did so, hooking their arms under my shoulders and hoisting my limp body against them, and someone else handed Woran a vial of the shimmery gold liquid that was more precious right now than any other substance, considering how sundew was all we had to swiftly replenish our power until the sun rose again.

Much of the Six Realms' emergency stores had recently been placed within East Fort's most heavily guarded cellar room just for this purpose. That cache, for all that it could fit within one large chest, was collectively worth almost more than the contents of the Crown Treasury, and we had been authorized to use all of it—a sacrifice of our most dear resource that would have been unthinkable two sevendays ago.

But then, the Devourer's second invasion was exactly the sort of unthinkable, cataclysmic event we had so carefully gathered it for all these many centuries, drop by precious drop. And we were here to give something even more precious for the Realms: our lives.

Even knowing Woran had full authority to give that vial to me for just this purpose, my face hardened as I eyed it, and I feebly lifted my hand to push it away as Woran brought it toward me.

I would recover...somehow. But that vial could be someone's salvation, and soon. Without that liquid, without the power it gave, healers like Woran could not heal people who were far worse off than I was. Without that power, we couldn't keep up the wards that strengthened the walls and kept the Devourer from forming darkrifts within them and the permashield that held flyers at bay above them. Without that power, we wouldn't last until dawn.

Taking it...felt like taking a life.

"No—"

Ben, torch you, Kor snarled silently, reaching me with a final stomp of his foot. *Drink it, or I'm telling Sarah.*

I had enough energy to wince now. I leaned forward, away from the person supporting me, and they let go. I settled myself into a cross-legged position as my eyes fell back on the vial, which Woran was proffering once more.

"Heir Koriben," he snapped, "as your head healer, I insist. We're going to need our Heir to be more than a limp rag when the wards fall."

My eyes flicked to Kor's in alarm, and he nodded grimly. *It's only a matter of time now, and not much of it.*

I felt as if the ground were giving way beneath me. *We're going through the sundew that* fast?

Yvera staggered over to us, grasping an elite's shoulder for stability as her blazing eyes darted between Kor and me. Her face was pale, her lips pressed thin. "What's this hellwinds I'm hearing about a *mogoth*?"

Mogoth. My flameheart sputtered at the word. The most powerful of the Devourer's magic workers save a lish, and quite nearly as feared, especially since they were, essentially, living shadows. One could have said that they were spirits...except spirits didn't consume whatever flesh they touched to leave only bone.

One hadn't been sighted in decades. And now one was *here*?

I grabbed the sundew and downed it in one gulp. Woran was right: if I wasn't back on my feet, as soon as possible...more people would die than could be saved by this vial alone.

It's warm, spicy liquid was too thick to flow through my parched mouth easily, but fortunately, Woran already had a water flask in hand that he gave me, and I downed a third of the contents in one gulp. Even through the lingering flavor of the sundew, I tasted the mineral and nutritional additives.

Kor no doubt deliberately delayed his reply until after I took the sundew, because only then did he turn to Yvera and silently answer, *There* was *one, yes.*

Before I could be relieved about the past tense, Kor clenched his jaw and continued. *It got in somehow.*

It was a good thing I'd swallowed most of my mouthful of water just before he said that, because I choked.

"What?" I spluttered.

Kor's eyes were blazing dark sapphires now. *We don't know how, or how long it was here. But a few dek before sunset, it began attacking the wall from the inside. Before I got to it, it had greatly weakened both the wall, and through it, the outer wards.*

Wait, Yvera said sharply. *You're saying* you *killed it?*

Kor shrugged grimly. *Yes.*

On any other day, that casual dismissal would have knocked me over. Kor could have gone down in history for single-handedly killing a mogoth, and he knew it. But on a day like today, it was only one of the many heroic feats that had been and would yet be required to save our Realms.

And even though it was now dead, the mogoth had just made that task tremendously harder. From the darkness in Kor's eyes, I saw how hollow his achievement felt to even him. There, beneath his mask, I saw only raging guilt.

I knew that kind all too well—the shame that screamed at you that no matter how much you gave, it never seemed to be enough.

"*Hellfrost,*" I breathed.

I knew our situation was dire, but this....

I downed the last of the water in the canteen to get it out of my hands and passed it off, then ran my hands over my face. I could feel the sundew at work, building up my flameheart once more, which in turn sent fire back through my blood, enlivening every enervated part of me.

And yet not fast enough.

How long can the wards last now? Yvera asked Kor.

They were still trying to figure that out when I left them, he replied wearily. *But if you want my rough estimate? A few deken,* if we can repair them before any *other catastrophic blows.*

He pointed to the eastern wall. Given the size of the fort, the wall was a quarter elden away, which was why I hadn't noticed the unusual concentration of drakón swarming there. Or the ominous dark line running down it.

But there's little we can do about that crack, Kor finished.

And that meant plugging and shielding it with magic, which meant it would be a constant power sink for us, draining us as surely as a crack in a vase would leak water, no matter how many times you filled it.

Kor was right. Our precious stores of sundew, which we had bet our very lives on...would no longer be enough.

Yvera cursed. Then swallowed. "I...had better get over there. Talk to Ulsa."

As the Heir's rightwing, she was one of the highest-ranking officers in the Warflight currently outside the Temple, technically higher than the East Fort commander who would right now be leading the defense against the siege beyond our walls.

I started pushing myself to my feet to join her.

"No, Ben," Yvera said, as she held up a hand and scowled at me. "You rest."

"Yv—" I began as I straightened. I didn't help my case when I staggered.

Some of her old fire reentered her eyes. "Let me do my job, Ben. You'll be needed to do yours soon enough."

She cast a glare at Kor, pointing a finger at him. "You stay with him, you hear me?"

Kor couldn't seem to help a smirk, as weary as it was. "Oh, so now that I've killed a *mogoth*, you think I'm sufficient protection for Ben?"

"You're the best I can spare right now, at any rate," Yvera said, scowling. "Don't let it get to your head."

She whipped around and strode away. "Ordran, with me."

My elite captain, who had joined us soon after Yvera did, nodded, casting me a strained glance as he left.

"I'll also be leaving him to your supervision, Leftwing Korinth," Woran said dryly. "Make sure he does indeed *rest*. And drinks."

Woran shoved another canteen in my hands with a pointed look.

"Yes, sir," Kor said with a cheeky salute.

Woran rolled his eyes but hurried away, his assistants following, leaving us with a handful of my elites standing in a loose circle around us at a respectful distance.

We were as alone as we were going to be right now, so as I uncapped the canteen, I looked at Kor and asked quietly, "Has a mogoth been sighted anywhere else?"

He shook his head, eyes darkening as I took a swig. "Not that I've heard."

After swallowing, I said, "Me neither."

And if one had been laying siege to the Temple before sunset, I *would* have heard, because I would have been called in to deal with it personally. So, unless the Devourer had another up its sleeve, it had used its second-most-effective slave not on the Temple...but on us.

This night's stand had been a gamble to begin with—one that I, Alyish, Avva, and the other Warflight strategists had made with a heavy heart. All the defenders trapped outside the Temple *could* have left through the sungate before Kaldrir had set, but that meant abandoning the Temple, our Tree, our King, and the Queen of Ice to their fate, allowing the Devourer to concentrate everything it had left on breaching their defenses.

Technically, there was little stopping the Devourer from doing just that, even now. We weren't in any position to defend the Temple from here, not as we were. But we had guessed that the Devourer wouldn't be able to resist spending at least *some* of its forces on us, especially with me here, and any small way we could weaken the Devourer could make the difference that saved the worlds.

Judging from the veritable army gathered outside the walls of the fort and the flyers still swooping overhead, we'd been correct about that much: the Devourer wasn't ignoring us.

But we didn't think the Devourer would press us so hard, nor so quickly. It made sense for it to be turning most of its efforts on the Temple. It made sense for it to save us for last, hoping to turn as many of us as possible to lish once the Tree fell and all hope for our worlds was lost. That's what all of us had assumed when we felt the rightness of this strategy settle into our flamehearts.

I looked up again at the swarms of dark shapes flying against the rapidly darkening sky, just waiting for the moment the permashield would fail so they could descend. I cast a glance at that dark crack in the wall. I listened to the crude war drums pounding outside, at the thunderclaps as the occasional troll or ahglen banged against the wards protecting the wall.

If the Devourer *was* turning its focus from us...it sure didn't feel like it.

"The situation at the Temple was the same as ever, last I heard," Kor said, following my gaze.

I glanced at him sharply. His dark eyes told me he knew exactly what I was thinking.

The Monarchs were ensconced within the Temple, safe from the Devourer's grasp. But that did not mean they were out of its reach. Not so long as it could use me to get to them.

Perhaps it hoped that it could lure one of them out, if I were in enough danger, and that was why it had been holding Solim back thus far: waiting for that most ideal of chances to get at the Blood it craved, the Blood that would allow it to end everything.

It had to be aware what a long shot that was. Even if Sarah or Avva could somehow get past the shields, no one would allow either of them to try. Monarchs or no, that kind of reckless self-endangerment recklessly endangered *everyone*. If either of them attempted to save me, Alyish would be fully authorized by our law to restrain them. Avva knew that so perfectly, I doubted he would try, even as his flameheart quenched for me.

At least I knew he would live. I'd waited the first few hours of the invasion in agony, wondering if my father was going to make the ultimate sacrifice, the kind that had ended the first invasion a thousand years ago. And perhaps if it were entirely up to him, he would have. But I thanked the Tree with every breath since noon that it *wasn't* up to him. Both Tree and King had to be in complete alignment for that kind of act. And surely if the Tree willed it, it would have happened by now. Sometimes the only thing that had kept me going that day was the growing confidence that Avva was *meant* to live. My death would devastate him. But my father, our King, would live to see the Realms through to the dawn.

Sarah....

My flameheart sputtered at just the thought of her, much less the thought of her so distraught that her elites would have to hold her back. I imagined her piercing silver eyes widening as she understood, then overflowing with tears as she sobbed and struggled against them while her tender iceheart broke.

I closed my eyes, agony at her impending pain coursing through me. For no other reason than to spare her that, I *ached* to live. I knew too well the burden of being the one to have to carry on alone. After so much loss just today, I'd momentarily gone mad with it.

I could only hope that one day...she could forgive me.

Another thunderclap echoed across the fort as something large and forceful slammed against the wards, interrupting my thoughts. I sighed and ran a hand through my hair, trying to steady myself. The drying sweat had made the strands clump unevenly, providing a helpful distraction as I worked my fingers through them and then tied them back.

More likely, this savage siege wasn't to lure one of the Monarchs out, and the Devourer truly meant to kill me, solely to hurt the ones who loved me or demoralize the Temple defenders. Or perhaps this was the Devourer's ultimate punishment for the challenge I'd supposedly thrown at it in my berserk insanity days ago, which I still could only vaguely remember.

It could have been for all those reasons and more. Whatever the cause, I saw in Kor's eyes that he'd guessed the same result I had: the Devourer would not let me live.

We—*all* of us—were about to die.

Except, perhaps...the one person whom no one could kill. Not if he were ready for them, prepared to escape. The one person who could fill the void I would leave behind me.

Perhaps the one who had always been meant to.

Agony coursed through me again as I thought of losing my star in that most final of ways, but I had to think of not just the good of the Realms but of Sarah. She would...she would...need him when I was gone. She cared for him. I knew she did. Instinct told me that she held the dimmest of embers in her heart for him, and it wouldn't take much for Kor to fan that into something more.

Perhaps that would be how she would finally forgive me.

Icy resolve filled my veins, despite the sundew's influence. Despite the two canteens I'd drunk by now, my throat felt as parched as ever. I cleared my throat reflexively, even though I spoke next with my inner voice. This wasn't something I wanted *anyone* else to hear.

Kor...can you get through the Temple shields?

His eyes narrowed, hardening. *Why do you ask?*

I slowly put my hand on his shoulder, clenching it as I gazed back at him soberly. *When...I die—*

Kor's eyes soulflared.

No, he said flatly, immediately.

Kor, let me finish, I insisted. I stowed the empty canteen in the ether so I could grip his other shoulder with my other hand. *I can't leave—*

You can just as well as I can, he silently raged. *You can surge away. And yet you won't. And I didn't insult you like this by suggesting you should.*

I clenched my jaw. *Because you know I have to live or die with them. I, their Heir, asked this of them, so I must share in their sacrifice. But you're my* leftwing, *Kor. It means something entirely different if you survive. You aren't even supposed to be* here, not really.

He'd insisted on it, but no one would have thought less of him if he had gone through the sungate after I'd sent him away, and certainly not if he had before the sun went down.

Kor just glared at me, for once too furious to even reply.

What a strange reversal of roles: me, trying to get my leftwing to think logically, to think of the good of the Realms. The irony of it steadied me somewhat, giving me the strength to face my immediate future...and the way my flameheart momentarily extinguished at the thought of it.

I took a deep breath. *I am honored to have you by my side to the end, as the best of friends and as the noblest of warriors. But when I die, the Realms will need you. Sarah...*

I couldn't help a swallow, nor my hands tightening reflexively on his shoulders. *...will need you.*

A muscle in Kor's jaw twitched. *No. They need* you. *Sarah will need* you.

Unbidden, the Tree's whispered words returned to me. *She needs you.*

I flinched. Kor took advantage of my hesitation to shake his head, lips pressed into a hard, thin smile, his eyes as dark and hard as flints.

I told you, Ben. She never wanted me. She only ever wanted you. Do you think I, the Tolsyon heir, would have let her go if she'd ever shown the slightest hint of preferring me over you? Flame Above, Ben, with her, I could have ended it all—

Kor stopped himself, his eyes darting away.

What? I demanded, flameheart pulsing.

Kor laughed humorlessly, still looking down. *Nothing. Nothing at all. Because I could tell from the first day the two of you met that she wanted you, and you wanted her, and I knew the two of you were meant. And for a time, it was all the same to me. I was happy for you both. It was only later that, against my better judgment, I....*

He swallowed, then closed his eyes.

Then, a moment later, he opened them and lifted his gaze to mine. His sapphires were now bleak. *Sarah would never forgive me, you know. If I came back without you.*

I don't know, I said, smiling thinly. *She's forgiven me worse.*

Hard to believe I was speaking so easily about my death, but ever since facing it, a kind of calming numbness had settled over me. Perhaps it was fatalism, but perhaps it was something...more. Some last, comforting touch from the Tree.

Perhaps it was because I could still see my star in my mind's eye, more beautiful than any of the lights appearing in the darkening expanse above, and knew she would be with me until the end. Mine...until the last pulse of my heart.

Kor echoed my thin smile. *No, Ben. I don't think she could forgive me, not for that. So you're wrong, actually. About everything. If you aren't meant to return to her, then I as sure as hellfrost am not either.*

I gazed back at him sadly, chest clenching. Before I could think of a counter to that, some way to make him promise me that *he* at least would survive, if only for Sarah....

We both felt it, the rapidly building pressure, the surge of power, and both our heads whipped to the side, looking east.

Both of us too late, too far away to stop it.

The wards abruptly gave out in a burst, releasing that pressure we'd felt build, and the sandstone wall around the crack exploded inward in a deafening blast, stone shrapnel flying all the way to us as we reflexively ducked, even though I'd just as reflexively thrown up a shield of golden energy in front of us.

When I rose again, it was to see hordes of consumed roaring as they poured through the gap, before the dust had even settled. An ahglen swung its stone fist at a Strongshield woman who was just staggering to her feet in a daze and sent her flying into the air—no doubt dead before she even landed. Three trolls ganged up on a Starkissed man, clubs raised.

And across the rubble slunk a humanoid shadow, going from corpse to corpse to replenish itself from such a sudden mass expenditure of power, leaving only bones and armor in its wake.

A *second* mogoth.

All previous thought, all former calm, all prior exhaustion shattered with the wall. My whole mind, my whole being, narrowed down on that shadow, on that breach that promised death to all.

I charged forward, my sword appearing in my hands and beginning to drip flame as I eyed that shadow.

And Kor was right at my side.

Chapter Twenty-Eight

LIGHT

SARAH

ALYISH WATCHED THE DEFENDERS' plight with a face set in stone.

He had known it might come to this. *They* had known it might come to this. He could have sent them through the sungate just before the sun set, to get them away, to save *them*, at least. And yet, even human as they were now, they were still doing some good for their Tree. Because the more consumed they could kill now...

...the fewer that would be pounding on our shields later.

I understood why he had done it, without anyone explaining it to me. I understood that if the Tree fell, *all* was lost.

All.

All Realms.

All Seven.

If the Tree of Flame fell, my *family* was inevitably lost.

There was a chance that the drakón's sacrifice could make the difference to save the Tree.

To save me and my family.

I understood.

And yet I could not understand.

That was *Ben* there, in that mass of drakón on top of that plateau miles away, in that fort that was now being overrun. I couldn't distinguish him anymore, but I knew he was there. I knew he wouldn't abandon his people now by surging away to an active sungate. He would remain...and fall...with them.

Which meant Alyish had just sacrificed him.

"How *could* you?" I whispered when I finally understood. Tears streamed down my face.

Alyish looked up at me. A kind of stillness had fallen over the entire command center. After all, *our* job was much simpler, now that our defenders were dying and the only thing we could do was keep the shields going and prepare for when they fell. A soft horror had fallen on everyone. As many as could fit had solemnly gathered around the fire table to watch the beginning of the end.

"I think you know why," Alyish said. His voice was rasping with unshed tears.

I just shook my head and began backing up.

"No. No. *No.*"

I turned and began shoving my way through the crowd.

I didn't even know what I was doing. I was just thrashing blindly, knowing I had to get out, get away, do *something.*

The only thought that rang in my head was *no.*

No. No. No. No. NO.

"Sarah!" Tyri shouted, her and the rest of my elites shoving through the crowd after me. "Sarah! Wait!"

But I was bursting onto the balcony. And there, what should greet me in that still, dark night air, but that moon that had hastened the death of my love.

I...*raged.*

I burned with an icy fire that surged through every particle of my being, that sucked in the dark around me and turned it into light.

With every step, I burned white fire.

And with every step, I glowed brighter and became surer.

Instinct finally took over my poor, broken mind and allowed my shattered iceheart to reign supreme.

And so, before my elites could understand, let alone stop me, I jumped with a force that cleared the balustrade....

And surged.

Not to a gate. Not into the ether. Not to Ben.

Into the sky.

I had simply *looked* at where I had wanted to go and then, in a streak of light, *went* there.

And stayed there.

I floated now, high above the desert. Beyond the shields that had held me back. Nothing could hold me back like this. Not even gravity.

Nothing could hold back light.

And that's what I had become, and with every second became more, and more, and more. I sucked in the dark like I had sucked in air before, and with every breath—no, with every pulse of my iceheart—my radiance grew.

My drakón needed their sun? Well, that much might be beyond me.

But I could give them a star.

CHAPTER TWENTY-NINE

STARHEART

KORIBEN

I HAD JUST SLICED the head off a krathen when I felt the impossible.

When *everyone* felt the impossible. I saw the shock go round everyone's faces. Even the consumed hoards we were facing—even the krathen pack that was now trying to cut me and my wings off from the rest—glanced, and the bright reflection in their eyes told me what was happening even before I heard the shout.

"The Moondaughter!"

My flameheart, even though it was surging with impossibly renewed energy, nearly went out.

"No," I whispered in abject horror.

Since I might as well use that energy for *something*, I blasted the krathen back with a wall of fire that sent them howling and scurrying. If they even could. Plenty of them lay still where they'd dropped.

Ben, Kor said in awe, even as he panted. I had never seen him such a mess before: armor chipped, covered in blood and fur and gore, bleeding his own sapphire blood from a cut on his cheek. But at his numb swipe, the blood was gone, and the cut healed.

Even though he, like all of us, had run out of spark long ago.

All of *my* cuts, bruises, and strained muscles were now working on overdrive to heal and had begun the second my flameheart roared to new heights and *flooded* the fresh energy through me. Which was how I had won myself the moment to stiffly turn and look.

Trembling in fear of what I would see.

A star, as if fallen from the heavens, now glowed in the air between us and the Temple. Though the center of that massive sphere of light was not visible, I knew who was inside of it.

She had always been my star.

Except now it seemed she had found a way to give of her potent energy to more than just me. I saw everyone healing: Avish with her broken arm, suddenly flexing. Orran, the gash in his side ceasing to bleed. Toreth, stumbling to his feet when he'd been still as death.

If their flamehearts felt *anything* like mine felt right now, it was as if it were noon once more.

Their minds, not so blocked with numb horror as mine was, quickly caught on to what that meant. Drakón began shifting right and left, the moment they could get far enough away from the others. Drakáfire once again broke out, sending the consumed around us scattering, collapsing darkgates everywhere that the consumed had left unguarded—because why would they waste the magic on defenses now? We were never supposed to reach them.

"Ben," Yvera said, putting a bloody hand on my arm. "Ben, we need to help. We need to change, get out there. With her, we might actually *win* this."

I almost didn't hear her. Her voice sounded distant. Everything was distant, dark, dim.

Everything but my star.

Sarah, I thought to her, flameheart trembling. *What have you* done?

Because in saving our lives...she had thrown away her own.

Without even giving them the command, my legs began to run and my arms pump. Then with a leap, I changed, forcing my flesh to expand, harden, burn—faster than ever before. I urged my wings to snap out and press down in a mighty blast of air that sent me into the sky, rocketing toward her.

Too late.

Too *late.*

The lish came from nowhere, his long, stretched, contorted black body snaking through the air toward my star. I roared with all my might, but Solim didn't so much as flinch. His black eyes just fixed on her, filled with greed for her Blood. His taloned hand reached for her, touching the outer rim of her aura.

As fast as I was pumping my wings, as much fire burned ready in my belly for Solim, as much as I was straining with my whole *soul* toward her.

I was...too late.

Solim grasped for her.

Then....

In a flash, she was gone.

My flameheart exploded in a supernova of raw power.

I crashed into Solim, spewing fire, raking my claws down his hide, expanding larger than I had ever been in my memory...before I understood why.

My star...was not gone.

Not entirely. Not yet.

Because she had surged...into me.

Into my flameheart.

My star...was now my *heart*.

And I...was now glowing like a sun.

A very, very large, burning, *raging* sun.

Who was daring to tackle alone the lish that would have killed her.

Solim and I grappled in the air, tumbling and roaring. Unfortunately, I couldn't just *bite* him the way I longed to do. His lish blood was poison, and it was bad enough that I now had some of it hissing away on my talons. Not nearly enough for my bloodthirst, though, and not nearly enough to do anything more than cause him a bit of pain.

His main disadvantage was my suddenly larger size, although he was doing his best to handle that problem by trying to snake his wyrmlike body around my torso and pin my wings. I lashed him away with my tail and spewed more fire into his face, but he darted to the side at the last minute. He spewed a fast-moving, poisonous white fog at me in turn, but with *this* much power inside me, I found myself able to do something no one had ever managed to do in drakáform before: shield.

The fog dissipated harmlessly against the gold field I threw out in front of me, and Solim reared back in shock, entirely disconnecting from me. I used that moment of advantage to rise up a couple wingbeats for momentum and dive forward, grabbing him in my talons and, with my full, tremendous weight, allowing us to fall....

Ramming him seconds later into a sandstone cliff. I breathed in deep, gathering all the fire in my belly for an inferno. His dazed black eyes blinked open. And then stared widely at me in fear.

And then he was gone, and I fell forward, with nothing in or underneath my talons any longer.

I *roared* in fury, making the world tremble with the loss of my prey.

I knew what had happened. Lish could surge to darkgates just as well as I could to my own. And he had more than his share to pick from now.

The hellfrosted coward had fled.

And I...with the fight dying in my blood...could feel myself weakening.

My...starheart weakening.

Even *she* could sustain a miracle for only so long.

I felt myself shrink back down, down in size and down on the cliff my forefeet had been pressed against. My front talons slid against the rock face as I shrunk back down to the ground my hind feet were on.

That...was not good. Even with Solim fled, we were surrounded by consumed and darkgates now. Eld away from the Temple. And drakón were once again losing forms and flocking together for protection as the power Sarah had given them had retreated from them long before it had left me.

Ben! Yvera cried at me, her inner voice dim with distance for all its helpless rage.

I knew that meant she couldn't reach me.

No one could reach us now.

And I wasn't just shrinking. I was losing my drakáform too. My starheart, comprehending at least something of the danger to us, tried with one last desperate act to send me another surge of strength. But it wasn't enough to stop what had begun.

I was becoming amá again. And her star inside me was going out.

No! I cried. *No! Sarah! You can't...you can't leave me!*

How shortsighted I was. She *should* have left me. That would have been a better fate than the one that awaited her with me.

Instead, I found that when I finally became fully amá, something had separated from me, and now lay limp and unconscious against me.

Sarah...was now in my arms. And I...was trapped against a cliff.

Surrounded by consumed.

Who were now approaching with greed and revenge glittering in their eyes.

I clutched Sarah to me and backed up as far as I could against that cliff in horror.

No, this couldn't be happening. No. *No.*

I couldn't fight them all—not an army of them, not like this. And I had no power to protect her with but the tiny surge she had given me just before she burned herself out. Only enough for a bit of fire or maybe a shield.

With only seconds to decide...I decided on a shield. Our only hope was if someone had the time to reach us. It was a dim hope, with only the last shield left over the Temple and most drakón who were still alive trapped far away.

But it was our only one.

At the very least, it meant never letting go of Sarah. Not until they pried her from my dead body.

To maximize the time that I could hold the shield, though, I would need as small an area as possible to cast it over. I scanned quickly and found just the thing: a sharp depression at the foot of the sandstone cliff—a crevice, really. I hastily laid Sarah inside it, trying not to feel as if I were laying her in her grave. Then I lay over her as a living shield and threw up the magical one over the crevice opening.

Not a second too soon.

Crude swords and spears and claws began banging and scraping on the gold shield, consumed shouting in frustration at being even temporarily denied their quarry. The shield held, though, and surprisingly well. I felt a flutter of treacherous hope. If I could only hold out long enough for Sarah to wake up...if she lashed us...I could surge us to an active gate. I could feel one close enough, yet in sunlight, around the rim of Ythra, glowing in my mind's eye like our last beacon of hope.

Sarah, I pleaded. *Sarah, please. You have to wake up. Please wake up. Please.*

And then the banging and scraping stopped. I felt a chill and craned my head to the side to look.

A vorpex leered over me, its insectoid face chittering. Then it raised its giant front leg, whose pointed tip I knew could spear an amá clear through.

No, I thought in breathless horror. I clenched my eyes shut and held the shield with all my might.

The vorpex hit it with a bang that made my eardrums ring. I trembled with the energy the shield had taken from me. But it held.

Though it wouldn't for much longer.

I was dead now. I knew that for certain.

And Sarah...my *sera,* my star, my heart....

Sarah, I said, clenching my eyes shut as I pressed my face against her neck. As I breathed her in for the last time.

The vorpex hit the shield, and I gasped, momentarily dizzy from the effort of holding it.

I would not last another time.

"Sarah, I love you," I gasped out loud. "I love you, my star—more than you will ever know."

Then....

I felt a burst of power originating from the Temple.

Shrieks. Guttural cries of alarm. Garbled shouts of panic.

"The gates, the gates!" one of the more articulate was shouting.

What?

Then a warm gold light washed over us, as if at the tail end of a mighty wave. I recognized the Tree's touch in it. It sent my flameheart roaring again.

But...*how?*

If the Tree could do something like this, She would have already. The only way She could have was if....

No.

No.

NO.

CHAPTER THIRTY

ENOUGH

KAVARIAN

KAVARIAN SUNFILLED, THE DRAKÓN King of the Six Realms, was dying.

And this time, there was nothing that could save him.

Because, for the very first time, he was in the arms of his Tree, who held him as he lay bleeding at the foot of Her base from a wound he had given himself. The Tree wept over him, Her tears of flame making scorch marks on his shirt wherever they landed.

He had always known it might come to this, and when he'd heard that his children were in danger, he knew there was no alternative.

Blood taken by force was powerful. Blood freely given to the Tree to save Her children...was far, far more so. And the Blood of a King or Queen for their people was the most powerful of all.

With that Blood, the Tree was able to extinguish every darkgate and rift not just in Her surroundings but surrounding every one of her Daughter Trees across the Six Realms, and to close those areas off from the Devourer's touch for another thousand years. The wave of power that did so also put a fire into the hearts of Her defenders that allowed them to lay waste to and scatter the consumed slaves, putting an end to the battle and siege, everywhere.

She had showed him this, as he lay dying in Her arms. Showed him what his sacrifice had done.

And the Tree wept.

Kavarian knew Her tears were for the dead who had already returned to Her. Many. Too many dead.

He knew Her tears were for himself. Something precious must be taken for something far more precious to be given. The life of Her faithful son and King was precious to Her indeed.

He knew She wept for the immutable law of the Creators that She only had the power to save Her children that Her children gave to Her to save them, through their obedience...and their sacrifice.

He knew the Tree wept for his son.

Kavarian wept for him too. Entirely for him. He saved no tears for himself, for he was at peace with what he had done, and he longed to rejoin his beloved.

But he knew Koriben might never understand that.

His final, halting thought to Her was of him. *Has not...my son...suffered...enough?*

Then his flameheart at last was extinguished, and the power that was his as King passed to another.

Almost immediately, a roar echoed across the desert and reverberated through the Temple Heart.

It was the agonized cry of one who had, just a moment before, been a boy and an Heir.

And had, in that moment, become a man and a King.

CHAPTER THIRTY-ONE

BREAK

SARAH

I SAT OUTSIDE THE chamber where they had placed the King's body for several hours. I didn't know what else to do. Or think. Or feel. I was simply numb. Helpless.

I...had failed.

Even though Tyri said many more drakón would have died had I not saved them. That Solim would have broken through the shields if Ben, with my help, had not driven him off.

I still had failed.

In saving Ben's life...I had cost him his father's.

Letting Ben die might have been more merciful.

So I sat numbly, pondering my failure. My selfishness. Wondering if there was anything else I might have done. Could have done. Wondering if, had I known what would happen, I could even have stopped myself. Or would simply have made the same selfish choice again, that time as a monster.

This was all my fault. I hadn't been enough. And what I had been....

I am...so sorry, I thought faintly as I looked at the chamber.

Ben slowly walked into view. I started, my treacherous iceheart pulsing even *now*.

Yet this was the first time I had seen him, really seen him, since the speech. I couldn't see anything while I was a star—just light. I had only *felt* Solim's darkness coming for me...and Ben's pull, made almost irresistible in his desperation, as he flew to save me. It had been all too easy to answer that pull and go into my gate. Inside him.

That's all I remembered until....

Ben's voice in the darkness. Telling me he loved me.

I had known then, with a fatalistic, dreamlike certainty, that we must be dying. I didn't expect to wake up.

And yet I did, in a guest room in the Temple, with Tyri once again watching over me and more elites waiting outside. She was the one who had told me what had happened. And had led me here, to where the old King lay.

I went in to see him then. Very briefly. Just to see for myself. But then I almost immediately walked out, the pain and guilt being too much. And yet...I couldn't just leave him. This was my fault. And it seemed like no one else except a couple of guards could be spared to keep vigil with him. It seemed so wrong for him to be left alone.

This much...I could do. So there, outside the chamber, I had sat, like the symbol I was, while the others, even Ben, made us safe.

Until Ben came.

He...looked about as I had expected. Like he'd been through hell.

The only surprise to me was that he must have showered and changed. His hair was damp, his skin and clothes clean. But he moved with the slow steps of someone who had the worlds weighing on his shoulders, and his eyes, though open, somehow looked more dead than I had ever seen them.

He barely glanced at me. He just stopped between me and the opening to the chamber. And stood there. Staring at nothing. As if he couldn't quite bear to face either one of us.

"Do you..." I rasped, then cleared my throat. "...want me to go with you?"

"Yes," he said emotionlessly. "But not in there. Come on."

He held out his hand, still not looking at me.

Startled, but relieved he was allowing that much contact, I stood, walked over, and put my hand in his. He gripped it tightly on reflex, then seemed to deliberately loosen the hold.

"Lash us, please."

"What?" I said.

Still not looking at me, still in that empty voice, Ben said, "It's dawn. It's time for me to take you home."

Oh.

I was too numb to know if that was what I wanted right now. Or what was right. Surely I should be here, with him and the others....

What *good* was I if I couldn't even *be* here?

"Sarah, please," Ben said tonelessly. "Do this for me."

"If...it's what will help the most," I said with a swallow.

"It is."

I let out a breath. Nodded my thanks to Tyri and the others, who nodded back. And lashed us together.

"Go ahead."

A moment later, we were standing in the chamber with the dual-natured gate, the one at Crownhold. We didn't even stumble. No feeling of being squeezed and shot through a cannon. The surging hadn't even been a blur. One moment we were somewhere else, the next moment we were here. That was all.

I blinked.

But Ben was letting go of my hand and turning. He gestured to the gate. Still not looking at me.

"Well. Go ahead."

I stared up at him. And finally, my icy numbness broke, and the tears came spilling freely.

How could the dead King look more alive than the living one?

Which one had I lost, in the end?

"Ben," I said in a choked whisper.

With terrible slowness, he finally turned his head, and his eyes met mine. And flinched, and looked away again.

I couldn't help myself. I threw my arms around him and held him with all my might. At first, he just stood there, and my iceheart truly began to crack.

And then he was pulling me up and crushing his lips to mine.

This was a different kiss than all the others. Urgent. Desperate. Demanding. As if he were slowly dying and I were the only thing keeping him alive. I clung to him with that understanding, giving as good as I got. Panted as he parted briefly to run his lips over my jaw, down my neck, across my collarbones. Then back to my lips, somehow with even greater hunger.

I love you, I told him.

The silent words slipped out before I could stop them. But as soon as they did, I could have killed myself for making *that* kind of mistake *now*.

Ben froze. Pulled back. And, even as he panted, and his eyes burned from want...lowered me to the ground.

"Ben," I said, aghast. "I'm...I'm—"

"Don't," he said, holding up a hand and closing his eyes tightly, blocking me off from those burning gold spheres. "Just...don't. You...have nothing to be sorry for. It's my fault, as usual."

I felt as if he had punched me in the gut. "Ben," I rasped. "*None* of this is *your* fault."

He didn't answer. At least, not until his breath stilled, and when he finally opened his eyes, they no longer burned. They were simply dead again.

"My mother died for me."

I stared, not even breathing.

He continued dully. "There wasn't enough power left in the Covenants. For sixty years after Avva was crowned, no Heir was born to the Sunfilled Clan. Sixty *years*. Then the Tree finally told Avva and Avvi why. And gave them a choice. They could live out their lives as they deserved, because they had been faithful servants, but knowing that when Avva passed, our people would be left without a Sunfilled Monarch, with the Covenants continuing to crumble down around them. Or...they could pledge some of their own flamehearts, and the Tree would give them a child. And that child...would be the Heir to restore the Covenants."

He looked away. "I think you can guess which they chose."

I nodded, unable to speak.

"It wasn't her time, Sarah," he said tonelessly as he stared at nothing. "Her flameheart might have lasted years more. Maybe even to this day, and beyond.

But instead, she gave some of it to me. My mother died for me. My father *was* dying for me...until you saved him."

I inhaled sharply as I finally understood.

Ben closed his eyes. "And now, Avva is...dead. Because of me."

"Ben," I breathed. The tears were once again pouring.

I now finally and completely understood *why* Ben thought he was a monster, that he was unworthy of love.

Because he thought he should never have even been born.

And that he certainly didn't deserve to live now.

I ached, I *burned* for him. But my mind and hands were empty of any words, any miracles that could save him from this kind of pain.

Eskala's words came back to me. *There is no way to convince someone that they are worthy of love.*

He took a deep breath and opened his eyes. His face was abruptly as hard as stone, and the golds of his eyes as ice.

"I didn't tell you this to make you feel sorry for me. I told you...to help you understand, and maybe one day forgive, what I am about to do."

With no other warning, he shoved me through the gate.

I stumbled back into my hold and fell hard on my rear. I was stunned not from the pain but from what he had done. Ben had never used force against me. *Ever.*

Through the ice curtain, I saw him reach to touch the arched edges of his gate, and I felt a rush of power, then a terrible....

Nothingness.

Separation.

The pull was entirely...gone. Not weak, not transferred.

Gone.

"Ben," I choked in pure horror.

I scrambled to my feet and to the gate...but my hands slapped against solid ice. My ice curtain was no longer a curtain. My gate...was no longer a gate.

It was only a wall.

I knew from how Ben met my eyes for one moment that he could see me. Which was the final mournful knell in my head that told me he had somehow, with his authority as King of Flame, put out the fire of his own side of the gate...and shut me out of his Realms.

All of them. I knew from the sudden deadness in every one of the six moongates around me that they would be just the same as this one if I opened them.

Stay where it's safe, Sarah, he said. *Far away from me.*

And then he turned and walked away.

"*BEN!*" I screamed with mind and voice, pounding on the ice. Loudly enough that, out of the corner of my eye, I saw members of my family come running.

But all I could focus on was Ben's back.

"*Ben! Don't do this,*" I begged him. "*Don't—*"

And then he was gone. Surged away without so much as a blur, in the blink of an eye.

Far from me.

I slowly slid down the wall he had put between us...and sobbed as my iceheart finally and truly broke.

For both of us.

AFTERWORD

This was a difficult book for me to write.

I write to work through the great emotions of my soul and the complexities of my mind, always struggling to find my way back out of the dark and toward the light. The only reason I ever have the courage to *share* that writing is out of the hope that it will add more light to the world, helping someone else do the same. My greatest fear about this book is that it will leave someone feeling darker than when they picked it up.

I hope these words help.

Let me be absolutely clear about one thing: I did *not* end in that way because of any supposed authorial "pleasure" in torturing my readers. I had none such pleasure, not in writing it, and not in anticipating others reading it. I, too, read because I need hope, light, and happy endings. I, too, was sobbing like the Tree at Kavarian's death, and like Sarah at her and Ben's separation. I longed to save Kavarian and to end this book in any other way, but I couldn't. No other ending for any of the characters would come to me...because this was the one *they* chose.

And this is like some of the chapters in many of our lives: deaths, disasters, endings, heartbreak. Sometimes there is no way to paint a silver lining around those moments, no way to end them on a note of hope and happiness. Those moments of pure sorrow are *not* the end of hope and happiness, but the sorrow of them must be fully acknowledged and felt before we may pass through them.

I could see no possible way to end this book on a positive note without making light of the pain these characters, whom I love, have just experienced.

Except...to promise you that this is not the end for them. In fact, it is the beginning.

You may be interested to know that the scene from the dream I had that was the kernel of inspiration for this entire series...hasn't even taken place yet. Because that scene is a raw moment of grief, uncertainty, reunion, apology, reconciliation, forgiveness, hope, healing, and light. A moment of such vulnerability and joy that could have come only *after* the darkest of days.

That moment...is coming.

So, though I cannot offer you a happy ending for *this* one book, this I *can* offer you: The darkest day is past. The dawn is coming.

And each book after will be brighter than the last.

ABOUT THE AUTHOR

Leah E. Welker graduated from Brigham Young University (Provo) in 2016 with a degree in English language and a minor in editing. She then edited for seven years and pivoted to writing in 2023. She is based in the DC area, where she lives with family and her rescue Australian shepherd, Wes.

You can connect with her at

https://www.leahewelker.com

Subscribe to her newsletter for updates, cover reveals, dog pics, and more:

https://www.leahewelker.com/follow

www.ingramcontent.com/pod-product-compliance
Lightning Source LLC
Chambersburg PA
CBHW020417030726
47495CB00006B/1548